A New Day at Paradise Pottery

Lynn Johnson left school with no qualifications. With determination and hard work, she ended her career as a Human Resources Manager with a large County Council. Born and raised in Stoke-on-Trent, she now lives in Orkney with her husband and six cats. Lynn is a member of the Romantic Novelists Association.

Also by Lynn Johnson

The Potteries Girls

The Girl from the Workhouse
Wartime with the Tram Girls
The Potteries Girls on the Home Front
A New Day at Paradise Pottery

LYNN JOHNSON

A New Day *at* Paradise Pottery

hera

First published in the United Kingdom in 2023 by

Hera Books
Unit 9 (Canelo), 5th Floor
Cargo Works, 1-2 Hatfields
London SE1 9PG
United Kingdom

A CIP catalogue record for this book is available from the British Library.

Print ISBN 978 1 80436 040 8
Ebook ISBN 978 1 80436 929 6

Look for more great books at www.herabooks.com

Printed and bound in Great Britain by Clays Ltd, Elcograf S.p.A.

1

To the women who were fore-runners in breaking into the world of pottery design in the Potteries

Part One

Chapter One

August 1913

Martha Owen arrived at Mr Sherwood's corner shop ten minutes after knocking-off time from Jackson's Pottery in Hanley. She was nearly fifteen now and had worked at Jackson's since she left school two years ago. She would probably still be working there until she got wed.

Calling in at Sherwood's had become one of her regular jobs and was a place of gossip, somewhere to be got over with quickly, if you had anything to hide. The bell tinkled as she opened the door. It was a bad time to go because most people called in on their way home from work. Still, she didn't dare go back empty-handed. Instead, she let out her frustration in a long sigh.

Mrs Sherwood looked up. 'Martha! Have you come for the firewood?'

'Sorry, Mrs Sherwood, I was miles away. Yes, please.'

'It's that bundle by the door. Already paid for. I hear your mother's had a nasty accident. What happened?'

'Oh, I left a cupboard door open and Mother banged into it. Got into trouble for it an' all. Still, I must go, I'll be late for tea.'

Martha shot out of the shop for the short walk home.

She had become quite accomplished at covering for Mother when the need arose. She didn't like telling lies. At Sunday school, they said lies were bad but as it was done for the best of reasons, Martha thought that God wouldn't mind.

Martha enjoyed her job at Jackson's. It was a local potbank making earthenware goods for the lower end of the market. Much of their ware was undecorated and sold with a simple white or cream glaze. Their decorated lines used transfers placed on the already glazed ware and fired again. Because they were fired twice and decorated, and were more costly to produce, they were aimed at people with a little bit more money than the majority in The Potteries.

Transferring was Martha's job – and she enjoyed it. She always thought people were pronouncing it wrong, but she had been told the correct way was 'trans – fe – ring'. She would take a tissue print supplied by a printer containing the appropriate pattern and, after trimming, carefully fit it to the piece of ware by rubbing it down until the glue – that was called size – stuck it firmly. Afterwards the paper tissue was removed by dipping it in a tub of water which dissolved the tissue and the water-based size, leaving the oil-based pattern untouched. Any tissue paper remaining was carefully sponged away. It was the only job she had ever done at Jackson's.

But there were better places she could work and better jobs she could do. Martha's supervisor at Jackson's was Beryl Turner and she was impressed with her work, so much so that Martha had shown her some of the drawings she had done at home. Beryl had looked quite surprised and told her to keep practising, for who knew what she could do in the future? Martha was tickled pink to receive such praise.

If the truth be told, she would like to become a paintress one day. A paintress was the most prestigious and probably well-paid job a girl could aspire to. Painting the ware freehand, but following company patterns, appealed to Martha's artistic leanings. She intended to keep working hard to make sure she did well. She might even get to art school one day.

The problem was, Jackson's didn't employ paintresses. She would have to get a job elsewhere and spend time and money training unless she could get a scholarship. After all, what did girls need a trade for – her father had said on more than one occasion?

Martha followed the alleyway. She turned into Dresden Street to find the twins, Daniel and Peter, playing football with a couple of neighbours, kicking a tin can along the road and using coats for goalposts. Issy stood watching the game with her friend Josie. They were both thirteen and had just left school. Josie had already got a job, which made things worse in Father's eyes. To Martha, they both looked so young. Martha's years at work had forced her to grow up and no doubt it would do the same for Issy. For now, she was her little sister.

As soon as Issy saw Martha, she ran towards her.

'Hiya. Hope they dunner break any windows, else they'll have Father to deal with.' Martha grinned. 'You'd think they'd have grown out of that now they're working down the pit.'

Issy tutted. 'They're boys and they're seventeen. What more do you expect? I'm glad you're home, Martha,' she said in a lower voice. 'Father and Mother are rowing again. Been at it ever since I got home. I wish we could go back to live with Grandma. We was happy at the pub.'

Martha reached out for Issy's hand. 'You know we can't do that. Dresden Street is our home.'

Issy thought for a few moments. 'If you could have seen what was going on when I got you'd have a different opinion.'

'Why? What did you see?'

'Father grabbed Mother by the arms and went to hit her. I had to get out.' Issy's huge dark eyes glittered. 'Why is he so horrible to her?'

'Oh, Issy, duck. Everybody argues.'

'Not like Father does. I hate him when he has a go at everybody, especially Mother.'

–

The twins followed the girls into the house, Peter joking with Daniel on how wide he needed the goalposts to enable him to score a goal. Mother was ready to dish up the tea. Father was sitting in his normal seat beside the fire grate.

Mother looked flushed, whether from the heat of the oven or Father going on, Martha couldn't say. Mother never had much to say when they were all sat round the table. It was always Father who determined what to talk about and, of late, it had been Issy's inability to get a job.

'Where've you two girls bin? Leaving yer mother to cook the tea.'

'We was just outside, watching the football,' said Martha, hoping to take Father's mind off another of Issy's unsuccessful attempts to find work.

'Never mind that, you should be here helping your mother get the men their teas. We've been working all day putting food on the table.'

'The twins seem to have plenty of energy, perhaps—'

'Dunner talk back to me, Martha. Do as you're told or else. And you boys should know better. Kicking a can in the street – if yer've got that much energy, the pit's not working yer hard enough. Issy, have yer had any luck in getting a job?'

Issy shook her head.

Poor Issy had been looking every day since she left school in July. Father would demand to know where she had been and why she couldn't get a job when everybody else was fixed up. There was no denying that Issy was intelligent, but the girl had difficulty concentrating and panicked about things. She had performed badly at school so her reference from them was hindering her search.

—

Martha and Issy went to bed about nine o'clock. Martha had an early start at the potbank, and Issy decided to go too.

'Martha, I'm worried about Mother. Have yer noticed she's getting quieter and doesn't say much when Father's around?'

Martha nodded as she brushed her hair in front of the mirror. 'I know. I wish she'd talk about it – but she won't. She'll be concerned Father'll find out and it might make things ten times worse.'

'Well, I wish we were all back at the pub. It was so much better. We was happy there.'

'So you keep saying.'

–

Martha couldn't sleep. Her mind was full of the changes that had taken place over the last few years. The Owen family had lived over The Potter's Wheel Public House in Tunstall, where their grandad was landlord, for as long as Martha could remember. Their father spent a lot of time away from home, 'defending the King's Empire' – his words. He'd only had two periods of time with his children before he left the army in 1908. The only substantial period was between May 1902 and February 1903, after his return from South Africa. At that time the twins were nearly six and remembered him fondly, she was three and a half and Issy under two years old – too young to remember anything about him.

In those days, he was a different man. Martha vaguely remembered being carried around the house on his shoulders and he smiled a lot. It was when he came back from India that things were different. Nothing was ever said – but something made him angry – most of the time. He got a job in Hanley and they moved out of the pub to this house in Dresden Street. The move from Tunstall to Hanley wasn't far, but far enough to mean going to a new school and making new friends. And all the while, missing Grandma and Grandad. She supposed it had been so good in those days and they had taken it for granted.

When she thought about life from Father's point of view, Martha might understand that casting privies on a potbank was nowhere near as exciting as being in the army and living in foreign lands. But it was no excuse for the change he brought with him when he came back.

All of the Owen children had been born at The Potter's Wheel. It was their home. The pub had been rented by Grandad's family for seventy years and he seemed to know everybody in Tunstall, from the draymen who delivered the beer, to the mayor. Martha had heard people say The Potter's Wheel was like the British Empire and Oswald Parker, their Grandad, its king. A traditional drinkers' pub, it had several rooms downstairs – a taproom, snug and a posh room for the more refined drinker. Behind the bar was a larger than average kitchen.

During their time at the pub, Martha's best friend had been Bridie O'Connor who lived next door and spoke funny because she came from Ireland. Bridie was the eldest and the same age as Martha. She never saw much of Bridie after they left apart from when she visited Grandma and Grandad. As the O'Connor's expanded and more children arrived, Bridie did not have as much spare time. The two school mates remained friends, but their chances to meet as they grew older reduced.

Dogs fighting in the alleyway let up howls as she lay there wondering why Father was like he was. On odd occasions, he seemed to forget his gripes with life and was even charming and she could see why Mother had fallen for him. Other times – well, most of the time – he was a different person altogether and not a likeable one at that. What would it be like when the twins were older and able to fight back? How would the family keep the peace?

Martha looked out through the grimy windows. It was starting to get light. The night-soil man and the knocker-up would be coming round shortly and it would be time for Father and the boys to go to work. She closed her eyes.

The next thing Martha heard was Issy using the chamber pot.

Issy smiled. 'Time to get up, sleepyhead.'

Martha groaned. She never normally had trouble getting up in the morning, but today she was exhausted.

—

When Martha arrived home from work, the house was too quiet – that's how she knew something was wrong.

Issy came running in. 'They was arguing again when I got home. I couldn't stand it, so I took meself off to Josie's, out of the way.'

Martha nodded and crossed to the door in the corner leading upstairs. She opened it slowly, listening all the while.

'Are you upstairs, Mother?' she called softly.

No answer – although she thought she heard a rustling of something.

'Mother?'

Again, her call met with silence. Then came Mother's voice – wobbly – not like her at all.

'I'll… I'll be down soon. Put kettle on for me will yer, duck?'

Martha turned and smiled at Issy. 'You put the kettle on and I'll go and see if she needs any help. There's no tea on and no sign of Father, so yer can start peeling the taters. Get yerself a piece or summat, if you're hungry. Won't be long.'

'I'm coming with yer.'

'Father'll moan if—'

'He'll moan in any case, miserable bugger.'

'Issy! Mind yer language.'

Issy stuck out her tongue. 'I'm coming up with yer,' she said, and followed Martha upstairs.

Mother was standing by her bedroom window, dabbing at her eyes.

'Mother! Whatever's happened?'

'Nothing, duck. Nowt for yer to worry yerself about. Where's our Issy?'

'I'm here, Mother.'

Issy moved from behind Martha and stood in the doorway, uncertain.

They had been ordered by Father never to enter their parents' bedroom and, even though he wasn't in the house at this very moment, Martha still felt uncomfortable stepping through the doorway into the forbidden room.

Mother bent her head and wiped her eyes on a handkerchief, a sniff escaping now and again.

'Is it Father? Has he—'

'Come in and close the door. You too, Issy.'

Then, Mother let go of the tears she was trying to hold back. Aghast, Martha and Issy threw their arms around her wanting to offer comfort, while taking solace from each other. Martha tried to swallow but something was lodged in her throat.

When Mother let them go, she pulled another already damp handkerchief out of her apron and dabbed her eyes, trying to smile. She turned her face fully towards them and there, on the side of her cheek, was a red and black bruise. Her eye twitched as if it was having difficulty remaining open.

'Mother!'

'Dunner say nowt. I'm all right. Nothing for you pair to worry about.'

'Did... Father... Did he do that?' asked Issy, almost as if she didn't really want to know the answer.

'He didn't mean it. Yer know how it is. I'd done summat silly. He wanted to go out but I'd spent this week's housekeeping money. I shouldn't have.'

Martha's eyes were wide. 'But... but you'd spent it on us.'

Mother shrugged. 'He doesn't see it that way.'

Martha swallowed. 'If he can do that...'

'Like I said, there's nowt for yer to worry about, our Martha. He'd never hurt yer – any of yer. Just make sure as you both look after yerselves.'

Issy stood, hands on hips. 'But he's always losing his temper – and it's getting worse, isn't it?'

'He doesn't mean to. He always says he's sorry.'

'Those times you've said as he loses his temper and shouts…? Yer dunner walk into doors or nothing like that, do yer? Even Mrs Sherwood at the shop knows that. She as good as asked me when I called in.'

Mother shook her head. 'It's first time he's hit me so hard where other folk can see it. Like I said, he's always sorry afterwards.'

Martha sat on the bed heavily, remembering back to all the times she had interrupted their arguments – which Mother always said were not really arguments. Mother listening until Father had said all he wanted to say. But it didn't stop there – she knew that now.

'Dunner you go saying nowt to anybody, Martha Owen. You an' all, Issy. It'll only make it worse for all of us. Keep it to yerself. Promise me.'

Issy licked her lips. 'Have yer told Grandad?'

Mother shook her head. 'No, and you're not to tell him neither, nor Grandma. No point in them getting involved.'

'But he's yer dad. He might be able to help.'

'Oh, I can take care of meself, duckie.'

'Mother, if this is you taking care of yourself – it's not working, is it?'

Trust Issy to be so bold, thought Martha, wishing she'd had the courage to say what she was thinking.

Mother attempted a smile, but the corners of her mouth wobbled. 'I know what you're thinking, Issy. But, like I said, don't you go saying nothing to nobody. It was, as likely as not, my fault any road.'

The three were silent for a moment. Martha stared at Issy. She might be wrong in her assessment of her young sister. She was growing up fast – and had a mind of her own.

'Come on, you two. Best get the tea on before your father gets home.'

Chapter Two

September 1913

The pottery industry was a staple in the area because of the abundance of marl, clay and coal near the surface. The coal meant they could generate the high temperatures needed for firing pottery, hence the importance of the second major industry – mining. Nearly all the workers in The Potteries were either potters or miners.

The Owens were no exception. After leaving the army, Father worked at Trent Sanitary Works making privies – the job he was doing before he went into the army. It was a man's job and was well-paid. It turned out the casting foreman was a former soldier and he'd done Father a favour.

The twins had worked at the pit since they left school and were now underground, working three shifts, mornings, noons and nights. It meant they only saw Father when they were working on the day shift, which ended at two in the afternoon. Father went to work at six in the morning when the slip started to pump and he returned between three and four in the afternoon. It was a relief they didn't meet too often because the rows between them had got worse as time passed. The whole family dreaded the weeks the twins were on days. During that time, their shifts coincided with Father's, leaving them with more time at home and more time for arguments. Once home and fed, they would disappear, returning at a time when it was reasonable for them to go straight to bed.

If only Issy could get a job too, then Father wouldn't complain. Life could be so much better – for everyone.

The twins had arranged to go out and were getting changed. Father had already left so they were larking about as usual when he wasn't around.

'Sure you'll be all right?' Daniel peered into Martha's eyes. 'Father's gone out.'

She shrugged. 'We'll be all right. It wouldn't be right for you to have to stay behind. Go and enjoy yourselves.'

There was a loud knock on the door and Martha ran downstairs to answer it.

It was Jeffrey Dean, her best friend Betty's elder brother, who worked at the same pit as the twins. They hadn't said they were meeting him here, so she had no time to prepare herself. Martha had always had a soft spot for him, a crush, but since Betty had gone into service she'd had less opportunity to see him.

'Hiya Martha, duck. Are the lads ready yet?'

'Hiya,' she said, almost breathless. 'They're coming. Nearly done.'

'How's things at work?'

'All right, I suppose.' If only she could think of something sensible to say. Something that made her feel grown up. She tried again.

'Where are yer going?'

'Hanley. Not sure after that. Summat'll turn up.'

They stood together near the front door – having run out of things to say. Martha was concentrating on Jeffrey and didn't notice Father coming up the street – until it was too late.

'Just a bloody minute, young man. What d'yer think yer doing with my daughter?'

Martha's face burned. She desperately hoped Jeffrey couldn't see it in the early-evening light.

'Don't, Father!' she burst out. 'He's here for the twins, not me.'

He had reached them. He grabbed Martha's upper arm so tightly, she cried out.

'Dunner you go flirting with my daughter – if yer know what's good for yer.'

He shook his finger right under Jeffrey's nose, his eyes glaring. 'The wench is only fourteen. Not old enough for the likes of you.'

'Hang on, Mr—'

'Father – please stop.' She didn't dare look at Jeffrey. She would never dare to look at him again. What must he be thinking?

'Mr Owen… I—'

'I said leave her alone, and gerroff home.'

'Father!'

It was Daniel, with Peter following. 'What's going on?'

'Ask yer friend here.' Father shouted, pushing Martha into the house, slamming the door behind them.

Whatever would she say to Jeffrey next time she saw him?

Mother's face was pale as Father pushed Martha through to the kitchen, him shouting, and Martha crying with shame.

'Percy – what's happening?'

'She's been flirting with a lad what's older than the twins and I told him to bugger off.'

'I wasn't flirting – honest I wasn't. It was Jeffrey come for—'

'Are yer calling me a liar, girl?'

Daniel and Peter had followed them into the kitchen so they must've sent Jeffrey away.

Daniel spoke up first. 'Look Father, there's nothing going on. Jeffrey was waiting for us and Martha was talking to him cos we weren't ready. She's only a kid. She wouldn't do nowt like that.'

'Shut up, Daniel. I know what I saw.'

'It's true, Father. I was only keeping him company until the twins were ready.'

'Keeping him company? Is that what yer call it now? Keeping a fella company can get a girl pregnant – or didn't yer know. Has yer mother not told yer yet?'

'Percy!'

Father rounded on Mother. 'And you've got a nerve to say anything, Fanny.'

Father stood with his back to the fire glaring at each of them one by one. Then, the stiffness seemed to leave him. He shook his head and walked out of the house without looking back.

'Bloody kids!'

–

With the atmosphere at home getting increasingly difficult and Father getting harder to live with, it wasn't fair that Mother should bear the brunt of Father's anger alone. Supposing something really bad happened? Martha said as much to Peter later that night.

'You're best staying out of it,' he said softly.

'What – leave our Mother to deal with everything so we don't get into trouble? Shame on you, Peter Owen.'

To be fair, he did look a bit sheepish and turned his head away.

Martha turned to Daniel. 'What about you?'

'I understand how yer feel, Martha. I really do. But I'm afraid that if I start on him, I'll be sure to punch him on the bloody nose. Mother's the best one to deal with him if he's in one of his... moods.'

'And look what it costs her to do that.'

–

The boys were allowed to pay board, which was a fixed sum every week for their keep and lodgings. Martha, being a girl and younger, was expected to hand over her pay packet to Father in return for pocket money.

As usual, Father counted it and frowned. 'Where's the rest?'

'There isn't no more this week.'

Father sat back in his chair and folded his arms. 'Why not?'

'They said as some of me plates was rejected.'

'They weren't good enough?'

Martha lowered her head.

'Wasn't yer concentrating, girl? Thinking about that Dean lad I caught yer with, I'll bet.'

'I told yer, Father, he was waiting for the twins, not me.'

'Yes, so yer say.'

'And I was concentrating but them transfers were not very good and wouldn't stick to the plates and it took me longer to get them done.' She didn't mean to be rude. She just wanted to stand up for herself. She was in the right. Surely he could see that?

He got to his feet and stood tall in front of her. She stood her ground. Then he swung his hand and caught her – hard – on her cheek. Her jaw jarred as if it had moved out of place. Her cheek smarted and she felt his hand as if it was still there even though it had only touched her momentarily. Her eyes were so bright she could barely see. She covered her face and backed away knowing there would be a red hand-shaped pattern on her left cheek, still tingling with the feel of his hand.

'You'll get another backhander if yer talk to me like that again.'

Martha rushed upstairs and slammed the bedroom door. Luckily, Issy was out so she had no explaining to do. She lay on the bed unable to believe that her own father could do such a thing. Then she heard loud voices rowing and one of them belonged to Father.

No one came upstairs to check on her.

–

Martha, having picked up bread and potatoes from Sherwood's, was later than usual in returning home from work. Raised voices met her as she opened the back door.

Her heart sank. Not again! How much longer could this way of life carry on? She wondered whether to go in or go for a walk until things had calmed down. No, she needed to be there for her mother and Issy.

It was Daniel on the receiving end of the words spewing from Father's mouth this time. Martha hurriedly took off her hat and coat and walked in as if she hadn't heard the argument. Daniel's face was almost purple whereas Father's was white, his eyes cold, his mouth pursed.

Mother rose the moment she saw Martha. Father pushed her back down again. That was all it took.

Daniel lunged at him and pulled him away from Mother, holding tightly to Father's collar, his fist under Father's chin, forcing his jaw upward.

Mother cried out. 'Daniel! Please don't.'

Immediately, he let go, just in time to receive a backhander across his jaw.

As quick as a flash, Peter jumped forward and, taking Father by surprise, pinned him against the wall, partly winding him in the process. He was quickly joined by Daniel. Now both of them were holding Father tight and Martha swore she could see fear in his eyes.

'Don't you ever touch Mother like that again. You're too fond of using yer fists!' Peter shouted into Father's face, their noses almost touching.

Father said nothing.

'In future keep yer fists to yerself, or else,' Daniel said quietly, but firmly.

His eyes were as cold as ice. Martha shivered. The fear she had seen turned to hatred.

The twins nodded to each other and let him go.

'Women shouldn't be treated the way you treat them,' hissed Daniel. 'What about our Martha and Issy? Will they be next?'

Mother opened her mouth, but Father thumped the table hard, with his fist.

Nobody spoke.

Martha's heart banged against the walls of her chest. She thought it might explode. Surely everybody could hear.

Father stood tall and took a deep breath. 'You two are no longer welcome in this house. You will leave now. You will have the weekend to take away your belongings – otherwise they'll be burned.'

Martha gasped as Mother cried out, but Father hadn't moved. He remained fixed to the spot.

Daniel turned pale. 'You're throwing us out?'

'I am.'

'But you can't.'

'Oh, yes I can. You're old enough to find yerselves somewhere to live.'

Daniel turned to look at Mother, who shook her head. 'I don't want them to go.' The words were spoken so softly even Martha could barely make them out.

'You can ignore yer mother an' all. It's my name on the rent book and I say who lives in this house. *My* house.' He stabbed his chest.

Father stormed out, stopping only to take his coat and cap from the peg near the back door. The door slammed. The crockery on the draining board protested.

No one moved. Peter's eyes were bright – Daniel looked shocked.

'That worked well. Not only have you two got nowhere to live, but us three are going to have to live with him on our own,' said Issy. 'Have yer seen our Martha, look what he's done to her, all because she was a few coppers short in her wages.'

'Oh, boys, what shall we do now? I begged you to hold your tempers.'

'How can we when he treats you and Martha like that? How could anyone worth his salt put up with him?' Daniel's eyes glittered.

Martha had never seen him so angry.

Mother slid into a chair with her back bent, her hands covering her wet cheeks. 'I don't think I can do it. I can't cope no more.'

Martha rushed to kneel by her knee. 'I'll be here, Mother.'

Mother smiled, a sad, watery smile, and stroked Martha's head. 'You're a good girl, Martha, but...'

As Mother's voice trailed away, Daniel shook himself into action. 'I'm sorry, Mother. I conner stay here. I think I'll only put you in more danger. I'll go and stay with Grandma at the pub for a while. Until things have calmed down.'

'Me too,' said Peter. 'He might calm down a bit in the next few days.'

'Don't go, please.' Martha felt tears welling up and was not able to stop them.

'We conner stay here, Martha, duck. Not now he's chucked us out.'

The boys went upstairs to collect a few things to take with them. Once the door closed, Mother's tears flowed unchecked. Seeing her mother in such distress started Martha off. It was bound to come to a head one day. How could they cope without the twins? And how would Father react now?

–

When they went downstairs for breakfast, Mother was in the back kitchen with a smile on her face, as if yesterday hadn't happened.

'Morning, girls. Get yer breakfasts down yer. There's only us. Your father's gone to play soldiers over at the drill hall for today, so we've got the house to ourselves.'

'Thank goodness, I was dreading what might happen if the twins turn up when Father is here.'

The two girls sat at the table. Martha watched Mother as she moved around the kitchen. As she turned to put the bread on the table, Martha noticed one eye was much darker than the other and looked swollen. Martha's eyes opened wide, quickly followed by a gasp from Issy.

'You've got another one, Mother,' said Issy.

'He blames you for the rows yesterday, doesn't he?' asked Martha.

'It's my own fault. I should have—'

'There you go, blaming yourself again. No mother should have to have a conversation like this with her daughters, but now it's out in the open, what are we going to do about it?' Martha was determined to be sensible.

'I know,' burst out Issy. 'If them lads can go and live with Grandma, then why can't we?'

'It's not that easy, duck. I made a promise when I got wed – "...to love, honour and obey until death—"'

'That should work for Father, an' all,' said Martha.

'That's as maybe.'

The boys arrived after dinner, relieved that Father had gone out.

'You're not really leaving us, are you?'

'No, Martha,' said Daniel. 'We're leaving Father. Surely you can't think we can live together after this. One or the other of us will do something we might regret. Father's ordered us out of the house, so what else can we do?'

'If yer want us, we'll be at Grandma's. She said we could stay as long as we wanted to. I don't think he'll be so bad if we're not around,' said Peter.

Daniel grinned ruefully. 'I seem to have the knack of rubbing him up the wrong way.'

'What were you two arguing about, any road?'

'Oh, Father had got it into his mind that we would be able to pay more board because the pit was doing well and he thought our tonnages would give us more money. I said that's not fair and just before you came in, he'd said some harsh thing to Mother and she was already upset – and you saw what happened next.'

'Yesterday, we were lucky. I think Pete took him by surprise and hitting the wall did wind him. Next time, he'll be on his guard.'

Peter nodded. 'Do you remember what he told us about the Boers?'

Martha said, 'I don't, what did he say?'

'The Boer men would carry out a raid on British troops and then disappear into the hills. When the British pursued them, they were ambushed and picked off by the Boer snipers. After a while, the British Army stopped their pursuit and just simply arrested all the Boer women and children in a village and took them to a concentration camp, as they called it. Father said it soon stopped the attacks.'

'I understand, I think,' said Martha. 'In the past when Father was angry with us he took it out on Mother knowing we'd keep quiet, for her sake. Yesterday, you took him on for the first time, and you crossed a line you cannot go back over. He's turned you out because he realises he can't take you on no more.'

Peter smiled and held her shoulders. 'That's right.'

'What if he turns on Issy?'

'You come and tell us and we'll get the police.'

Martha folded her arms. 'If we're not dead by then!'

'That's a bit melodramatic.' Daniel frowned. 'Dunner think as he'd go that far. Mother wouldn't let him. We're getting out of his way because we're a threat to him. You and Issy aren't a threat, so he has no reason to have a go. And that's why we have to leave. Now, d'yer see?'

Reluctantly, Martha had to agree.

Peter gave her a hug. 'Tell Mother to look after herself. You and Issy will be all right.'

'Chin up, Martha,' said Daniel.

The twins gazed around the room for one final check and made for the door. Daniel dropped a kiss on her forehead – and they were gone.

After the twins left home and moved back to The Potter's Wheel, things at Dresden Street seemed to calm down and good news arrived. Issy came skipping home from Hanley with the news that she had found a job — at Millward's Drapery in Parliament Row, just round the corner from Webberley's Bookshop. Their new store in Hanley hadn't long opened and they were looking for a junior assistant to help out. She was to start straight away.

'That's marvellous. Fancy our Issy working in a draper's,' Mother beamed. 'You'll be learning how to make yer own clothes before long. And you can make some for the rest of us.'

Issy laughed and shook her head. 'It'll be a good while before I can do that. I shall be the one who does all the jobs nobody wants — sweeping floors and cleaning windows, making sure the shop's spick and span for the customers. Dunner think as I'll be speaking to anybody for a few years. It's not very well-paid, and I'll be working six days a week, but at least I'm earning summat.'

Martha shook her head. 'Dunner be daft. You're so handy, you're bound to make a good impression.'

'We'll see,' said Issy, taking what was being said with a pinch of salt, knowing they were looking to support her.

She leaned over to whisper to Martha. 'And at least I'll be out of Father's way!'

Chapter Three

The Owen women were getting used to living with no men except Father. It meant there were times when Father was out, and they could get together to talk without fear of being interrupted. One of those times, Martha decided to take the bull by the horns and speak out. Issy had gone round to see her friend Josie, who had started to work at Jackson's a few weeks earlier.

Mother was darning socks and a pair of Father's work trousers while Martha was knitting a winter hat for herself. A single oil lamp was shining in the centre of the table.

'Mother – can I ask you summat?'

'Course yer can, duckie.'

Martha took a deep breath. 'You're so much happier when Father isn't around.'

Both flushed to the roots of their hair, Martha because she had raised such a delicate issue and Mother probably not expecting such a statement from her daughter.

Mother carried on darning, not lifting her head nor speaking.

'Mother?'

'I wouldn't say happier, I am just more relaxed. In any case, it's not for kids to hear about the problems parents have.'

On this occasion, Martha thought her mother was wrong. 'You must see how it's affecting us. Issy worries when Father's home, that's why she likes the job at the draper's. Father goes

22

out before she has to get up and she comes back at teatime and with any luck she can keep out of his way until bedtime, which is getting sooner every week. I do pretty much the same.'

'I agree, Martha, Issy would be here now if she knew Father had gone out.'

'We notice what is happening to you in just the same way. I don't see why you think your problems are not our problems.'

'I'm not saying they dunner affect you two, it just that it's down to me and your father to sort them out. Nobody else.'

'But sometimes even parents need help.'

At that moment Issy came in quietly through the back door. 'Father's out?'

'Yes,' said Mother, 'You're safe.'

Issy smiled, a little bit embarrassed.

'Go put the kettle on; Martha and me was having a chat about yer father. You might as well join us – when you've made that tea.'

Issy returned with teapot and cups. They sat for a few moments in silence and then Mother started to speak. 'I know what is happening is not good for us all, but you need to under-stand a few things about marriage. Once a woman gets wed, she and everything she owns is considered to be her husband's. If I left your father, I'd have no home and no children. You would have to live with him. Do you think I could bear that?'

'I didn't know,' said Martha.

'Why should I give up everything I've worked for?' She fingered the socks on her knee as she spoke, as if it helped. 'I talked to somebody. They said as divorce—'

The girls let out a simultaneous gasp.

'—if it should ever come to that,' Mother said quickly, 'divorce is biased against women. Best I could do would be to leave him but he would have the right to keep you kids until yer come of age.'

'That's not fair!' protested Issy. 'We should be allowed to live with who we want.'

'It's the law, nowt to do with fairness. It seems to put a woman in the wrong for wanting to leave the family – when actually, it's only her husband she wants to leave. If a stranger assaulted yer, he'd be put in prison, but if yer husband did the same thing to yer at home, the police dunner want ter know. I tell both of yer, be very careful of the man you choose to marry. You're giving him a lot of power over yer.'

Martha couldn't believe Mother knew so much about it. Who could she have spoken to? She had been so insistent that nobody should know. She didn't want people feeling sorry for her, or wondering what she'd done to deserve it.

'Well, I'm never going to get wed,' said Martha. 'No man is going to have that power over me.'

'You don't know what is going to happen,' said Issy. 'Look at our old teacher, Miss Rowley, she was really old, but suddenly she left to get married and had to give up her job. So, she must have been pretty sure. If I can't find the right man then so be it.'

Martha thought that for a thirteen-year-old Issy spoke a lot of sense.

'Trouble is, girls, you can see plenty of women married to thugs. No doubt they thought they'd chosen the right man. You can only know a man when you start living with him.'

'That's what a long engagement is for,' said Martha.

'You've got a lot to learn. A man will do and say anything to get inside your drawers.'

'Mother!' said Issy. 'Dunner say things like that. It's embarrassing.'

Mother continued. 'Once you're married or, God forbid, in the family way where you've got no choice other than marriage, it's too late to go back. Your vows do mean "till death do you part". Real life is nothing like them books you read, Martha. You need to remember that.'

'Why did you marry him in the first place, if you knew what he was like?' asked Martha.

'When you fall in love with someone you make excuses for their bad points. After all, you can change them, you think.'

'I can see that; Grandma tells Grandad to do something and he does it. But I've seen him wink at me as much to say he's doing it to keep the peace.'

'Oh yes, my mother knows her own mind, but my dad gets his own way when it really matters.'

This was the first time Martha had heard her refer to Grandad as Dad; you forget that parents have parents as well.

Mother sat back in her chair. 'We met at The Potter's Wheel. Your father was a soldier, young and handsome. He had a lovely smile. He was funny and really kind. We started to walk out together and then we got married. When he was away from the barracks we lived at the pub. He was stationed in Ireland so we got a chance to see each other when he was on leave. The twins came along and then you, Martha, and finally you, Issy. I was expecting you when his unit was posted to South Africa and he fought in the Boer War. He got a medal and was mentioned in despatches.'

'What does that mean?'

'It means he did something especially brave.'

Mother took a sip of her tea, clearly thinking about what to say next.

'It was nearly a year before his unit was posted to India and we spent a lot of that time together as a couple, and as a family. We was happy and you kids, although still young, enjoyed him being about the place.

'When he got news of his posting to India, he was excited. You see, a posting to India was one of the best postings in the army and we could all go with him.'

Issy looked surprised. 'Why didn't you go? India sounds far more exciting than Tunstall.'

'I worried what might happen if I got pregnant again or if any of us were taken ill. I also didn't want to leave my parents and The Potteries. India sounded so far away and so different from what I had been used to. Your father wasn't pleased.'

Mother sighed and was silent for a moment.

'He thought he'd finally made it. He would have married quarters with some servants. Plentiful supply of food. A regular wage. No rent man or tallyman to worry about. All I could think about was the weather being very hot and the dangerous animals. I knew it was a much better place to live with no bottle ovens belching out smoke, but "better the devil yer know", as they say.'

'Sounds so different. I would have liked to have seen it,' said Issy.

Mother's face creased as if a sudden pain had driven right through her. Martha and Issy couldn't bring themselves to speak at first. It must have been important to bring about such a change in her.

'When I said about getting pregnant again, you two should know that I was pregnant when we got married, but I lost the baby through a miscarriage.'

Martha put her hand over her mouth and looked at Mother and then Issy. Issy was the first to speak.

'You were expecting before you got married?'

'Yes, I'm afraid I was.'

'But how?' asked Martha.

'How d'yer think? Come on, Martha, you know all about that.'

Martha's face turned red. She hadn't meant it that way.

'Me and your father were planning to get married and, well, one night we were alone and – well, you know – one thing leads to another. Percy had a whole week off from the barracks and – shall we say – we made the most of it. Still, you girls remember that there are consequences if you lose control.'

More silence followed, everyone lost in their thoughts. Issy broke the silence. 'Oh Martha, "but how", I'll tell you how if you're unsure, you only have to ask.'

'Shut up, Issy.' The two girls licked their tongues out at each other.

'Can I carry on now?'

'Sorry, Mother, go on. I'll deal with my little sister later.'

'So I was concerned. If it happened once, it could happen again and I was too scared to risk it. After that, we grew apart. Father could've returned once a year on leave but he chose not to. His letters were informative but no longer romantic. He asked about you children, but I think his heart was no longer in the marriage.

'We were apart for five years and to be honest, I grew used to him not being about. I never thought he'd leave the army. You can imagine my surprise when he did. I was shocked and unsure what to do. A husband, who I didn't really know, returning home after five years. But it was my duty to make a home for him and I was determined to do my best. After all, we would be living at the pub and my mother would be there to help me.'

'He never wrote to you telling about him leaving the army?' asked Issy.

'Not a word. He only told me when he got home. He said he'd left the army so he could take over the pub when Grandad decided to retire. There was only me to pass the licence on to, so your father would be the logical person, being a man, to take over. I said he was mistaken. I could've told him my father had no intention of retiring. To be honest, girls, Grandad didn't like your father very much. He put up with him for my sake and until this point I don't think we had spent more than six months at the pub as man and wife.'

'I remember hearing Father and Grandad arguing in the bar while they were preparing to open the pub. It frightened me. They looked like two dogs sizing each other up for a fight,' said Martha.

'Oh yes, they didn't get on and when your grandad told him he wouldn't ever take over the pub, your father decided again without talking to me. He got a job as a caster which is what he had done before joining the army. Next thing we were moving here and the rest, you well know.'

'Well, I wasn't expecting that when I come in tonight. Thought I would have an early night. It's past eleven. He'll be coming home soon. I'm going to make myself scarce.' Issy hugged her mother. 'Thank you for telling us everything. It helps to make sense of it all, doesn't it, Martha?'

Martha nodded. 'I'll be up shortly once I've got me breakfast ready.' Martha had no idea what to say next. It was the most Mother had said about Father in all the years he'd been back from the army. In the olden days, fathers were to be respected and no matter what they did they were always in charge. Nobody interfered with what went on behind closed doors.

–

When Martha got upstairs Issy was sitting up waiting for her.

'That was a surprise. We could have lived a luxury life in India.'

'You'd have been called Lady Isabel. And all of them gallant officers would chase after you.'

'Don't be silly, Martha.'

'Seriously, I think I can understand why Father is so angry. He must have thought he had done everything right – a job in India followed by running his own pub – and then to end up making privies in a potbank in Hanley. He blames us all, but especially Mother and so he takes it out on her, knowing that we'll do as we're told so prevent Mother getting into trouble.'

'Well, I think we should tell Grandma and Grandad. She's their daughter, after all. I would want the same done for me. All this keeping secrets is no good.'

–

The back door slammed. That was Father's way of making sure his daughters were not late for work.

'Come on, Martha, time to get up.' Issy was already dressed in her plain black dress used for work. She didn't work on the counter but in the office and warehouse. Nevertheless, they still insisted she wore a black dress.

'You're early or am I late?'

'Need to get in a bit earlier this morning as we have a lot of cloth to wrap up for Holmorton Lodge. It is being collected at nine o'clock, sharp, as Mr Butterworth says.'

'Where is that?'

'Up Moorland Road in Burslem, by the park. They're having enough material to make curtains for half a dozen houses in this road – upstairs and down as well – and it's just for one room. Mr Butterworth says he'll give me a shilling. Father won't know about it so won't miss it. Dunner tell him, will yer? I'll be rich! And its payday as well.'

–

Issy normally worked until half past five on Saturdays. Martha was lucky, potbanks only worked until noon. By the time Issy had tidied up and walked home it was usually about six o'clock. So it was strange when there was still no sign of her by seven.

Naturally, they had eaten their teas, which was usually a light snack as the main meal was served at dinnertime at the weekend. Now Issy was working on Saturdays, the meal was still dished up and put between two plates. It could then be warmed up in the evening in the frying pan. Martha actually liked a meal cooked this way. It seemed to have more taste.

'Did Issy say she was going to be late tonight?' asked Mother.

'No. She left home earlier this morning—' Martha put a hand over her mouth; she had nearly let the cat out of the bag and would be in trouble with Issy if she found out. 'Well, I mean she looked ready to leave when I went out but she probably took the opportunity to have another cup of tea.'

Father did not make any comment, but said that Issy knew she had to come straight home from work on a Saturday as it was payday at the draper's. Martha thought that Father was likely to be looking forward to his money so that he could have a drink.

'Well, that's me, I've worked hard this week and I think I deserve a little drink. When that young lady comes home you give her a good telling-off, Fanny. And make sure she hasn't opened her wage packet. If she has and she's been out with her friends then there'll be trouble. Mark my words.' Father donned his cap and muffler and set out for the pub.

'Issy's too young to go into pubs, nobody would let her in, so where can she have gone, Mother?'

'I don't know. Nobody else we know in the street works in a shop in Hanley so we conner ask them.'

'After we had that chat last night, she said that it was wrong not to tell Grandma and Grandad about Father. She said to me that she couldn't understand why Daniel and Peter could choose to live with their grandparents but she was forced to stay here with Father. I think she's gone to see them.'

'Oh, that's where she'll be. I'll go up to Grandma's and see if she's there,' said Mother.

'Let's both go and find out what damage the little minx has done.'

Mother and Martha put on their hats and coats. Mother scribbled a note telling whoever came in first where they had gone, and locked up the house. They walked quickly up to the centre of Hanley and caught the first tram to Tunstall. They walked briskly through the square and soon could see the welcoming lights of The Potter's Wheel. They let themselves in through the back door. As usual, the kitchen was nice and warm and they were greeted by Grandma, who had just finished taking some cakes out of the oven.

'Hello, what are you doing here?'

'Hello, Mother. Have you seen our Issy? She hasn't come home from work yet and I'm worried about her.'

Grandma looked away and placed the last of the cakes into a tin and put it on the top shelf of the pantry. When she turned round, she had a slightly guilty look on her face. 'She's here. She arrived about half past six. She said she'd come here to see us as you were all out at home.'

At that point, Issy came downstairs straight into the kitchen and she stopped stone dead. 'What are you two doing here?'

'What do you think, you've not come home from work. Your father and me was worried about you.'

'I don't think so, he was probably worried about me wage packet. After all, it's Saturday night and he always goes to the pub.'

'What are you up to, Issy?' asked Martha. 'You were acting strange this morning.'

'Nothing.'

'You'd better tell them, or else I will,' said Grandma.

They all sat round the large kitchen table, which could easily sit eight to ten people.

Issy started to speak. 'I have decided that I am coming to live with Grandma and Grandad in just the same way as Daniel and Peter have. And if you two had any sense you would do the same. I've had enough of Father and I've told Grandma everything. I have just had a bath and there is plenty of room here for all of us. When Father was arguing and he threw out the twins he took great pleasure in telling us that it was *his* house, so in my opinion he's welcome to it – I'm coming back to *my* home.'

They looked at each other in turn. Grandma broke the silence. 'She arrived straight from work and told us that she had a problem. Fanny, I have to say I was surprised by what Issy had to tell us. I'm also disappointed that you didn't feel it was right to tell your mother what has been going on. And now I find out that Martha's just as bad as he's hit her an' all. I've got a lot of sympathy with this young lady. It took some strength of character to do what she's done.'

'She had no right to come here and to tell you about everything,' Mother said. 'It is up to me to do what I think is right for my family. What you've done today, Issy, will lead to lots of arguments with Father and it will make the situation worse.'

Issy shook her head. 'I don't see how it can get much worse. None of us dare say nothing for fear of Father losing his temper. He makes sure we know what'll happen if we don't toe the line.'

Mother folded her arms.

'Issy, you are coming back home with us.'

'I'm not, I'm stopping here with Grandma.'

'No, you're not,' said Grandma. 'You have to go home with your mother and sister. That's where you belong. What's happening between your mother and father needs to be sorted out, but it won't be sorted out by you coming to live here. Issy, promise me you will return home and I will promise you we'll do something about the mess.'

'What are you going to do about the "mess", as you put it?' interrupted Mother. 'Percy's the ruler in his own house and he'll not stand by and let you dictate what he does. It's the worst thing you can do.'

'Well, what d'yer suggest?' Grandma was sharper with Mother than they had ever seen her. Mother began to cry, softly. Through the tears Martha could hear Mother say that she'd had enough. She turned to Martha and Issy as if looking for some support.

Issy swallowed. 'I'll come back to Dresden Street, but I want Daniel and Peter to come back home as well. Father won't dare to do anything when they're about, and if he does—'

'No, that's not the way,' said Martha. 'You can't ask the twins to police what Father is doing. They're as scared as we are sometimes. Father needs to understand that his behaviour is wrong and he needs to make his own mind up about how to behave. Mother told us quite a lot about how things used to be and it shows that somewhere Father has some good qualities.'

Grandad came into the kitchen while Martha was talking. 'If Percy's got some good qualities he hides them very well.'

Grandad put his pipe back into his mouth. 'If he doesn't want to behave himself I know people who could make him feel the way Fanny feels when he's been having a go at her.'

'No, Oswald, that is not the way,' said Grandma.

'I agree,' said Mother. 'If you do that he'll only go to the police and get them involved and then you'll be in trouble, and you'll probably lose your licence.'

Grandad smiled. 'The people I know are the police. There's a lot of stairs in a police station and a man like Percy struggling when he's been arrested could accidentally fall down them stairs. Nowt would be said.'

Martha was shocked, their normally mild-mannered, fun-loving grandfather who always enjoyed a joke and had a smile on his face had a dark side. But when she thought about it later she realised that he knew a lot of people and you didn't run a successful pub if you antagonised the police. Perhaps Grandad was more worldly-wise than she had given him credit for.

'No, Oswald, I knew what you meant and I still don't think that is the correct way forward. But, if Percy continues this way then I think it might be an option to consider as a last resort.'

Grandma placed her hands palms down on the table. Martha recognised this gesture as signifying that Grandma was to be listened to without interruption. 'This is what I think we should do. Martha has got it right. Percy needs to find the solution himself, otherwise he will fight against it.' She paused.

'It makes sense that you all live together; that's you, Fanny, and your four children. So I think we need to talk to Daniel and Peter when they get in from their shift to see what they think—'

'But Mother—'

'Let me finish, I'll come down tomorrow with Issy and we can discuss with Percy the way he should be behaving towards you. I'm not stupid, I guessed that there was something like this happening. He was never the same when he came back from India. But we won't go into that. Suffice to say, he seems to be blaming everyone else for his shortcomings. He thought that he was going to take over the licence of this place and have a built-in income for the rest of his life. Perhaps he feels he deserves that. He needs to start being a father to his children, not a bully.'

Grandma looked at everybody around the table.

They were all quiet.

She nodded. 'We were just as surprised as everyone else how much he had changed over them five years out in India. He seemed angry to us and when he virtually demanded that yer grandad retire and sign the pub over to him immediately, that was the last straw. The rest you know.'

Peter and Daniel arrived home from work before she could say more. They were still covered in coal dust so a quick catch-up on what had happened followed. They agreed to return if Father allowed it.

It was past eleven o'clock and Grandma insisted that they all stay the night.

'What about Father?' asked Martha.

'He's old enough to look after himself. He can manage for one night on his own. He'll probably sleep like a baby. He usually does after a visit to the pub.'

–

The time had come that Martha was dreading – returning to Dresden Street and her father. Mother and Issy looked pale and Grandma determined as they set off for Hanley. Grandad stopped behind to open the pub.

They said very little on the tram, not wanting anyone sitting around them to know their business. What more could they say that hadn't already been said?

Martha stared through the window and Mother looked directly ahead, her chin up and not inviting conversation. Daniel and Peter looked thoughtful.

Mother let them all into the house and led the way through to the kitchen, where a surprised-looking Father sat at the table.

Immediately, Martha's heart beat faster at the look on his face as he twiddled his fingers.

'Welcome back, wife. What right have yer got – staying out overnight and leaving me with a skimpy note to tell me where you were.' He stopped talking when he saw Grandma. 'Ah! I see you've brought reinforcements.'

'We thought yer might have calmed down by now, Percy Owen,' retorted Grandma.

'Oh and you've brought the troublemaker back with yer.'

Issy looked him straight in the eye, but said nothing. Martha was relieved Grandma was with them. Grandma was used to getting her own way in most things.

'I suggest you put the kettle on, Martha, and we'll sit round the table like civilised people and sort this out.'

Martha nodded and took the kettle off the range to fill with water. She could hear murmurings from the kitchen but no raised voices so far.

'So, how are yer, Issy?'

'All right.'

'I wondered when you were going to ask about our daughter, Percy.'

'Well, I gather she's in some sort of trouble as you're all here. The little bugger isn't pregnant, is she?'

Grandma banged her fist on the table. 'No, it's nothing like that. You are the problem so don't start arguing – that's what started it all! Percy, I need yer to listen to me until I've finished because this is important.'

Her eyes bored into Father's until he nodded his agreement.

Grandma recounted everything that Issy had said, about his temper, the rows that went on behind closed doors.

'Issy left home because she's frightened of yer and she wants the twins to come back home to live.'

Father's lips thinned. 'She's a drama queen, that one. Always after her own way.'

'Percy – she's not yet fourteen and has been frightened out of her wits by the person who should be keeping her safe. She's seen you hit our Fanny and make her life a misery with yer rows. You've hit Martha and kicked the boys out. Nothing seemed to be improving so she decided you all needed help and she turned to me and Oswald. She wants you all to be together, but the arguments have to stop.'

Grandma's eyes swept around the table. No one, including Father, could bring themselves to look at her. 'Put yerself in her shoes, for Heaven's sake, Percy. With yer army work, that girl never saw yer until she was seven and even then she didn't see yer as her father but as a large angry man who had come to live with her family.'

Father's face was tinged pink. Martha could see him wet his lips with his tongue – as if his mouth was dry.

'When I came out of the army I thought I could help run the pub and eventually take over the licence.' He turned to Grandma. 'I came back with dreams that Oswald squashed. So here I am in a tiny house, in a smoke-filled town, making privies. Is it any wonder I'm angry?'

'You get angry most of the time,' said Mother.

Grandma nodded. 'I see, Percy. But we can't go on forever like this, it is no good for any of you. We talked last night and this is what's going to happen. Firstly, Issy wants the family to be together again, and I can't say as I blame her.'

'You're telling me what to do in me own house?'

'I am, Percy. And secondly, you need to find a way of controlling your anger. If you don't, Fanny and the children will leave and come back to the pub to live.'

Father turned to face Mother. 'And you agree to all this, do yer. You're threatening to leave me?'

Mother looked at Grandma as if for guidance but Grandma's face never changed. The answer must be Mother's.

'Yes, Percy. I am.'

Father got up from the table and left for the privy.

A half-remembered conversation between Father and the twins crossed Martha's mind. It was something to do with him telling the twins only to fight when they know they can win. He said, 'retreat, regroup and live to fight another day'.

When Father returned from the privy, he agreed that the twins could move back.

–

The twins returned home later that week when their night shifts finished. Issy's face was a picture of satisfaction, but Father's was a picture of defiance. Martha wondered how long it would take for him to return to his normal self.

What a week it had been. They had learned so much. Martha could not foresee what was going to happen with Father, but hoped that they had turned a corner and things might improve.

Chapter Four

Summer 1914

Father had been good to his promise. Maybe the thought of losing his family was sufficient. He began to mellow and join in conversations rather than cause arguments. Issy was still wary, but behaviour like they'd experienced never changed overnight.

For his part, Father held himself in check by walking out of the house when the pressure got too much for him to contain. He would disappear down to the privy with *The Sentinel* for longer than was strictly necessary. The rest of the family got to recognise his behaviour and stayed out of his way at these times. It was less than ideal, but tolerable.

–

Work was going fine, and Martha was earning good money. She didn't see much of Jeffrey these days. He tended to meet the twins at the top of the street since Father had a go at him. Her feelings for him were still the same. Hopefully she would have an opportunity to spend more time with him during the upcoming Potters' holiday and she was looking forward to it.

Although peace had broken out in the Owen family, the same could not be said for the royal families of Europe.

At the end of June, an event happened which was to have a massive effect on the whole world. A Serbian man had shot and killed the Archduke Franz Ferdinand, heir to the throne of the Austro-Hungarian Empire. Martha began to see headlines in the newspapers, talking about a European war and Britain's potential involvement.

'Why we would get involved in a war over there is beyond me. It's nowt to do with us.'

'Ah, that's because you're a girl, Martha,' Father said. 'Yer dunner understand matters of war.'

For the sake of keeping the peace, Martha kept her mouth shut.

Father continued, mostly addressing his words to Daniel and Peter. 'It's all to do with alliances. The French and the Russians have agreed they'll protect each other, so if anybody attacks France, Russia will come to their aid.'

'They are a long way from each other, so how could they help?' asked Peter, frowning.

'Germany hates the idea of a war on two fronts, so the threat of France attacking in the west and Russia in the east will make the Germans think twice. In turn the Germans have a pact with Austria to help each other. The idea is that these alliances will act as a check on all of them.'

'Sorry, Father, still don't understand why we would get involved, I remember you saying that we had a small army?' said a proud Peter.

'The foreign armies have conscription and a large reserve force which can be mobilised quickly. Despite the size of their armies, most of the fighting men are conscripts who don't want to be there, probably never seen active service and have a very low level of skill. Our army's not meant for large-scale fighting. It's there to maintain our Empire and has a much smaller reserve army. All of the men are volunteers and that makes us a very effective fighting force. If we do get involved it will be in Flanders and Belgium, making sure we keep the routes back to the Channel open – just in case. The real concern to us is Germany's growing navy. We depend on the navy ruling the seas to maintain our connection with the Empire and to deploy troops to areas where there is trouble. Even with a small army, we've got the largest empire the world has ever seen. If the Germans get a navy that can rival us, then it will put our Empire under threat.'

The four young people listened intently. This was a side of Father Martha hadn't seen before. He was trying to connect with his children. Even Issy, who didn't have any interest in what was going on in the rest of the world, was listening intently. He knew so much and the more he spoke the more animated he was becoming. Even though Martha *was* a girl, she found herself growing more interested.

She said, 'So we don't really want to go to war, we just want to protect the Empire, but the best way to do that is to be friends with France and Russia and therefore go to war.'

A look of surprise crossed Father's face. 'That's correct, Martha, you don't have to like your allies, you just have to have a common goal.'

Daniel chipped in. 'At school we learned all about our wars with France and how we beat the French to build the Empire. We also fought the Russians in the Crimea, yet now they're our allies.'

'Mr Wells told us it was the Germans what helped us to win the Battle of Waterloo an' all,' said Peter. 'And the royal family's of German descent.'

Father said, 'In the army we have a saying. When we're asked, "Why are we here?" we reply "Because we are." The army does not ask why, it just does its duty.'

Her father had never spoken up about the army before and Martha couldn't help listening. It turned out that her grandfather on Father's side was also in the army and was killed by the Zulus in South Africa when Father was only four.

Father sat back in his chair and closed his eyes as if transporting himself somewhere deep in his mind.

'Do yer miss the army?' asked Peter.

'I do, lad. There's summat about the army that brings out the best in men. I've seen it happen. You come to rely on yer fellow men to keep you alive. You lads should think about it.'

'You really liked being in the army,' said Daniel. 'It must have been a big decision to leave.'

'Aye lad, it was.' He shrugged. 'But, if we do go to war, I'll be called back because I'm a member of the Army Reserve. That's why I joined the Territorial Force. So as I could keep up me skills in case they was ever needed – and it looks like they will be.'

He was the first person Martha saw who actually looked happy at the prospect of war. Maybe she was beginning to see why Father changed so much during his life away and why he couldn't settle with his life at home. Martha desperately wanted to ask why he was violent towards Mother, but that was a question which could never be asked, let alone answered.

At that point he got up and left the room and never spoke of his time in the army again.

–

Father went off on his annual training camp at Cannock Chase on the Friday evening at the start of Potters' Week and everyone breathed a sigh of relief. It didn't matter how good a mood he was in, he still sometimes overreacted, but at least now he had learned to curb his temper – most of the time.

Fighting and mobilisation was going on all over Europe. *The Sentinel* reported daily, sometimes putting out special editions with extra news items. Only Britain had still to make up her mind whether or not to join the war.

Then, newspapers reported that the members of the Territorial Force had been ordered to report to their units and that failure to do so would be classed as desertion.

Unannounced, Father arrived home on the Saturday dinnertime. He had been told to return home and wait for orders. Immediately, the house became small and tense again, although for very different reasons. The excitement on his face was plain to see. It was where he was meant to be. Not this life at home with his family, but in the army, with his men.

'They've sent us back home as it looks like war. I am to wait here until I receive orders – by telegram, they say.'

He had a copy of *The Sentinel* which he had bought at the station. Martha just saw one headline.

SENSATIONAL NEWS – *warlike action by*
Germany

'Do you think we'll get involved?' asked Daniel.

For once, a thoughtful Father seemed to hesitate. 'I think so, son. It looks as though Germany thinks she can take on France and Russia at the same time, like I said before. Germany doesn't seem worried at the prospect of a war on two fronts.'

'Will the Germans attack us an' all?' asked Martha.

'No, my girl. The Royal Navy will give them short shrift. No need for you to worry. We'll sort the Germans out on their own doorstep. I'd best get meself packed ready, word could come any time.'

Father went upstairs. Now he was about to leave, he had become animated – mostly about the war and the part he might play in ending it.

Mother gave a faint smile. 'It'll suit him down to the ground. It's what he's wanted really – to get back into the army with the blokes in his platoon. He wants to be out there, fighting with like-minded people. He was one of those men who thought marriage might offer him all he needed only to find out, too late, that his former life had given him so much more. Now, he has the chance to relive his old life and has come alive again.'

Sure enough, at teatime on Sunday, Father received the telegram he was waiting for. It instructed him to report back to the North Staffords at Whittington Barracks in Lichfield by six p.m. on 3 August 1914 and to await further instructions.

'My old battalion's in India at the moment, so I'll probably join them or they'll join me if they are brought back to England to fight in this war.'

Issy did not ask any questions until she and Martha went to bed.

'Martha, are you awake?' whispered Issy.

'No!'

'What's going to happen?'

'I know as much as you, Issy.'

'Is it wrong to say I'm glad Father's going away?'

'No. I feel the same.'

'If the war goes on a long time, he might not come back.'

'Issy, don't say that. That's not nice—'

Issy covered her mouth with her hands. 'No, I didn't mean that. I just thought he likes the army so much he might decide to stop there and leave us in peace.'

Soon, Issy had fallen asleep, but Martha lay there thinking of what might happen and she felt ashamed that she too wondered what it might be like if he never returned.

—

Father was having his breakfast before starting his journey to war. No one was working because of the holiday so the whole family was sitting round the table. The men talking about the war, Mother and Martha listening, and Issy keeping her eyes on Father.

Everyone was there to see Percy Owen off to war. The first to leave in their street. Looking smart in his uniform, he stood proud, with his back straight and his chin up. Seeing him like that, Martha could understand why Mother had fallen for him in his youth. Even Daniel and Peter watched as neighbours took their turn to shake his hand and wish him well. His drinking pals made jokes about him not ending the war before they'd had a chance to join him.

Martha hadn't seen her father so happy in a long time. Again, she tried to think about their life from his point of view – living in The Potteries, making privies eleven hours a day, with a wife

43

and kids who had their own lives to lead long before he had come out of the army.

Her eyes watered. How did she feel about the possibility he might not come back? What was going through Mother's mind as she stood next to him? Her face was unreadable. He hadn't wanted anyone to accompany him to the station. He was off to do the job he had trained for and that was the end of it.

He gave Mother a hug, and while his arms were around her, he whispered in her ear. If only Martha could hear what he was saying. Her mother blushed. She even laughed, although Martha couldn't be sure whether that was for the benefit of the neighbours.

As the crowd around their front door thinned and the time for leaving arrived, Father appeared to take charge again and made it clear he would have to make a move or be arrested for desertion. He picked up his bag and, with a final nod, he strode off at a steady march. At the end of the street, he turned, gave a quick salute and Sergeant Major Percy Owen was gone.

–

Martha's heart was pounding as she followed Mother, Issy and the twins inside.

They sat round the table staring at each other with nothing to say.

Daniel was the first to speak. 'Well, that's it then.'

Mother's eyes filled and Daniel cupped her hand in his. 'Dunner cry, Mother. It was coming sooner or later. The papers are full of it.'

'What did he say... when he whispered in your ear?' asked Martha tentatively.

Mother's eyes were bright, her words ragged. 'He said he loved me – and that he was sorry.' She looked around the table and sniffed. 'He's never said he was sorry before. He wants us to write to him while he's away. All of us.'

Daniel raised an eyebrow.

'Doesn't want to be the only one not getting letters from home—'

'Peter!'

'It's true, Mother. He feels he's got his life back.'

'You should all write to him. We owe him that for what he's doing.'

Peter shook his head. 'Mother, we owe him nowt and neither do you.'

As usual, it was Daniel who had the last word. 'Father has changed this year – we don't know how long for. We can all hope that a better man comes back when it's all over.'

An ultimatum had been issued to the Germans that they should withdraw from Belgium by eleven o'clock that evening, otherwise a state of war would be declared.

The Germans ignored the ultimatum and the following day Martha woke to find that war had been declared.

–

Despite being at war, the Friday of Wakes Week became a celebration for both the Dean and the Owen families. Jeffrey, Mary-Ellen, Michael, Lily and Tommy Dean joined Daniel, Peter, Martha and Issy for a day out. Betty hadn't been able to join them, much to Martha's disappointment. The two mothers provided a picnic treat and there was lots of shouting, laughing and general enjoyment. They all walked together in the warm August sunshine. Martha didn't dare walk near to Jeffrey. The torch she carried for him was still there even though she hadn't seen much of him recently. She kept up a pace at the front.

Before long she heard his footsteps approaching. 'Somebody's in a rush today.'

She glanced across at him as he drew level. 'Hiya, Jeffrey,' was all she said.

'I'm glad you decided to come today. We'll have a great day won't we?' He breathed in deeply taking in the air.

'Course we will. We can forget about the war and just enjoy ourselves.'

And they did. The later part of the afternoon was spent at Hanley Park where the older boys provided another treat – the hiring of two rowing boats followed by a trip around the fair, laid on specially for the holidays. They split into two parties and took a boat each. Martha managed to get in the same boat as Jeffrey. It was a tight squeeze with lots of screaming and joviality as the boat rolled from side to side as each of them climbed aboard. Martha refused to scream – not while Jeffrey was around. She wanted to appear above that sort of thing. She even contrived to sit next to him, much to her delight. Her body against his gave her the strangest of sensations. Something she had not experienced before – something nice, very nice.

He was such fun to be with and even tried to show her how to row. It was easier than she had thought, although her arms ached by the time it was over. The key was not to put the oar too deeply into the water. It was the drag of pulling so much water that led to aching shoulders. As she grew in confidence, her strokes became lighter. What a delight to see the admiration cross Jeffrey's face!

All too soon the boating was over and they made their way round the fair, which she enjoyed too – but she had to share Jeffrey for the rest of the evening. On the boat, she was able to keep him to herself despite the others. It was as if the two of them could forget their surroundings and just enjoy being together. Perhaps Betty not being there hadn't mattered after all, for she doubted Betty would have let her spend so much time with her favourite brother.

For one glorious week in August, they were able to be themselves. For the first time, Martha was looking forward to growing up.

Part Two

Chapter Five

The first four months of the war did not go well for the British. The Germans made their way into France through Belgium, causing the British to retreat. All too soon the Germans were reported to be only thirty miles from Paris – closer than Stoke is to Manchester. Although the French and British halted the German advance in September, there was no way the war would be over by Christmas like many people had originally said.

The newspapers seemed to set a lot of store by the ability of the Russian Army but after some initial success, the Germans had inflicted a heavy defeat at Tannenberg in East Prussia, wherever that was.

The call for volunteers never abated. Posters and advertisements reminded them that it was their duty to support their country in its hour of need. Former suffragettes, who had laid aside their fight for the vote, tried to shame men into joining the Colours, much to the annoyance of essential workers like Daniel and Peter, and Jeffrey. Newspapers said that there had been three-quarters of a million men volunteering for the army.

Father had written a couple of times. He said he'd been transferred from the Second Battalion to the First Battalion, so he wouldn't be going to India after all. From the way he'd spoken before he left, Martha reckoned he'd be disappointed not to be fighting with the regiment he knew. The First Battalion had been deployed to Lichfield from Buttevant in County Cork at the beginning of the war. Then, after a short time in East Anglia, where Father joined them, they were in France.

Fighting had ground to a halt and, according to the papers, trenches reached from the English Channel to the Swiss mountains. Martha couldn't remember from her geography lessons how far that was – but it sounded a very long way.

–

Father sent a postcard at the beginning of December. It was preprinted with paragraphs that could be deleted if they didn't apply – on subjects such as health, whether he was in hospital, and confirming he had received their letter/parcel. There was no mention of his whereabouts, and if anything other than the printed information was added to the postcard, apart from his signature, the card would be destroyed. So all the family could glean was that he was 'quite well' and that a letter would follow 'at the first opportunity'.

Life went on much as usual. They did not seem as busy at work. Martha thought pots were probably not foremost on people's minds. For her, the real change came at home. The atmosphere had become so much lighter it took her back to the old days – when she was just a kid and the family was happy.

A week before Christmas the family received shocking news. Although Daniel, being a pit worker, didn't have to enlist, he had done just that. He was eighteen years and one month. He gathered them all together at home so he could get it over with.

He wasn't a fighter. She had wanted to scream at him but knew he had not done it lightly. All the time he spoke, he was looking at the clock, ticking away the time on the wall so he didn't have to look at their faces.

Afterwards, he spoke to Martha alone, in the backyard.

'I dunner think as I could've coped with telling everyone separately. Best get it done and out of the way.'

'Why did yer do it?'

'We had a visit from a sergeant in the Royal Engineers telling us how they need people with our mining skills. We was talking while waiting for the cage to take us down and a few of us made our minds up there and then to join up. It was the only way I could've done it.'

'What did Peter say when yer told him?'

'I didn't. I told him afterwards – before I told you lot. I knew he'd need time to get over it before the rest of yer. He said I was a silly sod, but I must do what I must do. *He* was happy to take his chances in the pit – he reckoned it was safer. I couldn't explain to him why I had to do it. I just knew I couldn't live with myself if I didn't.'

'Oh, Daniel…'

He hugged her. 'I need yer to be strong, Martha. You don't think you are – but you are. Peter isn't as strong as he makes out. You need to be here looking after things with him until I get back. Promise me.'

Martha nodded. He nodded back as if his job was done.

'Oh, and by the way, Jeffrey Dean joined up at the same time. We might even end up in the same regiment. We'll be able to look out for one another.'

Martha trudged back into the house, her legs leaden after receiving Daniel's parting words about Jeffrey. Betty said he'd promised not to join up. Did he get carried away listening to someone talking about a duty to his country? It was all so unfair. Why did people have to poke their noses in?

Mother was sitting at the table sobbing uncontrollably. She had coped with Father going – it would've been strange if she hadn't, given all she'd been through. But losing a son was something no mother should have to prepare for. He was eighteen and had only just begun to live and her heart was breaking into tiny pieces.

They sat and talked until the lamp needed some more oil.

'Best we go to bed. We're not made of money,' said Mother. After giving her a hug, Martha made her way up the stairs like an old woman. Her brother and her almost-boyfriend going together to war. How could she cope when any day might bring news she would not be able to accept?

It was during the week before Christmas when they received a letter from Father. Due to censorship rules he wasn't allowed to say much, but one thing was clear. From the postal address he gave he had joined the British Expeditionary Force and was now in France.

Most families had not yet felt the full horror of war. There had been deaths, especially in the early months when the German advance seemed unstoppable, but of late it did not seem too bad.

Ordinary working people in any industrial town had a basic diet, even at Christmas. Money was always put aside for a few extras and these were not in short supply unless they came from the Empire. Prices had increased a lot since last year and many families had to go without some of their luxuries. Dried fruit and other products for the traditional Christmas pudding and mince pies were available. Most people had a Christmas cake, of sorts.

Everybody did the best they could and the Owens were no exception. They were able to afford a chicken. Mother had decided to pool her resources with Grandma and all the family went to The Potter's Wheel for the whole of Christmas Day and returning on Boxing Day, after breakfast.

It was just like old times.

'I remember that last Christmas before Father came home,' said Martha.

'It was 1907 and you'd just had your ninth birthday,' said Mother.

'You bought me two purple ribbons and Grandma and Grandad gave me a purple scarf. We had plenty to eat and played lots of games. The twins seemed to like the toy lorries Grandad made for them.'

'I had a cloth doll and a pink rabbit. I've still got the rabbit,' chipped in Issy.

When the family sat down to Christmas dinner Martha wondered what they were thinking. Father fighting, Daniel about to go to war. They had all forgotten how Peter risked his life every time he went to work. The pits weren't safe and accidents happened regularly.

In the afternoon, they were all sitting in the upstairs lounge and Martha said, 'We've been very lucky to have such a good Christmas. I think that a lot of people had to make do with much less.'

Grandad replied, 'That's true. But as far as some people are concerned, we are living off the suffering of ordinary people by selling the demon drink.'

'Don't get him started about the Temperance people – it's Christmas,' said Grandma.

'They'll not be satisfied until all the pubs have closed down. They want to stop the working man from enjoying himself. They are all so bloody miserable, they think everybody should be the same.'

'Don't get yerself upset, just because you had another run-in with Mr Mellor on Christmas Eve. Let's forget it and have a quiet day.'

Mother and Martha smiled at each other and then Issy gave out an enormous snore and woke herself up. She looked startled, then embarrassed.

'We were very busy at work and I'm right tired.'

'Good job Michael Dean wasn't here – you'd have put him right off,' quipped Martha.

'On a serious note,' said Mother, 'girls, remember what I said about not knowing someone until you've spent a lot of time with them. When you're courting everyone's on their best behaviour, so just imagine the shock Michael would have had if he heard Issy snore for the first time on his wedding night.'

'That would have dampened his ardour.'

'Grandad, don't be so rude.' Laughter broke out all around. Martha did think afterwards that no doubt marriage was not going to be like Jane Austen would have them believe.

They returned to Dresden Street before dinnertime on Boxing Day. Grandma and Grandad had to open the pub as Boxing Day was usually very good for business. When they all got home, the house was cold; it had snowed overnight. But they soon got a fire lit in the range. Martha thought that no doubt Betty would be busy serving all of them toffs with their posh foods and drink. Still, she would be back in the new year for her Christmas.

Reports in *The Sentinel* said that there had been an unofficial truce declared by the men themselves in Flanders between the British and German opposing forces on Christmas Day. Fraternisation had happened and some reports even said that football matches had taken place in No Man's Land. Martha wondered whether Father's unit were involved. It would be nice to think they'd had one day off from fighting.

–

Martha hadn't expected to see Betty over Christmas. How had Betty taken Jeffrey's news? Martha thought Jeffrey would be pleased that his sister couldn't come for Christmas – she would have been hopping mad at him. At least Betty would be able to arrange a visit when he had some leave at the end of his training.

It was a surprise when, two days later, Michael Dean appeared at Dresden Street with a letter addressed to her from Betty. Martha heard Mother ask him to come in and give the letter to Martha himself. An embarrassed-looking Michael appeared in the kitchen. He glanced around as if looking for someone.

'Our Betty's asked me to give yer this letter.' He thrust an envelope at her. 'She was planning to come and see yer – but everything went up in smoke with our Jeffrey's news. So, her's bin and gone.'

'She's gone?' Without coming to see her?

'Her come to see Jeffrey before he goes and she had to go back straight away. At least she got two days this year. She's had a right go at him an' all.'

'But couldn't she have come round for a few minutes?'

'Who are you talking to, Martha?' Issy appeared at the bottom of the stairs and froze. 'Hello, Michael.'

'Hiya, Issy.'

The two youngsters looked at each other and from the light of the lamp in the kitchen Martha could see their flushed expressions. Well, well, well! Our little Issy has a boyfriend, she thought. Mother winked at Martha and shook her head, as if telling her to say nothing.

After a few moments, Michael sniffed. 'She dunner tell me nowt. Happen as yer should read the letter, Martha.'

She glanced at it, thoughtfully. 'Thanks for bringing it. How's everybody at yours?' What she really meant, but couldn't say, was 'How's Jeffrey?'

Michael shrugged 'So-so, given the circumstances.' he said.

'That's why she come home early.' He grinned. 'It probably says so in the letter. I'll have to go now, got things to do. See you around, Issy.'

'See you.' Issy gave him the most wonderful smile. Michael flushed and left.

The letter! Everything went out of Martha's mind at that moment – except the letter.

She ran upstairs to the bedroom and closed the door before sitting down to read.

28 December 1914

Dear Martha,

I am so sorry that I have not been able to see you for Christmas this year. We had Christmas early because

the Delhaven family thought it was important to visit our
families this year. I gave this letter to our Michael and
asked him to bring it to you. I hope you don't mind.

Martha's eyes felt sore. She blinked. Betty must have been
devastated Jeffrey was going. Martha remembered the relief she
had felt knowing that Jeffrey would be safe – or as safe as anyone
working down the pit could be. There was nothing between
them, of course, but Martha had felt they were getting closer
after the boating lake; he might begin to see her as a person in
her own right and not just as his young sister's friend.

She tried telling herself that she didn't mind that she wasn't
special to him. She couldn't be – otherwise he would've told
her he was signing up, wouldn't he?

She wasn't bothered. But her heart's reaction to the news
told her she was deluding herself. She read on.

> *He had to tell me in a letter because he couldn't tell me*
> *face to face as I may not have been able to get home*
> *for Christmas. He leaves on Tuesday, the same as your*
> *Daniel. There was nothing I could do about it, but Mrs*
> *Stone, the housekeeper at Stowford House, let me come*
> *home straight away so as I could see him before he went,*
> *so I did. I spent all the time I could with him. You had a*
> *bit of a crush on him at one time, didn't you? I suppose*
> *you're not so bothered now. Like I said, they both go off*
> *for training on Tuesday and so they'll not be fighting just*
> *yet.*
>
>> *I promise to call and see you when I next come home.*
>> *Hope you had a better Christmas than me.*
>> *Love,*
>> *Betty*

Typical Betty! Not once asking her how she felt about Daniel.
Surely she could have found time to pop round for a chat.

Martha would have done that if it had been the other way round.

From the outset Martha had been thankful that she knew no one at the Front except Father. She could just about cope with hearing the news coming out daily now. But this was different – looking for news of people she knew – of her own age. Lads who shouldn't have to think about killing – or being killed. It wasn't right. Now, she was all of sixteen and had both Daniel and Jeffrey to worry about and she didn't know if she could bear it.

Martha lowered the letter onto her knee. She didn't know where the boys would be heading, but their training would be in England, so they might be home on leave sometime before they had to go and fight. She swallowed with difficulty and stared at the wall. She had thought about finding an excuse to visit the Deans, but since Betty had left she had no reason to call on them. If only she'd known he was going to war. She would've found some excuse to go round to Wellington Road whether Betty was there or not.

Jeffrey was twenty now and too nice to be a soldier. Should she write back straight away and tell Betty that she had feelings for him and beg her for news? All she could do was pray both the boys would be safe – always.

–

Martha thought back to their arrival in Dresden Street and, particularly, her first day at the new school. She had gone round to see her best friend Bridie O'Connor to tell her they were flitting, but they would still be able to meet when Martha visited her grandparents.

The twins and Martha went to their new school the following Monday. Martha felt really lonely having no friends there, but luckily for her she was told to sit next to Betty Dean. She was no Bridie O'Connor, but she was the next best thing.

Over the next three years they became best friends and shared everything – well, not quite everything. Martha could not tell her about Father.

At school, Martha was what teachers called average at most of the subjects. She didn't want to stand out as brainy because others might call her a teacher's pet – or worse. No, she liked to be in the middle at everything. Her favourite subject was art. She liked to draw and paint and give life to the pictures she drew. She was good at copying things and her previous teacher said she had an eye for detail, whatever that meant. It sounded like a compliment.

In school, Betty didn't mind reading to the class from a book or singing loud enough for others to hear. Martha thought her voice was just as good and that she could read aloud as well as anyone in the class – she just didn't want to blow her own trumpet. That sounded stuck up, but it wasn't like that. By hanging around with Betty she could pretend she was as outgoing as her friend.

School had to end eventually for both of them. Betty got a job in service and Martha a job with Jackson's. That was back in 1911. Betty only had one day a month off from work. At the start she came home, but of late her visits were getting less frequent. Martha had always feared that Betty might forget their friendship as her life took her further away from Hanley and the home comforts of Wellington Road.

–

Mother had wanted to pack Daniel's bag for him but he insisted on packing it himself. Martha thought her mother needed to do this one last thing for him.

'Dunner werrit, Mother,' he said. 'Got to get used to this, haven't I? May as well start now.'

Martha could see Mother's hands twitching as she fought to stop herself from interfering. Turned out that each of them had their own battles to fight before they could let go.

He devoured his breakfast quickly because he said that Jeffrey was coming to meet him and they were travelling together. Issy watched him take every mouthful until it had gone. Martha thought Issy would miss him so much, just as she would.

Daniel got up suddenly, wiping his face with his hand.

'Jeffrey will be here any minute. Best get moving.'

Martha held out his jacket for him to slip into and turned him round so she could fasten the buttons, all the while staring into his eyes, wanting him to know that she too could feel his pain.

There was a strong knock on the door. Martha straightened her dress. She took a deep breath and opened the front door.

There he was. Jeffrey, his face pale in the light of the December morning. He came in, making some quip that Martha didn't hear. She smiled because everyone else was laughing.

Jeffrey cleared his throat. 'Ready, Daniel?'

'As I'll ever be.'

Issy was crying now – all thoughts of being nearly a grown-up gone from her mind. Mother's cheeks were wet and she wouldn't have been surprised if she had seen the same reflected on this brother of hers, too. No wonder Peter hadn't stayed to see him off. He had blamed the pit for not being able to be there, but Martha knew otherwise.

When it came to her turn, she reached up to kiss his cheek. She was right – there was a wetness there.

'Be careful, Daniel. Come back to us, won't yer?'

'I'll be doing me best, duck.'

She dared to look at Jeffrey and reached out for both their hands. 'Look after each other over there. Keep sending us letters to let us know what yer can.'

It was an excuse to hold Jeffrey's hand, she knew and she did it anyway, even if she wasn't walking out with him – yet.

Lastly, she turned to him. 'What I said to our Daniel, I'll say to you an' all, Jeffrey. Please come back to us safe and sound.

We'll miss you so much.' She was hiding behind the 'we' and she knew it. She hoped he knew it, too. What she really wanted to say was, 'I'll miss you so much.'

'Stay in touch with Betty an' all,' Jeffrey said. 'She misses everybody what with her being so far away.'

'I'll write and let yer know how things are back here.'

He smiled. 'Thank you.' It felt little more of a whisper, for her ears alone. He gave her a quick peck on the cheek.

'Goodbye, Jeffrey,' she said, returning the whisper.

There were a few people out on the street when they heard what was going on at number 34. Congratulations, jokes and well-wishing were plentiful. Daniel and Jeffrey strode along the street, turning twice to wave goodbye.

And then they were gone. Two boys, leaving their homes to fight for their country in a foreign land.

And the sixteen-year-old girl, at home, waiting for their return.

Chapter Six

Mother said she might look for a job. She might as well as she was still at home all day. It would get her out of the house. She even thought about going to work at The Potter's Wheel. Martha knew how Mother felt. She found herself thinking of Daniel and Jeffrey whenever she had time on her hands.

They'd only been gone a month, but it seemed much longer. Martha wondered what they were doing and, most of all, when they were going to fight. Mother worried that Peter might have the bright idea of following Daniel.

'I may as well do summat. No point in sitting here thinking of nowt but the war, in a house I never really liked. It'd mean I could bring in a bit of money to help us out.'

'What would yer do, Mother? Work on the pots?'

'Dunno yet, duckie. There's lots of jobs going in *The Sentinel*. Jobs yer wouldn't think of if there wasn't a war on. Any road, I'm just letting yer know as I'm thinking about it, that's all.'

–

A week later Martha received a letter from Jeffrey. She didn't recognise the handwriting and was delighted to open it to find his name on the bottom. She had been meaning to get his address from Betty, but she hadn't seen her to ask. Still, him writing to her suggested that he was writing because he wanted to.

She began to read.

30 January 1915

Dear Martha,

I hope you are keeping well and that everybody at home is also well. Daniel will no doubt have told you what we've been up to since we left. Training has been hard but seems to consist of a lot of marching. The bunch of lads in my training platoon include three from Stoke who joined at the same time. With me and Daniel, that makes five Stokie Lads in our platoon.

Can I ask a favour of you, Martha? Betty comes over as a strong girl who doesn't readily ask for help. But she's not as strong as she makes out. Could I ask you, as her best friend, to look out for her? I wouldn't dare tell her I've asked you so could we keep it between me and you? If something did happen, Heaven forbid, I don't trust her to tell me even if she needs my support.

Will you be my eyes and ears? I'm not asking you to spy on my family. I would just be happy to have some contact from back home. It might be a few months before I go overseas — but then again, it could be any time. I miss you all already.

If you would do these things for me, you will make me a happy soldier. It still feels strange to think of myself in those terms.

Yours sincerely,
Jeffrey
217755 Pte Jeffrey Dean
172nd Training Battalion
Corps of Royal Engineers — Chatham

She very nearly burst into tears when she finished. He wanted her to look out for his family. It was unexpected and must mean something. And he did say he missed us. She tried not to dwell on the 'us' word. She sat up and, by the light of a candle, wrote her reply immediately.

1 February 1915

Dear Jeffrey,

How lovely to get a letter from you. I will be happy to write to you and let you know what's happening at home. Having never been away from The Potteries, I can't imagine what it might feel like to go away, not knowing when you will return. I can't guarantee speaking to Betty, what with her being so far away, but I hope to see her fairly regularly and I'll try to speak to Mary-Ellen and Michael too. Issy is friendly with Michael so I might hear something from her.

Peter seems to be getting on all right; he is missing Daniel. He's right about us needing skilled men back here too. We shall all have to pray the war doesn't last too long and that we, at home, can welcome you all back soon.

Love,
Martha

There, she'd done it and taken the opportunity to include 'love' even if it did sound a little bold. She read it through twice. She didn't want to take anything for granted but she was pleased with her scribing and posted the letter on her way to work the next day.

–

It had been a cold and frosty day. The pavements were icy when she walked to work and were just the same now. It was dark and had started to snow. Martha was looking forward to getting home and being warm again. Her feet had been cold all day. The large windows in the Decorating Shop gave excellent light for working, but in summer you roasted and in winter you froze. It was even a pleasure to go to the drying room, even if you didn't have to, just to warm up.

Mother glanced at Martha as she walked into the kitchen. She said nothing, merely handed Martha a piece of paper. A brown official-looking envelope lay on the table beside her. It had a stamp of King George V with the words 'On His Majesty's Service' along the top.

'Came this afternoon. It's from the War Office,' Mother muttered. 'It says yer father's bin "missing in action" since 12 January. The theatre of war was France.' She looked up at Martha as if she couldn't believe it. 'That's it.'

'Is that really all it says, Mother?'

'Look for yerself.'

Martha's eyes skimmed the words. 'Oh, Mother.'

'How could it have happened so soon? He'd only just got there. He wasn't a raw recruit who knew nothing about soldiering. He knew what he was doing. If this can happen to your father, how's Daniel going to manage?'

Mother and daughter hugged each other, dry-eyed.

'They only say he's "missing in action",' said Mother. 'Other people have had letters saying, "missing in action, presumed killed". Does this mean they aren't sure?'

'Dunno, Mother, we'll have to ask somebody.'

Just then the door opened to admit Issy. The smile she was wearing disappeared as she took in their faces. 'What's happened?'

Martha passed the letter on to Issy. 'Here, read this.'

Peter arrived home shortly after and was told the news. The mood at Dresden Street was quiet – each of them lost in their own thoughts. It was difficult to know what to feel. How can you grieve for someone who is 'missing' – you can't weep for them because they may be alive, and you can't ignore it because they may be dead.

In the case of Percy Owen and the pain he had caused in the past, would it be wrong to feel relief? To be honest, Martha didn't know what she felt. Shock, then pictures of him floating into her mind, the smiling father as he was just before he left, and then the white-hot-with-anger father, which occurred more regularly.

'So he isn't coming back?' asked Issy, the first one to offer a truthful comment.

'We don't know yet.'

Martha joined them and Peter put his arms around both of them. The very act of closeness joining them together as never before.

Mother gently pushed Issy away. 'Maybe we'll hear some news soon,' she said. 'In the meantime we shall carry on doing what we need to do.'

–

'I don't know what to think, Martha,' Mother said. 'Every time I go to bed I lie down and wonder if he's still alive and where he might be. Is he suddenly going to walk in through the door as if nothing has happened? I conner settle to anything. I mean, should I start wearing black? If I don't, will people think I'm a bad wife for not mourning him? We can't even have a funeral.'

'That's because we don't know whether he needs one, Mother,' Peter reminded her. He gave a warm smile. 'How can we bury him if we don't know that he's... dead? I don't think any of the boys what's been killed overseas will get a funeral. There's talk of leaving them where they fell. We won't have nothing to bury and he'll be...' Peter shrugged '...who knows where.'

Martha shook her head. Her thoughts turned to Jeffrey and Daniel. What if she was having this conversation with Betty? How would they feel... if summat happened to them and one or other was left over there? All those thousands of young men – killed and buried, miles away from their families and loved ones. How would those left behind cope, never saying goodbye?

Her thoughts were too much. Quietly, she rose and entered the kitchen. A pot of tea just now would do nicely. Peter followed her.

'I can't stand it. The not knowing. Oh, Peter, when's it all going to end?'

'Anybody's guess, duck.' He leaned back against the wall chewing a fingernail grown black with the coal dust that wouldn't disappear. 'I wish I could feel upset, angry, but I just feel numb. Father only thought about himself most of the time. His family has only ever been the army. It's fitting if he should die doing his duty.'

He was only talking about Father, of course. He couldn't know it was Jeffrey in her thoughts now. She almost told him, then changed her mind. They were just friends – the brother of a friend, to be totally truthful.

Peter rubbed his face with his hands, his shoulders hunched, shaking his head. Martha held him quietly. This time they were both most likely thinking of Daniel.

The two of them stood there, together, each lost in their own thoughts.

—

'I need summat to take me mind off thoughts of yer father until there's more news,' Mother announced. 'I'm definitely going to look for a job.'

Peter shook his head. 'I told yer as yer dunner have to. We can manage. Think what Father would say.'

'But I want to. I want to earn me own money for meself. To prove to meself I can do it. It's especially important now he's missing.'

Martha thought she understood. It was likely that it would be Mother's only chance – if he did come home, Father wouldn't hear of his wife working because people would think he wasn't man enough to support his family.

Peter sniffed. 'It's early days, Mother. Happen we'll find out, one way or another, before too long.'

'I don't want Father to come home. I want us to stay just as we are.'

The words coming out of Issy's mouth were both shocking and truthful.

Mother's eyebrows shot into her hair in horror. 'Issy, you conner say that.'

'Why not? It's true. That's what you all think, isn't it?'

—

Mother went with Peter to make enquiries at the Ministry of Pensions office in Hanley Labour Exchange. She was informed she'd have to wait twenty-six weeks before her separation allowance would turn into a widow's pension. The authorities needed to perform checks – was he in one of the many field hospitals and clearing stations, was he held as a prisoner of war, had his identity disc or anything belonging to him been found to hold any clues as to whether or not he was alive. If he was still alive then he would continue to be paid as a soldier and she would continue with the separation allowance. If he was proved to be deceased then the army would stop paying him from the date of his death or, in the absence of a date, from the day he was declared missing, and his widow would be entitled to a pension from that same date.

Mother was shocked that it was all going to take so long. How could it be that a man could sacrifice his life for his country and the army only be concerned about not paying his pay any longer than his confirmed date of death. At least she knew that some people were still looking.

The Red Cross were helping to get information out to the many families back home waiting for news, but the sheer number of casualties on both sides made it difficult to get accurate information out quickly. Mother was told that the paper issuing her with a widow's pension would not be a proof of death, so she wouldn't be able to remarry on the strength of it.

'As if I want to marry anyone else,' Mother snorted when they got back home. 'Not after what I've bin through.'

A dark shadow passed by the kitchen window and Martha glanced up. It was Betty. She'd come down the alley because the curtains at the front were still closed. It's what folk in The Potteries did following a death in the family.

'It's Betty, Mother,' Martha called.

Mother was sitting in the front room and dashed her handkerchief across her eyes in a bid to hide the tears as Betty opened the back door into the kitchen.

Betty's face wore a sympathetic smile and she and Martha fell into each other's arms, until Martha felt an urge to blow her nose.

'How are yer?' Betty said in a low voice.

'Dunno how I feel right now. How am I supposed to feel? He was our father. I conner believe he'll never come home. The thought of being back in the army excited him.'

'How's yer mother taking it?'

'Same, but she feels guiltier. She says as she should grieve for him, but the tears won't come. *All* of us think it's our fault one way and another – because we were glad to see him go. Why should he make us feel like that, Betty?' Martha blinked. She couldn't say any more. She had already said too much.

'Are you all right for money?'

'With most of us working, we'll manage. Mother says she's going to get a job, to take her mind off everything.'

Betty kept her coat on all the time she was there. Martha felt a little jealous. It was easy to see that Betty had put on weight since she'd been working at Stowford. No shortage of food over there. No wonder she didn't come back as often these days.

Then they entered the front room.

'Hiya, Mrs Owen. I'm that sorry to hear about Mr Owen. I should've bin working but I managed to get today off so's I could call round.'

'Thank you, Betty dear. That's good of yer. It's all taking a bit to sink in. Any road, how's it all going in the posh place? We haven't seen yer for a while. Are you all right?'

'It's not so bad. Tiring, I suppose. But all work's tiring, isn't it?'

Martha could've sworn a cloud passed over Betty's face but she didn't say anything. The three of them carried on talking until dinnertime and it was only once Betty had left that Martha realised she had learned very little about how Betty was.

Chapter Seven

Spring 1915

Life in The Potteries was going on much the same as it had always done. They had not yet heard anything further about Father. They would just have to be patient, Martha supposed.

She was doing well at Jackson's and was starting to earn good money. Peter seemed to be getting on well at the pit, but was missing having his brother around although Daniel wrote home often. He was still in England but no longer at the same place as Jeffrey.

The weather had been fine most of the week and Martha enjoyed her walk home in the fresh air, after spending the day in the airless environment of the Decorating Shop. Although there were plenty of windows and lots of light, the ventilation was not the best. Dust was the curse of any decorator and unfortunately that was one thing you had everywhere in a potbank, so the windows were usually shut.

She had always thought the best jobs on a potbank were to be found in the Decorating Shop. Girls didn't get dirty and could wear ordinary clothes topped by a pinafore, or pinny, like Mother wore for housework. So, she was over the moon with her first job. She would've hated to be placed in the clay end – the dirty end, where the men worked and the girls were rather less refined. Girls in the Decorating Shop were considered posh and had little to do with anyone who didn't work in their shop.

Today was Friday and payday and unlike before she now paid board in just the same way as the boys had done. What was left of her wage was hers. She had even managed to save a little.

Issy was getting on well at Millward's Drapery, and was growing in confidence.

Martha opened the back door and joined her mother in the kitchen, dropping her bag on the table.

Mother looked up. 'Hiya, duckie. Had a good day at work?'

'As good as ever.'

'You're starting to sound like a real worker, moaning about their job.' They laughed.

'I've been doing the same job now since I started and will probably still be doing it when I leave. What a prospect.'

'That's what working is all about – yer dunner have to enjoy it.'

'Decorating Shops are full of women, and I hate to say it, there are a lot of little cliques. One bench doesn't like someone on another bench. Complaints about allocation of work. Just like it was at school. There always seems to be summat going on.'

'That's human nature.'

'Where's our Issy?'

'She'll be here shortly; she knows when it's teatime. She's taken to walking down Wellington Road on her way home from Millward's and calling at Josie's for a chat – outside of course so she can be seen from Michael Dean's house.'

'Her's too young to be interested in boys.' Martha retorted. 'I wasn't at her age; in fact, I still aren't.'

'Oh, is that so?'

Martha reddened; glad Mother was facing away from her.

'Do you want anything doing?'

'No, sit yerself down. I want to talk to you.'

Martha sat at her place at the table. She looked at where Father used to sit and wondered when they would hear anything about him.

'I was in Sherwood's this morning getting some potatoes. Mrs Sherwood was holding court, as usual.'

'She's such a gossip. Never misses a thing.'

'When it was my turn only old Mrs Goodwin was left and she was looking at each potato and muttering about how they were not very good and not worth the money.'

'Mother, what have yer got to tell me?'

'Sorry, duck, can't get used to not being interrupted. Everything comes out at once. She says Betty Dean's lost her job at that posh house. She's bin back home for over a week.'

Martha's mouth fell open.

'Yer didn't know?'

Martha shook her head. 'She never said she was having problems. Mind you, I thought she'd become too posh for the likes of us and too embarrassed to tell me she's lost her job. Wait till I see her.'

'Mrs Sherwood said that when girls get sent back from service it's usually cos they was expecting – or had got involved with people they shouldn't have. I said I knew nowt. I wouldn't have told her if I did. It's unusual though, she's not bin in touch. She came round to see you so soon after yer father went missing.' Mother nodded towards Father's vacant seat.

Martha frowned.

–

It was Saturday afternoon. Martha had a wash when she got in from work – as far down as she could – and as far up, that's what they used to say.

Issy came rushing in and flopped down on a chair.

'You'll never guess what I've just heard?'

'No I won't, so you'd better tell me.'

'Betty's come home. Michael's just told me.'

'We know,' Mother and Martha said in unison.

'Well, yer dunner know this bit. She came home two weeks ago. He said that the people where she works conner afford to keep as many servants and they had to let some go. Betty was one of them.'

'We know that too,' Mother and Martha said again.

'No, this is the new bit, but as you two seem to know everything, I'll not tell yer.' Issy went quiet.

'Go on, girl, tell us,' said Mother, beginning to lose patience.

'Don't think I should. I've just remembered that Michael said it was a secret and I shouldn't tell nobody.'

'Well, it's too late now and I'm sure he didn't mean us. When you tell us the full story we'll know what bits to keep secret.'

Although Martha was a little perplexed by the logic, it seemed to placate Issy.

'Well, Mary-Ellen's hopping mad now she has to share a bed with Lily and Betty, and Betty's put on weight since she left. Michael also said she was using the chamber pot often during the night and Mary-Ellen didn't take kindly to being woke up. Michael thought Mary-Ellen deserved it cos she's always moaning about summat.'

'She probably put on weight because of all the posh food she eats these days and is hiding away because of the shame of it.'

–

The more Martha thought about what she'd discovered, the more angry she became. Surely Betty could have found time to come round to see her. Then she remembered the letter Betty had sent at Christmas about Jeffrey joining up. She never sympathised with Martha about Daniel, it was all Betty and Jeffrey. Martha concluded that Betty had lost interest in their friendship and was too embarrassed to tell her 'best friend' she'd lost her job.

Well, two could play at that game. She would say nothing. She'd wait until Betty came to see her. Martha couldn't think of what possible excuse she might concoct to ride roughshod over their friendship.

Damn, shouldn't have had that last cup of tea. Martha got out of bed to use the chamber pot. She wondered what was happening at Betty's at the moment. She giggled. That'd teach her. She shouldn't have eaten all that posh food. A few weeks of normal food would soon slim her down.

Martha still hadn't heard anything from Betty and was more convinced than ever that their friendship was over. Again, Issy was the source of the latest news.

'Michael's just told me Betty's gorra another job. She's got work at a house near to Hanley Park and she's living in.'

'Did he say where?' Martha asked, casually.

'Yes, I just told yer. Near to Hanley Park. I must go, I've only come to drop my cardigan off. It was too warm.' She folded the cardigan and left as swiftly as she arrived.

'It looks as if Betty's fallen on her feet, as usual,' declared Mother.

'Mm,' said Martha.

'Perhaps she'll come round now she's settled. It's likely been upsetting for the girl. She'd have a lot on her mind. Be patient, Martha, and give her time.'

Martha decided to visit Betty. With it being Whit Sunday, Mrs Dean would be at chapel and it might be Betty's day off. It always used to be a Sunday.

Martha put on her best frock and a summery hat. This sounded grand but in truth they were the only thin things she had, the rest of her clothes were practical and more suited to colder weather.

Martha knocked on the front door. No answer. She walked around to the back and knocked on the scullery door. Again, there was no answer. It looked as if the whole family was out because it was locked.

With a final glance up and down the street, she left. At least I tried, she thought.

Martha always liked to sketch and since she'd been working had been able to afford a proper sketch book and some pencils. She had been up to the field where the horses were kept on Bucknall Road to try her hand at drawing them. On her return she chose to walk down Wellington Road, passing Betty's house. Perhaps she would be there? By Martha's calculations, it had been seven weeks and still no word from her. They only lived round the corner but she may as well have lived on the Moon.

Deep in thought and with anger growing, she rounded the corner into Wellington Road – and bumped into someone running in the opposite direction.

It was Betty. Martha resolved she wouldn't say anything. She would give Betty a chance to tell her.

'Hiya, Betty. Haven't seen yer for… whatever's the matter?'

Betty hugged Martha tightly and more tears flowed.

'I'll walk with yer. Have yer bin home?'

Betty nodded without looking at her. Was Jeffrey all right? A cold shudder ran through her body.

'So, why the tears? Has summat bad happened?'

'I can't tell yer. It's a secret.'

Martha was relieved. It wasn't about Jeffrey – Betty would've told her straight away if that was the case. So all the drama was about losing her job. Fear turned to anger. Martha very nearly pointed out that best friends don't have secrets from one another and she thought of leaving Betty to herself if she wasn't going to say what had upset her. There was a time when they told each other everything.

She softened. It must've been bad for it to upset Betty so much. Perhaps Jeffrey had been right that she wasn't as strong as she let on. 'Let me walk with yer then. Make sure you're all right.'

They walked in silence. What could she say to help if she didn't know what had upset her? Martha racked her brains for something to talk about as Betty fought for control. She was playing with her fingers as if by some magic spell it would help.

Martha took a sly glance, listening to the uneven breathing from her friend. She buttoned her lips to stop herself asking more questions, positive it was the only way to get Betty to talk.

'Martha – I'm expecting.'

It was a bolt out of the blue and definitely nothing like the words Martha was anticipating. She had been thinking of how she might react when Betty finally deigned to tell her what had happened. Now all of the planning was for nothing. Her mind went from anger to sympathy and back to anger. She had never thought for one minute that Betty would have done something like that.

She flushed violently. Betty wouldn't joke about such matters. 'Yer conner be, you're not married.' It was the first thing that entered Martha's head and she cringed. What a daft thing to say.

'I mean it, I'm expecting.'

Betty opened her coat and Martha's eyes almost burst as she saw the size of her swollen stomach. Martha let go of her as if she had burned her fingers. 'You're… Oh, no, not you.'

'Mother's just told the family. It was horrible, Martha. Really bad, and our Jeffrey's not speaking to me.'

Martha's thoughts flew to Jeffrey. He was – he's home! When can I see him, and then – what does he think of Betty's behaviour? Worse thoughts followed – would he think she might act in the same way? She'd hate that. It was summat she would never do. But then, she wouldn't have believed it of Betty, come to that. So Betty had had her fun and now Martha was paying for it. She would never be able to look Jeffrey in the eye again. No wonder he had asked her to keep an eye on his family while he was away. She didn't think for one moment it was the sort of thing he had in mind, any more than she had. So, Father was right after all. Being friendly with boys did get a girl into trouble.

Betty watched her intently.

What could she say? In the end, she said, 'Isn't he?'

'I don't want him going back to war with us not speaking. Supposing summat happens to him?'

Martha bit her lip. She could only speak the truth – as far as she saw it. 'It'd be your fault.' How harsh it sounded.

'What d'yer mean?'

Martha wished she hadn't bumped into Betty at all. What can you say to someone who had just announced they were pregnant and weren't married? Still, she had started down this road and there was no way back. She couldn't think quickly enough to make a difference. She bit her lip. 'I said as it'd be your fault.'

As she had more time to digest the words Betty had spoken, Martha's voice grew stronger. She couldn't take the words back. It was too late for that. 'What did you expect? You know what people think about girls who... go with men, never mind them what gets *pregnant*.' The last word hissed with anger.

Betty's face went pale, almost white. 'I didn't go with *men*, as you put it. We were walking out for a long time. He volunteered for the army and got himself killed.'

Martha felt a pang of remorse. She wanted to say 'sorry' but the word wouldn't come. Instead other words came to her lips. 'But yer still did it, Betty – and you're not wed. That makes you nothing better than a—'

'Don't say what's on yer lips. You don't know the full story.'

Betty's voice was threatening. Suddenly, Martha's temper grew. 'I know – I don't need no picture – you've done summat bad and there's no excuse.'

Her friend was still lying. She wasn't going to tell Martha about being sacked – about losing her job – and about being home and not even telling her she was back.

Betty's eyes bulged.

They were both so full of anger, it was unlikely anything could be resolved.

'Is that what you really think?'

'Dunno.'

It was true. Every time she saw Betty from now on she would think about what she had done and soon there would be a baby to prove it. A baby needing to be looked after, and raised. How could she spoil their friendship like that?

Even Betty looked shocked. 'How can yer say that? We're friends.'

Martha looked at her feet. 'Dunno what me mother'll say.' It sounded lame. What would it matter? Her mother would probably be the one person to sympathise, given the circumstances.

'You can't say nothing, Martha.'

Betty sounded panic-stricken.

A group of men walked in between them. Betty waited until they had passed. 'I've promised Mother I'll tell nobody. Promise me,' she said, urgently.

How could Betty expect her to keep quiet about such a scandalous thing? She could even be tarred with the same brush when word got out – if it hadn't already.

'She's like as not going to find out.'

Martha couldn't let herself be bound by any promise. She heard the talk about other girls in similar circumstances and it wasn't very nice at all.

Betty's face was cold. 'We'll have to see then, won't we?' She turned on her heel and walked away.

Martha put out a hand to stop her, but Betty was gone. Martha was rooted to the spot. Part of her wanted to run after her best friend – as was – but the other part wanted to steer clear knowing that when everybody knew what Betty had done, she would be talked about around the streets of Hanley and her reputation would be lost. She hated everything she had said, but it was all true. Even though when she closed her eyes she could still see the hurt in Betty's eyes. The abandonment, and the disappointment.

Tears of regret came to Martha's eyes for the friendship she felt was already lost. She hated herself for feeling as she did, and

Betty for bringing out the feelings she was ashamed to bear. Her best friend needed her help and support – and she wouldn't help.

Martha thought back to just before they left school. It seemed that they would both go to work in the potbank and find nice boys to marry. They talked about it – what happened in the bedroom – but it was only when a girl who had left school two years before was found to be expecting that both girls realised they were maturing. After that 'it' became a subject they never talked about. It was too rude.

Father's words, when he had accused Jeffrey of being too familiar, came back at that moment. How he had forced her back into the house as if he was ashamed of her, just for talking to a lad.

What would Jeffrey think when he found out about this horrible row? Their friendship by letter hadn't got off to a very good start, had it? Should she tell him she and Betty weren't speaking – or should she let Betty do the talking?

Martha didn't see Betty to speak to after the happenings on that terrible day. She thought about popping round to see Mrs Dean, but didn't dare. What would she say?

Chapter Eight

June 1915

The week after Martha and Betty's argument, Mother received a letter from the War Office stating that Father's identity disc and some personal effects had been found. The letter confirmed that, based on this latest information, the War Office had officially declared him as deceased. Father's final payment would be made shortly. She should obtain an official death certificate by taking this letter to her nearest Registry Office as soon as possible to avoid unnecessary delays.

That evening, Issy and Mother had a bit of a row – about something and nothing. Mother snapped at her, telling her not to be such a silly girl.

Issy's face contorted, her lips trembling.

Realisation of what she'd done hit Mother. She threw her arms around Issy. 'I'm sorry, I'm so sorry.'

She gave Issy another hug and then shut herself in the kitchen saying she would be better getting the tea ready on her own.

'I only wanted to help,' Issy said to Martha.

'Mother knows you did. She has a lot on her mind and now she's had the letter saying that she can draw a widow's pension instead of her usual allowance, it's upset her because it means that Father won't be coming home from the war.'

'After the way he treated her, I thought she would be glad.'

'I know, darling. But he's still our father and Mother was married to him for a long time. It'll take a bit of getting used to.' Martha stroked Issy's pale, mousy-coloured hair, the same colour as her own.

'But she *will* be all right, won't she?'

'Yes, duckie, she'll be all right. And Peter'll see we're all fine.'

Issy nodded and seemed to cheer up after that.

After Issy had gone to bed that night, Martha sat with Mother. They were both reading, a hobby that the two of them had in common.

Mother rubbed her eyes and sighed as if the weight of the world was on her shoulders.

'I'm sorry I lost my temper today, Martha. I think everything's been building up inside. Sometimes, I don't want to get up no more.'

Martha nodded. 'It's been hard, hasn't it.'

Martha wanted to say more, but what could she say to a woman who has just learned that her husband, who was violent towards her, wouldn't be coming back from the war because he was dead. She didn't even know how she felt about it herself. Could she, in all honesty, own up that part of her was glad? No, glad wasn't the right word. She was – relieved? It didn't feel right that she should feel anything else but wretched. No wonder Mother was muddled about her feelings.

'Yer father's money'll go down now so we'll need to work a bit harder.' She laughed, a harsh laugh, that wasn't funny. 'Widows are expected to economise, apparently.'

'I'll get a bit more when I turn eighteen – and Peter helps, doesn't he?'

'I know, duck. We'll just have to see how we can best manage everything. We'll cope.'

'Course we will.'

Mother looked as if she was about to say more, then changed her mind.

Martha looked up. 'What?'

'Nothing, duckie. Just bin thinking a lot recently. Things on me mind. Never you worry about it. We'll be all right.'

By unspoken consent, they each settled back into their reading, but Martha wasn't taking in the words. She was thinking about Betty. What would she have shared with her best friend about how the world had changed for them? She knew the value of friendship and was beginning to realise just how much she would miss sharing her life with Betty. She didn't even know when the baby was due. She thought about sending a letter – but what would she say? 'Hello, Betty, I'm sorry for calling you a fallen woman and to blame you if anything should happen to Jeffrey?'

It sounded horrible. Bitchy. Even evil. No wonder Betty walked away.

Martha was discovering that you don't miss something until you don't have it any more.

In bed, when Issy had gone to sleep, Martha allowed herself a few tears for all she had lost.

—

A week later all the Owen family were expected at The Potter's Wheel for Sunday dinner, which they would eat after the pub closed for the afternoon.

The family had received a couple of letters from Daniel and, according to what he wrote, everything was as well as it could be, given the circumstances. He said nothing about the fighting – only day-to-day stuff – which could put him anywhere. The last letter Martha had caused her to panic. He finished it by saying *we're off soon, pray for me.*

They walked briskly to Tunstall and The Potter's Wheel. Martha was starving – the walk had given her a real appetite. Woe betide anyone who was late and delayed their meal. Certainly, Grandma would give them 'what for' and no mistake. Martha couldn't help smiling at the thought of her grandma giving a strapping lad like Peter the sharp side of her tongue.

'All right, duck?' Grandad grinned as they walked in. He looked happier than she had seen him for a while. Come to that, so was Mother. Something had happened, and Martha determined to find out what before she left Tunstall.

She glanced at the food on the table and raised her eyebrows. There was a chicken! It was more like a special occasion than a normal Sunday dinner. Once the meal had been eaten, and everything cleared away, Grandad tapped the table, calling everyone to attention.

'Now, I want yer to be quiet for yer mother has summat to tell yer.'

The looks of surprise on all their faces told Martha that no one had any idea what she was about to say. Even Grandma's face showed nothing. Martha suspected that if Grandad knew, then so did Grandma, and she was just better at keeping secrets. Grandad made a gesture to Mother and sat back to let her take control – something Father never did.

Mother cleared her throat, her face becoming tinged with pink now all eyes were on her. She put her hands together as if she was about to start praying and took a deep breath.

'Things will become a bit tight now we've had news… about your father.' Her voice wobbled. 'The rent on the house is just about manageable with the money you are giving me each week. So…' She turned, this time to Grandad. '…Grandad has asked whether we should like to move back here – to The Potter's Wheel. There's plenty of room and we could save a lot if we didn't have to pay out rent on Dresden Street.'

'You mean for keeps?' asked Issy, wide-eyed.

The implications of the move ran through Martha's mind. In that minute or two, her thoughts went from shock to surprise to – excitement. Nothing was holding her to Dresden Street now that Betty had moved on. Their blazing row had parted them for good and there was no reason she could think of that she would miss that part of The Potteries – except she might never see Jeffrey again. Once the war was over, she would be able to pick up with him if he should want to call on her. Tunstall and The Potter's Wheel wasn't so far away from Hanley. She didn't kid herself that he would call on her – but the thought was there. It would also give her an excuse to look for the paintressing job she wanted.

'Dunno how long the war'll last, Issy,' Mother said. 'I think we shall all be better off living together – given that your father... your father won't be coming back.' She swallowed and Martha saw the Adam's apple in her neck move – the only indication that Mother was finding the conversation difficult.

Mother flashed a smile at Grandma and Grandad. 'They thought we could all help each other that way. Thanks to both of yer for suggesting it. What d'yer think?' She turned to face her children.

The smiles on all their faces told Mother she had made the correct decision.

–

Martha helped Mother to wash the pots and pans once dinner was over, and they had the opportunity for further discussion out of earshot.

'D'yer think it's a good idea, Martha? I never really liked that house. I never felt we belonged in Hanley.'

Martha nodded and took the opportunity to raise her new job idea. 'There isn't anything to keep us there now. I'll have further to travel but I can look for another job.'

'I thought you liked what you were doing?'

'I do. I asked ages ago if I could do some proper training to become a paintress. Beryl said as I was good enough but she didn't think they'd send me to art school to learn.'

'Why was that?'

'Because it costs money and they don't send girls because we have babies and they don't get their money back.'

'Seems a bit short-sighted, not to train paintresses.'

'They don't do any hand painting at Jackson's; they use transfers to keep the price down.'

'So it looks as though you will have to get a job somewhere else if you want to go to art school. Fancy that, my girl going to art school.'

Martha grinned. She might now be able to get what she wanted.

—

The move back to The Potter's Wheel wasn't too bad. This time the transport was more splendid than before. Martha remembered the rag-and-bone man turning up with his cart. They had loaded their possessions and walked with the cart, leaving the only home they had ever known.

This time, Grandad had asked the manager of the brewery in Burslem if he would lend them a dray. He had agreed and, on the Saturday morning, a magnificent shire horse pulling the brewer's wagon stopped outside 34 Dresden Street.

The drayman chose a different route to Tunstall. Instead of the banks of Waterloo Road and Scotia Road, they walked along High Lane which was on a ridge overlooking the towns. The weather was kind and Martha realised that she had never seen The Potteries from this road. Below them was the sprawl of Burslem and Tunstall where hundreds of chimneys and kilns belched out smoke. Here it was sunny and pleasant.

Martha was enjoying the journey but she was relieved to enter Tower Square, back at the only place she ever thought of as home. They made their way to the pub. Mother had helped Grandma to arrange the rooms during the past week. Martha and Issy were sharing one room, Peter, and Daniel when he returned, another, with Mother in the boxroom at the end of the corridor. Mother didn't need much space, she said. She would be quite happy in the little room that overlooked backyards shaded by a few small trees. Sometimes, she could hear birds singing, and that cheered her no end, she said.

'Besides, it has to be fair since there's only one of me.'

Everybody had laughed and the mood was so light-hearted it felt as if life was truly beginning all over again. Staying in Dresden Street, with all its bad memories, would always put a dampener to any happiness that might have come their way. Martha had thought about leaving a message for Betty but soon gave up on the idea. Apart from 'sorry', what else could she say when someone else might read it? No, if there was any chance of making up, it would have to be done face to face.

Bridie, her schoolfriend of old, lost no time in coming round on her way home, over the moon that Martha was back. The two girls hugged and Martha was glad they could see each other whenever they wanted.

On the whole, Martha thought, although this move had been forced upon them it could just be the thing that the family needed. A new start – and that surely must be good for everyone.

Chapter Nine

July 1915

On Sunday, Martha went round to see Bridie. They had kept in touch and usually spoke to each other on Martha's visits to Grandma and Grandad. But they had missed a lot of each other's lives. When Martha left, they were only just turned nine and schoolgirls playing with dolls; now they were young women, they had a lot to catch up on.

When Martha left The Potter's Wheel for the first time, Bridie had two brothers, Robert and Peter. This had expanded to five with the addition of Jimmy, Philip and Antony and the youngest, a girl, Theresa-Marie.

Bridie had changed a lot. She had become taller and had lost some of her Irish accent and picked up Potteries words. It made for a unique dialect. She had developed curves 'in all the right places', as she put it and had started to walk out with the local butcher's apprentice, Raymond. At least they would always have something to eat, she said.

Bridie, like Martha, was average at school. She was hampered because, along with her mother, she had to look after her younger brothers and sister. Her father worked at the steelworks and her mother took in washing and sewing. In fact it was Mrs O'Connor that had taught Martha how to sew years ago and it had come in so handy ever since. Mrs O'Connor would have bundles of washed and ironed clothes for them to deliver when they arrived from school. She always said, 'Don't forget the money.'

It was good to walk into their house. It had been busy when she was nine, but now it contained a fair few more people. But it was a happy house. Money was always tight for the O'Connors, but they managed. After all, hand-me-down clothes, if they survived, could be used for all five boys.

Martha had only been back a day, but somehow it felt like she had never been away. Most of all, the familiarity of the pub and the O'Connor house would help her to forget all that had happened at Dresden Street.

–

Martha had never liked the time just before her monthlies started. She felt horrible for the couple of days before. She was usually short-tempered and let things get on top of her easily. Only Mother knew the real reason for her short temper. Daniel used to say to her that she'd inherited it from Father. Sometimes, if she was lucky enough to be at home, she would get one of the stone bedwarmers and cradle it next to her aching belly, which felt as if it was about to fall out of her body. At those times she would moan to Mother and ask why it only happened to girls – it wasn't fair.

This month she was particularly anxious and felt like crying. It was not a good time for the inspector at Jackson's to reject her work. It would cost her nearly a quarter of her wages. She couldn't believe the inspector could refuse so much of her ware – unless the bosses were trying it on, to avoid paying the workers. She asked to go and see the work for herself. After all, she needed to learn so she didn't make the same mistakes again.

She entered the selection room and asked for Mr Cokeley, the inspector. He was a man in his forties, balding, and he always wore little round glasses. None of the girls liked him, but his word was final so they had to put up with him.

This was a noisy room with the rhythmical sound of pottery clattering against itself as ware was checked. The people who did this work seemed to be permanently bent over, looking down at the ware on the bench or on their laps. She could see why they were called 'overlookers'.

'Hello, Mr Cokeley.'

'Ah. Miss Owen, it's about your rejections, isn't it? Come into the office, it is too noisy here. These are samples of your work we've pulled out. The line around the edge is wavy. It seems to me you are working too quick to make your money. Shoddy work will always be rejected. It is not up to our standard.'

Normally Martha would have kept quiet and resolved to herself never to let it happen again. But today was the wrong day and something just snapped.

'There is nothing wrong with my work. They're no different than what the others are doing. This has happened to some of the other girls over the last few weeks. If the bosses don't want the work, that's their problem. I have done what I have been asked, so I should get paid the rate.'

Martha was shocked at the words and could hardly believe she had said them. What came next, in any event, was more unexpected and shocking.

'Don't you speak to me like that, Miss Owen. I am also paid to do a job to the best of my ability. So take note.'

Martha had learned something from her father – when to retreat, so that you live to fight another day when the odds are in your favour. She forced herself to calm down. 'Yes, Mr Cokeley.'

'Martha, if I may call you Martha. You are a good girl. I think you just need some extra tuition. I don't normally do this for everyone, but I would be willing to pass this work if you agree to stay behind this evening. I can show you how it should be done. A bit of personal tuition – you understand – if you get my meaning. Attend the training and I'll pass your work tomorrow.'

Martha couldn't believe her ears. She didn't need extra training and the plates and transfers were not that high quality.

There was a lecherous smile spread across his face. She knew exactly what sort of training he meant. She felt physically sick and stared at him, unable to believe her ears. How dare he suggest such a thing. For two pins, Martha would have thrown the plate she was holding at him, but she decided that would do no good.

'Mr Cokeley, for your information, I don't need any extra "training" – or whatever *you* choose to call it. You must do what yer must do if *that* is what yer are paid to do.'

She laid the plate down on the table, none too gently, and walked calmly out of the room, her head high.

'Whatever's the matter. Cokeley upset you?' asked one of the girls.

'Y-y-yes.'

'Offer you some special tuition, did he?' The girl stopped working and smirked at her.

'How do you know?'

'Most of us young uns know about him and his *special* tuition. It's the way things are sometimes. Yer dunner have to worry. He likes a fumble but never carries it further. Probably too afraid of getting a girl pregnant. Go along with him – it's the best way to earn a day's wage I know at this place. He soon gets bored, or worried, and moves on to another girl. After all, there are plenty to choose from and no one can afford to say no and lose pay. He can be vindictive if he's a mind to.'

Martha's work had been rejected, just as Cokeley had promised. She wanted to tell somebody, but who would believe her? She'd had a lucky escape. Knowing she wasn't the only one helped a little.

–

A week the following Friday, they were preparing to start work with the normal sound of chattering and plates being put onto benches when Beryl called to everyone to stop work and listen to an announcement. Her face was pale and she looked upset, as if she was forcing her voice to say the words.

'Because of the war and the downturn in the industry, the following people are being laid off immediately. If your name is called out, please collect your belongings and go to the wages office straight away, where you will receive what's due to you.'

There was a silence, followed by an outbreak of chatter.

Beryl read out the names.

Martha couldn't believe her ears when her name was called out – the last on the list.

'...That's it, ladies, back to work.'

Beryl turned on her heel and walked out as if she was heading for the privies.

Martha caught up with her. 'Why am I on the list?'

'I dunner know, duckie. You just are. It was what the bosses decided on. They usually pick the poorest workers with a lot of rejections, but not always.'

'Does Mr Cokeley have any say on who goes?'

'Why do you ask?'

'It doesn't matter – me job's gone and that all there is to it. Would yer give me a reference if I need one? Being laid off like this'll make me out to be a bad worker.'

'Yes, of course. I'll give you my address. Give us your book and I'll write it in there.'

Martha handed her book to Beryl. All the girls carried a book listing the work they had done each week and the prices they would be paid, so they could check their wages were correct at the end of each week.

'There you are. I'll have to get on or I'll be joining yer. I conner say no more, Martha, duck. But good luck. You're a talented girl – be sure you make good use of it and get yerself a job at a proper potbank.'

Martha walked home slowly, unable to believe the events of the morning. She was laid off because she would not do whatever it was Mr Cokeley wanted. She was sure of it. How could she even tell her mother the real reason she had lost her job?

She walked past the large houses on each side of Waterloo Road but didn't really take them in. After all, it was normal for people to be laid off at a minute's notice because there was no work for them, and this would be what she'd tell Mother. Jackson's had been less busy – and she wasn't the only one. Martha brightened up. It could be a blessing in disguise, if she was lucky.

Mother took the news rather well. These things happen all the time, she said. You just have to accept it and go and find yourself another job.

Now she'd have the chance to get the job she really wanted.

–

As had become usual since she'd moved back, Bridie called round to see if Martha wanted to go for a walk. After being shut in a pottery all week it was nice to get out. Bridie would always want to walk past the butcher's, in case Raymond was outside. Martha was only too pleased to say yes and Grandma said it was all right to go.

'I've been laid off from Jackson's.'

'Oh, I'm so sorry. I didn't know.'

'It only happened yesterday.' Martha told her what had happened.

Without any hesitation, Bridie turned to Martha. 'You could come and work at Paradise Pottery with me. I've bin decorating there for a while. It's a nice place to work and local. All down-hill, useful if you're late in a morning.'

'Are they taking on at the moment?'

'They are always on the lookout for good people. I can have a word with Mr Higginbotham on Monday. They might be interested. They set great store by recommendations. It could be fun, the two of us working together.'

Martha's eyes glowed. 'Are they good to work for?'

'Oh yes. I wouldn't have stayed otherwise.'

Martha wanted to ask if they had inspectors like Mr Cokeley, but decided against it.

On Monday evening, Bridie came round to the pub in her work clothes. Without waiting for Martha to say hello, she said, 'The bosses in the office said they were looking for trainee paintresses and were going to place an advertisement in *The Sentinel* after the Potters' holiday. It was lucky I called in, otherwise I'd have been too late.'

'Really? Well, thanks for mentioning me. I'll be over the moon if I get a job there – I really will. What do yer do?'

'Gilding mainly. That's what you'd probably start on. I'm hoping to get on to painting when I've got enough experience working on the flatware and hollowware. And we work on bone china, which is different than earthenware. It somehow makes yer want to do a good job.'

'What are they like to work for?' Martha was still concerned about Cokeley.

'They're good bosses – Mr Cyril Rhead is the owner but his son, Mr John we call him, works there an' all. He'll likely take over from his father when he gets older. I like it, and you will too. Any road, they said as they'd send you a letter saying when to go and see them.'

'Oh thanks, Bridie.' She went to hug her friend.

'I wouldn't do that; you'll get all dusty.'

They said their goodbyes.

For the first time in ages, Martha clapped her hands with excitement. She – Martha Owen – was going to do summat different with herself and if she did well, she could be creating beautifully decorated china.

–

'Why d'yer never see young Betty no more?'

Grandma was behind the bar while Martha collected the glasses as the pub had shut for the afternoon.

In the beginning, Mother had asked a few times why she hadn't seen or spoken of Betty since their move to The Potter's Wheel and she had always managed to avoid answering. Grandma was different. Martha could talk to her better than anyone.

'Betty's got her own life now. When she lost her job, she never came to see me. She's working somewhere near to Hanley Park. She's a housekeeper now.'

'No, there was more to it than that.' Grandma lowered her voice to a whisper. 'She was expecting, wasn't she?'

Martha nodded. 'How did yer know?'

'Your mother told me. She said it was the talk of the street and at Sherwood's shop. There was a lot of nasty things said about Betty. You know people, they like to gossip and if they don't know anything they make it up.'

'But the baby's father was a soldier and has been killed in the war.'

'So Betty and her mother said, but people talked about her as she did things the wrong way round. You remember, my girl, marriage and then that sort of thing.'

'Don't worry, Grandma. I will not be caught that way. After seeing what Mother and Betty have gone through, I don't think I'll be in a rush to get married.'

'Mm, with all these young men getting killed and injured so horribly you might not have the choice.'

Martha cleared the last table. 'Grandma?'

'Yes, Martha?'

'When I found out, I knew we couldn't be friends no more.'

'Was it because you were worried what yer mother would say?'

'No, not really. I would have been petrified if Father had still been alive. How he treated me after he caught me talking to Jeffrey Dean was bad enough, I don't know what he would have done if he had known about Betty.

'I was angry that she had been back home for so long and never come round to see me or tried to contact me. I got it into my head at first that she was too grand for us. When I found out she had lost her job, I thought she was too ashamed. And then her being in the family way was the last straw. What would people think about me? Would they say that I would be next?'

'Oh, my dear, that was silly. You are two different people. The likes of Mrs Sherwood gossip about one person until such time as they find someone else. And Lord knows they have plenty of things to talk about. You're too influenced by your father's concern about letting other people know your business, and you can see why. He had plenty to hide.'

'I was so hurt that she seemed to have cast our friendship away, so when I met her in the street that Sunday, I was in no mood to be friends. All I wanted to do was hurt her and let her know I knew all about what had happened. But when she said she was expecting it took the wind out of me sails. I didn't know what to do. I said some awful things.' Martha threw herself into Grandma's arms and sobbed uncontrollably.

Martha was slow to regain her composure. Grandma suggested a cup of strong tea and put the kettle on the range.

'I don't want to criticise my daughter, but right from the very beginning we didn't like your father. We couldn't see why she married him. There were some ugly scenes and we were glad to see the back of him when you all moved to Dresden Street. Afterwards, your mother hardly ever came to visit us and if she did she made sure any bruises were well hidden.'

'I remember those times. I remember what effect it had on Issy.'

'My point, Martha, is that you should always talk when you have a problem. Keeping things quiet because of what the neighbours would say is pointless. There's always someone to talk to.'

Chapter Ten

July/August 1915

The letter from Paradise Pottery Ltd came later that week asking her to attend an appointment at the factory at two o'clock on Monday, 26 July 1915, and to bring an apron or pinafore with her.

Martha hadn't expected to hear from them so soon and worried that she would not have enough time to prepare herself. Whatever was she going to say? Beneath the shock, there was excitement too. How wonderful it would be to tell Betty if she was offered a job. Then, just as quickly, she realised she couldn't tell her former best friend because that's what she was – her *former* best friend.

Although she liked Bridie and they got on well, it was at times like this she missed Betty most of all. It would be wonderful if she could tell Daniel and Jeffrey her good news, too. First, however, she must get the job. No point in getting carried away with her plans.

She turned up at the gates with ten minutes to spare and stood outside for a few moments taking in a rather long, drab building, laden with the soot and smoke from the kilns, like most of the buildings in The Potteries. Two rows of windows looked as if they hadn't been opened for ages. She hadn't really looked at it before. Now, she hoped that it would be more welcoming on the inside than it was on the outside.

She headed towards the sign that said Lodgekeeper. As she arrived at his window, the man in the office wished her a good afternoon.

'I've got an appointment for a job at two o'clock,' she said, remembering to smile.

He looked startled at first – then smiled back.

'Right, Miss. Go through the gates and I'll get somebody to come and see yer.'

She flashed another smile, remembering the importance of a smile even if she was trembling inside. He smiled back and winked – which surprised her totally. Had she seemed too flighty?

Soon, a woman appeared and walked purposefully towards her.

'Hiya, duck – you Martha Owen?' The woman wore her hair in a plait that fell down over her left shoulder. 'Me name's Vera Bell and I've come to take you to the Decorating Shop to see our Mr Higginbotham. Have yer remembered to bring an apron or pinnie?'

Martha held up her pinafore.

'Good. You'll probably be asked to paint summat and yer won't want to get it on yer clothes.'

'Have yer been working here long?'

Vera nodded. 'Since I was thirteen – that's twenty-one years. The old Queen, God rest her soul, was still on the throne.'

Martha was surprised and wondered just what Vera's story was.

Vera strode along a pathway and up a flight of stairs. Martha counted on her fingers behind her back. So, Vera was thirty-four, but her plaited hair made her look younger.

'Listen, if you *are* told to paint summat, take yer time – but not too long. Better that yer dunner make no mistakes. Yer can always get quicker with practice.'

Martha nodded and smiled, grateful for the advice.

Vera didn't say anything more after that. She opened the doors on the left which led into a room full of women, all dressed in white aprons, chattering among themselves but never looking up from their work.

Following her through the room, Martha was brought to an alcove where an elderly man, maybe in his fifties and wearing round spectacles, sat surrounded by papers and files. He didn't look up, but carried on writing. A wooden sign on his desk informed her he was Mr Wilfred Higginbotham, Decorating Supervisor.

'I've brought Miss Owen up to see yer, Mr Higginbotham, like yer asked,' murmured Vera.

'Mm. Thank you, Mrs Bell. You may get back to work.'

Still he didn't look up. Martha hadn't noticed the ring on Vera's finger, but she saw it as Vera opened the door to leave. She mimed the words 'good luck' as she squeezed past Martha. She was very nice and Martha mimed a 'thank you' back.

Martha licked her lips and moved her weight from one foot to the other. She thought it was rather rude of Mr Higginbotham to keep her waiting but there was nothing she could do if she wanted this job.

At last, he put his pen down and looked up at her. Quickly, she switched on the smile again.

'Miss… er… Miss…' He glanced down at his papers, swishing them about until he found what he was looking for. 'Ah… yes, Miss, er… Martha Owen?'

'Yes, Mr Higginbotham.'

'No relation of Oswald Parker, who runs The Potter's Wheel?'

'Yes, Sir. He is my grandad.'

'I haven't seen Oswald in years. Used to go in for a pint on me way home, but since the missus has taken the Pledge, I seem to have done the same – although I conner remember agreeing to.' He gave her a smile and a bit of a laugh.

Now the time had come to talk her mouth had grown dry and Martha couldn't for the life of her remember anything Bridie had said about the dos and don'ts of getting jobs at Paradise Pottery. Mr Higginbotham's name almost had her in fits of giggles – there had been a boy at school with that name and he got all manner of ribald jokes made of him. Had Mr Higginbotham had such a problem in his past?

He waved her towards a chair in front of his desk. 'Now, Miss Owen. I understand you have experience of working as a transferrer at Jackson's Pottery and that Bridie O'Connor has spoken for you?'

'Yes, Mr Higginbotham.'

'You will probably find that, while the job is basically the same as the work you were doing, decorating here is different. You might've noticed that this factory is actually called C. Rhead & Son. It's owned by Mr Cyril Rhead and his son. Mr John Rhead also works in the business. It's called Paradise Pottery because it's in Paradise Street. Some say it's paradise to work here.'

How many times had Mr Higginbotham said that – and still managed a smile when he'd finished.

'Mr Cyril's getting on in life and we expect Mr John to take over eventually. He has definite ideas on how he wants to run this factory. If you want to do well here, we expect you to pay close attention to everything as you go through your training. We do not send out shoddy work. That's why we are keen to take on employees recommended to us.'

'Yes, Mr Higginbotham.'

'No doubt you are aware of the type of pottery we produce here. It is the highest-quality bone china. We have provided tableware for royalty, and even provided the first-class dining crockery for the ill-fated *Titanic* as well as her sister ships the *Olympic* and the *Britannic*. Safe to say that, as far as I know, the latter two are still afloat.

'Apart from the tableware we also produce figurines, vases, spice jars and other ornamental ware. We use a number of decorating techniques such as tube lining, gilding and enamelling. But our best ware is all hand-painted.'

He stopped and looked at Martha. Was he expecting her to say something?

He continued. 'Now, what was the reason you left Jackson's?'

Martha thought – this is it. It may be the shortest interview in history. 'They laid me off because there wasn't enough work for us decorators.'

'Aye, that's a problem in wartime, things have to be practical not pretty, especially as how the prices of things have shot up.'

He continued to ask questions about what she had done at Jackson's and then, seemingly satisfied, he told her to sit at a bench in a corner of the main room and work on a sample plate and apply a transfer to it. She checked there were no spots of dust on the plate and then cut out the transfer carefully, and applied size to fix it to the plate. Then she dabbed it with a brush to make sure that there were no air bubbles and carefully removed the transfer. Casting a final eye over the plate, she took it in to Mr Higginbotham.

'Hmm, not bad.' He brought it up to his nose and examined it closely. 'You were a bit slow.' He raised his head and smiled thinly. 'But you'll soon quicken up once you're on piecework, when yer get paid for what yer make.'

Martha thought there was some praise in his words – although she couldn't be sure.

'Now, one last thing. I will need a reference from Jackson's. Who was your supervisor?'

'My immediate supervisor was Mrs Beryl Turner, but the department's supervisor has just taken the Colours. Mrs Turner is quite happy to give me a reference.'

'Oh, I know Mrs Turner. She's a good sort and knows her stuff, I'll send a letter to her asking for a reference.'

'I've brought these with me, I got them from school.' She handed him her school leaving certificate and reference from Mr Wells.

He glanced over them briefly. 'Very well. You may expect to receive a letter from us very soon. We will want you to commence employment on 9 August, which is the first day back after the holidays. I trust that will be satisfactory?'

Did that mean she'd got the job? Or did it mean she would receive a letter to inform her *if* she had been successful? She didn't dare ask more questions as he made definite moves to remove her from his tiny alcove.

Nevertheless, Martha grinned – or should that be smiled? She didn't know what the difference was – they both meant the same as far as she was concerned.

She went home a very happy young lady and kept her fingers crossed that Beryl was true to her word.

–

It was Friday teatime and a very special Friday being the last day of work before the annual Potters' holiday. The bar was full of men having a quick drink before heading home to their families and preparing for a week of doing nothing. Martha was in the back room reading a book, when Grandad walked in.

'You have a visitor, Martha,' Grandad announced.

'Who is it?'

'Come through to the lounge, Wilfred.'

To Martha's amazement, it was Mr Higginbotham.

'Hello, Martha.'

'Hello, Mr Higginbotham,' squeaked Martha in a little voice.

'I thought I'd pop by to tell you the good news. You can start a week on Monday, like I said. I spoke to Mrs Turner and fully understand the situation. Rest assured nothing like that happens at Paradise Pottery.'

Martha jumped up and clapped her hands. She almost threw her arms around him, but quickly decided it wouldn't be appropriate.

'I think I'll just have a quick drink with Oswald before I go. My wife knows I have to partake sometimes in business and she makes allowances.'

Mr Higginbotham took his leave with a friendly wink and returned to the bar.

Ten days later, Martha walked through the gates of Paradise Pottery as a worker, her head held high. She had used some of her limited savings to buy a new skirt and blouse and had bought four yards of white cotton material to make aprons. She had cleaned her shoes until they shone. It was with a happy though nervous heart that Martha set off to work that first day.

She had agreed with Bridie that they walk in together – something they might choose to do every morning. It certainly helped rid herself of the butterflies causing her belly to churn that first day. Bridie enjoyed a good blether and, in no time at all, they'd walked through the gates of Paradise Pottery.

'Hiya! Martha!' said an unfamiliar voice.

Vera was waiting for her. Her eyes lit up. She hadn't been looking forward to opening that door to the big Decorating Shop and walking in knowing no one, not knowing where to go, or who to speak to.

'I wish I didn't get so out of breath. I thought I was late and ran up the road like a madwoman,' Vera grumbled. 'I sit so long these days that I get out of breath walking up the stairs.'

Martha laughed.

Vera burst out laughing too. 'I wanted to meet yer outside – I know what I felt like on my first day.'

'Thank you, I appreciate that.' How nice of Vera to think about her.

Vera turned to Bridie. 'Hiya, duckie. I forgot – you two are neighbours, aren't yer?'

'Bridie spoke for me and I got the job.'

'You're a good girl, aren't yer, Bridie?'

'Course I am.'

'I've been told to show you the ropes, Martha – where everything is and what to do and who to see.'

'That's lovely. I was worried about going in all by meself.'

Vera nodded in the direction of the Decorating Shop and the three of them walked in together.

Martha held her head high and gulped. The buzz in the room was tremendous – even louder than she remembered – and *she* was going to be a part of it. The butterflies in her belly left her as quickly as they had come. She was going to enjoy this.

'See yer later, Martha.' Bridie crossed the room to her own bench.

Vera introduced her to a few of the women who would be sharing the same bench as she learned the art of enamelling. She would need to become competent with brushwork and learn the types of brushes she needed to use to gain the effect she was looking for. If all went well, she would move on to transferring. This work was hard, but it was work she was used to doing at Jackson's so she wasn't worried.

Vera introduced Martha to a girl who was one of the recent recruits to transferring.

'Martha, this is Cassie Mellor. She's been with us for – how long now, Cassie?'

'Hiya, duck, pleased to meet yer. Reckon I've bin here about seven months now.'

'Martha's started with us today but she's worked on a potbank before.'

Cassie nodded. 'Where were you?'

'Jackson's in Hanley.'

'Am sure you'll like it here.'

'Any road, we'd best get on, girls.' Vera moved back to her own bench.

Martha followed.

'You'll be starting on enamelling. Have yer done that before?'

Martha shook her head and then remembered to show her willingness to try things. 'But I've seen somebody doing it and I would love to try it out. I like painting.'

Vera smiled. 'Good – that's what we want to hear.'

Martha grinned. Good job she remembered what Bridie had instilled into her the other night when she paid a quick visit.

She was given a plate with a pattern in the middle and a blank plate and was asked to reproduce the design.

'You see the plate has the outline of the design on it?'

Martha nodded, hardly taking her eyes off the plate in front of her.

'I want you to paint that plate by filling in the colours so it looks exactly like this one.' Vera picked up a plate from a pile on a trolley that Vera had placed beside her bench. 'It's flatware painting and it involves shading the design more than painting, I suppose – but see how you go. You need to mix the colour powder with this fat oil and paint it onto the pottery using a brush.' Vera bent to pick one up. 'We call brushes "pencils". You are actually drawing with a brush. Got it?'

'Yes.'

'When you've finished painting, it will be fired and once that's done you conner change nothing – so be warned.'

Martha nodded.

They worked slowly until it was nearly dinnertime. A man who was sitting with the painters, the top men on the potbank, wandered over and stood beside Vera.

'Hiya, Eddie, come for yer dinner, have yer?'

He looked a similar age to Vera – early thirties.

'I should've told yer, Martha. This is my Eddie. My hubby. One of the top modellers in The Potteries. We were wed fourteen years ago. We started here at the same time, straight from school. Never liked him at school, he was a show-off. But we grew to like each other and now I conner get rid of him.'

'That's nice to know, Vera love.'

'Hello, Eddie,' Martha said. Vera had said nothing about children, so she would've been surprised if they had any. He seemed nice. He had one of those faces that always seemed to be smiling. They must have had plenty to talk about when they got home in the evening.

'Best get back else Jonas'll wonder whether I've scarpered.'

Vera chuckled. 'He knows yer better than that, Eddie.'

As Eddie walked away, Vera's eyes followed him. There was a warmness to her face and Martha could see the love written there.

'Jonas is the youngest modeller, but that's not saying much, as the other three, Enoch, George and Levi are all in their fifties.' Vera turned back again. 'He's a good bloke. Eddie gets on well with him.'

The girls arrived at their benches the next day and Martha was happy to note there were no butterflies in her belly or elsewhere. In fact, she hadn't given work a thought, apart from when she was eating her breakfast – then it was excitement rather than butterflies she felt.

She met Bridie outside and they walked in together.

As Martha was laying out her bench, Cassie stopped by her side. 'How did yer get on yesterday, Martha?'

'Fine – I think. I'm looking forward to today.'

'I've never regretted coming here. You'll have some fun with us.'

'Sounds good.'

'You're with Vera for the time being, aren't yer?'

'Yes. She didn't say how long for.'

'It'll depend on you and how good you are. If you're a fast worker and accurate, you'll be on yer own pretty fast. She's very good at getting the best out of people. You'll do well with her. She's trained a few of us and we're all on piecework now.'

'Hiya, Martha – Cassie. How's things?' Vera slipped out of her coat as she was talking. 'You must've done all right yesterday since you've come back today,' she grinned at Martha. 'The girls are nice and I love the ware, don't you?' she said, turning back to Martha.

Martha grinned. 'I do too from what I've seen so far. Like I said, I was working on Jackson's in Hanley decorating earthenware mainly but they were laying people off.'

The bell rang.

'Well, girls, much as I'd like to carry on with this conversation, we *do* have a job to do, so let's get cracking else we'll be laid off an' all.'

There was much banter as they put on their pinafores and took up their seats.

'Now, Martha. You've got the basic idea of what we want yer to do so I want yer to practise the brushstrokes and blending the colours. These are sable brushes. Look after them well and they'll last you for years. You'll miss 'em when they've gone. I warn you – you'll be bored by the end of the week, but practice is what yer need. Yer brushstrokes are key.'

'Yes, Vera. Thank you.'

Martha sat down and stared around as the girls – they were all called girls regardless of how old they were – started to work. Pity she hadn't been here all along. She could feel it in her bones, she was going to love it.

When they broke for a bite to eat, Vera told her more about the pottery and its owners.

'First you've got Mr Cyril Rhead. He's the owner and is closer to sixty than fifty, I should say. He tends to keep himself to himself but sometimes walks round the potbank with Mr John, his son. The boss is always known as Mr Rhead and his son as Mr John so we know which is which when we're talking. Mr Rhead's wife never comes here and Mr John isn't married. He'll have a bob or two when Mr Rhead dies and will be quite a catch for somebody – if you're looking?'

Martha shook her head. 'Not me. Probably be a spinster all me life.'

'Bit cynical at your age, aren't yer?'

'No, I'm realistic. I think I'm happy to decide on my future for meself without a man telling me what to do.'

She could see Vera had more questions on the tip of her tongue, so she shut up until she could change the subject.

–

It was the end of Martha's second week and she already felt at home at Paradise. 'Pottery' was usually left off, as Mr Higginbotham had already told her.

Mother and Issy met Martha by the clock tower to do some shopping after Martha had done her shift at Paradise on Saturday morning. When they got back to the pub, Issy went straight off to meet Josie in Burslem. Grandad and one of the men were sorting out some barrels ready for the drayman first thing on Monday.

Martha was helping Mother to put away the shopping when there was a clatter from the letterbox on the back door of the pub. Letters were always shoved through there. Mother picked up the post, which included an envelope addressed to her.

'I wonder who this is from, don't recognise the writing.' Mother twisted the envelope back and forth.

Peter came in at that moment. 'Seems to me you're not going to find out neither if yer dunner open it.'

'I know, Peter. I'm not daft. I just wondered who...'

Martha frowned at Peter and turned to Mother. 'Would yer like me to open it?'

'I'm all right. I can do it.'

Mother sat down at the table, took up a knife out of the drawer and slit the envelope open. She took out the pages — three in all — and turned them backwards and forwards. When she caught sight of the name on the last page, she threw it down on her knee.

'Are you all right?' Martha asked, unable to wait any longer. 'Tell us, Mother, please... what does the letter say?'

'It's from a Corporal Davies. He says he was serving at the Front, with yer father.'

Now it was Peter's turn to gasp.

Martha's mouth fell open. 'After all this time? What does it say?'

'Read it to us, Martha. Me eyes are not so good.'

It was an excuse, but Martha took the letter and began to read out loud.

15 August 1915

Dear Mrs Owen,

My name is William Davies. We have never met but I was a corporal in the Staffordshire Regiment and your late husband, Percy, was my sergeant. If he ever spoke of me he may have referred to me as Taffy. No doubt you will have received all of the formal paperwork from the War Office, but the CO, Captain Wilkinson, suggested that it would be good for one of his close friends to contact his widow as he often spoke of you and your family.

I served with Sergeant Owen in South Africa and with Sergeant Major Owen in India and we were good friends. When Percy left the army, I continued in service until recently. Percy was one of the best I was commanded by. He thought the world of his men and made sure that everyone in his platoon was looked after.

I was surprised in 1914 when he turned up at Lichfield Barracks ready to go to war. I thought he would be too old, but, like he said, he'd just sneaked in and didn't want to miss the opportunity.

We shipped out to France as soon as they could find transport and found ourselves on the Belgian border near Mons. We were together during the awful retreat and eventually ended up at Bapaume.

The day Percy was killed, there had been no serious fighting. The Huns were about 200 yards away from our forward trench. There had been some sniper action but, in the rain and snow flurries, neither side was too keen on leaving what shelter we had. Before tea, Lieutenant Fitzherbert came to Percy with orders to carry out a trench raid at two in the morning, under the cover of a nearby artillery barrage. Without giving away too many military secrets, this was a normal activity to collect intelligence on enemy positions and if lucky take prisoners. Both sides did it and occasionally the raids ran into each other.

It was a clear night but there was no moon when we headed through Piccadilly Circus – this is what we called the gap in the wire giving us access to some shell holes and No Man's Land. We were making slow but steady progress, being as quiet as possible and keeping our eyes open for enemy movement. Then all hell broke loose. We had stumbled onto an enemy patrol no doubt with the same plans that we had, but they were only just leaving their trench. Flares were sent up and firing started from both sides. Percy realised his vulnerable position and immediately ordered the platoon to return at all speed to our lines. Meanwhile, he along with myself and four of the men remained in the shell hole giving covering fire. After a few minutes things went quiet. Two of the lads who stayed with us had been hit and were in a bad way.

We moved out of our shell hole and into an abandoned observation post. We gathered ourselves and I started back to the lines with the other men. Percy said that he would follow on a few moments later in case covering fire was needed. We hadn't moved many yards when there was an almighty explosion. I turned round and saw Percy flying through the air. He disappeared into the German front trench. There was nothing that we could do. We returned to the British trenches and reported all that had happened.

After an attack we made several weeks later, both the British and German commanders agreed to a two-hour ceasefire to allow medical attention for the wounded and collection of identifying documents from the dead. It was when the identity discs were being sorted that we found Percy's.

I'm sorry but that is all we know. Your husband was a brave man, Mrs Owen, and much respected by his troops. We lost too many experienced soldiers early in the war. I hope that I was able to carry on the tradition

*that Percy had instilled into me to ensure the safety of
my men before my own.*

*I have enclosed my new home address, which is a
hospital in Oswestry, not far from Stoke. I am learning
to cope with both legs missing and we'll see how things
go.*

Best wishes
*Corporal William Davies, 75115, RAMC Hospital,
Oswestry*

'Oh.' The last paragraph almost took away Martha's ability to
carry on but she forced the words out. 'The poor man. How
awful.'

They sat in silence letting the words sink in. Mother was
pale. Martha squeezed her hand sympathetically, wishing she
could think of the right things to say.

'This corporal seems a decent bloke,' muttered Peter. 'But
it can't be our father he's talking about. I doubt Father would
even mention us.'

'Corporal Davies makes it sound like yer father was proud
of us,' Mother spoke up. 'But he certainly knew yer father well
if he served with him in South Africa and India.'

Peter's eyebrows had risen. 'Can yer imagine what Father
would say if he did talk about us?'

'Oh, I dunno what to think.' Martha's mind had gone blank.

'I believe Corporal Davies, and if we had any more questions
about whether or not yer father's still alive, I do believe they've
been answered.' Mother's bottom lip trembled and her voice
became croaky. 'And I don't know whether to feel sad or
thankful that it really is over.'

Chapter Eleven

Autumn 1915

Martha was getting on well at Paradise. The work was interesting and some of the designs, although a little old-fashioned, were complex and a challenge to get right, but satisfying once mastered.

'Just wait behind a minute, duck,' Vera said. 'Me and Eddie'll walk up the street with yer.' They packed up and sponged down their benches so they were ready to start the next day.

'What did yer want me for, Vera?'

'Nothing much,' she whispered. 'I wanted yer to meet Jonas Gray. You remember him, don't yer? Works with Eddie.'

'Why?'

'Well, you haven't got nobody and neither has he. I thought as it could be good for both of yer to say hello.'

'Are you matchmaking by any chance, Vera Bell?'

Vera pulled a face at her and then grinned as they walked out.

When they got to the door, Eddie was waiting with another man stood beside him.

Martha had felt a little annoyed. She'd said she wasn't looking for a bloke. Nevertheless, he was here and she should at least speak to the poor man. It wasn't his fault.

He was tall. She barely reached his shoulder. His eyes were dark and she couldn't see their colour in the evening light. His hair looked dark too although it was difficult to see under his cap.

'Martha, can I introduce you to Mr Jonas Gray? He works with Eddie in the modelling room. You'll see him about.'

Martha was sure her face was red. She squeezed out the words, 'Pleased to meet yer.'

Jonas looked as if he wished the ground would open up below him. He nodded and said he was pleased to meet her too.

They stood, looking at the ground wondering what Vera actually had in mind.

'I thought as it would be good for you two to meet as you're both on yer own. We like to go dancing, don't we, Eddie' – not stopping to give her husband a chance to speak – 'and next time we go dancing, we thought you both might like to come along too. We'd have a great time, wouldn't we, Eddie?'

Poor Jonas looked as if he had been ambushed and was at a loss on what to say.

The thing that annoyed Martha was that Vera had given them little choice in the matter. He looked older than she'd expected. How could Vera possibly have thought they could become friends, close friends, going by what Vera said?

Jonas suggested that he needed to get home. He didn't say why, nor where home was. 'Good to meet yer, Martha, and I'll probably see yer in Paradise,' he said.

Martha, seeing the funny side of his remark, burst out laughing.

He looked startled and then laughed too. His face changed and he looked proper handsome.

'Looking forward to it,' she replied. And, to Martha's surprise, she decided she was.

After that, Martha bumped into Jonas a few times at work but, apart from a quick nod and a smile in her direction, nothing more was said, thank goodness.

–

Issy came downstairs in her dark blue winter dress. She had decided to put on something warm. There was a chill in the air and it looked like it might go foggy later. Fog in The Potteries was not very pleasant as it tended to trap the smoke and soot, making it much worse.

'Where are you off to? Not a very nice day for walking.'

'I'm not, I just wanted to look nice. Michael's coming round. He wants some help with summat. He's got a form to fill in.'

'What sort of form?' enquired Martha.

'A blank one, I suppose.'

'Oh, we are the sharp one today, any sharper and yer'd cut yerself.'

At that moment there came a knock on the door, which was probably just as well.

'I'll go.' Issy rushed to the front door.

'Hello, Michael.'

'Hello, Issy.' They came into the kitchen and sat down at the table. Martha was doing her best to keep a straight face. Michael looked spruced up, too. Martha wondered if that was his idea or his mother's.

Michael took a brown envelope from his inside pocket and placed it on the table. 'I've got some news for you all. Our Betty's had a little girl, last Sunday. She's called it Hannah. With an "H",' he said as an afterthought.

Martha and Mother looked at each other. They were surprised even though they knew it was about the right time.

'Are they all right?' Martha had to ask.

'Think so, Mother's said nowt else. She had the baby at Mrs Shenton's and now Mother goes down each day to look after them and do for Mrs Shenton, until Betty's ready to start work again.'

Martha was thoughtful as she climbed the stairs to her bedroom.

It had actually happened. Even now she couldn't imagine Betty with a baby. It only seemed a short time since they were walking home from school and talking about how Betty would get a boyfriend; he would be handsome and ask her to get married. She would be all in white, with white flowers in her hair and a long white train. They would have children, at least two, a boy and a girl. They would have a nice place to live in the country and her husband would earn enough money so she didn't have to work.

On the other hand, Martha had said she would not be getting married and she would become an artist and live on her own. She would paint pictures of flowers and fairies and horses which would be sold in only the best shops like Burton & Dunn's.

How different was reality for Betty now?

–

Dinnertime was when most of the talking took place. Martha was keen to pick the brains of both Eddie and Jonas to enable her to find out as much about ceramic painting and decoration as she could. The more she found out the more she wanted to get a paintress job, but there were no vacancies. Now that she wasn't worried about Father having a go for not earning her money, she wanted to take every chance to learn. Talking to Eddie was relatively straightforward because he spent many a dinnertime chatting with Vera. Sometimes Jonas would be with him.

Martha didn't really understand what a modeller did but decided not to ask until later. She did not want to appear unknowledgeable. At first, she was a little concerned about talking to him knowing how important he was, but she needn't have worried. He was as down-to-earth as Vera. They talked about the current patterns and how they might need to change to suit more modern tastes in art coming over from Europe. He showed Martha some of the designs he was working on but was sworn to secrecy on disclosing anything about them.

Sometimes, when Jonas came along, they had discussions that fascinated Martha. She would think about the old Martha who wouldn't have spoken to these men, thinking herself to be too lowly to have anything of interest to talk about. At seventeen, Martha might have seen herself as too young to be taken seriously, but they encouraged her to talk, until she felt quite at ease and drew in information that might help her future. She loved it.

–

Martha was delighted when Vera stopped at her bench and asked if she would like to go to the dance at the Victoria Hall in Hanley on 18 December.

'Lots of people will be there and you'll have a good time.'

Martha wanted to ask if Jonas would be there, but she didn't know if she wanted to draw attention to her thoughts in that area just yet.

'I'll be going with Eddie, of course.' Vera gave her a sideways glance. 'And Jonas has said that he'll go if you're going.'

'He has?'

Vera nodded.

Martha couldn't deny a little pang of curiosity at the thought of spending the evening with Jonas. 'Go on then,' she said as if she wasn't too bothered, even though her heartbeats had increased dramatically.

Martha thought back to that first meeting with Jonas and how uncomfortable he'd seemed in her presence. He had been in good spirits when they parted, and at work he had been happy to talk to her about painting and answered all her questions. There was no doubting he was attractive. The more time she spent in his company, the more interesting she found him.

–

Grandad came up with a suggestion regarding the pub. He looked sad, but determined. Grandma sat next to him, and patted his knee from time to time. The whole family was gathered, except Daniel. It sounded serious when Mother asked them to be in the kitchen at five o'clock before they settled down to Sunday tea.

'Now listen to what I have to tell you because it's important you all know. But I dunner want yer to go telling nobody. We must keep it quiet until it's sorted. Is everybody clear?'

They all nodded. Martha wondered if it had anything to do with that letter from the sergeant they'd received a few months back.

'Yer grandma and me, well, we're getting on a bit now and we dunner know how much longer we can carry on running The Potter's Wheel.'

'Will we have to leave?' Issy said immediately.

Mother put a finger to her lips. 'Let Grandad finish telling yer, Issy duck, then you'll find out.'

'As yer know, I am the licensee of the pub. If I give up the licence then anyone can apply for it. The Temperance lot will try to persuade the council to cancel the licence, and then the pub would have to close.' He stared at each of them in turn. They were all hanging onto his every word now. 'Grandma and I have talked about you taking over the pub, Fanny, once we've got the financial and legal stuff finalised, and after a period of training, of course. It would set you up for life.'

'Oh!'

Instead of being happy with the suggestion, Mother's face grew pale. Her eyes bulged and worse still, her hand pulled at her neck as if she wanted to be sick or couldn't breathe. She scraped her chair back from the table. 'Father, did yer not think to ask me what I wanted first before telling all and sundry?'

'Whatever d'yer mean? I thought as yer'd be pleased to take it on.'

Mother shot out of her chair, shaking her head. 'I can't... I can't do it. And yer can't ask me to neither!'

She ran for the door, wrenched it open and, moments later, they heard the distant slamming of a bedroom door. The remaining faces stared at one another, aghast.

Martha rose to go after her but Grandma put a hand up.

'Leave her be. She's got a lot to think about. She needs a bit of time.'

'She should've jumped at the chance. It's not every day yer get the offer of a business.' Peter looked glumly at the table.

'Well, I'll tell yer summat. That mother of yours has got the strength to do anything she wants if she has a mind to it, no matter what *she* thinks. She has to believe in herself. And that's what yer father's knocked out of her.'

–

Mother was quiet for the next few days. As usual, she helped Grandma bake the pies they sold in the pub. The pies were selling well and Grandma needed an extra pair of hands most of the time. Mother and Grandma had talked about extending the kitchen and even opening a shop. Martha had been surprised when nothing came of it. It was a good idea. It appeared that Grandma and Grandad had been planning their retirement for a while.

On the Saturday afternoon before the Christmas dance, Martha could barely keep still. She was both excited and nervous and needed to take her mind off it otherwise she would never get through the rest of the day. The best thing she could do would be to take herself off for a walk – especially if she was accompanied.

'Mother, I have to slip down the road to get some painting brushes for work. Fancy a walk?'

All the pies had been made for the Saturday evening rush and the kitchen had been cleaned and everything in its proper place.

Mother wiped her hands on the now damp towel and nodded. 'The fresh air will do us a bit of good, I reckon.'

The day was dull but the shop windows more than made up for it with their Christmas decorations brightening the High

Street. It was a pity the windows couldn't be lit up in the evenings because of the blackout.

Having bought the brushes, the two women carried on walking towards the canal where they could talk without being overheard.

'Have yer spoken to Grandma and Grandad about the pub?'

'Only to say as I dunner want it. I've never wanted it, Martha. It was yer father's wish, not mine. They held onto it while yer father was alive, but once he was gone, I knew it would be only a matter of time before the subject came up again.'

'So we'll have to move out again when Grandad retires?'

'We will, duckie, but they won't see us homeless. They bought a house a good while ago cos they didn't know how long yer grandad would be able to carry on working. They rented it out and now they've given notice to end the rental.'

Mother's eyes focused on the path in front of them, her internal thoughts at odds with one another, as far as Martha could tell.

'After putting up with yer father's ways all these years, how can I commit meself to a pub? I'm surprised they can't see that.'

It suddenly dawned on Martha that Mother was right. Now Father was dead they had assumed Mother would jump into Grandad's place, not giving any consideration to what damage Father's actions had done to her.

'Actually, with the pies selling so well – dunner laugh – I've bin thinking about the possibility of baking them meself when yer grandma finishes.'

'What – making yer own and selling them outside of the pub?'

'That's right.'

'But where could you make them if we don't have the pub? Who'd buy them?'

'If I had a little shop with a kitchen, I could make and sell them.'

'A shop?'

'We've already proved people'll buy them – so why not?'

'But where would yer get the money from?'

'Leave that to me, but I think it would work. I'd need help. I know you've set yer heart on yer painting but our Issy might be interested in working with me in the shop. She likes helping cook the pies in the pub, when she gets a chance.'

The words coming out of Mother's mouth were quiet, pondering, as if she was talking it over with her own mind.

'It could work, Martha – I'm sure it could. And then I'll be helping women feed their families and not encouraging violent men to get drunk.'

As they turned to head back to The Potter's Wheel, Mother seemed to become more and more excited about the prospect she had been building, almost as if she was planning what to say to Grandad and Grandma when she got home. Help from them was likely to be the only way she could do it. So when they arrived, it was no surprise that Mother shot off to find Grandma. Soon after, Grandad joined them and the parlour door was closed.

How Martha wished she could have been a fly on the wall! She had seen a side of her mother she had not seen before. She was always too meek, with few opinions. Martha was sure that – in this mood – Mother could get anything she wanted, just like Grandad had said.

Whatever was talked about behind that closed door remained a secret for a week. No matter how hard Martha questioned her, Mother remained tight-lipped. All in good time – was the only answer Martha received.

Chapter Twelve

Christmas 1915

As the friends all lived in Tunstall, they met at the tram stop on the High Street and travelled together. There was a lot of jollity between them as they rode from Tunstall, through Burslem and on to Hanley. As they sat chatting, the first sign of snow appeared on the tram windows. Soon, they were covered in condensation and Martha gave up trying to look at the world on the other side of the glass.

Martha could feel the strength of Jonas's body next to hers on the small seat they shared. Vera and Eddie were sitting behind them and Vera periodically leaned forward to make conversation. Martha had the notion Vera was watching them to check they were getting on together.

They made the usual pleasantries. It was difficult to say much over the noise of the tram so their chatter didn't really happen until they got off and began walking to the Victoria Hall. The snow was growing thicker. She shuddered and shuddered and hoped it wouldn't stay like this, otherwise they might have difficulty getting back.

'Are yer cold, Martha?' Jonas said, close to her ear. 'Let me...'

He put his arm around her shoulder and pulled her towards him so he might link her arm. Whether it was the warmth of his body next to hers, or the fact she was warmer because she was walking, a glow spread through her. The snow no longer mattered.

Vera was right about the dance being busy. They had to queue to part with their outdoor clothes and then queue to get into the hall. Decorations had been hung for Christmas and Martha was looking forward to having an enjoyable evening.

There were no tables left, so they got a drink and stood watching. When the band began to play a waltz, Eddie led Vera onto the dance floor, took her in his arms and danced her away.

'Are you ready for this?' asked Jonas. 'I should warn you – I'm not the world's best dancer.'

'That's all right. Neither am I,' Martha retorted.

She was whirled away. He wasn't a bad dancer at all. She felt as if she was floating around the room and she was happy to follow wherever he led.

An hour later, they managed to get a table for the four of them and, while Eddie and Vera were still on the floor, Martha discovered a little about Jonas. He said he was the youngest of three sons and that his parents owned a green grocer's in High Street, Goldenhill, a mile or two further on than Tunstall, and had two market stalls, one in the covered market in Tunstall, run by his eldest brother, Robert, and a similar one in Burslem market run by David.

'How about you? What's your background?' he asked.

Martha was careful in what she told him. Nothing about her father's violence. After all, he was dead now.

'I've always loved sketching. In fact, Grandma gave me a sketch book for my seventh birthday, a year before we moved to Dresden Street. I like the canal and enjoy sketching the boats and the people. Best of all are the horses. They seem so tranquil.'

'It's hard to draw humans and animals. If you're not careful the drawing can look lifeless.'

'Yes, I wish I could do more.'

'We have lots of hand-painted ware. The competition's fierce for the paintress jobs – you'll need to work hard to get noticed. I'll have a look at some of your sketches when you feel able to show me them.'

Martha had never been asked by anyone to show them her work. She reddened and squeaked an answer. 'Yes, I'd like that. The more I see the more I want to have a career in painting.'

Jonas left to get them a drink. There was no hard liquor or even beer at these dances. Just fruit punch and cordials.

Vera plonked herself down in the next chair. 'I need to catch me breath. You two seem to be getting on well. Eddie says he's never heard Jonas talk for so long. He looks young for his age; he'll be twenty-four in February.'

'I didn't realise he was that old. Four years older than my brothers, and I think they're old.'

'Less of the old; I'm a good ten years older than him.'

'Oh, sorry, I didn't mean it to be an insult. He's just a lot older than I thought.'

Jonas returned with two glasses of cordial. Vera made herself scarce, saying she must find Eddie.

To cover her embarrassment at discovering Jonas's age she blurted out, 'So you didn't fancy working in the family business?'

'No. I've always had a hankering for drawing and painting. I went to work for Paradise straight from school, labouring in the decorating department. I was moved to the modelling room to be their labourer and Levi recommended to Mr Cyril Rhead I had potential. He talked to my parents about an apprenticeship and they agreed. I went to Burslem School of Art, three evenings a week, to learn all about the making of pottery. When I finished the course, I had been working in modelling as an apprentice for three years and so was pretty experienced. Mr Rhead promoted me to modeller under Eddie. I've done that ever since, and I love it.'

'What do modellers do?'

'When the company wants a new style of teapot, for instance, I sketch out drawings to show what the piece could look like when it's made and decorated. I can see if the colour scheme works and check that we can make the colour economically. Then I would make several full-sized models in clay. One of these models is decorated to see the overall effect. Once everyone is happy, the undecorated clay model is used by the mould maker, who produces a master mould in plaster of Paris from which all the moulds used in the factory are made.'

'Never heard of that before. It sounds really interesting.'

'It is, and it can be frustrating when things don't work out. The piece may not be substantial enough, the colours are too expensive, the parts may have difficult areas to mould which have to be changed and it may not fire properly. The final problem, after all of this work, is if it is not what we perceived the customer wants.'

Shortly after that they returned to the dance floor.

Martha grew hot. Whether it was the dancing or the company, she didn't know. He was older than the other boys she had been friendly with and, even at seventeen, she felt a little young to be flirting. She glanced across at their table and was relieved to see Vera and Eddie had returned to their seats. She walked steadily towards them.

'Are yer hot? Yer've got a right flush on yer cheeks,' Vera whispered.

Martha thought it was safest just to nod.

As the evening drew on and chatting was combined with dancing, Martha had a thoroughly enjoyable time and was disappointed when it came to an end. As they walked towards the tram stop Jonas linked her arm with his.

'Eddie and Vera are a grand pair,' he said. 'They've been together a long time. They think the world of each other – even more so, I think, because it looks like having kids is out of the question.'

'Oh, poor Vera.'

'They don't talk about it. Now and again one of them'll say summat and you can see the pain on their faces.'

'They would've made good parents. Vera's been very good to me ever since I started at Paradise.'

They approached the tram stop and caught up with Vera and Eddie.

'Can't say goodnight on the tram so I'll say it now.' Jonas took her hand and shook it. 'Thank you for a wonderful evening, Miss Owen. Hope you enjoyed it as much as I did.'

There was a warm look in his eyes, as if he was going to kiss her, but he didn't, thankfully. Hadn't Martha just told Vera he was too old to have such ideas about her? What on earth would she have said to him if he had?

She sat beside him on the tram and tried not to look at him, glad Vera and Eddie were sitting in front of them and there was no one behind.

As the tram drew into Tunstall, she turned to look at him before she rose from her seat.

'Thank you again for a pleasant evening,' she said.

Jonas moved aside to let her out of the seat and was sure she felt his lips brush her cheek. She couldn't believe he would do such a thing in a public place. She squeezed past him and descended from the tram behind her friends, their eyes locked together as the tram moved off towards Goldenhill.

Vera and Eddie walked Martha to The Potter's Wheel. All the time, her heart was pounding.

'He's a good sort, is Jonas,' said Eddie, grinning. 'I've worked with him for a few years now. Yer could do worse, yer know, Martha.'

'Be quiet, Eddie, less of yer matchmaking. That's my job.' Vera laughed at Martha's obvious embarrassment.

Martha said nothing. She would have to have words with Vera when they were on their own.

-

Martha said her goodbyes to Vera and Eddie and hurried into the house. It was late and everyone had gone to bed. She crept upstairs to the bedroom and as quietly as she could, slipped out of her clothes and into her nightgown. Issy never stirred, for which Martha was thankful. She wasn't up to answering all her sister's questions. She would have to face up to that tomorrow.

She sat on her bed and unrolled her stockings as her brain ran over the events of the night. She had enjoyed spending time with Jonas. Had he gone and spoilt it all with the kiss? She put her hand up to her cheek in wonderment.

'Did yer have a good time?'

Issy wasn't asleep after all. Martha sighed. She hadn't had time to work out her own response yet, never mind talk to Issy about it.

'Yes, I did.'

'I've been waiting for yer to come back so you can tell me all about it.'

'It's too late and you should be asleep.' But Martha knew there was only one way to shut Issy up and that was to tell her what she was desperate to know. 'He's very nice and good to talk to, just like at work.'

'And... are you going to see him again?'

'Yes, at work.'

'You know what I mean.'

'Haven't I said that I aren't looking for a man? I want to be a paintress. Besides, he's too old. Vera says he's almost twenty-four. Can you imagine it, Issy? I'll still be a kid in his eyes.'

'That's a pity.'

'And if we did get together and things went wrong, it would affect my job and I'm not willing to take the chance. Not now.'

'But Martha—'

'But nothing. Just go to sleep. Please...'

—

In the cold light of early Sunday morning, the kiss was the first thing to enter Martha's mind. With everyone in bed she could lie there and think what the implications might be, him working in the same potbank. Dare she speak against him if the kiss led him to think she was happy to receive one when they barely knew each other? She didn't want him to think she was that sort of girl. Besides, she'd already decided she wasn't going to wed, so it would be kinder not to get his hopes up.

Martha was bleary-eyed when she rose from her bed. She had tossed and turned during the night and got little sleep. She wished she had never gone to the dance, if he was going to invade her head like this.

When she joined Mother at the breakfast table, she explained the predicament Vera had put her in – no doubt with the best of intentions – and asked, 'What shall I do, Mother?'

'Mm, I agree he's a bit on the old side for yer, duck. You have to be careful. He might think he can rule yer and yer dunner want that. Whatever was yer friend thinking of – putting yer in such a spot.'

'She was trying to be helpful.'

Mother took the kettle off the range and filled the teapot. 'If yer ask me, I think as yer'd best stay away from him. Find somebody yer own age.'

—

When she went into work on Monday morning, Martha was dreading seeing Jonas again, but it was him who made the first move. She was taking her coat off when he came out of the modelling room – he must've seen her arrive – and hurried across to her bench.

'Before everyone comes in, I want to thank you for a very pleasant evening, Martha. It was good to talk to you and discover your ambitions, and I'd like to help in any way I can.'

She took a deep breath and was about to come out with the words she'd been rehearsing during her walk to Paradise—

'But, before I say any more, I need to apologise to you for my behaviour.'

'Your behaviour?'

'Yes. I never meant to kiss you. I don't know what came over me. Please accept my apologies. It won't happen again.'

'Oh, I see.'

A wave of relief flushed over her. He had made it easy for her – and she was thankful.

'It was the spur of the moment, I should think,' she said. 'We'd had a very enjoyable night. But working together… could cause problems, couldn't it?'

'Precisely. And thank you for your understanding.'

The Decorating Shop was beginning to fill with workers, who grinned as they walked past.

'I must get on with sorting my bench.'

'Of course, Martha. I'll leave you to it.'

As he left, she breathed a sigh of relief. She wouldn't have to think about it now. Ever the gentleman, Jonas had solved the problem for her.

–

Christmas 1914 had been spent at the pub, as visitors. Christmas 1915 was different – the pub was now their home.

Although there were shortages of certain things and some items were too expensive, they were lucky. Many families would not have been able to afford the new prices, some of which had doubled since the war began. As Grandma had always done, she managed to prepare a normal Christmas meal. Martha remembered the ornate menu Betty had shown her from Stowford House. Later, in her sketch book, she wrote out Grandma's Christmas menu.

Martha knew of Mother's plans but had been sworn to secrecy. Like any family's Christmas meal there was a lot of talking going on and Grandad had to bang the table with the blunt end of his knife to get them to be quiet.

'Now then, we have summat to tell you and you need to listen, for it's not very often we have good news in these unfortunate times. As yer know, Grandma and me have talked to you about what's going to happen when we retire. The pub has served us well over the years and we'll both be sad when the time comes to leave.'

He looked to Grandma who nodded back.

'We had thought that yer mother might take it on, but Fanny's come up with an alternative idea. Why don't you tell them, Fanny?'

Mother looked surprised and flushed with everyone quiet and looking at her. She began to speak. 'The pies what yer grandma sells in the pub do very well. But I've a feeling they might do even better if people could buy them from a shop, not just the drinkers who come into the pub. We miss out on a lot of people. There are plenty of women who won't go into a pub and would certainly not want to eat a pie from such a smoky atmosphere. You have also got Grandad's friends in the Temperance Society—'

'Dunner spoil me Christmas, Fanny. I was enjoying it until then.' Grandad had, like a lot of publicans, had clashes with Temperance people from time to time. Everyone burst out laughing.

'Even Temperance people must eat, Father. The shop next door has been empty for a while and could be the place for us to start. It'll need a bit of tarting up but should be big enough. I'll make the pies and run the shop. I'll need somebody to help me—'

'I'll help yer, Mother,' said Issy. 'I'm not bothered about staying at Millward's – I'm only sweeping, cleaning and packing and I can do that for you.'

'Are you sure, Issy?'

'Course I am. I could work behind the counter and keep the shop looking neat and tidy. Make people want ter come in. It would give yer more time for the baking.'

'That's the spirit, Issy,' said Grandad.

'What about if there are shortages or even rationing?' enquired Martha.

'Well, the ingredients for the pastry are all local. If we get short on meat we'll put more vegetables or potatoes in,' replied Mother.

There was a buzzing of excitement around the table which continued until it was time to dish up the pudding.

After they had finished eating, Peter said, 'What about the pub, Grandad?'

'Ah, yes. The pub. We intend to give notice on the licence on Lady Day and we shall leave the pub as soon as we can after Midsummer's Day. Keep your lips buttoned until 25 March. We bought a house for our retirement years. It's bin rented out. It has four bedrooms. We'll move there. The shop's got two bedrooms above an' all so, if we get it, they can be made suitable for somebody if we need extra space.'

'So, Father might have had his chance to take over the pub, after all.'

'Happen he might've.'

'Mother could take over the licence and me and Daniel could look after the pub.'

'I've already told yer, Peter, I don't want to take over the licence under any circumstances and you are too young. I don't think the King would be happy to let Daniel return just to look after the pub,' said Mother.

'You wouldn't get the licence automatically even if I wanted to pass it to your Mother or you. You'd have to convince the magistrates you knew what yer was doing, and suppliers like the breweries and vintners have to have confidence they are going to get paid. No, lad, you'll have ter make yer own way in the world.'

Peter looked disappointed.

'Peter, love. I thought about all these options before I made my decision. It wasn't made lightly.'

'I hadn't really thought about everything you needed to do. I think I'll stick to working down the pit.'

Mother squeezed his hand and smiled at him. Grandad also gave him a supportive nod.

Mother, whose eyes were bright and happy, spoke out. 'It'll be a wonderful opportunity for us. It'll be a business for the family. We can all play a part in it' – she looked at each of them – 'but only if you want to. I know what it's like to be forced into something you don't want to do.'

'I'm going to carry on with my painting,' Martha said, 'but I'll be happy to help out if I can.' She would have liked to be part of the venture, but her heart was set on painting.

Mother smiled. 'I know that, duck, and I'm happy for yer to do so. And if you can spare us a bit of time, all the better.'

'Haven't yer forgot summat?' asked Grandad.

'Oh yes, the shop will be called "Mrs Parker's Pies". After all, we'll be using Grandma's recipe so it's only fair that we name the shop after her – isn't it?'

Chapter Thirteen

January 1916

When Martha stood in the shop with Grandma, Mother and Issy, after Mother had picked up the keys, she stared around the empty rooms, dust and cobwebs everywhere. The whole place needed a damn good bottoming if food was going to be cooked without poisoning the customers. Martha pulled a face.

'I know what you're thinking, our Martha – how could anybody run this place as a shop in this condition... and I quite agree,' said Grandma patiently. 'It's been empty for many a year and nobody's taken an interest in it. The owner died and his son put it on the market early last year. It set me to thinking that it could be a good little earner. Grandad and the owner used to play darts together and he was a regular in the pub until he became too ill. When Fanny told us what she had in mind for the pies, Grandad had a word with the new owner, who was only too pleased to get a tenant for the property. The rental's very low as we'll have to carry out a number of repairs. Of course, we'll have to buy the ovens and counters and the like – but it won't take long to get set up.'

A spider ran across the shelf nearest to Martha's cheek and she jumped out of the way with a scream.

Grandma tutted. 'For goodness' sake, Martha. We dunner want that noise every time yer see anything. You'll be frightening the customers.'

Mother, who also wasn't a lover of spiders, chimed in, 'I should hope it'll be clean enough to discourage any creepy things from coming in by the time we've finished.'

'As it should be, Fanny. Hark what yer mother says, Martha – she knows what she's doing.'

Mother's face lit up – as if she had won a gold star at school. Martha giggled, which set off Mother and soon even Grandma couldn't help herself. It felt good to be there, with the two of them – and no men to tell them what to do. This is how it should be, thought Martha.

Everything was tidied up and the keys handed over to Mrs Fanny Owen on a truly momentous day for the family. To see Mother so happy almost had Martha in tears. She couldn't help thinking that this day would never have come if Father had been at home. She didn't like to say it but it was a day to be thankful that Father had not, and would not, return. It was the only way her mother could be truly happy. She knew that now.

–

Grandma had come prepared with mops and buckets and lots of bleach and carbolic soap. They had to finish early because they were without electricity. This involved Martha running back and forth to the pub for hot water until every inch of the shop had been cleaned to Grandma's satisfaction. The upstairs rooms could wait a little longer.

Grandma's idea was that she would continue to make pies in the pub until the kitchen area of the shop was ready. Mother would need instruction in taking orders for upurchases, dealing with cash and bookkeeping, while she, in turn, trained Issy to be her assistant. There would be a cleaning regime to follow each day as well as taking stock of the ingredients needed.

As Martha saw Mother and Issy chatting away about their plans, she couldn't help but feel she might have liked being involved too but, deep down, she knew she had to pursue her own dreams of becoming a paintress. She was working hard and was proud of the ware she was producing now. She was sure she would regret it if she didn't try.

She was doing more practising in her own time these days, wanting to be ready to show the bosses what she could do when she asked them to send her to the local art school.

Mother had followed her dreams. It was time for Martha to do the same.

–

Mother opened the door to Tunstall's newest shop in Tower Square at the end of January 1916, with the name Mrs Parker's Pies displayed in fancy lettering over the large window. What a grand day that was. On the morning of the opening, everybody who had helped them get ready for this day was nervous. It all looked so welcoming and entirely different from the shop they had originally walked into, which had been more of a home to spiders and mice.

Both Mother and Issy were wearing crisp, white pinafores made by Martha and, with Mother's hair tied back in a bun at the nape of the neck and Issy's in a single plait, they looked both clean and efficient and ready for work. Peter had put up shelving in one of the bedrooms to be used as a long-term store and Grandad had, following Grandma's orders, bought the ovens, counters and general equipment that would be needed.

When Martha arrived home from work that evening, Mother and Issy were full of themselves and how their day had gone. A queue of ladies had formed outside and appeared happy to chat to each other as the final touches to the shop were put in place and the first pies, meat and potato, were put on show.

As they continued to tell everyone about the day they'd had, Martha, with her elbows on the table and her head resting on the backs of her hands, listened avidly to their stories.

Never had Martha felt so proud of her mother than on the opening day of Mrs Parker's Pies.

Chapter Fourteen

Martha grew in confidence as she talked to Eddie and Jonas. Much to her relief, Jonas had not let the kiss affect their working relationship, as he had promised. He probably regretted it himself when he discovered she was only seventeen – he must've done. As a consequence, he'd gone up in her estimation. She couldn't have seen Father owning up to doing anything wrong. Eddie had said nothing, but had kept a watchful eye on his friend, perhaps blaming his wife for her self-professed match-making.

Martha soon warmed up to both men and she was sure that the kiss, as far as Jonas was concerned, had been forgotten. From then on she felt able to talk to some of the other painters, both men and girls, to get their views on the future of ceramic decoration. Often she would forget the time completely.

She made a couple of friends in the clay end who would get her odd balls of clay that she could experiment with, together with biscuit ware that was ready to be disposed of. Thus she could practise making ware, giving it to a kiln worker friend to fire, and then she was able to decorate it using a range of metal oxide pigments to experiment with colours.

She persuaded Jonas to add some of her better experiments to his own to get them fired, following which they would discuss their merits.

It was a wonderful time. She learned a lot and was convinced she had made the right decision in moving to Paradise.

Bridie pulled her leg, of course. Working in the Decorating Shop herself, she witnessed some of the time that Martha spent with Jonas and joked about it leaving Martha hot under the collar, hoping she wouldn't spread rumours that would cause Jonas to end their working relationship. Why were her friends so keen on making something out of nothing? Neither did she want them to give Jonas any ideas of a romantic side to their association which might require her to do some explaining. As it was, Bridie had more sense and picked her moments carefully.

Apart from Daniel away fighting, life could have been almost perfect.

–

'Martha?' Jonas said. 'D'yer think as I could have a word with yer later. At dinnertime?'

'Course yer can, Jonas. What d'yer want to talk about?'

'Tell yer later. Let's meet downstairs, in the yard.'

'Be a bit cold, won't it?'

'Make sure and bring yer coat.'

Jonas walked back to the modelling room, leaving Martha frowning. His face told her that it was not good news he wanted to talk about.

Vera wasn't at her bench when the bell went, so Marth grabbed her coat and headed off towards the door.

He was waiting by the warehouse, stamping his feet to keep warm. Summat was wrong. She hurriedly crossed the yard trying to control her coat because she hadn't had time to fasten it.

'Jonas – are you all right?'

'Can't actually say – although I half expected summat. I've been called up – to join the army.'

'What?'

'I've got to have a medical and then I'll join the army for as long as it takes.'

'Oh, Jonas. So soon.'

'Stands to reason. I'm an able-bodied bloke with no family and the right age. I've been expecting it. But now I've got me papers, it dunner feel real, Martha.'

A shiver ran through her body and it had nothing to do with the coldness of the February air.

'How's yer mother taken it?'

'Not very well. She's relieved it's just me – at the moment. Our Robert and David are older and have both got young families. They'll be called up later, if they are suitable. They're okay for now.'

Martha closed her eyes. Thoughts of little kiddies losing their fathers was unbearable, but it was a different sort of ache. 'Pray the war ends before they get called up an' all.'

They both stood in silence digesting everything that had been said.

'It won't feel the same without you there to help me with learning the painting.'

'Dunner be daft, Martha. You're a capable young woman. You can take on more than you realise.'

He'd taken out his papers and handed her a copy to look at. It was then that she realised the words on the page were blurred. She blinked in an attempt to stop the tears that had formed.

'I can't think what you must feel like, Jonas. I just wanted to say I hope you go on all right over there and wish you a safe journey.'

Jonas shrugged. 'Doesn't matter. We've all got to go and do our duty. Have you got anybody over there?'

'Our Daniel, my brother… and a friend's brother an' all.' It didn't feel right to call Jeffrey anything else – although even that hadn't been entirely true for a while. He had been a crush, nothing more; the first time she had feelings for someone, boy or man, outside of her family. They weren't true emotions. Just a shadow of the feelings that may come to her eventually.

She carried on speaking. 'Dunno what to say to yer. When our Daniel went…' She tried to talk but the damn tears got in the way 'It was awful, but we thought he wouldn't be gone long. But he's bin gone just over a year. Have yer told anybody yet?'

'I wanted to tell you first. You know what it's like when word gets out – it'll be all round everywhere.'

'Thank you. For thinking about me.'

Jonas held her hand and rubbed it as if to keep it warm. 'I'll think about the way you looked when we were dancing. Do you remember?'

She nodded tremulously. 'First dance I'd ever bin to.'

'You did very well.'

'We learned at school. When will yer go?'

'Soon as everything's sorted. Maybe a week.'

The distant ring of the bell sounded and reluctantly they headed back inside.

She returned to her own bench, glad he'd made the effort to speak to her first. In truth, she didn't know how she felt about him now. Her emotions were conflicting. Daniel was her brother and so it was to be expected, but Jeffrey – and now Jonas – were different. They were all on a similar mission for their country and carrying little pieces of her heart. How had she got herself into this position when she had told everybody, including herself, that she was never going to fall in love?

On Monday afternoon Jonas, along with two of the kiln men, left Paradise Pottery, leaving the potbank short-handed. It would only get worse as more were called up and others volunteered and replacements were difficult to come by. Men were relied upon in so many industries – the whole country might well grind to a halt. Many jobs in the pottery industry could be done by women, but had traditionally been reserved for men, as was the case with painting, with men designing and freehand painting, and women merely copying designs.

Martha couldn't go to see him off the following day, because it was a workday.

'Will yer think about me, Martha? I know we're only friends, but it would mean a lot.'

'Course I will. Might be over with before long.'

He laughed. 'That's the optimist in yer.'

'I'm not usually – but I hope this time it works out.'

'Look after yerself,' he said.

He pushed the door to the Decorating Shop open and left her to make her way back to her bench as he continued through to the modelling room to say his goodbyes.

–

Peter came back from the pit in the foulest of tempers. The weather had been bad and he'd been battling against the wind all the way home. The wind had blown most of the coal dust from his hair, cap and clothes. He complained bitterly when he arrived at the pub and told everyone he'd come to a decision – he was going to get lodgings near to the pit.

'I conner be bothered with all this walking in all weathers, Mother,' he said. 'You all have yards to go whereas I have miles. Besides that, I'm going on twenty. I shouldn't be living with me family.'

'But it's the cheapest if we all live together.'

'A bloke at work says as there's a room going at his place and I might get it if I'm quick. I'm going to look at it this evening. I can afford it.'

Martha caught him as he strolled up the path ready to meet his friends. 'Are you sure, Peter? We're fine as we are.'

'Yes, but you won't be when we leave the pub. And what'll happen when Daniel comes home? Could be any time. We have to be ready.'

'I hate this war. Yer conner plan for nothing.'

Three days later, Peter moved out and Grandad was the only man left in the house.

Chapter Fifteen

May 1916

Everything went on very much as normal during the following few months. Cassie had recently joined Martha's bench after one of the other girls had left under dubious circumstances. They'd all laughed when Vera told Cassie to watch what she was doing, for the chair could be contagious.

Martha continued to improve and still enjoyed her work, although she missed walking past the modelling room and seeing Jonas working away. Somehow, he had always known when she was there. He'd look up and smile at her and she had grown to look out for it. Now, her eyes still gravitated towards his empty seat.

It was a surprise to everyone when a visitor walked into Paradise on that day at the end of May. Mr John was talking to Vera, and Martha, half listening, had her back to the door so didn't see who walked in. It was when she lifted her head and noticed Vera beaming that she turned to see what had made her so happy.

Jonas had a huge grin on his face. Part of Martha wanted to throw herself into his arms but another part of her – the part that won in the end – told her to be cautious with everyone watching. She was happy to see him, but nothing more, she cautioned herself.

'Hiya, Martha.'

He nodded to Vera.

Martha got to her feet.

Mr John immediately strode over to shake his hand. 'Good afternoon, Jonas. It's good to see you back. How are you?'

'Fine, Mr John.'

'Glad you decided to pay us a visit. Do I take it that you've finished your training?'

Jonas nodded. 'Yes. When I get back, I'll be posted to – somewhere. Thought I'd pop in while I'm here.'

'Well – keep up the good work, Jonas. Your job'll be waiting for you when you get back.'

'Thank you, Mr John. I appreciate it.'

Everyone started talking again after Mr John left.

It didn't take them long to agree that they should meet later that evening, to toast Jonas before he went back to his unit. Whatever plans everyone had were changed and they agreed to meet at The Potter's Wheel.

–

Martha may not have feelings for Jonas, but she had to make the most of herself if she was going out with her friends. She had a dress she'd made that she hadn't been able to wear yet, a low-waisted pale blue with a hemline mid-calf, with a white collar. In her hair she wore a band with a flower made of the same material.

'Are yer sure you're not meeting some young man?' smirked Issy as she sat watching Martha dress.

'Nothing to do with you who I'm meeting.'

'It couldn't be that Jonas, could it?'

'You know he's away in the army.' Martha was not about to tell Issy the truth just yet, otherwise she'd never hear the end of it. She'd find out soon enough when he arrived at the pub with the rest of them.

–

The first to arrive were Vera, Eddie and Cassie, and Martha went to join them, sitting in the corner opposite the door. From where she was seated, Martha could see everyone who came in. It was about fifteen minutes later when Jonas turned up and immediately Eddie rose to get a round in.

'Jonas looks good, doesn't he,' whispered Vera in Martha's ear.

'Vera! Don't start that again. Otherwise, I shall have to go home.'

'You are home, duck.'

'I mean, I'll go through to the back.'

'Don't get angry. I'm joking.'

'Well, don't.'

Vera bowed her head and didn't say another word about Jonas, although Martha believed she was watching both of them like a hawk.

'What are yer going to be doing in the army, Jonas?' asked Cassie.

'Driving lorries mainly. I'll be in the Army Service Corps, so I'll basically move things to where they're needed.'

'Will yer be going over to France?' said Cassie.

Martha held her breath.

Jonas shrugged. 'I'll find out when I get back.'

Cassie shook her head. 'How awful for yer, not knowing where you'll end up.'

'It's something I'll have to get used to.'

'Hope you go on all right,' Martha said, then decided to clarify her words, for the benefit of Vera. She added in a quiet voice, 'I hate to read about battles in the paper and worry that someone I know may have been serving there.'

Jonas looked grim. 'It's the way of things.'

'Let's talk about summat happier,' grinned Eddie. 'We dunner want to send him back in the doldrums, do we?'

The men rose and went to get in more drinks.

'Are you going to say anything to Jonas – before he goes?' Vera asked.

'Say what?' Martha found it easier to act dumb on occasions.

'You know very well.'

'I've told yer, Vera. Leave things be.'

–

Martha was happy to see her friendship circle was growing, despite Jonas leaving.

Although she was beginning to feel she could talk to Vera about anything, it was Cassie she enjoyed being with, being closer to her own age. It was good to have such a friend, although it reminded her how much she still missed Betty. How she longed to talk to her about everything. Over her confusion about Jonas. She couldn't talk to Cassie, Vera or Bridie because they worked with him. Betty would've been able to give her an unbiased opinion – and a truthful one.

–

Martha arrived at the gates and clocked on, then ran upstairs to the Decorating Shop. Vera and Cassie were talking earnestly at the side of Cassie's bench and Vera was wearing what Martha called her 'serious face'.

'What's the matter, Vera, duck? You look ever so worried.'

Vera glanced at her and Martha picked up on the overly bright eyes and the handkerchief she held in her right hand.

'Eddie's bin called up. His papers come yesterday.'

'Oh, no.'

'We knew it was on the way as the government had said they were moving on to Eddie's group at the end of April, but with all this talk about the group system being on and then off and then on, we hoped it might be delayed. But sure enough, two days after mobilisation, he gets his papers.'

Poor Vera. Martha gave her a hug but said nothing. Just let the warmth of their friendship encircle her. No family to cling to, no children to look after and comfort. Vera had no one except Eddie.

Chapter Sixteen

June 1916

The day finally came when Oswald Parker left his beloved Potter's Wheel for the last time. The tenancy ended on Midsummer's Day. Under normal circumstances, a new tenant would have been available to take over immediately. But on this occasion, the council, no doubt prompted by the Temperance lobby, decided to defer the decision to grant a new licence until the autumn. It was not totally unexpected as several licensees throughout The Potteries had had their renewals held back for the same reason.

The owner of the building, Joseph Bosley, was also the owner of the shop housing Mrs Parker's Pies. Grandad had said that Mr Bosley had resigned himself to not being able to keep the premises as a pub and had plans to convert the building to shops with living accommodation above.

Their house on Park Terrace, which had been rented out for around twenty years, had been spruced up after the last tenant left in April. The kitchen had been updated with new equipment and each member of the family had their say on how they wanted their room furnished – although Grandma always had the final word. Items not required were sent to the second-hand shop in town where Grandma hoped it could benefit someone in dire need.

There was much sadness in those last few weeks. Grandad had never lived anywhere other than that pub and, together with Grandma, they had spent all their married life there. It would be such a wrench for them.

Martha knew how much leaving would mean to Mother, too. It had been her place of safety when things had gone wrong – as it had been for her and Issy. Now, they had the opportunity to forge new lives.

The Potter's Wheel closed its doors for business on the evening of the 21 June 1916, a Wednesday, and Grandma and Grandad moved out the following Saturday. Martha had asked Mr Higginbotham for the morning off to help with the move. With some reluctance, and a promise of Martha putting in extra hours to compensate, he agreed.

The new house reverberated with excitement when the van turned up with all their belongings, mainly personal things. The packed tea chests did not take long for the moving men to unload.

Mother stood by the front door of 99 Park Terrace supervising everything that entered the house, and Martha waited at the top of the stairs to direct the men to the relevant bedroom. Issy was in her element in helping and showing how organised she was now.

Once the move had been completed and all their possessions allocated to their rooms, Martha made a last visit to the pub while Issy, who remained at Park Terrace, made tea and sandwiches for their return. Everyone was bound to be hungry after their morning's work.

Grandma was standing outside the pub, arms folded.

'Hi, Grandma.'

'Oh, hello, Martha, I was miles away thinking about all the good times we've had at this place. Is yer mother not with yer?'

'She's just called at the market. Be along shortly.'

Martha detected a tear rolling down Grandma's face and gave her a hug.

'How's Grandad?'

'Go in and see for yerself. It might be a good idea, as when I came out he was stood at the bar as if he was expecting the normal Saturday dinnertime rush when the potbanks close.'

Martha entered the bar for one last time. 'Hello, Grandad.'

'Hello, Martha love,' he said in a croaky voice, his unlit pipe in his mouth. 'Just saying goodbye to the old place.'

'We've had such a good time here, Grandad; I'll always consider it to be my home.'

'Aye, girl, it's been really good to us, and even through the bad times I never once thought of giving up being a pub landlord. I enjoyed meeting the people and have made lots of good friends throughout the years... I was just thinking back to my first memory of the pub when my mother and father ran it. I think I was about three or four at the time, and my mother would set me on the bar as I liked to help her pour the slop trays into the bucket. I remember one time I decided that the sow that we used to keep in the field behind the pub—'

'Field behind the pub? I thought the houses had always been there.'

'No, lass, they were built about ten years afterwards. I was already working at the brewery. Father had been able to get me a job there and I learned all about making beer. I didn't start to work in the pub properly until I was thirty-two, but I worked here in my spare time. Father wanted me to take over the pub eventually, but he also wanted me to have a trade if things went wrong. I started my apprenticeship as a pub landlord. When he decided the time was right, he stepped back from running the pub and the licence was transferred to me. There was not so much palaver in the trade in them days. Your mother was sixteen when my name went over the door.'

Grandad paused as if thinking about times long past. Martha prompted, 'You were telling me about this pig that you had in the field at the back.'

'Yes, her name was Matilda. We used to keep pigs because they were good to feed all the scraps to and at the end we got some fine meat. My dad said that Matilda was the perfect sow; always had big litters. We always had a piece of pork at Christmas. I think I was six or seven at the time and I decided that Matilda could probably do with a drink as it was a warm day. I remember picking up the bucket and staggering out to the field and emptying it into her water trough, which was nearly empty. When I came back in my mother asked me what had happened to the bucket and I told her I'd given it to the pig. I didn't realise that the beer from that bucket was fed back into the barrel, so Matilda had a nice treat, and by the time I caught mother up the trough was empty. It didn't seem to do Matilda any harm, although she did spend the whole of that day asleep, and the following day Father said he could swear that she got a hangover, as he'd never seen her so miserable.'

Martha laughed. 'Did you get into trouble for it?'

'No, not really. Mother and Father saw the funny side of it. Still, that's enough reminiscing. It's time I locked this front door and started me retirement. I don't know what I'm going to do, but I dare say yer grandma'll have plenty lined up for me. Never was one for idle hands.'

Outside, Mother had arrived and was talking to Grandma. Along with Martha, the two women, three generations, watched Grandad shut the front door of The Potter's Wheel for the last time. They walked through the square to Park Terrace. They didn't speak; each was wrapped in their own thoughts.

–

A week had passed since the family had moved into Park Terrace. The house seemed so small compared with The Potter's Wheel. Everything was new. Grandma had only brought her most treasured possessions with her. Most of the furniture was from Burton & Dunn's, as was all the linen and crockery. The only household things she had brought with her were cooking utensils.

Martha still had to walk through Tower Square to get to work. She popped her head in at Mother's shop, but they were busy and she only stopped for a few moments. As she walked past The Potter's Wheel she thought how sad it looked, even though it had only been just over a week since the pub had closed its doors.

As Grandad had suggested, the Temperance Society was lobbying the council not to grant a licence on these premises. Nothing could be done until the next council meeting decided on its future. If the licence was refused then the contents and stock would be auctioned off.

As Martha entered Paradise Street she could see Bridie just coming out of her house. They chatted away, keen to stand in the warm sunshine of the beautiful July morning.

Bridie didn't take much notice of what was happening in the war. Although she likely had some relations who were fighting, she never mentioned them. It was different at work. Everyone was talking about the big battle taking place in France in which the British and French had jointly attacked the Germans along the River Somme. The newspapers reported spectacular gains along the whole Front, but as the week went on 'spectacular' turned into 'substantial' which turned into 'significant'.

—

One Monday dinnertime, most of the Decorating Shop took their dinners outside into the yard to take advantage of the sunshine and fresh air. They were chattering in groups and Vera mentioned that Eddie would soon be ending his training and she hoped he wasn't going to be sent to fight straight away. She said her Eddie didn't have a violent bone in his body, so she worried how he would get on. Martha also thought about the three men in her life already out there. Jeffrey and Daniel had been over there for a year but had written letters back home regularly. She didn't know if Jonas had gone over to France or whether he was still based in England. She called them her men because she knew them – not because they were actually her men.

She looked around the yard and knew that every one of the women and girls she could see had got a father, son or brother fighting this war.

–

On Friday morning at the end of August, Vera told Martha and Cassie that Eddie was coming home on a weekend pass, having completed his training.

'It looks as though you are going to have a good weekend, Vera,' said Cassie with a mischievous grin on her face.

'I don't know what you mean, Cassie Mellor.'

The friends laughed.

Martha's mind went back to the day in July when the girls from the Decorating Shop were eating their dinners out in the sunshine. She now looked at that same group of women and realised that at least three of them had lost a loved one in the Somme and others were wounded, suffering horrific injuries. Although Martha didn't say anything, she felt extremely concerned for her men in France.

Martha, Cassie and Vera walked home together that evening, their spirits high. As they walked through the gates they passed a group of women consoling one of their number. It was the wife of one of the kiln men who had left at the same time as Jonas. He had been killed.

–

Once Eddie left, Cassie and Martha gave themselves new duties: to look after their friend and make sure she wasn't forgotten or allowed to fade away. They took it in turns to call by the house or arrange a night in for a natter. They had taken to knitting and to sending treats to cheer up the soldiers as the war continued.

In the intimacy of Vera's house, they talked about all manner of things, both funny and sad, as their friendship deepened and confessions were drawn out. Why Vera and Eddie had no children. It wasn't for the want of trying; she had laughed and faced the ribald jokes about how much she must be missing it – the trying. But beyond the laughter was the hurt and pain of a lost chance of motherhood now made worse by the two of them living in different countries. Why Cassie wasn't walking out with anyone, despite her being the prettiest paintress on the potbank, ordered by her parents to have nothing to do with lads they hadn't approved of.

Finally, it was Martha's turn and she told them what she had told no one else – the role her father had played in her life and why she had been so determined not to get wed. And lastly she told them how she had lost her best friend and why there had been no forgiveness between them.

They made a promise to each other that they would not tell another soul about what they had discussed, but each felt better for it.

Chapter Seventeen

November 1916

Throughout the summer of 1916 the three women enjoyed themselves when they could shake their thoughts off the menfolk, but those thoughts were never far away. *The Sentinel* carried lots of news, some good, some bad, and published casualty lists of those killed, injured or gassed. Gas was widely used now, causing damage to the lungs and ultimately, death. The lists were there to be looked at with eyes closed, if that made any sense. A need to read – while desperately hoping not to come across any recognisable names.

Then came the day when Vera didn't turn up for work – totally unlike her, for she was never late. Word came from her neighbour who thought that her employer might want to know that Eddie Bell had been killed in action in France.

The news soon got round the potbank and everyone who knew Eddie and Vera sent their condolences. Martha and Cassie decided to call on her that evening after work. She needed to know everyone was thinking about her and that she was not alone.

They knocked three times without getting an answer.

'Surely she won't have gone out,' said Cassie.

She stepped back from the door to look up and down the street as if expecting Vera to come waltzing round the corner at any moment.

'I don't think so. I think she's hiding inside.' Martha bent down and put her lips to the letterbox and called and then looked through to see if she could see any movement.

'Vera! Vera! It's Martha and Cassie. We want to make sure you're all right and then we'll go away.'

They both listened but there was nothing. She tried again and this time, Martha saw something move.

'Vera, darling. Please say you're all right. We need to know.'

A body moved towards the door and it opened slowly to reveal Vera, still in her dressing gown.

'Oh, Vera. I'm so glad you answered us. May we come in?'

Vera stood aside to allow them entry, Cassie first with Martha following.

They entered the parlour and stood looking at each other. Then, with huge gulps, the tears came and the three of them stood in the middle of the room holding onto each other, desperately needing the closeness of another human being.

Eventually, the tears subsided and they sat huddled closely together on the large settee that dominated the room.

'You don't have to say anything, Vera. We can just stay and keep you company – or we could go, if you prefer it?'

Vera whispered. 'No, don't go.'

After that, Vera let out all her fears: the lack of a body, no place to go and mourn, no funeral. Things you did not think about until landed with such terrible news.

Once Vera had exhausted the pain she was carrying, the three of them sat talking about anything and everything other than the war. It was more difficult than Martha had thought. Hadn't she felt it for the first time when Daniel left? What she would do if she received such news she couldn't bear to think about.

Then Cassie said, 'Do you remember when I first started at Paradise, Vera? Somebody told me to go and get a bucket of fresh air and off I went, trying to be helpful. When I got to the warehouse, the bloke there told me I'd best get back to work cos I was on a fool's errand, and didn't I feel a fool when I got back. Eddie was the one who told me to be on my guard in the future. I was so grateful to him.'

'Just like my Eddie, that was.'

And Eddie was back in the conversation again. Martha groaned inwardly – but somehow, Vera was laughing. Maybe she needed to talk about Eddie, not closet him away. Clever of Cassie to think of it.

More anecdotes followed until they were all chatting away.

As Martha and Cassie were about to leave, Martha asked if Vera had Jonas's address so she could let him know about Eddie.

'I was going to write to him when I felt a bit better. I can't face it at the moment. Thank you, Martha.'

When Vera returned to work, the workers pulled together as workers do, to support and protect one of their own.

–

22 November 1916

Dear Jonas,

It is with great sorrow that I am writing to you. There is no easy way to tell you, but Vera received a letter today to say that poor Eddie has been killed in action. As you can imagine, she is distraught and will take time to get over it. At the moment, that's all we know. I'm sure we shall be in touch once more is known.

I got your address from Vera so I could spare her the distress of writing to you with the news. I am sure that, now you know, she will appreciate hearing from you.

I am so sorry to be the one to tell you. If you would like to write back to me too, I would be pleased to hear from you.

Yours,
Martha

–

1 December 1916

Dear Martha,

Thank you for letting me know about Eddie. I cannot believe it. I knew things like this would happen but it is no less of a shock when it does.

I have written to Vera at the same time. I'm sorry my reply is so late, but our post goes to our home depot, and my unit spends a lot of time away.

Look after Vera for me. I know you will. I don't know what Vera is going to do without him. They have been together so long.

Can you try to make sure Vera is not left on her own over Christmas? She will be so sad.

I will write again soon.

Best wishes,

Jonas

Chapter Eighteen

Summer 1917

It had been six months since Eddie had been killed. Vera had returned to work the day after receiving the news. She had to earn something to pay the rent and feed herself. In any case, she said she didn't want to stop in the house; she needed to be busy.

Christmas was the worst. Vera refused all offers of spending Christmas with friends or work colleagues. She didn't want to intrude on people and their Christmas. She had already planned to be on her own, with Eddie away. Martha walked up to see her on Christmas morning but it was clear that Vera wanted to be alone, and she left after about half an hour.

As winter turned into spring, Vera started to get back to her old self – being there for people when she was needed. On the outside she looked normal, but her close friends could detect the underlying sadness.

What it must be like to love someone and lose them at any time. How could a person ever get over that, Martha asked herself.

–

Martha was surprised when Mother told her that she was going to convert the upper floor of the shop to living accommodation.

'Why yer doing that?'

'Well, with all of the early starts and late finishes we have, both Issy and me feel it would be better to live over the premises.

Some days we make several journeys to and from the shop, and sometimes by the time we have taken our coats off and had a cup of tea it is time to get back.'

'What will Grandma and Grandad say?'

'Oh, they're happy with it. They always appreciated living over the pub, so they understand why I've got to do it.'

Martha paused for thought. 'Would you be expecting me to live there as well? It would be closer to work.'

'It's up to you, but it'd be cramped. Grandma says that you're welcome to stay here as long as yer want. I thought that now you're older yer might want a bit more freedom.'

'Well, that's a surprise. Usually it's the child that tells the mother they're leaving home, not the other way round.' The two women laughed.

'It is going to take some weeks to get the outside store and cold room built. We can install a marble stillage to help keep the meat, and the new building for the dry goods will be more secure against pests. So there is no rush to make yer mind up.'

Later that night, Martha concluded that it would be a good idea to remain at Park Terrace. She would have independence and also somewhere to work, if she ever made it to art college.

—

On her way to work, Martha called in at the shop as usual. Both Mother and Issy had been working since five o'clock and Martha could see the benefits of converting the upstairs to live in.

They passed the time of day, while Issy served a customer.

'Listen, Martha,' Mother said, 'the pies are going so well that I've decided to make extra for tomorrow. I'm going to put a couple of hours in tonight and—'

'Can my lovely big sister stand in for me tonight?' Issy interrupted. 'I'm meeting Josie and a couple of friends from Dresden Street.'

'I don't finish until six, and you want me to do a shift here for you, an' all?' Martha replied.

'Josie said that Michael Dean might be there.'

Martha recognised the pleading in Issy's voice 'All right, I'll cover for you this time, but don't make a habit of it.'

Mother hid a smile.

'Can I borrow your new shoes?'

'Don't push yer luck. Your shoes are perfectly good enough.'

Issy turned away with a little pout on her face and went to serve another customer.

–

Martha wished she hadn't agreed to stand in for Issy. It was a lovely summer's evening. She had been stuck inside all day and now she was going to be inside till who knew what time.

She arrived at the shop to see a soldier standing outside the entrance. She crossed over. For one moment, she thought it might be Daniel, then she noticed the crowns on his shoulder. He was an officer.

'Can I help yer, sir?'

'Good evening. Does Mrs Percy Owen work here?'

'Yes, but we're closed now.'

'You know Mrs Owen?'

'I'm her daughter.'

'I would like to see Mrs Owen, if that is possible?'

'Who're you?'

'Captain David Munro from the Corps of Military Police. I was told she works here. I saw someone moving so I thought I would take the opportunity. I need to see Mrs Owen as a matter of urgency.'

'Best come in then.'

He was about six foot tall, with black hair going grey at the sides. He walked with a stick, and his left leg didn't bend, suggesting to Martha that he might have an injury or maybe even an artificial leg.

Martha unlocked the door and they entered.

She shouted, 'I'm here, and you've got a visitor.'

Captain Munro gazed around with interest. A tray of pies had just been completed and would be ready to bake for busy workers first thing in the morning. Mother dried her hands on a towel. Her face, flushed from the heat of the oven, grew pale at the sudden arrival.

'Lock the door again, Martha.' She attempted to smile at the captain. 'Don't want anyone thinking we're open, do we? I'm sorry we haven't got no chairs down here. We could go upstairs – we have some up there?'

'There's no need, Mrs Owen, but before we go any further I have to be certain I'm talking to the correct person. Can you confirm that you are Mrs Fanny Owen – previously Parker – and married to Sergeant Major Percy Owen of the Staffordshire Regiment?'

'Was married. That is correct.'

'And you used to live at 34 Dresden Street, Hanley?'

'Yes.'

'Good. I have a matter to talk to you about of a very delicate nature. Are you happy for the young lady to remain, or would you prefer somewhere private?'

Mother's face turned grey in the dim light of the shop. Martha knew her mother would be unlikely to want to talk to any man on her own. Sure enough, Mother told him she was happy for her daughter to stay.

'What I'm about to tell you is going to come as a shock. You must understand the difficulties of getting this type of information in the midst of war. About three months ago, the War Office received a list of prisoners from the German army via the Red Cross in Switzerland. This has been normal procedure throughout the war and, in the early stages, it worked quite well. But of late it has become rather less reliable given the numbers involved.'

He cleared his throat and then looked Fanny directly in the eyes.

'On this list there was notification of a Sergeant Percy Owen, with his correct serial number.'

If Mother hadn't been holding onto the counter, she would, almost certainly, have collapsed. Martha looked at him in horror.

'This has obviously come as a great shock, but I must caution you on building your hopes up.' Munro looked at Mother and Martha in turn and then paused to check something on his papers. He asked Mother to tell him what she had been told about Percy's disappearance and any other information she might have.

'I've received a letter from his corporal who was on the mission with him that night, Captain. He saw Percy's... demise personally.'

'I too have read the report and spoken to Corporal Davies. You must understand that casualties have been on a greater scale than expected and it's not always possible to identify soldiers who have been killed. Often a soldier is declared dead on the basis of probability.'

'What does that mean?' asked Martha.

'Well, young lady, if twenty men go out on a mission and only eighteen return and we find two bodies, which we cannot recognise by sight, but we find effects that indicate these are the two souls who have lost their lives, then they are declared dead.'

'So they did that in Father's case?'

'Not entirely. You see, we never found a body, only his service rifle – identified by its serial number – and his iden-tification tag.'

'But finding them together must mean he's dead?' Mother said.

'Not necessarily. They were not found at the same time or location.'

Mother was starting to show signs of agitation. This must all be very confusing for her. Martha broke the silence.

'So what you're saying is that Father may be alive despite evidence to the contrary.'

'Put simply, yes. I'm afraid there is one other problem, and it's the main reason I've got involved. You see, my Sergeant Owen was captured on 19 March 1917 at a place called Vaux, about 110 miles south of where your husband went missing — and two years later.'

This took a moment to sink in.

'So, are you saying it *is* Percy or it isn't?'

'We don't know.' He handed Mother a piece of paper. 'This letter will be sent to the Red Cross and I hope they are able to make further enquiries with the German authorities and obtain a photograph of this person. Have you a photograph of your husband I can take?'

'I've got a tin box upstairs; we had a photograph taken when he returned from India.'

As Mother went away, Martha commented, 'I don't think you really know who this man is.'

'No, Miss Owen, we don't.'

'So you raise people's hopes for no good reason.'

'It may appear so, but we do need relatives to help with identification.'

Mother returned and passed over a photograph. Martha had not seen it before. It was a picture of Mother sitting with Father standing behind her, his hand on her shoulder. Mother was dressed in a very grand-looking dress and Father was in his full dress uniform. Martha remembered that photographers often had a selection of clothes that a person could wear for the photograph.

'Thank you very much. I will make sure it is returned to you as soon as possible.'

'I would like that.'

'Mrs Owen, forgive me, but you seem troubled at my news. I understand—'

'Troubled? That's an understatement. I have rebuilt my life, and now you come along and tell me my husband may be alive.'

'Well, I can only offer you my sympathy and I understand how difficult this interview has been.'

'You're a policeman,' Martha said. 'Has Father done summat wrong?'

'No. Or should I say I don't know. In this case it is the discrepancy between both the date and the place of his capture that gives the CMP concern and it has landed on my desk. My department sorts out unusual happenings and it's possible that we'll only get to the bottom of it when the war ends and prisoners are returned. You must understand that information in wartime is greatly hampered and from time to time it will get delayed or lost. Also, clerical errors are possible. Under normal circumstances the appearance of your father's name on a pris-oner list after two years would be unusual, but not uncommon.'

'In the meantime, what will I do?' said Mother.

'Carry on your life as you are doing. I would ask you to keep this information as quiet as you feel able until more is known. If we get a reply from the Red Cross or I have something more concrete, I or someone from my department will get in touch with you.'

Captain Munro stepped forward and shook Mother's hand. He did the same to Martha. Martha went to unlock the door for him and he smiled at her. 'Look after your mother.'

'I will.'

He saluted her and left. Martha locked the door to the shop and returned to her mother.

'Oh, Mother.'

The two of them clung together, refusing to let go, until they were spent and there was nothing left.

'What if Captain Munro's right?' Mother said. 'He wouldn't have come if he wasn't sure of his facts?'

Martha shrugged. 'He probably thought he was bringing happy news. He couldn't know what it would do to us.'

They stood beside the table, doing nothing but holding hands.

'Martha, we'll tell nobody. Daniel can't do anything about it and if we tell Peter he'll insist on telling Daniel too and it'll only upset them both. There's no point in setting hares running with Issy neither. After all, we don't really know anything for certain. It has to stay between me and you.'

–

At eleven o'clock in the morning, Mr Higginbotham came out of his office with Vera following him. She had been with him for around an hour, with the door to his office closed. Martha had kept an eye on them. What could be taking up so much time? she wondered. He didn't like his workers to be away from their benches too long because it meant the potbank was losing money. Once in the middle of the Decorating Shop, he stopped and banged on the nearest bench until he had everyone's attention.

'I am pleased to announce that Mrs Bell will be taking over as Painting Supervisor with immediate effect, to replace Ernie Williams who is leaving us next week to take the Colours.'

A cheer went up from the paintresses. The few male painters left, none of whom were eligible for conscription, didn't look too happy. It had always been a man's job and this war had changed everything.

Vera's face had taken on the appearance of a bad dose of sunburn.

'I'm sure you will, as always, do your best for Mrs Bell.'

Once the boss had left, Martha jumped out of her seat and gave Vera a big hug.

The words 'creep' and 'teacher's pet' were heard.

There was always someone to make a sarky comment, but Martha didn't care. 'Congratulations, Vera. You've done so well. You'll make the best supervisor ever, and your Eddie would've been that proud of yer.'

Vera's first job in her new role was to get a group of excited paintresses back to work – a job she did admirably.

Martha was cleaning her bench on Saturday dinnertime; she had finished her work and was preparing for Monday when Vera came to her.

'That's good to see.'

'Getting ready for Monday. I hate it if I have to start a new day clearing up.'

'Best way to work is to start with a clean bench, I always say. Tidy bench – tidy mind. And it's good to pass it on to the people yer work with an' all, don't yer think?'

'Yes, it's what me mother taught me.'

'She did well, Martha. I've a question for yer now and I want yer to think about it. We need a new paintress to take over my bench. How are you fixed?'

Martha stared at her. 'You mean me – become a paintress?'

Vera laughed as Martha tried to take it in. It's what she had always wanted. Her, Martha Owen, become a paintress for Paradise Pottery!

'You're not kidding me, are yer?'

'We're at work, Martha. I dunner kid about work. Happen you'll need to think about it. You'll be back on day rates for a time so yer wages might not be as good, but I reckon you'll pick it up quick enough? D'yer want to let me know when you've thought about it?'

'Yes! I've thought about it and I definitely want it.'

'Sure?'

'Never been surer about anything, Vera.'

'Right. I'm glad it's what yer want. Go to your normal bench on Monday morning and I'll sort out your new place then. In the meantime let's get our skates on, it's gone twelve o'clock – we're on our own time now.'

Martha hugged herself. At long last she was very nearly where she wanted to be. Who would've thought it?

They walked up Paradise Street together. Martha could have floated up; she was so pleased.

'Thank you again, Vera.'

'You're like the cat what's got the cream.'

'It's what I've wanted all along. I know I still have a lot to learn but I won't be happy until I can work on the vases and jars.'

'Dunner get too carried away. It'll take a long time, and that sort of work is usually done by the men.'

'A girl can dream, can't she?'

'I think it would be nice if you wrote to Jonas to tell him. He'll be pleased to get a letter with some good news.'

'Oh, you think he'd be interested?'

'Yes, of course. He thought you'd got real potential and told me to keep an eye on you. Encourage you to keep on with your painting.'

'He did?'

'Yes. I'm not kidding.'

'I haven't had a letter from him since before Christmas. Don't you think it might be a little forward?'

'He's written to me a few times and always asks about you.'

Martha was both surprised and pleased. 'I'll write to him this weekend. Is his address the same as when I wrote to him about...'

'Yes, but don't expect a quick reply. It sometimes takes days for letters to catch up with him.'

Martha beamed all the way home and everyone she passed smiled back. What a glorious day it was.

That evening she put pen to paper. She was surprised how nervous she felt. She wanted to make sure she said the right thing.

Dear Jonas,

I hope you are keeping safe and well.

Vera seems to be getting better, but you can still tell she is sad underneath. I suppose it will take a long time for the wounds to heal.

This time I have good news — well, at least for me. I have been promoted to a paintress. I start on Monday. I was beginning to think I'd never make it. I've worked hard and it has paid off. It is you I have to thank for this. If you had not shown such faith in my ability, I might have given up. I hope I don't let you down.

Vera will no doubt be writing to you, but briefly, Ernie Williams has been called up and Vera has got his job for the duration.

Keep safe and well, wherever you are, and thanks for your encouragement. I will make you proud.

Best wishes,
Martha

How could painting involve using so many different brushes? Thin, thick, flat, bushy? Martha spent a lot of time drawing straight lines, which she'd had experience of doing when she was gilding. It invariably meant drawing a perfect line around the edge of a cup or plate, using gold. It was so expensive that even the tiniest bits of gold were picked up to be melted down and reused at the end of each day. Each part of the hand-drawn pattern had to be perfect in every way, otherwise it would be placed on the seconds shelf and the worker, whose initial appeared on the bottom of the piece, would be paid a pittance.

Then she went on to enamelling. The paintresses mixed fat oil and turpentine with powdered enamel paint and painted flat colour inside patterns drawn on the biscuit ware. It coated hands and fingers and there was always the smell of the turps.

−

It had been two weeks since Martha had become a paintress, and she was delighted to receive a reply from Jonas:

29 June 1917

Dear Martha,

Congratulations on your job. I told you you could make it. And now you are a paintress you can look towards your next goal.

Thanks for telling me about Vera. I got several letters yesterday on my return to the depot and there was one from her too.

I am keeping well and as safe as I can be. No point in telling you anything about what I'm doing, it would only be censored. I can say that I like the driving job.

Please write to me again. It is so nice to have letters out here − it keeps you in touch with the real world.

Look after yourself and Vera as well.

Best wishes,

Jonas

−

'Well, the buggers have gone and done it.' Grandad pointed at a page in *The Sentinel*. 'It says that at the council meeting today they endorsed the licensing committee's decision not to renew the licence for the former public house, The Potter's Wheel, in Tower Square. They stated that there were sufficient establishments in the town and so no need for the licence to be renewed.'

'So you was right then,' said Grandma.

'Yes, and listen to this. I quote, "the council has agreed to the conversion of the former public house, The Potter's Wheel, to shops which they hoped would bring much-needed business into the centre of the town". You have ter hand it to old Bosley, must have done a deal with the council. He's got his building converted into shops, which are likely or not going to give him more rent than I used to pay, and the Temperance people are happy now they've managed to close another pub. So it looks as though everybody is going to benefit from my retirement.'

'D'yer think that's going to be of any benefit to my shop?' asked Mother.

'I think so. When I was speaking to Bosley he said that he could get three shops in that space, and it is an attractive position being at the top of the square. No reason why we shouldn't get our trotters in the trough. I'll have a word with Bosley to see if he'll paint the front of your shop so that it matches the new shops and try to get a nice sign out of him.'

Grandad was as good as his word.

It was the Friday before the annual Potters' holiday. Martha called at the pie shop as usual and Mother was talking with Mr Rafferty, who had done all of the conversion upstairs and given the whole place a coat of paint.

'Well, missus, we finished on Monday, so everything should be dry and ready to use. I thought I would call round to see if everything was satisfactory.'

'And it is the last day before the holidays, so I expect you'd like to be paid.'

'Aye, me men need their pay, they conner live on fresh air.'

'I think you've done a really good job. I have your money here, for the agreed amount.'

'Thanks, missus, I wish you a good holiday.'

He doffed his cap and left the shop. Mother turned to Martha. 'There goes a happy man, and in a few hours there'll no doubt be happy publicans.'

Mother put the closed sign on the door and they went upstairs. Now the place was finished, it looked so nice. The main bedroom and sitting room were at the front overlooking the square. The second bedroom and kitchen at the back. But best of all they had managed to include a privy with the latest flushing toilet. As far as Mother and Izzy were concerned, this was the best part. No more chamber pots and no putting on your coat to go to the privy in midwinter.

Martha was really proud of her mother. She would never have thought she could be so confident. Her business was thriving, and for the first time in her life she had somewhere to call her own. In fact Martha thought that Tower Square now had a new queen to take over Grandad's title of King of The Potter's Wheel, from his days at the pub.

—

The following day, Mother and Issy left home to move above the shop. Apart from their personal possessions and clothes they had very little to move to the flat. They decided to take up Michael's offer of help. He turned up with the vegetable cart complete with horse. They piled on their possessions and they were gone.

Martha had been down to the stationer's to buy another sketchpad. When she returned home, it seemed strange. Grandma and Grandad liked sitting in the back room over-looking their little garden. This left the front room free most of the time and Martha had taken to sitting there watching the passers-by. The green area in front of them was an open space, but mostly it was used by children. Much better for them than playing in the street.

Martha glanced across to the buildings on the right-hand side of the green, one of which was Tunstall School of Art.

She wondered whether she would ever get there. Further down Greengate Street there was the new swimming baths, and then around the corner was the public library. What more could she wish for?

Chapter Nineteen

Winter 1917/18

One afternoon in early December, Martha might have been sitting at her bench but her mind was miles away. She was now able to do her work without thinking – which was a good job, otherwise she would have definitely lost money that week.

'Your brother seems like a nice bloke. How's he coping on his own?' piped up Cassie. 'He must be missing his brother.'

'Sorry…?'

'You're not listening. I was just saying as Peter must be missing his brother.'

'We all are. We don't see as much of Peter as we used to since he moved into his lodgings.'

'Does he go out very often?'

'Dunno. He dunner say much.'

'If he hasn't got a girlfriend, d'yer think you could get him to come to the Christmas Dance?'

The annual Summer Dance, so long a regular date in the Paradise Pottery diary, had not taken place since July 1915. This year, Mr John decided that a Christmas Dance would be in order, albeit a lower-key affair.

'What d'yer mean?'

'I would like to have somebody to go with for once in my life. I'm nearly twenty-one and never been taken to anything by a man who was not my father.'

'Oh, I see. Well, I'll ask him. He may have a girlfriend at the moment, he does not keep me apprised of his social life. But I'll try.'

'Thank you, Martha, you're a real pal.'

–

Martha rarely visited Peter at his lodgings. His landlady had looked very suspicious the first time she had called, but was used to seeing her now.

'Peter. Will you escort me, Cassie and Vera to the Works' Christmas Dance on Saturday?'

Peter was sitting in his room reading *The Sentinel* and looking for the latest news from Flanders. He dragged his eyes from the page and glanced up, irritated. 'I usually go out with the lads for a drink on Saturdays.'

'It'll be fun. Think of all those single girls waiting to meet some handsome blokes. But in their absence, you'll have to do!'

He grinned, then pursed his lips. 'That's not the right thing to say if you're asking for a favour.'

'Oh, go on, Peter. You like dancing.'

'Okay. This once, but you can bake me a cake to take home with me.'

'That's blackmail.'

'D'yer want me to go with yer or don't yer?'

–

The following Saturday, Martha and Peter walked over to Tunstall Floral Hall. Peter was proudly wearing his suit and displaying prominently his badge indicating he was an essential worker. What a pity Jonas wasn't here. Once Martha had managed to pair up Peter and Cassie, she could sit with Vera. It had become normal at entertainments that women would sit or dance together because of the lack of men.

Martha and Peter met Vera and Cassie outside the hall as agreed.

'Cassie, Vera, this is my brother, Peter, our escort for the evening.'

Peter blushed a little and shook both of the women's hands. 'Please to meet yer.'

Martha noticed that he never took his eyes off Cassie and held her hand a little longer than necessary.

'Pleased to me yer, Peter.' Cassie linked arms with Peter, leaving Martha with Vera. 'It's too cold to stand out here, let's get inside.'

'Martha,' Vera said, 'you go on about me matchmaking, but I think you've done a good job there. He certainly noticed her.'

'I saw that, also. I had to bribe him with a cake to get him to come.'

'It looks as if he might have his cake and eat it! They make a nice couple, don't they? Cassie is so much fun at work and she really enjoys herself when she's out. It is a pity about her parents. Mr Mellor's a staunch Presbyterian as well as a member of the Temperance Society. The family go to chapel. Cassie has gone every week since she could walk there. From what I know, they think anything that is fun is sinful. I often wonder how they managed to conceive a child of their own – perhaps they did it with the lights off and their eyes shut.'

They both laughed.

'So how does she manage to get permission to come here?' Martha asked.

'Because it's a works dance, and even Cassie doesn't tell them everything.' Vera lowered her voice. 'Over the years Cassie became a regular visitor to our house. Mr and Mrs Mellor approved of us. I suppose Cassie made up for the us not being able to have children of our own. As she got older and Mr Mellor got more severe, she would use our house as a safe haven where she could meet school friends. Eddie would have given her more freedom, but I insisted we would not help her to meet boys. It worked well over the years, but the poor girl has never really had many friends.'

'She must be glad to have a friend she can rely on.'

At that point, Peter and Cassie returned to the table and the conversation moved on. The evening was a great success. Peter and Cassie seemed to get on very well. Their party was one of the last groups to leave. Martha was relieved as she had expected Peter to make excuses to leave as soon as he could.

The four of them walked back into Tunstall. Cassie said goodnight to Peter and exchanged a few words before parting.

'I'll make sure there's no chance that Mr Mellor will see any sign of Peter. He usually waits on Summerbank Road and has got good eyesight and hearing when it comes to sin,' said Vera.

Martha and Peter turned away and walked back to Park Terrace where Peter was staying the night. It was a clear and frosty night, and for once you could see the stars. They said nothing to each other, both lost in their thoughts.

–

Martha was about to start work on Monday morning when a smiling Vera appeared at her bench.

She took up Martha's hand and looked her in the eye. 'Thank you so much for insisting I came out with you on Saturday night. I felt guilty, I thought I shouldn't put me head through the door until the war was over. But I enjoyed myself so much.'

'We all need people to share our highs and lows with. Don't bottle it up. Go out, see people. I believe we'll need others if we are to get through all this.'

'I realise that now. You should be very proud of Peter. He took care of Cassie all evening, quite the gentleman.'

'I wish our Daniel could've bin there. Mind you, he's not one for the dancing. Prefers his own company – or reading a book, to be honest.'

Martha's thoughts turned to all the lads who had gone to war; all ready to do their bit on the battlefields of Europe, not knowing when, or if, they would see England again.

–

'I'm right looking forward to being twenty-one,' Cassie chirped up, disturbing Martha's concentration on the flower she was painting. Not to upset Cassie, Martha carefully and surreptitiously wiped the spoilt design off the plate she had been working on.

'Yes, are yer doing anything special?'

'What d'yer think? It'll be the same as any other Saturday. We'll have our tea and then pray for the souls of the drinkers. Father doesn't like Saturday nights. On reflection, he's not too keen on any night where drinking might be involved.'

'That's a pity. After all, it is a milestone in anybody's life.'

'I think my mother will make sure I have a cake with a single candle. Father says that God knows my age so there is no need to show off.'

'Doesn't it get you down? It must be an awfully dull life with them.'

'It is! They took some persuading to let me go to work. They were concerned that my morals would suffer. You know, access to men and swearing and the demon drink. But thanks to this war, they did and they are happy with the money I bring in.'

Martha thought to herself that perhaps their fathers were really no different after all.

—

On the way home that evening, Cassie had a surprise for Martha.

'I wanted to tell yer before, but I couldn't take the chance that someone might find out.'

'Find out what?'

'I've been seeing Peter since the Christmas Dance.'

'You have?' If Martha could've whistled, she would have done so. 'Our Peter's not one for keeping secrets, but he's done a grand job this time.'

'I'm sorry I made him keep it quiet. My parents set great store that nothing should happen between a man and a woman until the age of consent, and by that they mean even seeing each other. He asked me at the dance to see him again, and I agreed. He came around to Vera's house after Christmas and we talked. He said he would like to walk out with me. I explained my position and we agreed to say nothing to anyone, except Vera, until my twenty-first. I promised him that we would tell everyone then. I wanted you to be the first to know.'

'Congratulations.'

'It's been only twenty-two days, but it seems like an eternity. We have seen each other a few times at Vera's but you can't relax in case one of our neighbours sees and tells. Some of those who go to the same chapel would take great pleasure in my father's embarrassment.'

'Oh.'

'Please don't be angry, Martha. It was the only way we could think of. If Father got even an inkling, it would all have been over.'

'I suppose so.' Even to Martha's ears her response sounded childish – just like she had been with Betty. She wasn't going to make that mistake again, and let herself be comforted by Cassie.

'So we're telling my parents on Sunday afternoon, before chapel. I will let the parents get used to him before telling them about your grandfather. I think there have been some heated exchanges between the two of them over the years. I'm hoping that Father'll be magnanimous now that the licence for The Potter's Wheel has been refused.'

'I'm not surprised. It was Grandad's life's work. How would your father have felt if Grandad had tried to get your chapel converted into a pub? I remember him using some very choice words to describe the Temperance people.'

'So you can see why we've been so secretive.'

–

Vera and Martha were having none of Cassie not having a party, and they organised a little celebration on Friday lunchtime along with the other girls in the department. Cassie was old enough to do whatever she pleased and that was worthy of celebrating, if anything was. Of course, there were some coarse remarks flying around, but it was taken in good spirit.

–

Peter walked into the kitchen at Park Terrace in his Sunday-best clothes looking like a man about to be executed.

'Peter, lad. Yer look like a trussed-up chicken,' proclaimed Grandad. 'Bit dressed up like a Saturday night. I think there's a girl involved.' Grandad had a smug smile on his face. He struck a match and relit his pipe.

'Do I look all right, Martha?'

'Let me tidy your collar. And is that the best tie you've got? It looks like you're going to a funeral.'

'It is me funeral tie, the other one's too bright.'

She reached up and tidied his collar, brushed his lapels and stood back satisfied. 'That'll have to do. I hope you enjoy wherever you're going.' Martha winked at her brother.

She went with him to the front door and wished him good luck and hoped that Cassie's introduction of Peter would be greeted favourably. Cassie seemed confident that she would be able to persuade her parents to accept Peter. Martha thought she'd better keep her fingers crossed, just in case.

–

'They seemed to like him,' Cassie said to Martha at work on Monday. 'He's allowed to see me only when my parents are present, or when we are in a public place – so we don't have the opportunity to get too close and cause embarrassment to anyone.'

'I assume that Vera's services will still be required as a meeting place?' said Martha archly. She was sure that this would be the type of subterfuge Peter might enjoy.

-

A few days later, it was Cassie's turn to be put on the spot as she was introduced to the Owen family at Park Terrace. Martha had no doubt that her family would be pleased to meet the woman who had captured Peter's heart sufficiently to bring her home to introduce to his family. Martha looked suitably surprised so as not to embarrass Peter and Cassie.

-

Martha and Vera had started to chat to Cassie about when they were going to announce their engagement. Cassie said that they were not ready for that sort of thing as they had only been seeing each other for a few months.

During one of these conversations Cassie mentioned that when they did get married, they were going definitely to move to Northwood; she wanted to get as far away from her parents as she could. Martha was concerned that her brother might rush into marriage and determined to have a word with him the next time they met.

Chapter Twenty

June 1918

Mother and Issy usually came to Park Terrace for Sunday dinner. It was Grandma who suggested that Sunday was a day of rest and that Mother, Martha and Issy deserved to be looked after. Martha had started to take an interest in cooking and Grandma was pleased to teach her.

It was about four in the afternoon when Mother decided to return to the shop as she usually used these couple of hours to 'do her books'.

Martha said she would come along and help Mother and keep her company for a little bit. She would then walk to the park.

'Yes, that would be nice.'

No sooner had they got to the shop and started to work than a knock came on the shop door.

It was Peter, dressed smart, but looking nervous.

'I didn't think you'd be here, Martha.' He threw her a glance. 'I've got some news for yer. Both of yer.'

They sat at the kitchen table, Martha and Mother, smiling. Peter put his hand to his shirt collar as if he needed to breathe. If his news was good, why was he so nervous? The smile left Mother's face.

'Go on then, out with it.'

'Cassie and me – we're getting married.' Peter looked down at the table waiting for their response. Martha and Mother stared at him and then at each other.

'That's good news – we've been expecting it. Congratulations.'

Peter remained silent.

Mother tutted. 'Judging by yer face, my boy, there's a bit more to it than you've told us.'

'She's expecting, Mother.' His face was riddled with anxiety.

'She's what?'

'I said she's expecting.'

'Oh, no, not Cassie. She wouldn't,' blurted Martha.

'How d'yer know? Yer didn't believe Betty would get herself pregnant – but she did,' Peter retorted.

'How could yer bring that up?'

'It's true, isn't it?'

'Now then, you two. I'll have none of that in this house.' Mother turned to Peter. 'How dare you land such news on our doorstep? I've brought you boys up to know better. Do you love her?'

Peter rubbed his hands through his hair. 'I think I do.'

'You *think* you do?' Martha demanded.

'No, I mean I do, Martha. I like her a lot, but I didn't think of marrying anybody for a while yet. I conner get me head round it—'

'Maybe yer should've thought about that before you went and got her pregnant then, me lad,' Mother said.

Peter winced at her harsh words.

'And yer'll have to find somewhere for the pair of yer to live.'

'Cassie thinks her folks might even throw her out.'

'Were you thinking she could stay at Park Terrace until you're wed? There's a limit to how many of you yer grandad'll be prepared to put up with.'

'Cassie could have Issy's old room,' said Martha.

'No. It is up to your grandparents, even though it would only be for a few weeks until the wedding.'

'Then where will we live?' asked Peter.

'You'll have to do what others do. Find somewhere to rent. You're both earning good money for the moment and when the baby comes, you'll still manage on your wages. You've rented somewhere before; you can do the same again.'

'Suppose so,' mumbled Peter.

He sounded petulant. He was a grown man. His brother was fighting for his country, putting his life at risk every day, and Peter needed to be told he would have to rent somewhere for his family to live.

Mother paced the floor. 'You're just like yer father, you are. Not thinking of the consequences of yer actions.'

'It's not like that, Mother.'

'Well, my boy. Whatever it *was like* is of no consequence now. You haven't even got the excuse that you were leaving for the Front, have yer?'

Again, Peter winced at the harshness of Mother's words. With his arms on the table and his hands covering his ears, he groaned.

'You'll marry the girl and have done with it. You'll not bring shame on this house by shirking yer responsibilities. Cassie will have to find somewhere respectable to live, and I don't mean your digs, until you're wed. It'll be a quiet, no-fuss wedding. No church, just get it over with.' Mother lifted her head. 'I'll ask you once more, Peter, and think hard before you answer. Do you love Cassie?'

'Yes.'

'And do you think Cassie's trapping you?'

'No, I've never given that a thought.'

'Right.' Mother went to her bedroom.

Martha shook her head and motioned for them to go down the stairs and out into Tower Square so as not to disturb Mother.

'Oh, Peter, what have yer done?'

He sat on a bench near to the clock tower, looking meek and lost, with Martha beside him.

'One night, we'd both had a little too much to drink. And...'

Martha closed her eyes and shook her head. 'So, you're saying as yer got drunk and one thing led to another.'

'It wasn't like that.'

'Yes – and it was me what introduced her to yer.' Martha's anger rose as she laid into him. 'I feel as if it's partly my fault. I can't believe you would go with a girl, let alone one of my closest friends.' She shook her head. 'You're all the same.'

'She's a nice girl. You know that – you're her friend.'

'Yes, I know. But she must be more to yer than "nice", Peter. Surely you can see that. You have to love her and want to spend the rest of yer lives together. Otherwise yer'll end up like Mother and Father.'

They were both silent, trying to take in what had just been said.

Martha began again, in a calmer voice. 'Didn't yer think as there'd be consequences?'

'Have you never lost control, Martha? Thought what you might do if you were attracted to someone – and couldn't stop yerself?'

Instantly her mind flew to Jeffrey and that day in the park on the rowing boat. She could easily have lost control then. She knew her face had flushed because Peter's face held a look of triumph. She insisted, 'I wouldn't.'

'How d'yer know that?'

'I… I mean… I… just know I couldn't.'

'Betty did, and she was yer best friend – but you just ignored her. You forsook her. Will yer do the same with Cassie and me?'

Martha didn't know what to say. He was making this whole thing about her. 'Now you're being unfair.'

'How? Same things happened. Boy meets girl – boy and girl do what boys and girls do, boy and girl face the consequences.'

Martha was dumbstruck. That her own brother should come out with such horrible words—

'Look, Martha, I meant what I just said to Mother. Me and Cassie are going to get married. I shall do the right thing by her.'

For a moment, Martha felt proud of him as her thoughts turned to Cassie and what she might be going through right now. She found herself thinking of Betty, too, although her future was different because her future husband had been one of the fallen. Were their thoughts so very different? How brave of both of them in telling their families. Did either of them truly love the father of their baby?

So many questions and words left unsaid. At the time, Martha hadn't been able to forgive Betty. She wished things had been different. Knowing what she knew now, she couldn't do the same to Peter and Cassie.

What a complicated world this was.

At that point, Peter donned his cap and stood up. 'We're going to tell her parents after chapel. I'm not looking forward to that!'

'We shall all be at Grandma's this evening, so when you're finished, come round and tell us what's happened.'

–

The whole family were sitting in the back kitchen of Park Terrace chatting about the events of the day when Peter returned looking as if he was about to burst a blood vessel.

'Bloody parents! Call themselves Christians!'

'What's happened? I gather they haven't taken it very well?'

'They threw me out.' He paced the room thumping a fist into his splayed-out hand as if planning to use it against Cassie's family. Martha's thoughts jumped to poor Cassie.

Mother got up. 'Sit down, love, and tell us what's happened.'

Martha wasn't sure if he heard, but he remained standing.

'Cassie wanted to do the talking because it would sound better coming from her, she said. So, I let her. She introduced me as her intended. I didn't know she was going to do that, but it probably sounded better that way.'

'Her father stood up to congratulate me but said I should've asked him first. He was about to shake me hand when she blurted out that she was expecting. That was when it blew up in our faces. I tried to say me piece but he was having none of it. He told me to leave and not come back. I said, "What about Cassie?" He refused to speak to me and showed me the door.'

'Oh, poor Cassie.' Martha closed her eyes.

'I could hear her crying and thought it wouldn't be good for the baby if she was so stressed, but they refused to let me stay.'

'They're devout Christians and Temperance people, Peter,' Grandad muttered. 'You shouldn't be surprised at their reaction. I wouldn't be surprised if they threw her out.'

'That's what she's frightened of. I'm going back round to see her in the morning. See what's bin decided.'

Martha scraped her chair back. 'Should I pop round now?'

'No, Martha.' Mother sounded adamant. 'She needs to sort it out with them. You should be ready to help pick up the pieces afterwards.'

Shortly after that, Peter left for his digs.

–

Martha barely slept that night thinking of the burden Cassie now carried. Would she be in work tomorrow? What would everybody say? For once, she wasn't thinking of herself, but of the girl who would, hopefully, become her sister-in-law.

Martha enjoyed having the house to herself in the early morning and was eating her breakfast when there was a knock at the back door. Surprised at the early visit, she opened the door to Vera and Cassie.

'Hello, is everything all right?'

'Yes,' said Cassie. 'We've come to tell yer what's happened. I know that Peter told you and your mother yesterday and that things went reasonably well.'

'I wouldn't say that.'

Vera shrugged. 'Better than it did for Cassie.'

'Yes, but we did give Peter a hard time. We were both shocked. I think we said all the usual things. Parents seem to forget you may be their child, but you are not their possession and forcing you to adhere to their beliefs is wrong and cruel. Mother's told Peter that he must get married, not for his or your happiness but for propriety, and for the sake of the child. Do you want to get married?'

'Yes, it feels strange to think of marriage,' Cassie said. 'I don't feel old enough and I'd need more time to get used to the idea. Your grandfather being the landlord of The Potter's Wheel all these years was always going to be a stumbling block but I hoped when they saw how much we loved each other, they would relent. But that wasn't the case. If anything they're more upset about my association with the grandson of "a demon who makes money from the misery of others" than my condition.'

Cassie looked as if she was about to burst into tears, so Vera recounted what happened. Cassie had pleaded with her parents to listen to what she had to say but they were so disgusted they wouldn't listen. They said she was nothing more than a whore and how could she expect to stay under the same roof as God-fearing folk.

'Oh, you poor thing, Cassie. What did yer mother say?'

'She was quiet. She always does what my father says. She never has an opinion of her own. They attend chapel, go to Bible classes and other meetings. They spend their spare time raising money to send missionaries to the colonies "to teach the heathen about God" and how they should behave. What's happened over the last day is definitely not the way anyone should behave.'

'What did yer do?'

'I was so upset; I could hardly think straight. I decided to go round to Vera's. Being as she lives on her own, I knew she'd have a spare bed. I couldn't come to yours, Martha. Just turn up on yer doorstep and explain to yer family what'd happened. Any road, Vera's letting me stay until I can get things sorted.'

'No, Cassie. I said as you could stay for as long as yer want to.'

More tears followed, but these were tears of relief.

'We'd best get off to work, otherwise we'll have some explaining to do to Mr H,' grinned Vera.

Chapter Twenty-one

The wedding was set for 10 August. Peter had sent a letter to Daniel, but had not yet received a reply. There had been a lot of fighting over the spring and summer on the Western Front. First a major German offensive almost broke through the Allies and the Germans got as close to Paris as they had done in 1914. But recently the British and French, along with help from the Americans, had stopped the attacks and in a counter-offensive seemed this time to be making 'substantial' gains. The news was good, but more fighting meant more chance of receiving a letter like Mother had received in 1915.

There had been no contact between Cassie and her parents. Cassie tried not to seem too bothered, but Martha suspected that she would miss her mother in the coming weeks. Outwardly she looked happy at the prospect of being married and having a baby, but there was still a sadness in her eyes.

Peter seemed to have taken to the prospect of married life quite well. He had been searching the second-hand shops for some bits of furniture and other things. Grandma seemed increasingly excited by the prospect of becoming a great-grandmother.

Vera had offered Cassie and Peter a room at her house, sharing the costs and the jobs. This was a relief for all involved. Vera now had some company and soon would have the sound of tiny feet. She was looking forward to being Aunty Vera in the future. Cassie and Peter would have the larger room with plenty of space for the cot. Vera would move into the back room, which was plenty big enough for her needs.

Issy and Michael seemed to be growing closer together, too. This prompted Martha to have an embarrassing conversation with Issy, advising her not to do anything with Michael no matter how she felt. Issy was most indignant and said she had no intention of doing what Betty and Cassie had done. She was going to follow the example of her big sister. Issy did confess that she hoped the war would end soon. Michael would be eighteen in next March and eligible for call-up.

Thanks to Michael and Issy, Martha knew that Betty had become a clippie on the trams; she was not married and there didn't seem to be a boyfriend. Her daughter, Hannah, was living at Wellington Road with her grandmother. Betty lived on her own somewhere in Hanley. Martha wondered if Michael could be persuaded to give Issy Betty's address, but she couldn't bring herself to ask and she did nothing more about it.

The next letter Martha received was from Daniel. Martha sat by the fireside, even though there was no fire, and tore open the envelope. Two pages slid out. She hoped it contained good news – although there was little chance of that.

Holding onto her chest, she unfolded the pages and began to read.

He must have received Peter's letter. He knew about Peter and about the wedding too, and that Cassie's family had disowned her. Peter must have poured it all out in one fell swoop. Goodness knows what Daniel's response was – most likely a burning wish that he could be there. The rest of the letter contained Daniel's day-to-day activities and other general news.

Relief flooded through Martha. She hoped that the war would end very soon and decided that she would reply to this letter after the wedding so she could tell him all about it.

Once again, she gave thanks that they had kept the news about Father away from Daniel. With all that had happened, he had more than enough to think about.

When they were on their own, Mother and Martha talked again about what might have happened to Father. Was that prisoner really him? The two years' delay Captain Munro talked about did seem very strange. Mother had heard nothing from him over the last year, so it did not look like the Red Cross had received any information that was worth passing on to her. What would happen when the war was over? Would it be Father who returned or was it just a clerical error, as Captain Munro had suggested?

–

The wedding took place on Saturday 10 August at Hanley Registry Office. Both Martha and Vera acted as witnesses. Issy insisted on Cassie carrying a posy of flowers so that she might look after them for her during the ceremony – as if Cassie was a real bride – at which Cassie had burst into tears, not because she wasn't a real bride, but because Issy was trying her best to make their day special.

Vera admired Cassie's dress. Secretly, a panel of material had been sewn into the back to allow it to fit her expanding figure. Though not a proper wedding dress, it was, nevertheless, better than anything Cassie had worn before. A long silk shawl covered the back and most of the front.

Martha had laughed and Cassie's tears quickly changed to laughter too. Issy was amazing and had made light of a situation everyone had found difficult. Since Issy had been working at Mrs Parker's Pies, she had grown in confidence and had turned into someone who could be relied upon. Mother had said, more than once, that she didn't know what she would do without her youngest daughter.

'We all do our bit, Mother, and you say that about all of us,' Issy said, but the praise had had its effect and Issy beamed with appreciation.

'Peter can look so handsome when he's a mind to it,' Mother sighed. 'I wish Daniel was here. He should be Peter's best man.

He'll be devastated not to be here. Even yer grandad looks smart.'

At that moment, the door of the Registry Office opened. In the doorway stood Daniel, in his army uniform, looking as if he had just popped by.

'Not too late, am I?'

Martha was sure a little scream had escaped from her mouth as her eyes lit on his. Peter left Cassie momentarily to rush to his brother's side and crush him with both arms. Daniel shook hands with him and whispered something in Peter's ear – at which point Peter's face reddened. Last of all, Mother just stood there as if she didn't believe her eyes. Daniel walked steadily towards her and gave her a hug that lifted her off her feet. He turned to Cassie and lifted her hand to his lips and placed a kiss there.

'Best get the service over with before they chuck us out, hey, Pete?'

Peter grinned. 'If I remember right, it was always you what held things up.'

Everyone laughed. And the ceremony continued without a hitch.

Martha couldn't take her eyes off Daniel as he stood beside his twin. He had come home to stand by his brother's side on the most momentous day of his life. How Martha wished she could be stood next to them. To touch him to make sure he was real. He looked older and thinner since she last saw him and his face had a sharper look to it.

The reception was a small family do, held at home with a few friends. Mother had invited Cassie's parents to come along as witnesses in the hope it might bring them together as a family, but they declined.

'Poor Cassie – having no one from her family at her wedding.'

Peter was attentive to his new wife, surprising Martha at both his consideration and his gentleness. It seemed that, having got used to the idea that they were to be married, he actually began to feel it was what he wanted. He even talked about the baby – to those who had been taken into his confidence. The rest, he chose to ignore.

A good time was had for the rest of the day. Everyone remained close to Daniel, but Peter wasn't bothered. That his brother had made the trip, to be back to support him on this day, was all that mattered.

Daniel had news. 'I was called to headquarters and told to take my kit and tools with me. When I arrived there were lads from Staffordshire, Yorkshire, Lancashire, Durham and Nottingham. We were given a medical examination. We guessed pretty quickly what was happening – it turned out we was all miners. An officer came in and told us that we would be transferred back to England if we agreed to return to our former jobs – back down the pit. A cheer went up. I think everyone accepted. Technically I'll still be in the army, but my unit will be Northwood Colliery. I'll be demobbed when the war's over. We were driven to Le Havre and waited for a boat back to Portsmouth. In the end we hitched a lift on a destroyer.'

'How many of you were there?' asked Peter.

'About fifty. When we got to Portsmouth there were lorries waiting for us. We went to Aldershot Barracks where we received another medical and were given our papers and travel warrant. I arrived at Stoke station at midday and left my kit in the left luggage office. Had a chance to get a shave and walked straight up to Hanley.'

'Does that mean you're home for good?' asked Issy.

'Yes, just got to find somewhere to sleep. How am I fixed, Grandma, got room for me?'

'Of course, we'll find you somewhere...' Grandma's voice tailed off as she started to cry. This set Martha, Mother and finally Issy off.

So many tears – but these were tears of joy.

Later, Daniel said he was going to the station to get his kit. 'I'll come with yer, Dan. I'm sure Cassie will let me go with yer.' Peter smiled at his new wife.

'Yes, you go with your brother. But come back straight away – no stopping on the way.'

'I'll make sure he does, Cassie, can't have the groom in trouble on his first night.'

Martha watched the two brothers, united again, walk down the road towards the tram stop.

–

'You know, Cassie really does love Peter, I'm sure of it. She would never have given herself to him if she didn't,' Vera murmured when she was alone with Martha tidying up the kitchen after Daniel's departure. 'The way she looked at him – all starry-eyed and happy as she came in. You wouldn't think there was any prob... they were as happy as any other couple I've seen get wed.'

'I'm so glad you're here, Vera.' Martha took Vera's hand in her own and her eyes watered.

'Oh, Martha, duckie. Come here.' Vera opened her arms to Martha and the two held each other tightly, one happy to give support, and the other to receive it.

Somehow, all Martha's troubles with Betty came tumbling out: how close they were, the terrible argument, and how awful it had been since they had parted. How convinced she'd been that Betty considered herself to be too posh to associate with her friends in The Potteries. In telling Vera, she had begun to realise that this wasn't all about Betty's behaviour, but about her own, her shame in not being there when Betty needed her and being too adamant that Betty's reputation had been well and truly lost.

'My goodness, Martha. What a heavy burden you've been carrying all this time.'

'Don't feel sorry for me. I don't deserve it.'

'Stuff and nonsense. Everybody makes mistakes. Don't we talk of forgiving our sins? Where would we all be if we couldn't be forgiven?'

Martha reached for her handkerchief. Of course, Vera was right. It was her own attitude about it all that upset her the most.

'I always thought of meself as a forgiving sort of girl while all the time I've got this evidence that it's the last thing I am.'

'No, I'll not have that, Martha Owen. That's you feeling sorry for yourself. Think about others. Think about what they're going through, and then think how you might help them. Only when you've thought about all of those people should you think about yourself. Trust me. You are a good friend. You just have to believe in yourself.'

Martha swallowed and hugged her dear friend, thankful for the wisdom of this older woman. 'Well, thank you for believing in me.'

All this time she had spent thinking about the friend she had lost – instead of recognising the friends she had gained.

–

Daniel dawdled in the kitchen after his first day back at work at his old job at Northwood Pit. He was staring into space.

What was he thinking about? Martha wished she could read his mind.

'How was yer first day?'

He shrugged, but didn't speak.

'Did it feel good to get back to what you know?'

He stared at her and then turned his head to look through the window at the blue sky just visible over the roofs of the houses.

'Is everything all right, Daniel?'

'Just savouring me time, that's all. A bit of time for meself for a change.'

Martha smiled. 'I can understand that. Must take a bit of getting used to.'

There was something different about him. She wished she could put her finger on it. He was quieter than she recalled – brooding almost.

'Yer would say – if there was summat wrong, wouldn't yer?'

'Why should there be anything wrong? I'm one of the lucky ones. I'm back home, all in one piece, working. Why would there be anything the matter?'

'I don't know, but—'

'Leave it, will yer. Just give me time, Martha, please.'

She nodded. It was bound to take some adjusting. And it was his first downer – that she knew of. What had she expected? He would hardly come back singing and dancing after a hard day's work. All she could do was to be there for him if and when she was needed. She might ask Peter how things went when she could get him on his own.

Chapter Twenty-two

November 1918

An armistice had been signed and was all over the newspapers. Not many people worked that day, judging by the number of people in the streets. News reached *The Sentinel* offices by telephone at half past ten in the morning, and a special early edition was rushed out saying the armistice had been signed at five o'clock that morning. Hostilities were to cease on all fronts at eleven o'clock the same morning, pending the drawing up of a peace treaty. The war would finally be over – there was a profound thankfulness for the Allied victory.

Martha, Cassie and Vera were working away as best they could when the news reached them.

Mr Higginbotham and Mr John appeared in the Decorating Shop and announced that a ceasefire had been agreed starting at eleven o'clock.

'I want us to take a minute to think about our colleagues and friends who lost their lives during this conflict,' said Mr John.

The whole of the shop stood in silence.

Martha looked across at Vera, who appeared surprisingly calm, but very proud of her Eddie.

'This isn't a day for working, so get off home to be with your loved ones.'

A cheer went up.

He shouted over the noise, 'Clean up properly before you go because tomorrow is a working day. Make sure you're on time!'

It was a noisy crowd of excited workers that left Paradise that day. Crowds had gathered in the streets as the news spread. Most of the factories had knocked off work and a general holiday mood set in. No doubt the bosses realised there would be little work done that day. Or it could've been that the joy was so considerable it brought out the best in everyone.

Garlands of flags decorated each of the six towns and thousands of children waved Union Jacks as fast as they could. There was much merriment as the bells joined in.

Bridie went home, thankful that none of her younger brothers would be involved. Vera and Cassie said they needed to go home, too, so Martha called in at Mrs Parker's Pies to see Mother. The shop was sold out, as most people seemed to have treated themselves to something they could eat while they celebrated.

Mother and Martha shared an embrace. Martha, in a quiet voice, asked Mother if she was all right.

'We'll know shortly, no doubt,' she said with a weak smile. 'Captain Munro said we will get to know only when the war was ended, but he also said that it would take time, so we may not hear anything just yet. Go and have a word with your sister, she's a bit upset about summat.'

Issy was in the kitchen cutting up the last of the onions for the next day. She sniffed and tried to hide her face. After much cajoling, Issy admitted that they were tears of relief. Michael Dean would be eighteen in five months' time and she couldn't believe the weight that had been lifted off her shoulders.

When they got to Park Terrace, Grandad told them that the twins had come home and gone to see the celebration in Hanley.

–

Everyone in the Owen household went out after dinner to celebrate in their own way. Issy persuaded Martha to go with her to Hanley where she was hoping to bump into Michael.

Mother wasn't too bothered about going out, but Grandad and Grandma persuaded her to walk with them.

For those with the strength to continue celebrating into the evening, lighting restrictions were removed. Streetlamps and shop windows were lit up for the first time since the war had begun.

Martha's mind turned to Jonas. What did soldiers do on such a great day? What must they be feeling after all this time?

There were people all around. Groups were singing and dancing. Even the bobbies were joining in.

Martha and Issy were walking on Percy Street and for the first time that day, Martha was hit by the realisation that Father, if indeed it was Father, could be on his way home shortly. But she soon put those thoughts to the back of her mind. This was a day for rejoicing.

Issy spotted Peter and then Daniel, and ran over to speak to them. Martha followed, beaming.

'It's a great day. We've won!' exclaimed Peter.

They talked about the joyful scenes they were witnessing. Daniel was a bit more thoughtful, talking about what his comrades in the platoon might be doing at this moment.

'At least I'll get demobbed now. I think I'm no longer a soldier from today.'

Issy glanced around. 'Where's Cassie, Peter?'

'She's stopped at home with Vera. She was too tired after walking back from work and Vera was too upset. They said they would go out later.'

Martha asked what her brothers' plans were for today and was not surprised by their answer.

'We're going to the Grapes and then the Trumpet and finally the Angel. By that time we'll have had enough.' The brothers had spent so much of this war apart, they had plenty to celebrate.

Martha and Issy continued down Percy Street, threading their way through the crowds. Issy suddenly rushed off and leapt into Michael's arms and they kissed on the lips. Martha almost shouted to her sister to behave herself and to come back immediately. But the thought only lasted momentarily. Issy was sensible and it was a special occasion, after all.

Suddenly, she was gazing straight into the eyes of Betty Dean, who was standing with her mother.

'How are yer, Martha?' asked Mrs Dean.

'I'm fine, Mrs Dean. Hello, Betty.'

'Hello,' mumbled Betty.

There was an awkward pause and Martha tried not to look at the pram. Mrs Dean's cold attitude put Martha off saying something about Betty's daughter.

'Best get a move on,' said Mrs Dean. 'Come on, Betty.' Betty started to push the pram away.

Martha was on the verge of calling her when she overheard Mrs Dean, saying in a loud voice, 'There was no way I was going to let that little madam ignore us with her high-and-mighty ways.'

That was it. People would never forget that Peter and Cassie had to get married. Events like that are not easily forgotten in such a close-knit community. Unfair, perhaps, but reputation was everything.

There was no hope that things would ever change. Martha knew exactly what Mrs Dean thought of her and now Betty knew that even Martha's own family weren't above getting themselves into trouble. Thank God they didn't know anything about Mother.

She rummaged through her coat pockets desperately trying to find a handkerchief to dry the tears on her wet cheeks. She couldn't find one. Instead, Martha put her head down to hide her face and hurried towards Parliament Row to look for Issy.

–

In early December, the government announced its plans for demobilisation of the army. Soldiers with essential skills, like miners, were to be first. Some, like Daniel, had been returned home to work, but were still considered soldiers. The government treated the rest of the soldiers, whether they were volunteers or conscripts, on their length of service. In practice this would mean that volunteers usually returned before conscripts. The last to return would be the eighteen-year-old conscripts of 1918.

Somewhere in all that, might Martha's father be returning too?

Chapter Twenty-three

January 1919

Cassie had stopped working at Christmas and, with Vera still at work, Grandma had taken to calling around each day to make sure everything was in order. Cassie went into labour on 8 January, a Wednesday. The poor girl's labour pains started at two o'clock in the afternoon and went on for nearly twelve hours. The women took turns to sit with her, while Peter and Daniel waited anxiously.

At just after two o'clock in the morning, Cassie's little boy was born. Everyone was concerned because she had such a rough time of it, but once the little chap had arrived, that changed. He was a right bonny-looking lad.

Peter and Daniel both had to go to work, although they hadn't had much sleep. Vera also went to work and no doubt told everybody the good news. Great-grandma Parker was delighted to look after Cassie and the baby.

When Martha got home, she quickly changed out of her work clothes and, along with Mother and Issy, walked up to Vera's house in Henry Street.

The door was opened by a jubilant Peter, who had already wet the baby's head a few times.

'Mother, we've got a boy. He looks just like me, although Cassie thinks he looks like her. I don't care as long as he's healthy.'

'What a pity if he looks like you, Peter.' Martha grinned. 'How's Cassie?'

'Tired but in good spirits. It's been a long labour and she's exhausted. Let's go up to see her.'

Martha was overcome. She'd never seen such a tiny scrap even though she had been assured that he was a good size. He was wrinkled and had no hair, just pale and blotchy skin which, those in the know insisted, would be a beautifully soft pink in a day or so.

Mother was given the honour of holding her first grandson. Gazing at him, she was overcome with tears that wouldn't stop.

How wonderful it must be to hold your child's child, Martha thought, almost in tears herself. He turned out to be heavier than she expected when Martha took her turn to hold him. She stared at his face, took in his tiny ears, and the delicate eyelashes surrounding deep blue eyes. What a beauty he was. He would charm everyone he came into contact with. For a moment, she held his tiny hand. It closed around her finger with a strength that surprised her. It that moment, she swore to herself she would do all she could to protect the new addition to their family.

'We're calling him Andrew, Peter's middle name.' Cassie beamed at Peter who was too emotional to speak.

Martha's heart thumped powerfully. She was this little lad's aunty. How much stronger would Betty's feelings have been for her little Hannah? A bond so strong nothing could break it. The more she learned of people, the sorrier she was that she had been so harsh in the beginning.

Martha helped Vera to prepare a huge pan full of lobby. The stew would be good for any hungry visitors expected to call to see little Andrew. Daniel arrived back from the pub on the corner with bottles of ale, to help wet Andrew's head later.

They had just finished eating when a knock came on the door.

'I'll go,' said Martha. Vera was washing up and Issy and Martha were drying and putting away.

She opened the door and came face to face with Cassie's mother. They hadn't formally met, but Martha had seen her around Tunstall and recognised her.

'Mrs Mellor! How nice to see yer. Have you come to see Cassie and the baby?'

'She's had it?' A pale and anxious Mrs Mellor stepped over the threshold and into the hall.

'Who is it, Martha?' called Vera from the kitchen.

'It's Mrs Mellor,' Martha shouted back.

Quick as a flash, Vera appeared in the hall, not bothering to wipe her dripping wet hands.

'Good evening, Mrs Bell. I'm sorry to call unannounced but I've come to see my—'

'Of course you have.' Vera smiled. 'What mother wouldn't want to see her first grandchild? I'll take you up to see Cassie. I must warn you that she's very tired. It was a long labour.'

'I just want to make sure she's all right, Mrs Bell.'

'Please call me Vera. I'm sure we can call ourselves friends after today's event?'

Surprised, Mrs Mellor's face relaxed a little. 'There weren't any... complications, were there?'

'No. Your daughter's strong and resilient, Mrs...'

'Adeline, please.'

Vera led the way upstairs. Martha stayed downstairs. Cassie's room wasn't big enough for them all. She heard a cry from Cassie as her mother walked into the room.

Vera appeared a few minutes later. 'I thought it best to leave them to make their peace. Peter looked a bit shocked to see his mother-in-law.'

'Fancy her coming round here on her own. I wonder how she got Mr Mellor to let her visit. Perhaps he doesn't know.'

'Yes, I thought that the minute I saw her. But I haven't got room for her if he throws her out an' all!' Vera laughed as she was speaking. 'She said she was sorry for not being there for them, but that was her husband's doing rather than hers and she has every intention of seeing her grandson in the future.'

'What good news. I'm glad.'

Martha would've skipped back to Park Terrace that night if she hadn't been so tired herself. The day had been perfect, in every way, and she couldn't have been more pleased.

Chapter Twenty-four

When Martha got into work on Monday morning, everybody was going through their normal tasks of getting their benches ready for the day's work. She looked across at Vera who looked sad.

'What's up?'

'A few of the women have received notifications that their husbands or sons are coming home. There must be about a dozen of them. So at last ordinary soldiers are starting to be demobbed. It got me upset thinking about my Eddie.'

Martha comforted her friend.

When she got home that night there was a letter from Jonas waiting for her on the hall table.

Impatient to hear any news he might have, she opened the letter and scanned the contents.

31 January 1919

Dear Martha,

Sorry it has been a while, I just thought that I would send you a quick note to let you know that I am safe and well. I hope you are keeping well yourself and continuing with your art. Now you are a paintress you will have lots of time to develop your skills.

It looks as if I'm going to be one of the last ones to return, even though I've got a guarantee of a job. The Royal Army Service Corps is being demobbed at a slower pace than the rest of the army because of the work we have to complete over here. It is understandable; it took us four years to accumulate our supplies and equipment, and we've got six months to get it back.

Since the Armistice I have had a couple of forty-eight-hour passes, and although it's impossible to get home in that time I have been able to take the train to Paris. It is such a beautiful city. Its boulevards are wide and there are trees everywhere. No wonder artists for centuries have painted this place. I do wish you could have seen it. The countryside around Paris is beautiful. Some of the French drivers we met say that it is glorious in spring and, thanks to Mr Lloyd George, it looks as if I will get the chance to see it.

I think if the British Army has been anywhere over these last few years, I've been there as well. I am at Ypres moving stuff back to Calais for the time being and our base is at Langemark, which was behind the old German lines. You could drive through the whole of the battlefield at Ypres in under an hour. It is so sad to think that thousands of men on both sides spent four years fighting over this piece of ground. On the battlefields there are hardly any trees, all the houses seemed wrecked and the ground is a sea of mud. Trenches are everywhere, empty now, of course. It's unreal. So quiet. But people are returning to their villages, trying to pick up their lives. I have done a number of sketches. I have posted them to my family, and hopefully one day will feel able to show them to you.

It surprises me how much I am looking forward to my return to Paradise Pottery and my friends.

Best wishes,
167852 Lance-Corporal Jonas Gray
RASC Aldershot

Martha was disappointed to read that he wouldn't be returning immediately. It seemed unfair as Jonas had been one of the first conscripted, and now it looked as if he was going to be one of the last to be demobbed.

The letter reminded Martha that she would need to speak to Mr Higginbotham or Mr John soon if she was to go to art school in September to study painting. Her eyes had been opened to the work she could get involved in if she learned as much as she could about painting pottery. It would show she had ambitions and make the bosses believe she meant to succeed. Before Jonas went into the army, she would've talked her ideas over with him and valued his opinion. Nobody had shown so much faith in her before and she had missed his encouragement. She couldn't rely on Jonas to be back. She would have to make the running for herself. It was time for her to take control.

She settled down to write a reply. Would it be too forward to tell him she was looking forward to his return? In the end, she wrote in general terms and mentioned that Paris sounded beautiful.

Martha and her mother were in the sitting room at the flat. Martha was reading *The Sentinel*.

'Mother, have you read this about the prisoners returning home from Germany? It says most of them are back now, but some are being held in recuperation centres because of the flu.' She laid the newspaper on her lap. 'Did you never hear back from Captain Munro?'

Mother shook her head. 'Not a word. I'd have told you if I had, duck.'

'It's been almost two years since he promised to let us know.'

'Perhaps he's not heard anything. He must have hundreds of men he's looking for.'

'Do you think the army made a mistake in telling us he might be alive, or d'yer think they're still looking for him?'

'Your guess is as good as mine. If I haven't heard anything by the end of June, I'll write to him and give him a piece of my mind.'

'It's not his fault, Mother.'

'That's as maybe, but we can't live like this forever, wondering if yer father's going to walk through the door.'

'When are yer going to tell the others?'

Mother shrugged. 'Never – unless I have to.' She picked up her knitting and there was silence for a minute or two. Then she glanced at Martha as if she had made some sort of decision.

'Martha, what d'yer think about another shop?'

'Instead of this one?'

'No, things are going well here and I know I could make double what I do now if we had another shop. I thought of Burslem, on Queen Street or Market Place, where there'd be lots of passing trade.'

'There are plenty of potbanks in Burslem. A warm pie or oatcakes would go down well after a busy day.'

'That's what I thought. Issy thinks it's a good idea too. I think she's got enough experience to run it. She's good with people, whoever they are.'

'Have you got a place in mind?'

'Not as yet. I'll have ter be patient.'

'A pity to miss out on those sales.'

Listening to Mother speak gave Martha a warm glow. She had blossomed since those first days setting up and running the pie shop. Building up her own business had rebuilt the confidence Father had knocked out of her. And it looked like Issy, now eighteen, was a natural saleswoman too. Martha had seen her at work ensuring nobody left the shop without buying something and many left buying more than they had planned.

Chapter Twenty-five

May 1919

Peter and Cassie were getting on well at Vera's, and she was grateful for the extra money. Cassie had taken motherhood to heart and had even begun to think about having a second before too long, so she had whispered to Martha in confidence. She had laughed and said that she couldn't tell Peter because he was still getting over the first. But he was a good father, she gushed, surprising Martha no end. He could be selfish at times, but Cassie and baby Andrew were certainly having a positive effect on him.

The same couldn't be said about Daniel. He was fine, though quiet, when he first came home, and it was clear that he *was* glad to be back. However, once he'd gone back to the pit, he seemed to go into himself. Martha had thought that the camaraderie in the pit might have helped him to ease his way back into a normal life. It didn't. Even Peter commented on it to Martha when she went to visit them.

'So, what d'yer think we should do, Peter?'

'I've never seen him like this. It's as if he's here, but he isn't. If yer think he's bad at home, you want to see him at work with the lads. He hardly gives them the time of day. I've sympathised with him and told him it'll get better but he just snorts and walks off shaking his head. Then I tried being angry and told him to pull his socks up. But honestly, Martha, I don't know what to do with him. What's he like at Grandma's?'

'Same. He spends a lot of time in his room. Mother has had some heart-to-hearts with him but, knowing Daniel, he's probably said nowt for fear of upsetting her.'

'Before the war, we could tell each other anything. Now, he finds it difficult to talk, even to me.'

'I'll try to talk to him. See if I can find out what's really the matter.'

—

'Fancy a walk?' It was about an hour before tea. Martha decided it was a good time to approach Daniel. 'Come, we both need a bit of fresh air. It'll do us good.'

'I've just walked home from Northwood, that's enough fresh air for me.'

'Oh, come on. Let's go and watch the ducks in the park. We don't often have a chance to talk together.'

'I dunno, Martha. I'm tired. To be truthful, I dunner think as I can be bothered.'

'But I've got nobody else to walk with, Daniel. Surely a short walk around the park won't give you any more aching bones than you've already got?'

He gave in. 'You're enough to drive a bloke crazy.'

'Sometimes, yer have to be cruel to be kind,' she muttered under her breath as she bent to fasten her shoes, but she was smiling again by the time she stood up.

They didn't say much as they walked. A bit about the weather being cool for May. Martha mentioned how well things were going at work and how she aimed to get the job she always wanted at the potbank. Daniel said how well Issy was coming along in helping Mother in the pie shop. The one thing she cottoned on to was that he didn't say anything about his own work: neither the army, nor the pit.

She took a deep breath and set out on her mission. 'I bet it feels good to be home doing all the stuff you used to do before the war, doesn't it?'

'I suppose so.'

She waited for something else to emerge. It didn't.

'Did yer make any friends in the army? Only, yer never speak of them.'

'The two what I trained with both died. One was shot by a sniper and one got one of his legs shot off. He lost too much blood and...'

Daniel stopped there as if his mouth had rusted up and refused to move.

'Oh, Daniel. That's awful.'

He shrugged. 'Well, you wanted to know.'

'No, I don't mean it's horrible... to be told,' Martha faltered. 'I... I mean awful for you to see. Your friends—'

'That's why I dunner say nowt. It's too much for me to remember and it's pretty shocking for those who weren't there to imagine. I dunner want to upset yer, but that's the way it was. Other men have said the same. We can talk together because we don't have to explain. We just know.'

There was a harsh reality in his voice and after the first words came out, others followed.

'I'm so sorry,' she whispered. Tears began to well up, and she dashed them away. She would not let him see how his words were affecting her.

She swallowed. 'Did yer meet any Germans?'

He nodded.

'What did yer do?' Her voice was barely a whisper.

'The first one... we'd bin told "shoot or be shot" – so I did. After that I only saw them when we took prisoners, which wasn't very often in my work.'

'What did you do most of the time?'

'Sit and wait and try not to get killed. I remember one time we got caught out in No Man's Land. I had been sent to lay some charges to demolish a building which was more use to the Germans than us.'

'Was it somebody's house?'

'Well, I presume it had been but after two years of war, to us it was just a good place for German snipers and shelter if the Germans attacked.' He stopped. His hands trembled. 'At that point a star shell exploded and lit up the whole of No Man's Land. The next thing, Harry, one of the lads in my crew, was shot in the chest by a sniper. Our side opened up covering fire and the rest of us got trapped in a shell hole. The noise was deafening. I couldn't see a damn thing. Just heard the continued shelling and the whizz of bullets. We lay there until it got quiet and we could get back to our line. Harry didn't make it; he was one I mentioned earlier. I have nightmares. I'm glad I'm not sharing me bedroom with Peter no more. At least he conner hear me cry.'

'Oh, Daniel!' Martha threw her arms around him until he stopped shaking.

'That's why I'm best on me own.'

'But we can help yer. Look after yer till you're feeling better.'

'No, Martha, you don't understand. We went away to do our duty – and we came back – most of us did, any road. The burden is ours to carry, not yours – or anybody else's who wasn't there.'

Martha looked at him – her big brother who had put up with their violent father for so long, reduced to tears that threatened to flood his whole being.

They were entering the park and Daniel had his head down as if watching his legs moving along the pathway beside the lake.

'Let's have a seat.'

Martha sank down as if the walk had tired her. Daniel sat beside her staring at the ducks swimming back and forth, the odd one or two chasing each other, squawking to show who was boss.

She took in the view – the trees fast growing their greenness back. Pink and white blossom, their petals already over, turning brown as nature returned their goodness to the ground.

'You know, Martha? I could easily have stayed over there after the war ended. Those areas that weren't obliterated by the fighting were good places. The weather was good. The fresh air so amazing. I actually enjoyed my job.' He grinned. 'Even learned a few French words an' all. Although, knowing some of the people I met, I couldn't be sure they weren't swear words.'

It was good to see him smile again, so Martha decided to tackle the other subject she wanted to talk about.

'What about yer job down the pit?'

'What about it?'

'How's it going?'

Another shrug.

'Same as ever.'

He stared across the water although she had the idea that he wasn't taking in what he saw. His face had darkened. The smile had gone. So, there was something.

'What is it, Daniel? What's wrong at the pit? It's bound to take a little time to get back into the swing of things.'

Still he kept quiet. She put a hand on his arm and rubbed it. 'You may be my big brother, but I'll always be here for you. You do know that?'

Still nothing, but she could feel a tightening of the muscles in his arm.

'What is it – please?'

'I hate the pit. I hate the job. I hate the cage. I hate—' His hair stood on end where he had pulled it in his frustration to get the words out.

'You hate it? But you've bin there for ages. I don't understand.'

'I never liked it. Every day, I hated going down and I hated coming back.'

'You got Peter his job – you never said.'

'When you're a miner, you eat, sleep and drink coal. Your neighbours are miners, and you drink down the pub with miners. And we're all down there – together. That's the good part. The queue for the cage is the opposite. We queue to get in it and we queue to get out. We cram ourselves in and when the door's closed we drop like a stone. I can't tell yer what it feels like. Best I can say is that you think you've left yer belly up top.'

'We walk underground with the weight of the Earth between us and daylight. And then we walk to the coalface all the time knowing that the bloody cage is waiting for yer. Only, when yer leave the bottom of the shaft, yer belly stays down there. By the time daylight hits yer, you feel as sick as a dog.'

'You've felt like that since yer started in the pit?'

'It's bin worse since I've gone back the cage also reminds me of the war. When we dug mines under the German trenches, they were shallow compared with a pit, but the feelings of being trapped were just the same. We knew the Germans were hunting for us, just as we were for them. We never talked. I tell yer, Martha. I dunner have it in me no more. I never want to go down there again. I only went back because we needed the money and it got me out of the army. But I tell yer. I've reached the end of me tether.'

She couldn't hide her horror She tried to stay in control but couldn't. Her pain must have echoed his. Daniel froze and then pulled her into his arms.

'I'm sorry! I'm sorry! I'm sorry,' was all she could get out of him.

Two couples, followed by a family, passed them. The couples tried to avert their eyes, but the family stared until the mother urged them on. Martha didn't care, she only had eyes for Daniel.

She spied a wooden seat beside the park keeper's shed where they would be less noticeable and pushed him gently towards it. When he was seated, she took a clean handkerchief out of her pocket and pushed it into his hands, not taking her eyes off him.

'I'm sorry, Martha.'

'You have nothing to be sorry for. Nothing in the world.'

She sat beside him staring at the spring flowers coming into bloom, flooding the park with colour. Bright, bold colours that lit up the place, making it happy after the darkness of winter. Their colours were becoming bolder as the strength of the sun deepened. That's what must have attracted insects to drink their nectar. Martha could do with bright colours like that to get her up each morning. Yes, bright, happy colours.

She shook her head as an idea was forming. It was to do with work – painting. But that wasn't important just now. Daniel needed her and she wanted to make damn sure he was what she was concentrating on most of all.

He sniffed and put the hankie in his pocket, promising to wash it.

'You know, while I was over there, I couldn't wait to get back, to see everyone and get things back to normal. Now I'm here, I'm wishing I was somewhere else.'

'What do you mean? It isn't all about the cage, is it?'

'The pit in general takes me back to the war. The noise, the dirt, the whole atmosphere. In the war, I didn't have a cage to worry about but it has become muddled up in my brain – with the Germans and the war, the sweat and men held against their will to do what no man should be asked to do. Now, every time I go into that damn thing it's all I can think about.'

How bad he must have felt since he came back – keeping it all locked inside himself so as he wouldn't upset anyone. But she might have known Daniel would always think about someone else before himself. That's why she loved him. That's why he—

'I'm thinking of going away, Martha.'

'No! You've only just come back. Mother won't have it.'

'That's why I've told yer. I need yer on my side. This time when I go, yer won't have to worry about me. I'll be doing what I want, when I want, with whoever I want. That's all I'm looking for.'

'And what about Peter? Does he know any of this?'

Daniel shook his head. 'I've tried to keep it to meself. Pete's got his own family now. We'll miss each other, sure as hell we will. But it's not the same since he's bin wed. He'll be all right.'

'And our Issy? She'll be ever so upset.'

'She'll get used to it. She's doing well with Mother in the pie shop. They'll look out for each other now there's no Father to worry about.'

'And what about you? How will you get on without us?'

'The honest truth? I dunno. I do know that I have to try.'

She stared at his earnest face. He meant all that he said. He couldn't go on like this; it would break him.

'Where will you go?'

He shrugged. 'Not too sure, but I'm thinking of Canada or—'

'Canada? But that's the other side of the world almost! How'll yer get there?'

'Towards the end of the war I worked with a lot of Canadians. I got friendly with a group of them and they said there are always opportunities in Canada for skilled people. One of them, Calum, lives in Nova Scotia and I've written to him. He replied a few days ago saying that there are some Canadian Government schemes for former soldiers and their dependants being talked about. These schemes are mostly in farming and are open to Canadian and Empire residents. I'm going to make some enquiries. He also said I could stay at his parents' farm which is not far from Halifax, the capital of Nova Scotia, for a few weeks with free board in exchange for work. All I'd have to do is find me own passage. He says that some blokes have worked their passage, but I can't see there would be much call for a miner on board ship.'

Martha's mouth fell open.

He leaned over and put his hand under her chin to close it. He was grinning now. 'I need yer to help me, Martha. Promise you will?'

Never in her wildest dreams had she anticipated having such a conversation with him. And worst of all, he was asking her to help him.

Martha nodded and took his hands in hers.

'I've never seen you so unhappy, Daniel. Not even when we were going through the worst with Father. If going away will help you, I can't stand in yer way.'

They hugged, each taking comfort from the other.

'What are you really looking for in life, Martha?'

'I've been a paintress since 1917 and what I'd really like is to do some of the stuff that men do. It's more challenging and satisfying. Vera thinks I'm good enough to go to night school to learn all about painting pottery. I'm thinking of speaking to Mr Higginbotham about it, but I dunner want to sound pushy.'

'You mustn't think like that. You must go for what you want in this life. That's what I'm trying to do and you must do the same. We only get one chance at it.'

'I've mentioned it before to one of the modellers called Jonas, but that was a long time ago. He's waiting to be demobbed and should be back in a few weeks. He was a painter originally, and very nice. He helped me when I first started at Paradise Street and has encouraged me with my drawing and painting. I'm looking forward to him coming back. He'll give me sound advice about art school and stuff.'

'The Martha I used to know wouldn't have considered going to art school, so I reckon he's done a good job.'

'Dunner look at me like that. He's just a friend and a lot older than me. He worked with Vera's husband before he...' She couldn't go on.

'How much older?'

'Seven years.'

Daniel shrugged. 'I wouldn't let that stop me if I was interested in someone. No other lad on the horizon?'

'I don't need nobody. I'll be content to fulfil my ambitions with the painting. Being what *I* want and not beholden to any man. My experience of men only reinforces that.'

Daniel shook his head. 'And you know a lot about men, don't yer?' He laughed. 'You'll change yer mind one day, our Martha, and I'll take great delight in reminding you of this conversation. In the meantime, keep yer eyes open for that special person. I'm sure there's some bloke out there, young or old, what's looking for somebody like you. And if yer find him – dunner shut him out.'

Chapter Twenty-six

June 1919

That morning as Martha worked through the ten-inch plates with the Cotswold design, she had her future in mind and what she might do with it, brought on by her talk with Daniel. He'd never talked about girls, not in the way Peter had, but he sounded so knowledgeable when he told her not to shut anyone out. She appreciated his words, but she wasn't ready to commit to a man – even one as nice as Jonas, if he was interested in her. She had been only seventeen the last time she saw him, and he, twenty-four. They had both changed a lot since then, she was sure.

Martha would concentrate on her work and her ambition to paint pottery. She had contacted the art school in Burslem and obtained details. She knew of other girls who had attended the course and had got on very well. The art school stipulated that they required an endorsement from a manufacturer and an undertaking to pay all the fees. So, she needed the support of Mr John. All she had to do was work out how she was going to achieve this.

When Martha heard footsteps behind her, she glanced up, knowing they belonged to Vera.

Martha beckoned her closer. 'I need a word with yer at dinnertime.'

'Okey dokey.'

The more Martha thought about it during the morning, the more she began to doubt the wisdom of her idea. So, when dinnertime came, she very nearly told Vera she'd changed her mind.

'Dunner be daft, Martha. You obviously wanted to say summat. Come on, out with it.' She glanced around her. 'Let's go for a walk up the street.'

Vera led the way outside. They both squinted in the bright June sunshine until their eyes had grown accustomed to the light after the dullness of the Decorating Shop.

'Now then, what is it yer want to say? You're not pregnant, are yer?'

Whatever was Vera thinking? 'No, I'm not!'

That was when Martha knew she had to tell her what she had come to say. No point in waiting for things to happen. She should go for it and, if it went wrong, she'd have the knowledge she had at least tried. She either had ambitions – or she didn't. Her choice.

'I want to go to the art school. To study painting.'

'Mm. I can't say as I'm surprised, Martha. I know you mentioned it a while ago and Jonas was certainly taken with your drawings. You do pick 'em, most of the skilled painting is done by men – pays the higher wages. Course, we lost a few in the war, "God rest their souls",' she murmured.

Blast! She'll be thinking about Eddie now, poor bloke.

'But even men had to start somewhere, Vera. I know I have a lot to learn, but could I go and see Mr Higginbotham and show him my work?'

'I've known him for a long time. He doesn't take many risks but he'll always listen to what you have ter say.' Vera studied her carefully. 'Are you asking me to speak to him for you?'

'Would you?'

'No, but I'll come with yer. If you're going to ask the company to help it'll sound better coming from you.' Vera smiled. 'Bring in some drawings and paintings. Might be useful to copy a design from work an' all – to show your copying abilities.'

Martha's eyes shone. 'Thank you so much, Vera. I'm so happy to think you have some faith in me. I'll bring them in tomorrow. No messing!'

'I'm not the only one who's got faith in yer, duckie, believe me.'

Her heart was singing when she went back to her bench and her smiles lasted all day. She had wondered who Vera was referring to with her last comment, but it went out of her mind before she could give it much more thought. Instead, Martha went through everything she'd done at home, trying to decide which of her pieces to show. It was a golden opportunity to shape her own future.

–

At home that evening, Martha pulled together all her work and pondered over which of the drawings, paintings and cups she'd decorated over the past year, best showed her capabilities. She roped in the family too but didn't tell them what she was doing. She merely asked for their opinions.

Armed with around a dozen items, she carried them in a shopping bag to the potbank. She deliberately arrived early so no one would question her on the contents of her bag, which she shoved under her bench. By the time the other girls arrived, she was well into decorating her third plate.

–

When the bell went at twelve, Vera nodded to Martha and they walked over to Mr Higginbotham's tiny office and knocked.

'Mm – come in.'

They stepped inside to find him adding up columns of figures and looking harassed. It was obvious that now was not a good time to interrupt him.

'Sorry to disturb yer, Mr Higginbotham. Martha and I wanted to have a word with yer about summat.'

'What's that, Vera?'

'Well, we can see as you're busy. Probably best if we slip back later?'

'Indeed, I am busy now. Come back after knocking-off time tonight, will yer?'

'Yes, Mr Higginbotham. Much appreciated. Thanks.'

Vera ushered Martha out of the office and together they returned to their benches to eat their dinners.

–

Throughout the day, Martha practised in her head what she wanted to say to Mr Higginbotham. Earlier, Vera had whispered words of encouragement advising her to be bold, but not argumentative, and if he seemed to waver, to press on. He didn't like to say no because he wanted to keep the workers happy.

Martha jumped when the knocking-off bell sounded. She let some of the girls go before reaching under her bench for her shopping bag. She took a deep breath and strode over to the supervisor's office behind Vera.

They had done well to wait. He looked less agitated than earlier.

'Now then, ladies. What can I do for you?'

'Martha has been thinking about her future with the company, Mr Higginbotham.'

He frowned. 'Why? You're not thinking of leaving us, are you, Miss Owen?'

'Oh, no. Nothing like that,' said Vera. 'Quite the opposite, Mr Higginbotham. Martha wants to do more. And I believe she has the talent to do it. Martha, tell Mr Higginbotham what you said to me.'

Martha gave Vera an anxious glance.

'Go on, Martha.'

Vera sat in the one chair available leaving Martha with little choice but to stand.

Martha took a deep breath and launched herself into the speech she had being saying over and over all day. 'You see, I always wanted to be a paintress, and I was so glad when I got me job and I love it. But now I've got experience, I want to do more. I want to do full freehand painting like the men.'

'Why do you want to do a man's job?'

'But it doesn't have to be a man's job, Mr Higginbotham. If a girl proves she can do the job well, then it shouldn't matter.'

'Maybe it shouldn't – but it does. How would yer feel sitting with a group of men all day?'

Martha shrugged. 'It wouldn't matter, cos I'd be working, wouldn't I?'

Mr Higginbotham's eyebrows raised. 'You girls are always nattering when I come through the Decorating Shop.'

'They work very hard an' all, Mr Higginbotham.'

Vera sounded protective of her girls. With renewed confidence, Martha carried on.

'I've brung along some of my drawings and paintings to show yer what I can do.' She emptied her shopping bag across his desk, covering up everything that belonged to him.

'Sorry, I didn't mean to do that.' Nevertheless, she spread out the papers so he could look at them.

He picked them up one by one and scrutinised them, occasionally nodding to himself. She wanted to say more, but felt she should give him time to take in what he was seeing.

When he'd finished, he looked up and smiled. 'Very commendable. So, what do you want from me?'

'I've heard as you send girls to art school to learn all about ceramic painting. I've checked with the art school and they said as I need to be put forward by the potbank and somebody needs to pay for the cost of the training.'

'Doesn't that bother you? It could involve up to three years of training. Suppose you want to get married?'

'Oh, I don't, Mr Higginbotham.'

'It's all very well for you to say that now. But what about—'

'No, Mr Higginbotham. This is important to me. I won't be getting wed, and I know you've been short of painters during the war. Could you talk to Mr John? Ask him if he'll consider me for one of the places and pay the fees?'

'Very well, Miss Owen, I'll organise an appointment. Better still, as you've got your work with you, we could speak to him now. We always have a word on Friday evenings.'

Martha's mouth dropped open. See Mr John right now? How could she? She'd thought he would see Mr John on his own.

'Grab your belongings, Miss Owen, so you don't have to come back here. That'll be all. Thank you, Vera.'

Vera nodded and patted her on the shoulder as she went out.

—

Martha trailed after Mr Higginbotham, down the stairs, across the courtyard and up the staircase to the posh offices. She had never had call to go beyond the Wages Office before. The main offices were well cared for, with wood panelling on the walls and glass panels for each office door to let some light into the corridors. Each door informed callers of the person's name and/or occupation, in gold lettering. Most of the offices were empty now and few lights were lit. Their shoes echoed in the silence surrounding them.

Martha had thought she was in control of herself as she strode behind Mr Higginbotham, her head held high. Now she knew differently – she might well go to pieces. He stopped outside a door towards the end of the corridor which said: 'Mr John Rhead, Factory Manager'.

'Ready?' whispered Mr Higginbotham.

Martha bit her lip. 'As I'll ever be.'

'He won't bite. Just answer his questions. You'll be fine.'

He gave the door a polite knock.

'Come in,' said a deep voice from the other side of the door. They went inside.

The room was much bigger than that belonging to Mr Higginbotham. It didn't surprise her – given he was the big boss. Seeing Mr John in his office made him appear much more important than the odd times he had passed through the Decorating Shop. He was wearing a smart suit with a white shirt and dark tie. When he came through the Shop, he always wore a brown overall to keep his posh clothes clean. He was in his late thirties, his dark hair tinged with light grey about his ears.

His office was wood-panelled too, and overlooked the courtyard. The evening sun spread a comfortable orange glow into the room.

Mr Higginbotham introduced her. Mr John surprised her by shaking her hand. Mr Higginbotham went on to explain their presence and Martha's request.

Mr John gave Martha a wry smile. 'I imagine Mr Higginbotham here has informed you that our top painters are men?'

'Yes, he has, Mr John, but I believe that you should allow women to paint all the ware that the men do. After all, there are lots of women artists, aren't there?'

'Oh, is that so. Do you think that other skilled jobs like modelling and mould-making should be done by women as well?'

'I don't see why not. It's not heavy work, but you have to learn how to do it properly.'

Mr John rubbed his chin.

'Miss Owen has brought some of her work to show you.'

They spent time looking at her work and talking and after a stuttering start Martha gave a brief description of each piece, gradually becoming more animated as she warmed to it.

He looked keen and listened intently to what she had to say.

'You've put a lot of effort into it, Miss Owen. I can see you're passionate about your work. Why don't you leave it with me? I need time to think about it. There's a couple of people I'll need to talk to before I make up my mind.'

Martha arrived home buzzing with excitement that evening. She didn't want to tell anybody just yet in case it didn't happen, but the thought that she might get the chance to go to college in September was delightful.

Daniel was alone in the front room of Park Terrace when she joined him. She closed the heavy wooden door behind her so they could talk freely.

'You look happy.'

'I am. You'll never believe what happened today.' Before he could open his mouth, she told him of the events of the afternoon.

'That's really good news. At least you've made a start, and that's often the hardest part.'

They sat in silence for a few moments and then, in a low voice, she asked the question she was dreading. 'How're you getting on with your plans for Canada?'

'Quite well. I sent a letter to the Canadian Embassy in London asking about the schemes they're offering, and it looks really promising. They're mostly for farming in exchange for free passage to Canada. I could even get a chance to buy some government land at a very reduced price, with a mortgage at a low rate of interest to be paid off over twenty-five years.'

'Oh, that sounds like ages.'

'It is, but at the end it'll be my land and my home. Better than paying the rent man every week.

'To get the free passage, I'll have to spend two years on a Canadian farm learning all about farming. Evidently, there are several specialists in areas such as dairy and crop-growing, and they'll inspect my progress. Classes are held in some of the large towns, like Halifax, where I can learn the technical side of farming an' all. So, if all this goes through, both of us could be doing some learning over the next few years.'

'Sounds wonderful. What happens next?'

'I've filled in the application forms and posted them to the Canadian Embassy, along with my army information. They'll no doubt check my service history and then, hopefully, I'll get a letter telling me if I've been successful.'

'That's amazing, Daniel. I didn't think you were that far with yer planning. Have you told the rest of the family yet?'

'No, but Grandma's probably seen some of the letters, when I haven't managed to get to them first.'

'It must cost a lot to get to Canada, so they must be keen on getting people out there.'

'From what I've read, most of the immigration into Canada has been to the industrial cities, and farming's missed out. It's a massive country and they are wanting to expand the population. It's probably worth the cost of a free passage to get people out there. Most of the land is out in the Prairies, as they call them. If you look on the map, you'll see that just one of these Prairie Provinces is five times bigger than Britain. It's supposed to be very good for growing wheat, which everyone wants for bread-making and, I suppose, pie-making. So perhaps one day Mother'll be making pies with flour I've grown.'

They laughed at that.

'But are you sure it's what yer want? It sounds exciting, but also a little bit frightening.'

'I'm as sure as I can be. Calum, the Canadian soldier I told yer about, said I'd feel at home because Nova Scotia looks a lot like Scotland, but as I've never seen Scotland that was not much help. He said Nova Scotia has a nicer climate and the land's very good for dairy and beef cattle. All he had to say about the Prairie Provinces was they are very warm in the summer and very, very cold in the winter. In some places there's snow on the ground from September to April.'

'You said you'd have to spend two years on a farm – would you be able to do that at Calum's farm, or would it have to be done in the Prairies?'

'No, I could do it in Nova Scotia if Calum's father is willing to sponsor me; after all, he owns the farm. But at this stage,

I'm hoping I can spend a few weeks with them before I have to decide. Back to your news, Martha. Has your Mr John given you any idea of when he'll let you know his decision?'

'He wants to talk to a few people first. It's a big step to send a woman on a ceramic painting course cos women are generally not employed to do the best ware. But he was impressed with my work, so I'm keeping my fingers crossed. They lost a couple of painters during the war, and Eddie, of course—'

'At the park, you mentioned a bloke called Jonas who was in this line of work. You said he was waiting to be demobbed. Do you write to each other then?'

'I wrote to tell him about Eddie, and we've exchanged letters on a few occasions since. He told me the RASC was going to be demobbed slower that the rest of the army because of all the equipment.'

'I'm not surprised. Everywhere yer looked there were vehicles, carts and loads of packing cases with who-knows-what in them.' He looked at her keenly. 'And when you see him, what's going to be your reaction?'

Martha felt her cheeks burn as Daniel's questions kept coming. 'What d'yer mean?'

'Do you think there might be a reason why your face has gone all red?'

Her whole face grew even hotter. 'I don't think of him in that way, Daniel. He's told me a lot about painting – that's all.'

'Ah,' Daniel winked.

'I've told yer. I'm determined to make a life for myself. If I do get to go to art school, I'll have to hold down a job as well as attend evening classes. I won't have time for any romantic entanglements. I never want to be in the same position as Mother. I'll decide what I want to do for myself.'

'You'd put your job before romance?'

'Yes. He'd have to allow me to work and even when we had children, I should be able to choose to work if I want to, and he would have to be prepared to wait for marriage until at least the end of my studies.'

'A saint, in other words.'

'No, Daniel, just an understanding man, and if I can't find him I'd rather be alone.'

'Well, don't hold out too long. I'm not speaking from experience, but common sense tells me that we were not meant to live alone in this world. Once you're able to spend time together you will know which path you want to follow.'

—

Two weeks later, Martha had another letter from Jonas waiting for her when she returned home.

14 June 1919

Dear Martha,

At long last I am on my way home and this time it's for good! I was beginning to think the day would never come. I was in our depot near to Rheims when the sergeant told me I was being demobbed. He handed me my papers. My last assignment was to drive myself and fifteen other demobilised men to the Dispersal Centre in Rouen and await orders. We arrived in Rouen, but we had a spot of bad luck. Some of the men were showing signs of flu and we were all sent to an isolation hut until we were given the all clear. It was pretty bad in there and a good few men in the camp didn't make it. I will be glad to get on my way again.

We have been told to expect transport to the docks tomorrow and I will be transferred to Harrowby in Lincolnshire. That is the Dispersal Centre for Stafford-shire. Don't ask me why — it's the army.

Believe it or not, I found myself singing this morning when I had a wash and shave.

Martha chuckled as she read. He sounded in a different frame of mind than Daniel, thank goodness. She tried to picture him in the bathroom, having a shave and trying to sing. What he said was true – only happy people sing while trying to shave – although it wasn't necessarily a good idea!

> *It feels good to do normal things again. I will spend a few days at Harrowby, probably three or four, and then it's back to The Potteries. I can almost taste the oatcakes and it feels good.*
>
> *I shall have a month's leave before getting back to work. Vera has told me you're getting on well and are thinking of going to night school. That is good news. I am looking forward to seeing how your work has progressed since I last saw you. Perhaps we could get together during that time to talk about night school and look at your work. I will write to you when I am back in The Potteries, and we can arrange a date.*
>
> *That's all for now. Here's to getting back to England – and sanity.*
>
> *Regards,*
>
> *Jonas*

Martha was longing to show him the same artwork she had shown to Mr John, and other ideas inspired by the spring flowers in the park – to show she had listened to his advice. Most of it was drawing. Jonas had told her she needed a steady hand and one way of practising was to draw with a brush as if it was a pencil, with lines of varying thickness, just as they did in school. Being in total control of the brush – or the pencil as they called it at work – would be the key to her future.

She had practised whenever she could, taking paper and pencil with her on some of her walks and drawing what she saw. She enjoyed sitting alone, taking in the industrial land-scape around her, growing to know more about the six towns surrounding her than she ever thought possible. Yes, when Jonas got back, she would enjoy showing him some of her work inspired by the world around her. She thought he would welcome that.

Daniel's talk about Jonas was on her mind constantly as she worked. It led her to wonder if she was about to start walking the same road with Jonas as she had with Jeffrey, mistaking his helpfulness as summat more than it was.

–

Martha received a letter a few days later confirming that Jonas would meet her at the clock tower on Sunday at two o'clock. Today was Monday – she had nearly a full week to prepare herself.

Martha was busily sorting through all her work on the dining table. Issy entered, carefully avoiding the sheets of paper lying on the floor.

'Can I come in?'

'Yes, but be careful, don't move anything… please.'

'What on earth are you doing?'

'I'm sorting out my work, ready to show to Mr Gray. It's about me going to art school and he wants to see my work.'

'When's this going to happen? I'll get Michael to bring around the horse and cart to move all this stuff down to Paradise Pottery – you'll need it.'

'He's coming here to see it and I want to make sure I show him my best work.'

'This Mr Gray you're talking about wouldn't have the Christian name of Jonas, by any chance?'

'Yes, but it's to do with work. He needs to see how I've improved since he last saw me.'

Issy, looking down at her sister's ample bosom, said, 'I think he'll be very pleased at your progress.'

'Don't be coarse. It's nothing like that. I told you, it's work.'

'What are yer going to wear? Your work clothes?'

'If you're not going to be serious then get out!'

'Come on, Martha, I'm only joking. I've never seen yer so het up about a man before.'

'It's important to me.'

'Sorry, so what are you going to wear?'

'I thought my long grey skirt and that nice white—'

'And look like a Sunday school teacher!' Issy thought for a moment. 'I think your light blue dress and a matching scarf. We could shorten it to the latest length.'

Martha stared at Issy for a moment and then gave her a massive hug.

—

Thankfully it was a glorious summer's day. Martha arrived at the clock tower a few minutes early. She couldn't believe how nervous she was. Would Jonas travel down on the tram, or follow his normal route to work? She placed herself where she could see both the tram stop and Summerbank Road and waited.

'Hello, Martha.'

She spun round to face him. The years he'd given to the army had added character to his face. There were lines around his eyes she hadn't seen before. A little older, and slimmer than she remembered. She couldn't take her eyes off him. 'Hello, Jonas, it's good to see you.'

'Good to see you an' all. I never thought I would be so glad to see this place. It's changed a bit now the pub's gone. Your mother's shop is looking very nice. Is it doing well?'

Martha glanced towards the shop and the upper floor windows. Sure enough, two faces stared back at her, smiling.

'I thought you could come to Park Terrace, I've laid everything out in the dining room, if that's all right with you?'

Martha turned towards the Town Hall and they began to walk.

'That's a nice shade of blue, it suits you.'

'Thank you. I've worn it before.'

'Yes, I remember. It was the last time we met before I went to France.'

They talked casually until they arrived at the door. Grandma must have been watching as the door opened immediately. 'Come in, you two. Nice to see you, Mr Gray.'

He shook Grandma's hand. 'Jonas, please. I'm not used to being called anything else.'

'Nay, lad. I bet in the army you were called summat else. Like "hey you, you horrible little soldier".'

Martha sighed. That had to be Grandad, he always had some little joke ready.

Martha steered Jonas towards the dining room.

'Sorry about Grandad. He likes his little jokes.'

'Not to worry. He's right, I have been called a lot of things.'

'Are you looking forward to going back to work?'

'Oh yes, I've missed it so much as there aren't many jobs where you get paid for doing something you love. But I'm concerned how I'll feel when I'm stuck inside all day, after years of being outside. It'll come as a bit of a shock, but at least I won't be shot at. Once the Armistice was signed and we had a bit more freedom, it was a pleasure to be outside. When the spring came and I saw parts of France which hadn't been touched by the war. It was so beautiful. I could see how it came to provide inspiration to artists throughout the centuries. You should see it, Martha, the colours and the light.'

'I would like to see it one day, but I think I'll have to paint an awful lot of pots to afford it.'

'Yer never know what's going to happen in the future. I remember you saying your brother was over there. Dare I ask if he's back yet?'

'Oh, yes, and he's back – but he can't seem to settle.'

'He worked down the pit, didn't he?'

'Yes, he came home earlier as part of the scheme to get miners back underground.'

'I remember I transported several groups back to the port. I might even have transported him.'

'He's talking of doing summat different but hasn't said, or won't say, what yet.' Martha thought it was up to Daniel who he told.

'I can understand that. The war does funny things to yer mind. It changes you.' Jonas went quiet.

She put a tentative hand on his arm. 'And you, Jonas – what about you?'

He shrugged. 'My mind fills up sometimes with pictures I can't get rid of. I try to shake them off – but they won't always go. Early days yet, I suppose. Any road, how's yer painting coming along?'

At that point Grandma knocked politely and entered with a tray of tea and home-made cake.

'Thanks, Grandma. You should have shouted me; I would have brought it through myself.'

'That's all right, duckie.'

Martha tried to hide a smile as Grandma was clearly checking on Jonas as she poured out the tea and offered him a slice of cake.

'Now then, have yer got everything yer need?'

She had still not taken her eyes off Jonas, who squirmed a little under her scrutiny.

'Wilma!' came Grandad's rough voice from the kitchen. 'Come out of there and leave the pair of them alone.'

'Yer grandad dunner know how to treat guests. You'd never think as he'd run a pub all his life, would yer, Mr Gray?'

Without waiting for an answer, Grandma shook her head as she went out of the room leaving an embarrassed Martha to fill her own cup.

Martha cleared her throat and resumed their conversation. 'My painting's coming on very well. I've been practising that hard I haven't got enough hours in the day.'

Jonas laughed.

She stopped talking and stared into his eyes. She told him about her meeting with Mr John, and that she thought it had gone well. Now she was waiting for his answer. 'He said he wanted to have a word with someone before he made his decision.'

'I dare say I'll hear all about it when I get back. Mr John wrote to me. He said I was not to think of work or visit the potbank until the day I return to work. He thought I'd need the rest.'

They moved over to the dining table and began to look through her work. He took up the sheets and scrutinised them, one after the other, not saying a word. The ticking of the clock on the sideboard grew louder with each minute that passed until she wanted to say something, anything, to break the silence and reduce the sound of the clock.

At last, it was over.

He kept his eyes on the last drawing. It was of him, working. She hadn't shown it to anyone, for obvious reasons.

'It's me.'

She grinned. 'It's just summat I did quickly. To make yer laugh. I thought as yer might want cheering up on your first day back.'

He dragged his eyes from the drawing and back to her face. She wasn't quite sure, but she thought she saw a tear in the corner of his eye. It was her turn to look away. 'You can keep it if yer like.'

'But yer might need it – to show people what yer can do.'

'It doesn't matter. I can do another one.' She didn't tell him that she had committed his face to her mind and could probably draw it again with her eyes closed.

He turned away and coughed to clear his throat.

'So, you're still determined to go to art school to study ceramic painting then?'

'More than anything else in the world. I'm nearly twenty-one, Jonas. If I don't do it now, I may never get the chance. You do understand, don't yer?'

He nodded. 'These are very good, Martha. You've come on a lot as a paintress while I've been away. I'm just not sure that painting course is right for yer.'

Her heart sank. She'd been so convinced he would be pleased for her.

'I'm thinking of asking Mr John to put you on the general ceramic course – the same one I did.'

Her frown was immediately replaced by a look of incredulousness, rapidly followed by a smile that stretched from ear to ear.

'You mean me – training as a modeller?'

He smiled and nodded. 'Don't sound so shocked. You're good. The art in ceramics is to receive an idea, or request for a piece of work, to draw it out, paint it and make a model of it. Only at that stage will we see the result and, if all goes well, a new piece will be added to the range.'

She kept shaking her head. 'I can't take it in, Jonas. Why me?'

'Like I said, you're good. You can say it's a bit of advanced planning. Two of the modellers are coming up to retirement, so we'll need new modellers and they don't grow on trees.'

Martha brought her hands up to her face. 'Do yer really think as I can do it?'

'I wouldn't have suggested it to you if I didn't have confidence in your abilities. But you need to be fully committed. It'll take three years, and Mr Cyril asked me to agree to stop at Paradise Pottery for three more years after that.'

'Why?'

'It's only fair. What if they are paying for you to attend and then you leave and get a better-paid job at a place like Jackson's, who don't train anybody? Jackson's and the like then get the benefit of our company's investment.'

'I wouldn't want to work anywhere else.'

'In your case, Mr John will also have concerns about you getting married and leaving to have children. People can control when they marry, but not when they have children. Most men don't want to see their wives working and assume that marriage will give them a servant for life.'

'Yes, my father was like that.'

'That's why you don't see many women modellers, designers or painters. I've been painting for seven years, but I wasn't as good as Eddie. He said he was always learning.'

'You're saying that if I want to go on this course I have to be prepared to wait for marriage and children until I'm twenty-seven.'

'Yes.'

'I can do that. I have always said I am not interested in men. I won't give a man control over my life like Mother gave to Father.' It was time to describe her ideal man and see what he had to say. 'My ideal man would have to be happy with me going to work and having a career of my own. He wouldn't stand in my way when I wanted to better myself. He would have to be considerate in marriage, and if children did come along, be happy to help in their upbringing.'

He whistled. 'A long list! I think you'll take longer than seven years to find a man fitting those criteria.'

'Jonas, I am fully committed to my career. I know I'm setting very high standards, but I've resigned myself to a single life. Even more now with the tragic loss of men during the war. I won't be the only one – I fear.'

Martha heard the front door open and close and, moments later, Daniel entered the room. She introduced him to Jonas and the pair reminisced about their wars and talked about their plans. Daniel mentioned nothing about Canada, just that he wanted to do something different.

Jonas left shortly after that. It was a rather dazed Martha that returned to the kitchen to tell everyone that she might be going to Burslem School of Art in September to study ceramics with a view to becoming a modeller for Paradise Pottery.

Chapter Twenty-seven

July 1919

Martha walked up Paradise Street. It had been a lovely day and she was still in her work clothes and pinnie. She hadn't bothered with a coat. Issy was still serving people in the shop when Martha got there.

'Hiya, Issy.'

'Hi, Martha, Mother's upstairs and I've got to serve these customers. I'll be up when I've shut.'

Martha climbed the stairs. Mother was sitting in her usual chair looking out over the square. 'You look thoughtful.'

Mother turned towards Martha and beckoned her to shut the door.

'What's the matter?'

'Have a look at this letter. It's from Captain Munro.'

Martha gave a little involuntary squeak. She read the letter to herself.

21 June 1919

Dear Mrs Owen,

At long last I have been able to resolve the situation we talked about over two years ago. It appears that the soldier who was using your former husband's details was a deserter who had assumed your husband's identity to avoid being punished on his return. As a result, the army endorses its original view that Sgt Major Percy Owen died on the 12 January 1915 in the service of his country.

*I understand that this may not be the news you were
expecting and offer you your country's condolences at your
sacrifice.*

*This department is being wound down. However, you
can contact the War Office at any time should the need
arise.*

Assuring you of our best attention at all times.

Yours sincerely,

Captain D. Munro

They looked at each other, saying nothing, not wanting to take
any risk that Issy might hear what was going on. Mother asked
Martha to take the letter with her and keep it somewhere safe.

'It looks as if it's all sorted out.'

'Yes, I think it probably is, although I don't suppose we'll
ever know for sure.'

Martha left, hardly able to take it in. The long saga was now
over.

–

The day Jonas walked back into Paradise Pottery was a special
one. He was the last of the men to return. Mr John collected all
the workers in the yard. He said a few words and then asked for
a minute's silence for the fallen. When Martha looked around,
she could see in her mind the faces of the men who would never
return, the widows and mothers who were mourning the loss
of husbands and sons, no matter where they worked. Mr John
said he'd be placing a plaque with the names of the dead of
Paradise Pottery in the reception area as a lasting memory of
their sacrifice.

–

Martha woke up on Sunday morning knowing that today
was going to be a sad one for their family. Daniel had been

accepted onto his scheme. Yesterday he received a large brown envelope with all the necessary papers. His boat would sail from Southampton on 6 August and should arrive in Halifax on the fourteenth.

Daniel promised he would break the news to everyone after dinner and warned her to look suitably surprised. She thought she was the only one who knew. She suspected Grandma would have been intrigued at the large envelope and would've inspected the postmark. Martha laughed to herself as a picture rose in her mind of Grandma trying to steam the letter open.

After dinner, just like the time when Grandad announced he was going to retire from the pub, there was a tapping on an empty beer bottle and Daniel stood up. Martha had to admit that he handled the situation very well. He explained what he had been feeling since coming back from the war and his dislike of working down the pit. Although the faces around the table betrayed their feelings, they were either too shocked or too respectful to interrupt.

When he announced that he'd be leaving home to travel to Southampton on the 4 August to make a new life for himself in Canada, there was complete silence.

Issy got to her feet and walked purposefully around to Daniel. Martha thought she was going to hit him. Instead, she put her arms around him and gave him a big tearful hug.

'I wish you all the best. I may be the youngest, but I saw the Daniel that came back from the war was not the same as the Daniel that went. I could tell, and I am fairly sure that all of us expected something, but perhaps not this.'

Martha felt like crying. She didn't know which upset her more, Daniel's decision to leave or Issy's speech.

For the rest of the afternoon the family talked, asking Daniel all manner of questions. Martha was surprised Mother had taken it so well. She learned later that Grandma had told her about the envelope so she was prepared for something to happen.

A smartly dressed woman walked through the Decorating Shop. She didn't look at, or speak to, anyone but they all knew it was Miss Emily Norton, Mr John's new spinster secretary. Martha thought that, likely as not, she was nervous in walking through a shop full of people where all the chatting suddenly became a whisper at the entry of a newcomer. As an office worker, she would be used to working alone. Word had it that she had been a secretary to the manager of one of the tram depots, but had to give it up when the war ended and the men came back.

Miss Norton knocked on the door and walked into Mr Higginbotham's office. The chatting started up again when there was a realisation that nothing exciting was happening.

Moments later Mr Higginbotham called across the shop, 'Martha — can you go with Miss Norton? Mr John wants a word with you.'

The whole shop went quiet. All heads turned towards her. She took a deep breath and walked confidently over to where Miss Norton was waiting. Together, the two women left the shop and heard the gossip start up as the door closed behind them.

Miss Norton was quiet and nervous from what Martha could see. She barely spoke as they walked side by side until they arrived outside Mr John's door. She must've picked up on Martha's anxious face because Miss Norton patted her arm.

'It'll be all right, Miss Owen. You've nothing to worry about. Ready?'

Martha nodded.

Miss Norton knocked and walked in. Martha followed.

'Here is Martha Owen, Mr John.'

He smiled. 'Ah, Miss Owen, take a seat, please.' It was only when Miss Norton smiled and left that Martha saw Jonas sitting in one of the two chairs at the desk.

Mr John got to his feet. 'I've asked Jonas here for a reason, which I'll come on to in a moment. What we are about to discuss is strictly confidential and must not leave this room.'

Then why was she there? thought Martha. She had assumed it was about her art school request.

Mr John began. 'My father is retiring from the company tomorrow and I will be taking over. Also, Mr Abel Lodge, our chief designer, is retiring at the same time. We have appointed Jonas Gray to the job, which is why he's here today.'

She knew she was grinning from ear to ear, but she couldn't help it.

'As a consequence, we will be short-handed in the modelling room. You gave me something to think about when you came to see me… and, of course, I had to speak to Jonas before I could decide on the right way to approach matters. I believe he's spoken to you briefly?'

She sat with her hands holding each other on her lap. It helped her to concentrate. She nodded and waited for him to continue.

'I was very impressed with your work. I have no doubt that your painting skills are highly satisfactory. You are quite a capable young lady. Having discussed the matter with Jonas, my proposal is that you would benefit from instruction on art and ceramic design rather than painting. We want you to move to the modelling room to work with Jonas to update our pattern book with exciting new designs. At present, our order book is looking healthy, but we must prepare for the future – the sooner the better. To do this, Jonas will need a skilled assistant.'

Martha fidgeted in her chair, barely able to contain herself. To work with Jonas and learn from him would be the icing on the cake. She couldn't wait to say, 'Yes, please.'

'We would, of course, pay for your training, which would require you to attend Burslem School of Art for three years for three evenings per week. It will be hard work but, I think you'll agree, it'll be worth it. However, given the commitment we are showing, we would require you to sign an undertaking that you would remain with us for three years after the end of the course. If you do leave, you will be required to repay the money.'

'Oh, thank you, Mr John.' She felt a glow inside. She'd had some compliments recently but these from Mr John pleased her no end.

'The new intake to the School of Art begins in early September. It seems you have fallen lucky, Miss Owen. So, we will move you to work with Mr Gray after the Potters' holiday. You will be paid a day rate equivalent to your current earnings and your wages will increase substantially as you gain experience. We shall review your work in six months.'

'Oh, Mr John! Thank you ever so much! This is so much better than I could ever have dreamed of.'

'Do I take it that you will be accepting the job?'

'You bet I will.'

The two men laughed and Martha was more than happy to join in.

Mr John rose, followed by Jonas and then Martha.

'Jonas will take you through everything from now on. I hope you'll be happy in your new job.'

She was still nodding as she walked out of the room with Jonas following. They walked through the empty offices and out into the street.

'Thank you so much for speaking for me, Jonas.'

She could feel the blushes rise. She was glad he was happy for her. If it hadn't been for him, she doubted she would have come so far.

When she returned from the office the Decorating Shop went silent. Everybody looked towards her. Martha hurried back to her bench and shared with her friends that she was moving to work with Jonas. The rest, she kept to herself as requested. The girls were at once pleased for her but disappointed she would be leaving them. She had sat with the same group of girls since she had become a paintress. They had become friends *because* they sat together and for no other reason. This was normal for pieceworkers. There was no time to socialise. But she would miss them.

—

Daniel left on Wakes Monday. It seemed like a return to the day he went off to war in 1915. This time he was going because he wanted to start a new adventure and a new life whereas before he was heading into danger and possibly the end of that young life. Who knew whether she would see him again?

He held a party for his family and some of his close friends on the Sunday evening at Park Terrace. He said his goodbyes that evening because he had an early start.

Despite Daniel's request that they not get up to see him leave, the whole family were waiting for him in the kitchen when he rose at six o'clock in the morning. Because it was the Potters' holiday, Mother didn't open the shop until later. Issy was holding Andrew who was sleeping. Peter and Cassie stood together, and Grandma and Grandad stood by the range.

Daniel had a word with everyone and then announced it was time to go. They said their goodbyes and he turned to leave.

Martha was putting on her jacket ready for the walk with him to Tunstall station. He didn't object; perhaps he did want a little bit of company at that moment.

'Well, that was a surprise. I should have known you wouldn't stay in bed while I left.'

'Come on, Daniel, we're potbank workers and miners, we're used to early starts.'

'Whose idea was it?'

'Peter's. He said it was wrong to let you leave without saying goodbye. After all it might be the last time we see yer.'

'Let's try to write to each other as often as we can afford, but don't spend all your money on stamps.'

She nodded, feeling tears welling up.

'Dunner cry, Martha, else you'll have me in tears an' all.'

'I'll miss yer so much.'

'And I you. Yer never know, yer might wed a bloke with money in his pockets and then sail out to see me.'

'Chance would be a fine thing.'

'I meant what I said, Martha. Dunner let the chance of happiness pass yer by. Not every bloke's as bad as Father. Yer might even find somebody as good as me.'

He grinned and she punched him back. Not too hard.

His train was on time; he seemed to be the only one getting on at Tunstall. Probably because of the holiday. She waved him goodbye, and he was gone.

Chapter Twenty-eight

It was a bright and cheerful Monday in August when Martha moved into the modelling room, and she couldn't be happier as she walked swiftly to work. She had purposefully set off early because she had to move her belongings into the modelling room and get her bench set up.

With everything packed into a wooden box that previously held large bottles of paint, all she had to do was pick it up and say her goodbyes to her friends, even though she would only be along the corridor and would see them every day.

'Oh, I hope you're doing the right thing, Martha,' said Bridie. 'I thought as you'd be a paintress for ever. It's what you always wanted.'

'And I'm glad I did it – but I've got opportunities I never thought about and I must take them. I have to try.'

'Well, remember we're here, if yer want us.'

'I'm hardly likely to forget. I'll be walking past yer every day.'

Even so, everybody gave her a hug and sent her on her way.

–

Martha, carrying her box of assorted tools, brushes and other tranklements, struggled to open the door to the modelling room. She peered through the window trying to attract attention. One of the old men looked up at her but carried on working.

Annoyed, Martha kicked the bottom of the door with her foot and Jonas, who had been talking to one of the other men, rushed to open it for her.

'Sorry about that, but I had to attract attention. This box is bloomin' heavy.' She said nothing about being ignored – she had to work with these men and complaining on first meeting them would do no good.

Jonas pointed to an empty bench in the corner and told her to get herself settled and he would introduce her to her new colleagues. She glanced around. Only Jonas looked young enough to have his own teeth! She could understand now why Mr John said they would be short of modellers soon.

Martha laid out her bench and sat waiting for Jonas to speak.

'You will probably all know Miss Owen from the Decorating Shop. She will be working with us and attending the Burslem School of Art's ceramics course. I believe—'

'A young lass takin' a man's job? Are yer in yer right mind, Jonas – or has your head been turned by a pretty face.'

'Dunner know whether you're joking or not, George, but we'll have less of that talk.'

George folded his arms, but his mouth remained shut.

'Martha will be learning from all of us and I hope you treat her well.' Jonas turned to introduce her to George Longshaw, Levi Cohen and Enoch Walmsley.

'Now, let's get to work.'

-

A sharp knocking on the door of the modelling room made Martha jump.

'What the bl—'

'Language, Enoch. Lady present,' piped up Levi.

'Typical. See, this is what happens when yer give men's jobs to women,' sneered George.

Seeing Bridie's face lurking through the glass in the door, Martha hurried to speak to her, muttering apologies as she went.

She slipped through the door.

'What is it, Bridie?'

'I had ter tell yer. They've just given me your old job. I'm going to be painting from next week. So, I hope as you'll settle in and not want it back again.'

Martha gave her friend a hug, but her mind was on George Longshaw. She hoped, for all their sakes, she didn't need it back again because he was making her life difficult. She needed a plan to overcome his dislike. She couldn't allow Jonas to jump to her defence each time she had a problem.

—

At dinnertime, Martha visited the butcher's on the High Street. Bridie was courting a young man, Raymond, who went to war in 1914 and returned to his job at the butcher's in 1919. His job suited him perfectly and he could often be caught singing in the back of the shop as he worked with his cleaver.

'That'll be three shillings, Martha. Hear your brother's gone to Canada.'

'Daniel wanted to get away from the pits and try something new. He had a bad time in Flanders. It must have been bad for you an' all, Ray, cos you were there all the way through.'

'Once they knew what my job was they put me into the catering corps, gave me a rifle and an apron. Cooking meals for whoever was around to eat them. That was my war. Never shot my rifle in anger. Only had to dodge shells on odd occasions, and that was usually a mistake. Worst thing what happened was when a German aeroplane came over and dropped a bomb. It landed in a big boiler of porridge and exploded. The porridge was so thick it muffled the bomb and blew porridge everywhere.' He chuckled to himself.

Martha could never tell when he was joking so she played safe. 'Well, I'm sure Bridie's glad to have yer back.'

–

At knocking-off time, Jonas walked up Paradise Street with Martha and filled her in about her colleagues.

'George Longshaw was not very kind to you this morning. He's like that with everybody, but I'll keep an eye on him. He was none too keen on me when I started. He doesn't like change.'

'I'll make allowances for him an' all, but working on piece-work has taught me to look after meself.'

'Levi Cohen's a nice man. He's good at his job and unlike George rarely complains. He'll help you if you ask him. That leaves Enoch Walmsley. He's like Levi, but his arthritis is getting bad. Mr John is going to find him somewhere else to work unless he wants to retire.'

'Mr John never asked me about my plans. Did you speak to him about what we talked about?'

'I assured him of your commitment and outlined your plans generally and he was happy to take my word.'

'So, if I get married, he'll blame you.'

'Yes, unless I get married to you.'

'Is this a proposal?'

Jonas went red – he stuttered out a resounding 'No', and then said, 'Sorry, that sounded a bit harsh. I just meant—'

'It's all right, Jonas – I'm pulling your leg.'

They both laughed and continued to chat until Martha went into the shop.

–

At last, they received a postcard from Daniel. It had taken him nearly two weeks to complete his journey from Tunstall to Milford Station. Martha felt she could relax now she knew he was on dry land again. The card was short but gratefully received.

17 August 1919

Dear all,
    Just to let you know I have arrived safely at Calum's home. Very warm welcome. Will write soon.
    Love, Daniel

On the front of the postcard there was a photograph of the centre of Halifax.

Part Three

Chapter Twenty-nine

It was with great delight that Martha set off from Paradise Street to enrol at Burslem School of Art in Queen Street in early September. Emily had completed and delivered all the paper-work to the school. All Martha had to do was enrol and provide her personal details. She was told there would be assessments and reviews each year and an exhibition at the end of the course to which local dignitaries and manufacturers were invited. It was a showcase for the students' talent and to show employers their money had not been wasted. For those not yet employed in the industry, there was the possibility of getting a job at its conclusion.

Martha had plenty to think about on her way home. For the first time she realised that she was taking a step which she hoped would ultimately lead to designing ware and the security of a trade. But there was a long way to go.

—

Martha walked from Park Terrace to the Wedgwood Institute, where the School of Art was based, a matter of three miles. She could have used the tram but decided that the walk would give her a chance to think about that evening. It had been agreed with Jonas that, on college days, she would start to work earlier in the morning and leave at five o'clock.

The Wedgwood Institute was a magnificent building of two storeys of red brick, with several windows with castellated turrets and a coat of arms. Martha had walked past it many times but hadn't really taken it in. Now, she was going inside and would be learning in this amazing building. She glanced up and let her eyes take in the wonder of it all before she opened the great doors and slipped inside. She was told to go to the door at the end of the corridor. When she opened it there were a number of people inside, mainly men around her age and older.

'Right, students, please be seated.'

He stood by a table waiting until the noise had stopped.

'My name is Mr Wingate and I will be one of your tutors during this first year. I will ask you all in turn to introduce yourselves, not just to me but to your fellow students. I do recognise some of you from before the war, and am very pleased to see you here tonight.'

When it came to Martha's turn, she took a deep breath and spoke as confidently as she was able to a room full of people she had never seen before. 'Hello, me name's Martha Owen, I work at C. Rhead & Son in Tunstall. You may know it as Paradise Pottery.'

Her fellow students seemed to represent most of the big pottery manufacturers locally including Royal Doulton, Royal Edward, Wedgwood, Spode and Minton. The list went on and she was part of it. A thrill of anticipation ran through her.

Mr Wingate continued. 'In this class you'll learn all the skills relevant to decoration and finishing in the ceramic industry – more than you ever thought possible to know about the humble clay we use to practise our art. Techniques of decoration, including brushes and brushwork, colour work. You'll need a good eye and a steady hand. You will develop the skills to draw and paint what you see. You will become fed up with drawing line after line for hours on end until you can produce perfection, not once, but every time. Once you have shown you have these skills, and only then, will you be allowed to work on the ware.'

He paused for breath. Martha swallowed. He was committed to his craft; she had no doubt at that. His intenseness was spellbinding. She glanced across the room, smiling to witness the same awe on the faces of all the students.

'You will now pick up a pencil and paper and choose something to draw from the shelf at the back of the room. I want to check the dexterity of your hands.'

The students got up from their seats and moved to pick up the necessary equipment. She was glad she had been able to practise before going to the college, and concentrated on the small vase she had picked up, studying it intensely, taking in the light and shade and the pattern etched within the clay.

'Miss Owen, you haven't drawn anything yet. Do you need assistance?'

Mr Wingate was standing at her shoulder.

'Er… no. I'm looking at how the patterns could be made interesting in black and white.'

'It's fairly… nondescript, isn't it. What colours would you work in if you were to paint it?'

'Bright. Bold. A more interesting pattern. I think people are after summat that makes them smile, these days.'

'Mm, I see. Well, you'll have an opportunity to put it into practice next week.'

She stared at him and then down at the empty sheet of paper.

'I suggest, Miss Owen, that you commit pencil to paper, lest you are not prepared for next week's class.'

She smiled at the thought of learning. That, after all, was why she'd come here. 'Yes Mr Wingate.'

–

The next day, Jonas asked how her first class had gone.

'There were three other girls. The rest were men. I counted sixteen in total. It was a little sad in some ways – three of the men were about my age and clearly had artificial limbs and one man only had one eye.'

'At least they've returned.'

'Yes. I thought about Eddie. He would have been pleased to see me there.'

'And there are four women on the course. When I was there it was all men. Same everywhere, Martha. Women do the decorating. Men do the painting. It's beginning to change but it takes time.'

She told him what Mr Wingate had said about her taking time to plan out her drawing.

He laughed. 'Sounds like Old Windy. He can be a bit sarky, but he only does it to those he thinks he can work with. Consider it a compliment.'

She thought Jonas was joking but, as the classes continued, she watched Mr Wingate and, true enough, he did talk mainly to those he seemed to be encouraging, offering his advice and getting them to explain the why, as well as the how, of art.

Martha's world had begun to change since obtaining support to study from Mr John. She had begun to find her way about the modelling room and had painted several of the models being worked on by the others. They said she needed the training, but she knew they thought her painting was the best.

As the autumn evenings grew darker, Martha made the most of it. She enjoyed being in the modelling room and her three evenings a week at the art school. It kept her busy. She enjoyed going in to work and discussing her ideas with Jonas. She had spent some of her wages on pencils and brushes and stayed late at work – on the two evenings she was not at art school putting into practice some of the techniques she had been studying that week. She particularly liked drawing patterns on the large holloware pieces for the paintresses to finish off. In one class, they were learning about decorating, both the practical techniques she was good at and the theory, which was complicated. Jonas was only too willing to help her.

13 September 1919

Dear Martha,

I hope you are well and enjoying your course. I always knew you could do it, and Paradise Pottery seems to think so as well. I am proud of you.

Can you pass my best wishes on to all the family? I will send you all the letters in the future in one envelope and you can give them out. It's cheaper that way.

I've discovered I hate sailing, by the way. The ship was basic and cramped but landed at Halifax after two weeks. I was seasick for the first two days but once we got out into the ocean, I seemed to get used to the constant rocking. After leaving Southampton, we called in at Le Havre in France, where I landed back in 1915, and Queenstown in Ireland. Most people on the ship were heading for a new life away from the destruction and carnage of Europe. There seemed to be people from every country. I also met some Germans and we found out we had probably faced each other in 1917.

Once at Halifax, I spent two nights in a hostel while my papers were checked and prepared and, just like the army, I was given a medical. They are still concerned about the Spanish Flu but thankfully, I had a clean bill of health.

I hope you received my postcard. I wanted you to have a picture of where I was going to call home. Lots of places over here are named after towns in England and Scotland.

Milford Station is a small town with mainly settlers from Scotland. Most have been here since the middle of the last century. The farm is about ten miles out of town in a valley facing north-west, which means we will get more snow in the winter.

Calum's family are really nice. They were born and bred in Nova Scotia, but his grandparents came from

Sutherland. I felt really embarrassed when he had to show me where it was on a map of Scotland. His grandfather had told him that the countryside in Nova Scotia was very much like Sutherland.

Their farm is an average size, but you still need a horse to get around.

Calum has two brothers older than him. The elder one, David, was killed at Vimy Ridge, but the younger one, Rory, came through the war. He also has a sister, Catriona, about Issy's age. All the family work on the farm. Mr MacLeod, Calum's father, also runs the town's sawmill.

I have a room at the top of the house, and it is amazing to wake up in the morning to fresh air. It overlooks the hills which are starting to turn purple with heather as the autumn sets in. Another spectacular sight are the trees. I have never seen so many colours as the leaves get ready to drop.

I know it is early days, but in the short time I've been here I think working on the land will be considerably better than working under it.

My two years officially start at the beginning of October. I'm looking forward to it, but with some trepidation. Will I make a farmer?

Your loving brother,
Daniel

Martha was so pleased to hear from him, and a little surprised at his words as Daniel had never seen the countryside, let alone wanted to live in it. She replied to his letter telling him all the news, but especially her news about the first weeks at art school.

Chapter Thirty

Martha couldn't believe she was about to enter the party for her twenty-first birthday. It had come along so quickly. It wasn't so long ago that Cassie had been talking about her own. At that time, twenty-one had seemed old to Martha. But now it had caught up with her, she didn't feel any different.

Her birth date was yesterday but today, Saturday, was a better day for the party so that everyone could be there. Martha had invited Jonas. He had been part of her life for so long, she wanted him there to celebrate with her. Issy could say much the same about Michael, too. He'd been helping in the shop when he had time. The party would be at Park Terrace where there would be enough room for everyone. Mother and Grandma agreed that both men would be welcome.

Peter and Cassie arrived at four o'clock with little Andrew. Cassie volunteered her help while Andrew slept through the early evening and Peter caught up with Grandad.

Once everything was laid out to Grandma's satisfaction, Martha and Issy disappeared upstairs to get themselves ready. Issy had brought clothes to change into so there was no chance of anything spilling over her best dress. The girls would also dress each other's hair.

Martha had treated herself to a new dress, wanting to make an impression on Jonas. She hadn't realised how important this was to her until she had seen the very dress she was looking for – a pale lilac organza, trimmed with deep lilac ribbon and a lace collar. She had never spent so much on a dress before and had felt quite guilty. Wearing it, she felt grown up and, with Jonas on her mind, she knew she had to have it.

Issy whistled as Martha drew the dress out of its bag and hung it on the picture rail. 'Must've cost yer a month's wages. You're definitely wanting to impress Jonas, no matter what you say.'

'I do like him, Issy. I want him to see me, not Martha the paintress who he works with every day.'

'You've changed yer tune.'

Martha flushed. 'He's a very nice man. I've known that all along. I thought I would be happy to have him as a friend. Turns out I might've bin wrong.'

As Issy slipped her head into her dress, a floral cotton, she said, 'I told yer ages ago that wouldn't work. I've seen him a few times now and I've watched the way he looks at yer. He doesn't look at yer as if you were just a friend.'

'When I decided to go to the art school I told him I was committed to my work and that I wasn't interested in having a man in my life. I promised Mr John at work that I would not get married or leave for three years after the course finishes.'

'No one should have the right to make you promise that, Martha. It's not fair.'

Martha shrugged. 'I was desperate to go to art school. Jonas and I have been friends and worked together for only four months. I thought that when he came back from the war everything would continue as it was before.'

'So, what's changed?'

'He has. I have. Oh, it's complicated. Before he went to war, I also told him I wasn't interested in walking out with anybody because I was too young and he seemed to accept that. Since his return, he's not made any advances towards me. Hasn't attempted to kiss me. He hasn't done anything.'

'But you want him to?'

Martha thought. 'Yes, I do.'

'And that's why you've spent a fortune on that dress.'

Martha nodded. 'I wanted to show him that I was a woman, not that seventeen-year-old girl I used to be, who was frightened of the prospect of an older man.' Martha slumped onto the bed. 'Now it's too late. I can't expect him to wait around while I play at painting, can I?'

'First of all, you're not playing at painting. You're a paintress and a very good one. Jonas has seen that and wants to help you achieve it. Most important, he's still with you and he's coming tonight. Does that sound like a man who isn't willing to wait for a woman to make up her mind?'

'I did ask him once what he would think of a wife who wanted to keep her job.'

'What did he say?'

'A woman should have the right to both. She shouldn't have to choose.'

'There you are then. You're worrying about nothing.'

'I'm worrying that he might have changed his mind.'

'You'll never find out sat in this room, will yer?'

The girls walked downstairs together.

Martha opened the door to the sitting room and entered first. Michael had already arrived but there was no sign of Jonas. Issy immediately went to Michael. It was easy to see the admiration in his eyes. She wished she could say the same about Jonas. Perhaps she'd been too forceful. In future she needed to do less talking and more listening.

Just then there was a knock on the door and Martha hurried to get there first. It was a smartly dressed Jonas. With the light of the hall shining on his face, she could see every part of it. His eyes widened as if unable to take in what he saw. Admiration and awe, followed by a wide smile. She returned his smile and bade him enter, taking a deep breath as she closed the door behind him, her face burning with an intensity he must've seen. He was carrying flowers, which he presented to her as she turned to face him.

Looking into his eyes, her stomach turned over. Her body was reacting in a way she hadn't felt before. Each breath she took came quicker than the last. How was she going to get through the evening feeling the way she did now?

She took a breath of the flowers' scent. 'Thank you, Jonas. They're lovely.' She looked into his eyes to find him staring at her as if for the first time.

'Best come into the sitting room and meet everyone,' her voice squeaked.

He followed her and was soon in the midst of her family. She introduced him.

Grandma seemed delighted to see him again and was the first to shake his hand.

'It's good to meet you again, Mrs Parker.'

'Our Martha's been in a bit of a state, I dunner mind telling yer.'

'Grandma!'

Mother shook her head. 'Mother, don't embarrass the girl. It's not every day yer get to be twenty-one.'

'I know that. Her's bin working very hard, and it's about time she enjoyed herself – is all I was going to say.'

Without further ado, Martha introduced Mother, Issy and the rest of the family, feeling very much under scrutiny having never done it before. Would they see her in a different light from now on?

Martha looked at Jonas from underneath her eyelashes. His eyebrows had risen.

'She loves anything arty, don't yer, Martha?' Issy was quick to jump in.

Beginning to think this party was all a mistake, Martha led Jonas over to the table brimming with food. They had managed to buy everything they wanted – even the eggs to make the sponge cakes, which were Peter's favourite.

'I'm sorry about my family, Jonas.'

'Don't be. There's a lot of love in this house. I can feel it.'

She smiled again, wondering if he could feel the love that was trying to burst out of her at that very moment.

There was no doubt about it. She did love him. Perhaps had loved him for a while, except she was too busy with her job and her art classes to give much thought to romance. How could she go against all she'd said to Mr John?, but on the other hand, could she afford to wait until art school was over and then confess her love? There were plenty of surplus women who would happily step into her shoes – was she prepared to take the risk?

Everyone appeared to have a good time. Martha put her questions to the back of her mind, determined to enjoy this party, the one and only time she would be twenty-one. She lapped it up. The rest she would leave to another day.

Another day never seemed to come.

She continued to work comfortably with Jonas. Several times she thought about talking to him but couldn't bring herself to open the conversation. Would he think her too fickle for changing her mind so readily?

Her art school course was going well. She was surprised to find she could understand and master the complicated chemistry if she put her mind to it. Perhaps at school she had not been able to devote all her energies to classwork because of her home life.

She was keeping a careful eye on Jonas for signs of a burgeoning relationship with anyone but, at the moment, he seemed content with his life and happy with their friendship. He made no demands of her. He helped with the academic side of the course, but more and more this assistance was required by Martha as an excuse to be with him, rather than a supplement to her own knowledge and ability.

Chapter Thirty-one

Despite working different hours to her friends, she took the same dinner break when she had the chance. Vera was sitting on her own eating a butty when Martha entered. She headed over and sat down next to her friend.

'What's the matter with you today? You've got a glum look about yer,' Vera said.

'Oh, it's nothing. I've got summat on me mind and it won't go away. It's nowt to do with work. Well, it is – depending on how you look at it.'

'No one can hear. What's the problem?'

'I don't know how to start.'

'Usually, when a girl starts off a conversation, it's about a man. Is it Jonas?'

'I don't know what to do, Vera. I've been pondering about it ever since my birthday.'

At that moment two of the girls from the next bench returned and struck up a conversation with them. As others began to return, Vera whispered, 'We can't talk here. I'll come round to yours in the next day or so and we'll talk then.'

Martha nodded. Yes, that would be better. It would give her time to think what to say without feeling stupid. 'Come for yer tea. Grandma loves a bit of company.'

–

Grandma asked Vera all sorts of questions, while Grandad was happy to sit listening. Once the meal was over, Vera and Martha took a tray of tea and cake into the front room. They sat side by side on the settee, Vera waiting for her to speak. She wasn't going to make it easy, Martha felt.

Martha thought about all she had to say – that Jonas was on her mind all the time, that she had more feelings for him than she had let herself believe back in August, that she was horrified about her feelings after promising to Vera and Mr John, and even Jonas himself, that she aimed to go to college and there was no love in her life that would prevent her from achieving her ambitions. When Jonas had spoken to her of the responsibilities of going to art school and of receiving support from Paradise, she had happily agreed that she did not have a young man, therefore she wasn't about to run off and get married. Neither was she about to have any children. Jonas himself said as it would be embarrassing for both of them if she should change her mind. He had assured Mr John that Martha was dedicated and, on the strength of that recommendation, Mr John took the risk of agreeing to send her on a course which Paradise had never sent a girl on before. 'I can't think how I'm going to resolve it. I feel so foolish—'

'Duckie, it's written all over your face every time he walks into the room.'

Martha covered her burning cheeks and felt tears gathering.

'I shouldn't worry. It's only because I know you so well. Any road, you've discovered you've got feelings for him what you didn't think was there, I gather.'

Martha nodded again. 'I would never have asked to go on the training if I thought me and Jonas…'

'And you would've lost out an' all. Martha dear, when you asked to go to art school, you did so with belief in what you were agreeing to and that's a responsibility, but you can't let it rule your life if your feelings change in the future. I'm saying that as a friend, not as a boss.'

'You don't think I'm not to be trusted?'

'When me and Eddie introduced you two, it was because we felt you'd be good for each other. You got on well and you were both into art. Jonas had a bad time few years ago. He had a young lady – Doreen Wilmott was her name. They'd been to the same school and ended up working at Paradise. Jonas was quiet, took his work seriously and loved drawing. Doreen was different. She enjoyed a good time. Loved going dancing. They were so different it was a wonder they ever got together, but they started walking out. Jonas was earning good money and Eddie thought Doreen wanted to mould him into the man she wanted him to be. Anyway, he decided he was going to ask her to marry him.'

Martha's mouth opened wide. 'I didn't think he was married.'

'He isn't. Never has been. She ran off with some bloke from Royal Edward's potbank and went to live and work somewhere in Longton. It didn't last, and I believe she moved to Manchester. Got a job in a cotton mill. Course, Jonas felt stupid. It took him a bit of time to get over it. Since then, he's never taken no interest in a girl – until you.'

'Poor Jonas. How awful for him.'

'Me and Eddie could see he was interested in yer and decided he needed a bit of help. He wouldn't ask you out cos he knew you were committed to getting to art school. But we both could see he had feelings for yer.'

'But he never said nothing.'

'It's the sort of man he is, duck. He wouldn't put his happiness first.'

Martha was stunned.

'If yer want my opinion, you're both as bad as each other. Talk to him, Martha. He'll listen and will probably be a lot more understanding than you think.'

'Thank you for telling me, Vera. I won't repeat a word, but I'll think about what you've said.'

'One of yer has to say summat, else you'll get nowhere!'

Chapter Thirty-two

January 1920

Martha put a great deal of thought into what she should do about Jonas. Should she really speak to him and tell him of her changed feelings only six months after swearing that it was the job she was interested in? She was floundering – of that she had no doubt. Vera didn't bring up the subject again. She seemed to be letting Martha come to her own decision.

Towards the end of January, Martha received a letter. It came totally out of the blue. She arrived home from work later than usual and went straight in to eat her tea, which Grandma had put on the hob to keep warm. Taking a cup of tea with her, Martha then went up to her room with the typewritten envelope. It looked very official and she opened it carefully. Much to her surprise, it was from Betty Dean.

Her handwriting was far neater than she remembered.

21 January 1920

Dear Martha,

I hope you are well. It seemed as good a way as any to start a letter but now I'm not so sure. Anyway, when I was up in The Potteries at Christmas, I decided it was time I reacquainted myself with friends I have lost touch with.

I'm sorry it's been so long, but Michael will have told you that I only come home periodically and that is taken up seeing my daughter, Hannah.

We have so much to catch up on. Could we meet
at the tea shop on Parliament Row in Hanley at three
o'clock, on Saturday 31 January 1920? I do hope you'll
come.
　　Looking forward to catching up with you again.
　　Yours sincerely,
　　Betty

Martha sat for a few moments. She hadn't expected to hear
from Betty after all this time. Martha dashed off a quick letter
confirming she would be there.

—

Martha and Jonas walked through Tunstall that Saturday dinnertime after work. She wanted to know his opinion on the subject
that had been on her mind since receiving the letter. She
explained that she was going to see her friend, Betty, later in
the afternoon. Briefly, she told Jonas they'd argued and hadn't
seen each other for ages.

'I have no idea what I'm going to say.'

'Let her do the talking – she's asked to meet you.'

'Should I say, "I'm sorry, Betty" and take all the blame?'

'Does it matter who's fault it was?' Jonas said.

'What d'yer mean?'

'It seems to me the real question is d'yer want to be friends
– or don't yer?'

'So what—'

'You need to talk to her and see if you still want to be friends.
There are kids we knew at school we thought would be best
friends but as we grow older, we hardly recognise them. You
make new friends. Just go along and see how you feel. You'll
know what you want to do afterwards.'

His face clouded. Martha remembered what Vera had said
about the girl called Doreen and bit her lip, wishing Vera had
said nothing.

'Jonas – listen to me.'

He stopped with a grin.

'You make it sound so simple.'

'Pardon me for stating the obvious, Martha, but it is. D'yer want to be friends with this girl – or don't yer?'

–

Martha wore her very best skirt and white blouse, with her dark blue three-quarter length coat buttoned up. A dark red hat she had bought recently went well on her mousy-coloured hair to complete her outfit.

It was cold and raining. Martha made sure she was well wrapped up. She took the tram to Hanley and to her first meeting with Betty in five years.

–

She hurried up the street and into the tea shop and found a table by the window. The window was covered in condensation and she couldn't see a thing through it. The place was full of dripping umbrellas, and everyone seemed to be wearing their thickest coats. Already hot when she got there, Martha unbuttoned her coat to gain some relief.

'Good afternoon, miss, what would you like?' the waitress asked cheerfully.

'Pot of tea for two, please.'

A few moments later, Betty breezed in and immediately caught sight of Martha and came straight over.

Martha stood up and the two former friends gazed at each other, looking at how much they had both changed. Betty looked a little plumper and was very well dressed. Quite the modern woman, Martha thought, in contrast to her own plain appearance.

'Hiya, Betty.' Martha had been determined to be the one who spoke first. 'It's good to see yer.'

'Hiya, Martha.'

The pair sat and Martha poured Betty a cup of tea.

'I bet you was surprised to get my letter.'

'To be honest, Betty, I thought it was high time we talked. I've really missed yer, and I was hoping we could be friends again.'

'I'm glad to hear that. I've missed you an' all. I should say I—'

'I want to say—'

They laughed as they both tried to speak at the same time.

'Let me go first, Betty.'

Betty nodded.

'I'd got it all planned, what I was going to say to yer when we met, and now it seems I can't remember nothing.' Martha's voice got softer as she spoke.

'I'm sorry an' all—'

'No, Betty. Stop.' Martha held up her hand. 'Let me talk first. I was so shocked when yer told me you were…' She lowered her voice. '…expecting, I just didn't know what to say, and blurted out the first thing that came into me head. I said all the things I'd heard other people say. When I think back, I reacted like an enraged father in a Victorian melodrama.'

'Being pregnant came as a big shock to me an' all, I don't mind telling yer.'

'I was so angry with you that day, Betty. We were best friends and had agreed we'd keep in touch, but gradually, we got together less and less. I knew it'd happen as soon as you got the job in that big house.' Martha didn't wait for Betty's reply. 'It proved to me that I wasn't good enough for yer, and that's why I was so angry. To be honest, I wasn't angry that you were expecting. I was angry because I felt I'd lost yer as a friend.'

'I never realised that you felt that way about me getting the job at Stowford House. I wish I'd known. I expected we'd both work in the potbank. When Mother told me about the job in service, I didn't think anything about it. We would still see each other.'

Martha paused and took a sip of her tea. 'It sounds silly when you talk of it today, but at thirteen I thought I was losing a part of meself, like losing a sister.'

'Oh Martha, you should have told me.'

'I didn't want to. It would make me seem clingy and it wasn't like that.'

Betty poured them another cup of tea. This gave Martha the chance to compose herself for the next part.

'Yer knew we was having a lot of trouble at our house with Father. It got worse as we grew older. All through the time we lived in Dresden Street he was – a bugger, a bastard, and Mother was frightened of him. He hit her and browbeat her and made her look small in front of us. He threw my brothers out of the house after an argument, terrorised our Issy and even hit me once.'

'Oh, Martha.'

Martha shook her head. 'Mother wanted to keep it a secret. It was Issy that sorted it eventually. She told Grandma and once she waded in – you know what *she's* like – everything was out in the open and the family had to face its problems. The war, coming when it did, probably saved us all. We were glad when Father was called up, but it was nothing compared with how glad we felt when he went missing.'

Betty stared, dumbstruck. 'You mean you were happy he was missing?'

'Not happy, relieved.'

They paused to take in what had just been said. Martha carried on. 'All through this time you were one person I could depend on. When Father was being awkward or angry, I knew I could come round to see you and things would be better. It made Father tolerable. Your leaving for the job in service made me feel I had no one. So, you can see why you being back for such a long time without contacting me made me angry and I just wanted to lash out at someone that day.

'It took me a long time to realise what I've just told yer. I kept saying to meself it was because of the baby, but I knew deep down it wasn't. When I met yer on Armistice Day, I was ready to talk about it, but yer mother was so cold towards me and couldn't wait to get away – that was obvious, and she made damn sure I heard her remarks about Peter and me. I thought you must've told her and didn't want to see me no more.'

'What I told her, when we got home, was that she shouldn't have said what she said.'

'I was angry with meself for everything I said. I didn't mean any of it. I should never have said those things to you. I'm so sorry.'

Betty called the waitress over and ordered another pot of tea. The two women sat in silence for a few moments gathering their thoughts. The tearoom was quieter now and the tea arrived quickly.

'Shall I be mother?' The two of them burst into laughter, the same laughter they had often shared at school.

'How *is* Hannah?'

'She is so bonny, Martha. She is growing all the time. You'd love her. She turned four in October and will be starting at Wellington Road School in September.

'It wasn't the best time of my life, Martha, but Mother and Father were so good. They took care of her for me so I could get a job where I could earn enough money to take care of her. I was lucky to get the job with Iris Shenton as her housekeeper. She was a lovely lady and helped me no end.' Betty recounted the story of that time. 'Then I managed to get a job on the trams – which was great because I was able to bring home a man's wage. Once the war ended we had to give up our jobs, but then I got a job in Birmingham and it's been like that ever since. I don't get to see Hannah as much as I'd like – but you probably know all about it through our Michael and your Issy. It's rather nice that they are sweet on each other, isn't it?'

'He's a nice lad. Very helpful.'

'Who would've thought it.'

They both laughed. After that Martha had run out of words, other than the question at the forefront of her mind, and took a breath. 'Aren't yer coming back to The Potteries?'

'Only if I can get a job like the one I've got. I don't think there's much chance of that. But there is one other complication. I met this boy in 1916. He was in the Royal Artillery and was being posted overseas a few days later. He asked me to write and we exchanged letters through the war and when he came home we had to get to know each other properly. He's named Duncan. What about you? Have you got a young man?'

Martha couldn't tell her about Jonas, not yet, so she shook her head. 'Not me, I'm a paintress now. I'm studying at the art school in Burslem. I wouldn't want to give it up.'

Martha was trying to digest all that she'd heard.

'Betty, why did you not tell me you had returned?'

'When I told my mother, she swore me to secrecy. We never told my sisters and brothers, only told Father. I knew if I called to see you, I wouldn't be able to stop myself from telling you everything. I didn't have any idea of how you felt. I assumed you'd understand.'

'If only we'd talked more, we could have saved ourselves a lot of heartache. After Father went missing, Mother said that a lot of the troubles she'd had with him might have been resolved if they had talked more. That is what made them the people we knew as girls. Mother's so different now, you wouldn't believe it.'

Betty picked up the bill. 'My treat.' And she moved towards the till.

Together they walked to the tram stop. The girls hugged each other before going their separate ways. Although Martha was happy with the knowledge that this could be the first of many meetings, she realised they might never become the friends they once were.

Chapter Thirty-three

Spring 1920

As it was, Martha had to wait until April before meeting Duncan and Hannah. Betty had been busy, and it was difficult to fit in with Martha's classes.

Today, Easter Sunday, the weather was fine and sunny. The family, without Peter and Cassie, had got together for Sunday dinner and for once Martha was pleased not to see her nephew. She never understood how a little mite like Andrew could make so much noise and cause so much disruption. She sat on the chair in the window and started to read her book from the library.

The next moment, Grandma came rushing in. 'Martha, Martha, you've got visitors. It's young Betty and her daughter, and she's got a right handsome man with her.' It took several moments for Betty to comprehend what Grandma had said.

'Can they come into the front room?'

'Of course, I'll bring them through.'

Martha stood up and waited. Betty was the first to enter, followed by a man she assumed was Duncan, and the most gorgeous little girl, which was obviously Hannah. 'Come in, sit down. I was reading and appear to have dozed off. I'm so glad to see yer again, Betty.'

Betty and Duncan sat on the settee with Hannah standing between them. She was looking at Martha and then looking around the room. She held her first finger on her lips. Betty explained that they had decided to take Hannah on the trams and where better to visit than Martha? She had told Hannah all about her.

Betty said, 'This little minx here is my daughter, Hannah. Say hello to Martha, Hannah. We knew each other at school – the same school as you'll go to – when we were just a little bit older than you.'

Hannah was partly hidden by Duncan. He tried to encourage her to put out her hand to take the one Martha offered her.

'She'll come round. She's always a bit shy the first time.'

Martha bent down until she was the same height as the little girl.

'Hello, Hannah. We haven't met before, but I'm so pleased to see yer. Do you think we might become friends – like I was with your mummy?'

The girl's blue eyes pierced hers and Martha was taken aback by their beauty. Her long red hair, arranged in ringlets around her head, was surprising. As far as Martha knew, there was none in the Dean family, so she must take after her father.

Hannah nodded without speaking – which was a start.

'And how old are you?'

'Four.' The voice was barely a whisper, but it was a voice and therefore an improvement. Relieved, Martha rose and was finally introduced to Duncan. He got to his feet and held out his hand.

'Hello, Martha. I'm glad to meet you at last. How wonderful for the two of you to get together after all this time. You must have had a lot of catching up to do.'

'Pleased to meet you too, Duncan.'

Hannah grinned and nodded her head. 'Yes, Duncan.'

They all laughed and the intensity of the moment dissolved.

After a brief chat, Duncan and Hannah went into the back kitchen as Grandma said there might be a biscuit in there if she could find it.

'He's a very nice man,' smiled Martha.

'He is,' Betty replied. 'I think the world of him.'

Any further conversation was interrupted as the door to the sitting room banged open and in charged Hannah followed by an apologetic Duncan.

The two women were delighted. As Martha dashed away the hint of water in her eyes before they became full-blown tears, she was thankful to be sitting there – with her former best friend.

'What do you do for a living, Duncan?'

'I'm a traffic manager on the North Staffordshire Railway. I work in Stoke, just above the station.'

'Betty says you wrote to each other during the war. It sounded romantic.'

'I don't know how I would have got through it without her.'

Betty beamed. 'We'd better go now. It's been a long day for Hannah.'

'Well, thank you for coming today. It's been lovely to see you, Duncan – and you, Hannah.' The little girl was already half asleep in Duncan's arms.

Martha kissed Hannah's soft cheek as they said their good-byes and turned to Betty. 'It's been good to talk and to meet your family, Betty.'

Betty hugged her. 'Yes, and it's been good to see you too.'

As Martha waved them down the street, she smiled. Yes, it had been good to straighten things out with Betty. It was only as she closed the door that she realised there had been no talk of meeting again.

Chapter Thirty-four

Martha had been out sketching after work. She had a lot on her mind and felt angry when she looked at her drawings. They weren't very good. This evening was not a time for sketching. She had been drawing the station – and her thoughts had strayed to Betty and Duncan. She had enjoyed meeting Betty but now they had made up, their friendship didn't take on the same degree of importance it once had.

She was about to start her second year at art school. Surely everybody would see her commitment. She had done so well in the end-of-year examinations. Now would be the time to tell Jonas her feelings for him and hope they were reciprocated. But the usual doubts and concerns crept back into her thoughts and, in the end, she was back at the same place. She liked the way things were currently and didn't want to disturb them.

Martha let herself into Park Terrace to find another letter from Betty waiting for her on the sideboard. She opened it on the spot, eager for news.

14 June 1920

Dear Martha,

I'm engaged! I couldn't wait to put pen to paper. Duncan arranged for my mother's house to be empty when I returned from a dress fitting for Hannah, who will be a bridesmaid at my friend Connie's wedding.

It was so romantic, he got down on one knee and asked me if I would do him the honour of becoming his wife and I said yes.

We have not set a date yet, but I will keep you posted.

Best wishes

Betty

It was to be expected, and Martha was thrilled at the news. So it looked like Betty was going to get married first, but then again she was bound to, as Martha had committed herself to her course and hopefully her career.

For the first time, Martha wondered if she had done the right thing.

–

When they left work on Saturday lunchtime, Martha and Jonas walked together to the top of Paradise Street. Both were in a thoughtful mood. Normally Jonas would turn left onto Summerbank Road to go to Goldenhill, but today Martha decided they could spend more time together.

'Have you ever tried our pies?'

'No.' Jonas looked surprised.

Martha grabbed his hand and they crossed the street to Mrs Parker's Pies. They waited in the queue and when it was their turn to be served, Mother looked up, surprised.

'Hello, Martha.'

'Hello. Can I have two of the small pies please, Mother?'

Mother looked quizzical. 'Feeling peckish, are yer? Afternoon, Jonas. Nice to see yer.'

'Good afternoon, Mrs Owen.'

Issy's head popped round the door. 'Thought I recognised those voices. Lovely to see yer, Jonas.'

'You too.' He smiled.

Martha noticed how, whenever she was in the shop, everyone had a smile for Issy.

'Going anywhere this afternoon, you two?'

It was plain that Issy was fishing for information, and Martha was equally determined to give nothing away.

'Here.' Mother handed over two individually wrapped hot meat and potato pies. 'Get these down yer. Expect you'll be needing it after working all morning. When will we see yer next, Jonas?'

To save any embarrassment, Martha jumped in with a reply. 'I'm sure he'll pop by when he's got time, Mother. I keep telling yer how busy we are.'

A few more words were exchanged, and they left the shop, and a disappointed Issy. They walked through the square and turned onto the High Street, which would lead them to Gold-enhill. By unspoken agreement they continued to walk, eating their pies and enjoying each other's company, talking about things in general.

'You know, Martha, I never thought I'd see the day when I would be walking through Tunstall eating a pie.'

'Why ever not?'

'We were told not to, and we obeyed. Besides, I never had much money in my pocket. I didn't see why I should spend my pocket money buying food when there was plenty at home.'

The more she found out about him, the more she liked him. The thought of him as a child, under the thumb of his family, sent her into fits of giggles. When he grinned back at her, her heart turned over.

They reached the point where Summerbank Road joined the High Street and Jonas stopped walking.

'Would you like to come for tea on Sunday?'

Martha stared at him. 'What'll yer mother say?'

'She suggested it. She said how we were spending a lot of time together, what with us working with each other. She said it'd be nice to put a face to the name.'

'You talk about me?'

A faint flush came to his face. 'Well… yes. It'd be hard not to when they ask me about work.'

It was Martha's turn to flush.

'Yes, Jonas, I would like that very much.'

They arranged that Jonas would call for her at four o'clock and they would walk up through Sandyford to the centre of Goldenhill. She was glad Jonas had suggested doing it this way rather than have her turn up on the doorstep.

Travelling from Tunstall to Goldenhill, Gray's Grocery Shop stood on the right-hand side of the main road with Jonas and his parents living above the shop.

It was a double-fronted affair with the entrance door in the middle. Being Sunday, the shop was closed but Martha was curious, never having been in there. The Owens got their groceries from the covered market in the centre of Tunstall. Probably from Jonas's family stall. She didn't know. That was Grandma's domain.

Jonas walked down the side of the shop and used his key to open the door while Martha brushed down her coat and tried to ensure her hat was on straight. She felt a good impression was so important.

'Hello, lad. Are you all right?' came a woman's voice.

'Yes, Mother.' He turned towards Martha. 'This is my friend Martha – she's the paintress I work with at Paradise.'

'Oh, pleased to meet you, Martha. Jonas has spoken a lot about yer. I almost feel as if I know yer already.'

'Pleased to meet you too, Mrs Gray.'

'That's all right, duckie, but you must call me Ruth.'

At that moment, two men, older than Jonas, entered the kitchen. His brothers. She recognised Robert from his stall in Tunstall market. He wore a patch over his left eye, having lost it when a piece of shrapnel hit him in the face. He was lucky because most of its momentum had been absorbed by the soldier standing in front of him.

'This is the lass our Jonas has spoken of,' said David, the other brother.

Martha moved closer to Jonas, who had a look of astonishment on his face.

'What are you two doing here?'

'We're here to sort out the horse for Monday, and Mother told us you was coming for tea with a young lady. And – well, we couldn't miss it, could we, Rob?' said David.

'Now you lot... dunner you go matchmaking and embarrassing the girl,' Ruth tutted. She took Martha's coat before herding everyone into the front room where his father, Enoch, was waiting. He jumped up as she walked in and took her hand, welcoming her on behalf of the family.

Martha sat next to Jonas listening to banter between the brothers, who were both married with children of working age. It turned out that Robert and David had been keen to meet her and Ruth had agreed, provided it was just the two of them. She didn't want Martha to be overawed by the whole family on her first visit.

It was a happy meal. Everyone got on so well, a true family. Martha soon relaxed and was even a little disappointed when it was time to leave.

As she was putting on her coat in the hallway, Martha heard Ruth talking to Jonas in the kitchen.

'She looks a nice girl, Jonas. Bit on the young side, but that's not such a bad thing. Doreen was the same age as yer, and look how that turned out. Perhaps this one, being younger, will be less inclined to leave yer.'

Martha's hands stopped working as she listened, unable to move. She wasn't eavesdropping – if there was something she could learn about him that would help their friendship head closer to love, then it would be best if she knew about it, wouldn't it? All that Vera had said about this Doreen – it was true. In some ways, Martha was relieved she did know about it, otherwise she might've said summat she might regret.

Jonas appeared in the hall. He stopped when he saw her, no doubt wondering how much she'd heard.

'Nearly ready, Jonas.'

His face was pale. Martha felt a little sick at the thought of ruining such a good evening. She should've made a noise to warn them she was there.

They said their goodbyes and headed through the back door and onto the main road back to Tunstall.

'Sorry to have put yer through meeting up with Robert and David an' all. It was meant to be just Mother and Father.'

'Don't worry. It was good to see them. Perhaps the best way, cos I didn't have time to worry.'

They continued in silence for a couple of hundred yards as Martha fought with herself on whether or not to mention that she knew about this Doreen, and that he needn't say anything if it was too painful.

'Martha, I need to say something—'

He looked as if he was struggling so she blurted out words she would later regret. 'It's all right, Jonas. I know…'

'You know what?' Jonas's face closed down. The happiness of the evening was destroyed with the utterance of those words.

'I know about Doreen.' Her words were barely a whisper as Jonas's eyes glittered.

'How?'

'Vera. She told me. And I heard yer mother talking about her when I was putting on me coat.'

'You've talked to Vera about my private life. She told yer something she had promised to keep to herself?'

This was a side of Jonas she hadn't seen before. They both stopped walking. There was no one near them, apart from an old lady on the other side of the road, walking in the same direction and unaware what was going on.

Panic set in at the anger in his voice. Martha stepped back, but he followed.

'What did she say? Come on, Martha, you can't stop now. Tell me. She had no right talking about me. I would've told the whole world if I wanted people to know.'

She shook her head. 'Please don't. Vera only said summat because she wanted to help.'

'She had no right, Martha. It wasn't her decision.'

Martha couldn't breathe. Her shoulders stiffened. He must've seen something in her face – her eyes, maybe. He stopped talking.

'I'm sorry, Martha.' He frowned. He put his hand out to her. She ducked.

'Martha—' He lifted both hands in front of him, palms towards her. 'Martha, dearest, please don't get upset.'

Martha swallowed, rubbing her hands together as if she was giving them the wash of their lives.

Gradually she relaxed. The horror must have gone from her eyes. His arms came round her, begging for forgiveness.

'I'm sorry too, Jonas.' The words crept out of her mouth. 'It was my father. He used to lose his temper regularly. We couldn't… I couldn't…' Tears filled her eyes as he took her shaking body into his arms.

'Oh, my love.'

They stood together. The old woman on the other side of the road had long since disappeared.

Calmer now, Martha was able to relax. 'I'm sorry, Jonas. It wasn't your fault.'

'Oh, but it was. I lost my temper with you for no good reason.'

'Vera was only trying to help us both. Please don't say anything.'

'Martha, love. I promise you I will never, ever lose my temper with you again. You are too important to me. I couldn't bear to lose you.'

'Thank you, Jonas. You don't know how much that means to me.'

279

'Before I take you home, can we talk? Not here – somewhere more private. The church, maybe?'

Though surprised by his suggestion, she nevertheless agreed and, a few minutes later, they were standing outside Christ Church with its tower and large arched windows, its stone darkened by years of soot. Jonas opened the door for Martha. The church was empty. They crept inside and took a pew on the left.

Martha stared around, looking at the magnificence of the holy place instilling her with peace. To be sitting here with Jonas was all she could wish for. She had tried to keep him at a distance but knew it was beyond her. When Vera told her about Jonas and Doreen, her heart had suffered for Jonas, but also for herself. If she believed she could live her life without him, she was fooling herself. She knew that now.

Jonas picked up her hand. 'My dear Martha. There are things I have wanted to say to you for so long, but for any number of reasons it was never the right time. I think that the right time… is now.'

She kept as still as if she was made of the stone that surrounded them.

'We have come a long way, you and I,' he said, softly. 'But then again we have taken only small steps. I say that because I think we are frightened – for reasons that only each one of us can know about. From the first time I saw you I thought you were the one for me, so imagine my delight that we would work together and spend time in each other's company. I thought that would be enough – I'd been hurt before – and I didn't plan to go through that again.'

His eyes darkened. 'When you've been hurt like that, you don't want to put yourself in the same place a second time. I decided to wait because, apart from my own problems, I knew you were far too young to be interested in me. It would give me the chance to make my own mind up, too. Then you began to talk about not getting involved with anyone and wanting to follow ambitions that were more important to you than any man. I thought you were warning me off, but soon realised that you meant what you said. I couldn't do anything but bide my time. I thought that if I was always there for you, you would begin to see me in a different light.'

Martha covered his hand with her own. 'You're right, Jonas. I was attracted to you when we started working together and I did think you were old.' She laughed at the affront on his face which turned easily into a smile. 'I had wanted to become a paintress ever since I knew I would end up working on a potbank. It's the pinnacle for girls like me. I loved drawing and painting and I often go out by myself to draw, even now. Once I thought there might be a possibility of becoming a paintress, I knew I had to try my best to succeed. So, I did and you were so encouraging, I knew I was doing the right thing.

'When you came back from the war and I saw you again, I realised my feelings had begun to change. You were in my thoughts but I still yearned to go to art school. I thought I could finish my training before I committed to anything else or anyone else. It turns out to be very hard to turn feelings off and on.'

He had begun to smile. 'Martha Owen – are you telling me you have feelings for me?'

Her face must've turned bright pink judging by the look on his face. 'But don't you see, Jonas? How can anything come of it? I've told Mr John that I'm going to put all my energy into the art course and that I'm not planning to get married or have children until that's over. He'll think I only said it to get the training. How could I face him if I have to tell him I've changed my mind?'

He edged closer until his nose was almost touching hers. 'If you're saying what I think you're saying, Martha, then I can tell you that I think I love you. No, that's not true. I *am* in love with you.'

Martha looked into the eyes so close to hers – and smiled. 'And I know I'm in love with you too.'

She slid into his arms and was content to stay there.

'But what shall I do about the training? Will Mr John be very angry?'

'I'll speak to Mr John when the time is right. In the meantime, we'll keep it to ourselves.'

'Can I tell Vera? I've a feeling she had a part in arranging all this. If she hadn't told me about Doreen, we wouldn't have had a row and we wouldn't be sitting here like this.'

'In that case, I suppose we have no choice. But she'd better not say a word to anyone, or else—'

At that, Martha jumped up and pulled him up behind her. 'Come on. Let's go.'

Together, they walked out into the bright sunshine, convinced they had everything worked out for a new life.

–

On the Monday after what had turned into the best Sunday ever, Martha went in to work early to catch Vera before the rest of the workers arrived.

She waited by the large sinks just inside the door until she heard Vera's recognisable footsteps. She walked towards the door, causing Vera to jump.

'Martha, love – you gave me a fright.'

'I'm sorry, Vera, but I have to talk to you.'

'There's nothing wrong, is there?'

'Jonas knows that you told me about Doreen. I'm so sorry.'

'You mean you told him?'

'I didn't mean to. He invited me to tea at his house.'

Vera's eyes opened wide. 'He did?'

Martha nodded. 'We had a bit of an argument on the way home. I got the idea that he was going to tell me about her but he looked too hurt, so I said I already knew and he... he... got angry. I swear I was only trying to help. I wanted you to know. I managed to sort it out and we... made up.'

Vera looked at her curiously. 'Is there more you want to tell me?'

'We... we are going to be... seeing each other... regularly.'

'But that's wonderful news, Martha! It'll be worth taking a few harsh words from him to see you both happy, in my view.'

'You can't tell nobody, Vera. We aren't telling nobody until Jonas has had a word with Mr John – when the time's right. After all, I promised I wouldn't be thinking of going out with anybody until after my course has finished, at the earliest.'

The door opened as workers began to trickle in.

'Any road, I wanted yer to know – but you're to say nothing.'

Chapter Thirty-five

Jonas caught Martha as she was leaving for the night. She had deliberately stayed late pretending to be tidying her work so she could speak to him alone.

'What is it?' she asked.

'I thought we might go somewhere on Tuesday. Somewhere we can be ourselves without the likelihood of bumping into anybody we know. I thought Manchester would be good.'

'I've never been there.'

'Even better. I'd love to show you around. We could visit the art gallery.'

It was an exciting prospect. Her first outing with him. What could be better?

–

It was all arranged. They would meet at Tunstall railway station and catch the train to Manchester's London Road station. Apart from the art gallery, they could visit the large department stores to look at their ceramic displays – a working visit, which is what Martha told her mother the night before. Issy was out with Michael, otherwise she would have been quizzed endlessly.

The city of Manchester was considerably bigger than anywhere Martha had been before. She was in awe of the number of shops and the beautiful buildings in which they were housed.

Their first stop was at Manchester City Art Gallery where both were keen to look at the masterpieces on view to visitors. Her teacher at the art school had encouraged everyone to see art first hand, whether it was ceramics or paintings. Only then could the work be fully appreciated.

Martha had taken books out of the public library to learn more about painters such as the Pre-Raphaelite Brotherhood and the ceramics of Minton and Wedgwood, and the more recent art movements. She appreciated all she saw. From time to time, she could feel Jonas watching her. At first, she was a little bashful, but then became so caught up in what she was seeing, she took little notice. After all, she might never see the like again.

When their visit ended, they called into a cafeteria to have a bite to eat. Afterwards they strolled through the huge department stores of Lewis's, Kendal Milne & Co and Paulden's to view their ceramic ranges. There was a mixture of the traditional seen together with the more exciting, in Martha's view, newer geometric designs she was beginning to hear about in her classes. In fact, it was difficult to draw her away from the beautiful, but often expensive, ware on show.

'That's what I want to paint, Jonas.'

His eyebrows lifted. 'Mm, a radical painter then.'

'No, it's the use of colour I like. Summat different. What makes you smile when you see it.'

With a pretend look of horror, Jonas said, 'Whatever will Mr John think I've introduced him to!'

By the end of the afternoon, Martha was exhausted and looking forward to the train journey home.

'I believe you enjoyed your visit today, Martha.' Jonas smiled.

'Oh, yes. More than anything. Fancy being able to look at such beautiful stuff as often as you like. I think I'd be in these places every single day.'

'I know what you mean. It was good to come here today. Our first outing together and not under the prying eyes of friends and workers.'

Martha nodded. 'I did feel more relaxed.'

They jumped on the train already waiting to take them back to Tunstall. It was a compartment train; once inside, travellers remained in the same carriage. Many of the carriages were full so they climbed inside the first with empty seats and sat, not looking at the other two people already in there.

Martha didn't know who was the most surprised when she thought about it later. The two people they would be sharing the carriage with all the way back home were none other than Mr John – and Emily Norton.

'Good afternoon, Jonas, Miss Owen,' he said, startling them both. 'It would seem we all needed a break from The Potteries today.'

'Mr John! I never expected to see you on—'

'No, Jonas, I don't suppose you did.'

Martha was mortified and covered her cheeks, although she was relieved to note that Emily was just as shocked as she was.

'This is… unexpected, to say the least. Have you enjoyed your day out?'

'Yes, we've been to the art gallery and around the bigger department stores looking at what's new.'

Jonas had obviously decided that little could be done about their meeting, so they may as well talk on the way home.

'Miss Norton and I – oh, who cares.' Mr John threw his hands in the air. 'Emily and I have been working long hours recently and I thought a day out was the least she deserved.'

Jonas nodded. 'Same here.'

The men discussed the pottery ranges in the department stores while Martha and Emily talked about Manchester – a place neither had visited before. By the time they reached Tunstall, Martha thought she knew Emily considerably better. She was really very nice. It was her job that kept her aloof. She liked a laugh as much as anyone.

After their initial discomfiture, even Mr John could see the funny side of their meeting and a tacit agreement was reached that nothing more would be said.

It was one of those late August days. The weather had been nice for a while and Martha walked home from work slower than usual. She had called in to see her mother but the shop was busy. Mother had started to sell home-baked cakes. They were just bread rolls sliced longways and filled with buttercream and covered in chocolate. It was only cooking chocolate, but nobody seemed to mind. They helped sales, which tended to fall in the summer.

Martha let herself in through the front door at Park Terrace and noticed another letter from Betty. Two letters in quick succession could only mean one thing – they had set their wedding date. She opened it eagerly.

21 August 1920

Dear Martha,

It seems a long time since we spoke in April. How are you and how are the evening classes going?

I have some news. I have broken off my engagement. It was nothing to do with our feelings for each other. On my part I still think the world of him, but we couldn't agree about work.

I always said that I would not return to The Potteries unless I could get a better job. His sister, Susan, had warned me Duncan expected me to give up my job after marriage, but I didn't believe her. He wanted me to move into his family home with Hannah and generally become an unpaid housekeeper for them all. For my part, I assumed Duncan would be happy to get a job on the railways in Birmingham, where the prospects are better.

We had several arguments. He thought he could change me to be the wife he wanted me to be. I realised deep down he would not change. I knew I could never compromise. It would be an open sore between us. So, we parted.

Take this as a warning, Martha. You need to be very
sure that what your man says is what he really feels.

Hannah will continue to live with her grandma and
grandad for the foreseeable future. She is happy and
settled. After all, she doesn't really know any other life.

Please write with your news.

Best wishes,

Betty

Poor Betty, it had only been a couple of months since they got engaged. Duncan had seemed so nice and had got on well with Hannah. It showed Martha that, no matter how careful you are, you can never tell whether you have chosen wisely. Betty seemed to have gone down the same road as Mother had all those years ago. Ominous feelings made Martha's belly curdle. If Betty couldn't keep Duncan, what chance did she have of keeping Jonas?

–

Martha hardly slept that night. A picture of Betty and Duncan together, laughing, had invaded her mind. Then came shouting and arguments, each wanting their own way. She tossed and turned but couldn't budge the scenes from her mind. Supposing it happened to her and Jonas? After all, she wanted the same as Betty, didn't she? Her job and her family?

She woke up with a start, hot and flustered, her heart thumping in her chest. She needed to speak to Jonas. What if it came to choosing between her heart's desires? He always said he wanted what she wanted. She remembered her mother saying that a man would say anything to get what he wanted.

–

She was up early the next morning. She brushed her hair and was shocked to find a pale face with dark eyes looking back at her. She looked awful, but she had to go to work. She had to talk to Jonas.

It was one of the few days when Jonas was late arriving at the potbank. All the modellers were at their benches when Jonas walked in. She waited for him to take his seat and then picked up the vase she'd been working on and walked over to him.

'Jonas, could I have a word with you?'

'Of course.' Jonas laid down the papers he had picked up. 'What can I do?' Both were careful not to give anything away.

She whispered, 'I have to see you. I need to talk to you.'

'Are you all right, Martha?' He looked anxious and pretended to turn the vase over. 'How about dinnertime?' he whispered. 'Meet me outside, away from prying eyes.'

'Very well,' she said in a louder voice that could be heard around the room.

She walked back to her seat. She needn't have worried. She doubted any of the men had looked at her.

As soon as the bell went, Martha picked up her coat and rushed out of the room. She waited by the coal hole near the end of the building and waved to Jonas as he emerged.

'Martha, love, whatever's the matter?'

'Oh, Jonas. I have to talk to you. I've had a letter from Betty. She's broken off her engagement.'

He frowned. 'That's unfortunate. Poor Betty. But why are you so anxious? Are you not feeling well?'

'I haven't slept. I kept thinking about us.'

'What d'yer mean?'

'I'm the same as Betty. I want a career and I want to be with you. Promise me you'll never make me choose between the two. We're a team and we should always do what is best for each other. There'll be times when we'll have to compromise, but I want to be sure we'll be honest with each other. None of this saying one thing and meaning another. Please, Jonas.'

'Oh, Martha. We are not the same as Betty and Duncan. We're different people. I want what's best for both of us. I understand your desire for a career and fully support it. I agree we must be honest and always say what we feel.'

'That's why I love you.'

He kissed her tenderly.

'Like I said, I'll talk to Mr John and assure him you will be staying here to finish your course – whatever the future holds for us.'

–

Jonas called in at Park Terrace on his way home. Martha knew he had arranged to see Mr John and was waiting anxiously. He arrived just after seven o'clock.

Martha rushed to the door and let him in. 'Well, what did he say?'

'Mr John wishes us every happiness. He's surprised it's taken us so long. I think that more people at Paradise know what's in our hearts than we do. He's not worried about your commitment and knows you'll do yer best.'

'That's a relief. I was so worried.'

'Martha, dear, now we know it's an open secret, why don't we just go ahead and announce our engagement.'

Martha stood for a second hardly taking in what had just happened. 'Are you proposing to me?'

'Yes, of course.'

'Then I'm accepting.'

They embraced each other and kissed like they had never kissed before. And Martha's eyes brimmed with tears. Gently, Jonas wiped them away. They were together, and they would stay that way always.

Chapter Thirty-six

The first days of September were hectic. It took a good few days to tell everyone, but by the end of the week their engagement was common knowledge. Martha was surprised how readily everyone had accepted their news.

One of the first things she did was to dash off a letter to Daniel, admitting happily he had been right all along. This was followed by a letter to Betty.

–

A few days later, Martha received a lovely card from Betty congratulating her and Jonas on getting engaged. On the back of the card she had written, 'It's a funny old life isn't it, Martha. I was the one who always wanted to get married and you were the one who didn't. And look at us now – you will be the first to become a married woman and I will probably end up a spinster.'

Martha was glad to receive Betty's congratulations and to be remembered by her friend. She smiled at the note Betty had written on the back of the card. Sadly, she realised that the Betty she had known at Dresden Street would have come to see her personally and they would've celebrated together.

She had no doubt now that their friendship would continue, but it would be in the form of exchanged letters, Christmas and birthday cards and on other special occasions.

Part Four

Chapter Thirty-seven

June 1922

Martha came home from work on Monday evening. It had been a pleasant day, but had started to cloud over.

'Had a good day, Martha?'

'Yes, Grandma.' She flopped into a chair. 'And now I am going to spend all evening revising for next week's examinations.'

'Well, yer mustn't work too hard. Yer've been so busy recently.'

'Don't worry, I won't. These are the final examinations for my course and I want to do well.'

'Have yer tea and a bit of a rest. You'll study better with summat in yer belly.'

Martha was glad of Grandma's advice. As soon as she had finished her tea, she felt ready to work.

The time flew by. It was soon ten o'clock. The sky had cleared and although the sun had set, there was a lovely glow in the west. What with the classes taking up three nights a week, working during the day, helping Grandma in the house and writing letters to Daniel and Betty, there was little time to do anything else if she wanted to see Jonas too.

She laid her book on her knee, as Daniel came to mind. He'd been away for nearly three years now and had finished the two years he'd committed to with Mr MacLeod at Milford Station. Originally, he was obligated to buy land designated out on the Prairies, but with the support of Mr MacLeod and other leading businessmen in the area, the authorities relented and he persuaded them to allow him to buy a piece of land in Milford Station. Fairly early on, Martha's keen eyes had noted his letters contained lots of references to Calum's sister, Catriona, and had wondered if she could have been the reason he wanted his land in Milford Station. She had found herself hoping so even though it would likely mean he would never come back to England. He deserved to be happy.

Her mind automatically moved from one brother to the next. Peter's life had changed so much since the end of the war. He'd become quite the father, and Martha was proud of him. In the early days, she had worried that, lovely though Cassie was, she might have trapped Peter into marriage in order to get away from her dominating and stifling father. But Martha had been wrong. Peter and Cassie were devoted to each other and made fine parents to young Andrew who seemed to grow and look bonnier every time she saw him.

Cassie's mother had continued with her visits and regularly called upon them. She loved to take Andrew out to show him off to her friends and had become a true grandma. It gave Cassie and Peter time to themselves. Mr Mellor no longer had Adeline – it was still strange to think of her as such – under his thumb as a result, and that could only be good for her, Martha knew all too well.

Martha breathed out slowly. She looked down at the ring on her wedding finger – a solitary diamond, small but beautiful. She was used to being engaged now although it had seemed strange at first, especially with them working together. Of late their wedding seemed to take up everyone's interest, probably because no date had yet been set. Martha continued to tell them that it was her wish to finish at the art school before she got wed, as she had promised Mr John, and that they were saving to buy a house. It wasn't much better at home. Hardly a day went by without Issy raising it. Peter wasn't so bad because he had his hands full with his family.

A knock on the door brought her out of her reveries. The door opened and Grandma appeared.

'Hope I'm not disturbing yer, duckie. I thought as yer might like another cup of tea.' She entered the bedroom with a little tray on which stood a teapot, cup and saucer, and a small plate holding a piece of fruit cake.

'Grandma, you shouldn't. I should've made one for you and Grandad. I didn't realise it was so late.'

'It's no bother. You're the only one left for me to look after, so let me indulge yer now and again.'

'I think that's enough revising for tonight, my mind's been wandering.'

'Oh, yes? Such as?'

'Lots of things, but mainly the family. You know, the twins being away and settled. And even me and Jonas – engaged and almost there, but not quite.'

'Jonas is a good man, our Martha. You'll do well to hold onto him.'

'I know, Grandma, and I'll be so pleased when we get wed.'

'I'm that proud of yer, lass. I hope as yer know that.'

Martha gave Grandma a hug. 'Night, night.'

'Dunner stay up too late. Night, night.'

Grandma ruffled Martha's hair just like she used to and left her to her revision.

–

Yes, thought Martha as her head returned to the textbook, it was a good time for the Owen family. She hoped they would all be settled before too long.

Her revision took her back to the last two years at art school and how much she owed to the Rhead family. It had been a sad day for Paradise when Mr Cyril Rhead passed away in October 1921. The factory had closed for the day to show respect for the family. Paradise Pottery was left in the full control of Mr John. After an initial concern that it might be closed down or sold, Mr John convinced everybody that he wanted to retain the business and make it grow, and said he had ideas for taking it forward.

During the course, she had learned about the modelling side of ceramics and how to take an idea or design from a sketch to a finished article. Not only to replicate the sketch but also to make sure the most efficient solutions were considered. She understood the art of the mould maker and the way clay reacted to drying and firing. She had even worked for a couple of weeks in the mould maker's room – another totally male domain – where she acquired a considerable number of additional words to the English language.

A lot of time was spent working on colour palettes and how to reproduce shades consistently when an item went into production. The science behind firing the ware was fascinating and so many variables had to be considered in both placement and position of the pieces. She was able to put what she learned into practice and had got into the habit of asking questions to ensure she understood what she was doing. She wouldn't have been surprised if George, Levi and Enoch had moaned privately to themselves and to Jonas. However, Jonas had winked at her when she mentioned it. Most men liked to be asked questions and the modellers were only too pleased to impart their knowledge.

She sipped her tea slowly. Mother's business was prospering. She had opened her second shop – this one in the middle of Burslem, just below the Town Hall, and wasn't short of customers with Issy in charge. Her sister was loving it. Someone had told Issy she could sell Mrs Parker's Pies to the king himself if she set her mind to it. Whatever Father would've thought about Mother's pie shops no one would ever know – but Martha chuckled as she pictured what his face would look like. It felt good to know she could laugh about him now.

After the examinations, the end-of-course exhibition was next. It was a chance to put her work in the public eye. Mr John would finally see what he had paid for and she hoped he thought it was worth it. Even with the praises Jonas showered on her, Martha had butterflies in her belly at the thought of it all.

Thinking about the passing of Mr Cyril brought to mind the most poignant event of 1921 – the unveiling, by the Earl of Dartmouth, of the Burslem War Memorial in Swan Square. It stood sixteen feet tall and carried a life-size figure of a bare-headed soldier, with his helmet at his feet, facing Waterloo Road. It was erected to the men of Burslem who had sacrificed their lives with the inscription 'They died that we might live'.

All the Owen family went to see the momentous occasion. Martha was unable to take her eyes off the figure of the soldier looking down at them. Father came to her mind and she felt a pain that grew inside. Even if he could have been a better father, no one should ever have to go through what these soldiers did. She thought of Daniel who was now living far across the sea in a foreign land, in his attempt to forget his soldier's life that no one should ever have to bear witness to again. Then there were many others, the likes of Eddie Bell who she knew well, to the likes of Betty's young man who she didn't know at all. Today was a coming together of so many people to help those who had lost loved ones, friends and relations to remind everyone of the heroism and sacrifices of so many.

When it had all ended, Martha had hurried home and let herself in. No one else had returned, so she knelt in the silence of her bedroom thinking about all those people she'd seen in Burslem that day and how important the remembrance seemed to them. Tears on solemn faces, men in wheelchairs, others unable to see being led by their companions to touch the memorial raised to friends they would never see again. She had prayed with all her might that those who bore witness to the silent grief of the day would never experience the like again.

Those were her final thoughts, the sad but momentous end to 1921. Here she was, in 1922, with the promise of everything she could wish for in life only months away, and she was happier than she had ever been. Perhaps the time was right to set her wedding date.

Chapter Thirty-eight

July 1922

Who would ever have thought that she, Martha Owen of Tunstall, in The Potteries, would ever be celebrating a day such as this? Today was the day of the exhibition of the Burslem School of Art. It would see the culmination of her work of the last three years. She wanted to please Jonas but, most of all, she wanted to be proud of her own achievements.

She arrived at the school's main hall in plenty of time. She hated being late – for anything. They had set up their displays the night before, so it was just a case of making sure everything was perfect. Throughout it all, Jonas had been by her side.

Martha was displaying a range of her work, from drawings and paintings through to the ceramic ware that would be part of her work from now on. Her favourite was her dining set, *Sea, Sand, Sun*, with its bright colours of blue, orange and yellow, in the irregular patterns characterised by the Cubist movement.

She reviewed everything she had laid out to maximise the impact and moved pieces around the table until she was satisfied. Jonas was due to arrive a few minutes before the exhibition opened and was to help her show off both her work and Paradise Pottery.

Bridie, who had promised to help, breezed in with about fifteen minutes to spare.

'Bridie – where have you been? I thought you weren't going to come.'

'I had a couple of problems to sort out with me younger brothers, but I'm here now. I have made sandwiches and we have some pieces of cake. I've also brought some glasses and a bottle of cordial.'

Martha grinned. She should've known better than to question Bridie's timekeeping.

Jonas turned up at that moment and gave Martha a hug, eager to calm the nerves that were threatening now she had nothing left to do. With ten minutes to go, the three of them wandered around the large hall and looked at the various pieces on show. There were paintings, drawings, models, pottery ornaments and ceramics of all sorts, each with a special beauty of their own. Martha could have stayed all day just looking – and maybe talking. She was not usually one for talking, but where art was concerned she could put her feelings to one side and lose herself in the beauty surrounding her.

She was quick to notice that the pottery ornaments, toby jugs, figurines and ceramics were made by men of varying ages. No women were represented. Women were represented in the drawings and paintings. She was sure that women could hold their own if they were allowed to try for themselves.

A bell echoed around the hall informing the exhibitors that they should return to their tables, as the doors were about to open to the public. Martha and Bridie hurried back to their display and stood ready to be polite and welcoming to the attendees.

Soon, a steady murmur lingered in the hall as the exhibitors were questioned by those people wishing to discover more about their work. As Martha watched well-dressed men and women pass by or stop at tables, she believed they were delighted to have the opportunity to question those responsible for making the individual pieces that had aroused their interest.

When there was nobody at her table, Martha asked the lady on the next table if anyone would be coming to see her display.

'Yes, my employer. What about you?'

'The same.'

Martha wanted to say more but just at that moment, a gentleman stopped at her table. He asked a couple of questions about where she got the inspiration for her work, sniffed, and moved on. Not a good start.

'A friend said she hoped to pop along,' Martha said. 'She was the one what got me to go to art school in the first place. S'only natural she should want to come to the exhibition – if only to see what I've bin up to! I work with her. Her name's Vera.'

Vera arrived at quarter past eleven and it had just begun to rain. She wore the same hat she wore to work and it kept most of her head dry.

'My word, Martha, you haven't half bin busy, duck.'

She was looking at a drawing in charcoal that Martha was particularly proud of. It depicted workbenches, with paintresses hard at work. One of the paintresses was holding a brush and staring through a window where a sparrow sat on the sill staring back. The bench where the paintress was working held lots of brushes of different sizes, and small pots of paint. The dull brown sparrow looked as if she was staring at the paint pots and begging the paintress to give her some colour – any colour, except the dull brown she was wearing.

Martha held her breath as Vera looked on. After what seemed like minutes, Vera lifted her head, wet with tears.

'It's beautiful, Martha. How clever you are.'

Bridie smiled over Martha's head, nodding in agreement. Martha gave a contented sigh hoping that others who looked at it would give the same kind of response.

'And this is the design you've bin working on.' Vera looked long and hard, her head turning one way and then the other as if to change the angle. 'It looks fine. You should be well satisfied, Martha.'

'I dunno whether anyone understands it, to be honest. I think people expect to see a design that means summat. Like sprays of flowers, or animals or scenes. Perhaps I was wrong to pin my hopes on it.'

'No you weren't. I have every faith in yer and I'm not, and never would be, just saying it to make you feel better.'

'Mr John said he would ask a couple of board members to come, but I wouldn't know them from Adam!'

A well-dressed gentleman who had been standing at the back of the group moved forward and lifted his hand to attract her attention.

'So, you see a future in this sort of ceramic ware?'

'I certainly do, sir. Designers need to get their ideas out into the world to the customers who are buying the stuff.'

'Isn't that what happens?'

Martha shook her head. 'No, sir. Most of the pottery is sold to wholesalers and they in turn supply shops. It is the wholesaler who has made the decision to buy, not the customer. If buyers choose not to stock our ware, how will customers find out about it?'

'How could we ask everyone – don't be absurd.'

Those standing around Martha stopped talking, aware something was happening.

'I'm sorry. That's not what I meant,' she said apologetically, refusing to be silenced. 'We just need to put our designs out there where people can see them, in places such as shops, and advertisements in magazines, to show them what they're missing. Then, they will tell their friends... and so on...' She trailed off. Mr John had attached himself to the back of the group. How much had he heard? Whatever must he think – her, a paintress, trying to act like summat she wasn't?

'I agree with Miss Owen,' said an elegantly dressed lady. 'These designs are what modern middle-class women are looking for to adorn their tables. They are refreshingly different.'

'Yes, madam, but that's not how business works,' the man insisted. 'Our job is to make the ware and it is our wholesalers' task to sell it.'

'I beg to differ. I am Ursula Dorn, the household commissioning editor for *New Woman* magazine, and I for one think this is just the sort of product our readers are looking for. This is elegant and practical. Something for every day, not just for major events.'

As the group finally split up, Mr John came forward. 'Good to hear your explanation of how things should be happening, Martha. That was a stroke of luck, Miss Dorn arrived just at the right time and she has given me her card.'

Martha's face was well and truly burning with excitement.

The well-dressed gentleman she had been talking to took Mr John's hand and shook it.

'So, this is what we're resorting to, is it, John. Having our workers shut out our buyers and run our company for us?'

'Of course not, Mr Curtis. But Martha, here, has a point. The closer we can get to our customers, the better our sales would be. You only need to take a look at the large department stores. I have seen new designs from smaller potbanks than ours in prominent places, yet we cannot get our ware into those locations.'

Mr Curtis took another glance at Martha's display. 'And this young lady is...?'

'I beg your pardon. Let me introduce you to Miss Martha Owen, one of our recently qualified modellers, and Mr Jonas Gray, Chief Designer and one of our most experienced and talented modellers, who has been supervising her work. Martha, Jonas, this is Mr Curtis, one of our board members.'

'It's been... interesting, Miss Owen. You have given me food for thought.' He shook her unresponsive hand – and moved on.

'Oh, Lordy! What have I done?' Martha covered her face.

Mr John gave a wry smile. 'Martha Owen, you are one of the few people I know who has rendered Mr Curtis speechless!'

Surprisingly, Mr John stayed at the exhibition for most of the afternoon, and for nearly all that time he had a broad smile on his face.

Jonas helped her to pack everything away.

'So, how did you enjoy your first exhibition?' he asked.

'I loved it. I was scared at first – but when I got into it, it felt wonderful.'

'You looked wonderful too – you took to it like a duck to water.'

'D'yer think so?'

'It's what I like about you, Martha. You can do just about anything, but you don't push it. Sometimes, I feel you need pushing because you don't sell yerself.'

'You think I should sell meself?' She frowned as if she didn't follow. 'Shouldn't I wait until I've lost me job, before resorting to that?'

He came to stand by her side. 'Not in that way – and you know it.' He grinned. He put his hand on her arm. 'You did well today, Martha. I'm very proud of you.'

She smiled. He looked so earnest. She pulled him behind the large display board behind them and kissed him, because if felt the right thing to do. The only thing to do. She closed her eyes, not to blot out the picture of him, but to savour the moment when her body might respond to his.

His arms came round her and he held her tightly.

'Oh, Martha,' he groaned. 'All that time I kept my distance because you didn't want me to get close to you. You don't know how much it cost me to do that.'

'Thank you for putting up with me. But now I think we must stop this and remember we're in a public place. It would never do for Mr John to catch us like this!'

So much longing had come with that kiss. He had done so much for her. And now she could pay him back.

–

Mr John sent for Jonas and Martha the following Monday. He looked happy, pleased with the exhibition and the feedback he had received.

'And by the way, Martha, Mr Curtis was very pleased with what he saw and heard – and that is all down to you.'

'Oh! He asked a lot of questions. I thought he didn't like any of it.'

'He doesn't like to show his hand too early, our Mr Curtis. He's a card player, you see.'

She didn't see but nodded anyway.

'I've called you here to tell you what I am going to do. Our business has always had two distinct parts to it. There is the bone china dining ware. Many of the patterns and shapes have not changed since the turn of the century. The range of shapes are many and the patterns are usually bespoke to the customer. Our ware adorns exclusive hotels, country houses and even some of the royal palaces. The other side and by far the most lucrative is the vases and jars. These are highly decorated items which take a lot of work and command high prices in the market.'

'As you know,' Jonas filled in, 'we only make small numbers of each shape and pattern combination which adds to their attractiveness. People like to have something exclusive to show to their friends.'

'I am proposing we revamp our existing patterns on all of the vases and jars. Our traditional colours tend to be dull and dark, so we are going to take the ideas you're advocating, Martha, to brighten up our offerings in this area. When it comes to new shapes, we want you to come up with a complete range of household pottery designed for prosperous workers and the middle classes, based on some of the designs you exhibited at Burslem School of Art. These products will be marketed directly through magazines to create demand, forcing our wholesalers to stock our items. Finally, once we have solved the technical issues, we'll go ahead with a line of modern designs for general use.'

Mr John took a deep breath and paused.

'All these changes need to be available at the British Industries Fair at the end of February and the beginning of March 1923, at White City in London. It's a prestigious trade show and our new lines will take centre stage. Jonas, you'll be in charge of the whole project.'

'I've already got a lot of ideas for the vases and jars, so I'll concentrate on their redesign,' said Jonas.

'Of course, while this is going on we need to keep the existing business supplied with designs and patterns to our usual standards. There's so much to think about. It's a huge step for us. It'll mean changing a lot of what we do. Setting up and investing in new machines, building stock and outlay on advertising. There is a board meeting in two weeks on 24 July, when I will present my strategy to them. I would also like you to produce sketches – those you exhibited will be perfect – on some of our existing shapes to give substance to the designs.'

Martha could not believe what she was hearing. They were going to go ahead with some of her designs, but, best of all, it was going to be a completely new range designed by Martha Owen.

Mr John sat behind his desk, rubbing his chin. Martha could almost read his thoughts as he turned things over in his mind.

'Some of the board are still very loyal to my father's memory. Those directors may see any change as a betrayal of my father.'

'I understand, Mr John – but times move on. Paradise Pottery will have to do the same else people won't buy it,' Martha said with a boldness that surprised her.

'Jonas has been telling me the same for a while. I didn't want to change anything too soon because I thought it would upset the workers.'

'To be truthful, Mr John, the only thing that would upset the workers would be losing their jobs because nobody wants to buy nothing.'

'You have a blunt way of putting things, don't you, Martha?'

'Not really. I try to tell the truth. Sometimes it gets me into trouble. But there's no point in second-guessing anything when the truth's plain to see.'

'Mm. Starkly truthful, but you're right – unfortunately. Now it is my turn to be starkly truthful. Whatever we do has got to succeed or the business might fold. I have already had offers from other businesses, but at a fraction of the company's potential worth. I am determined not to sell and see this change of direction as our best and only route out of our situation.'

Martha went cold at the thought of everyone in the factory depending on her designs.

–

Jonas and Martha walked back to the Decorating Shop in silence. She thought about what Mr John had told them. The task was enormous and failure could mean the end of the business.

Instead of turning down the corridor towards the shop floor, Jonas said, 'Come on, let's go for a walk outside, we both could appreciate some fresh air after what we have just been told.'

It was sunny and getting warmer. They turned out of the gate and walked down the hill towards the canal.

'How d'yer feel?'

Martha shrugged. 'I dunno, Jonas. Building up to the exhibition was wonderful and I had so much to concentrate on and now all I can think about is people losing their jobs because of me.'

'Mr John knows what he's doing. Your project wouldn't have got this far if he didn't think it would work. It can be a problem, when you try to do summat different, exciting, there's always a possibility of something going wrong. And you have to deal with that. But it isn't the end of the world. Everybody in the company will play their part in making it work. Trust me, if you want summat to happen, you'll make it happen, Martha.'

They returned to the modelling room and as she opened the door the three wise men, as she called her fellow modellers, were anxious to know what had gone on. Between them, they had a wealth of experience, but would have to be nurtured carefully to make the best of it.

'What's happened?' whispered Levi.

'Oh, Mr John wanted to congratulate me on the exhibition, that's all.'

George said loudly, 'Was Jonas congratulating you, an' all? We was all watching you two walk down the street.'

'Leave the girl alone. She's allowed to walk down the street with her fiancé,' said Levi. 'I hear congratulations are in order, lass. You did well at the exhibition. I hear there's going to be a piece in *The Sentinel* about you and the factory. Good for us all.'

Martha beamed. 'Is there? I didn't know.'

'Dunner think we've ever worked with a famous person, have we, Levi?' said George.

'No, I think not.'

'I'll have to find someone else to make me tea.'

Martha laughed. Ever since her first day, if Martha was making herself a mug of tea, George had said he'd have the same, and he had always been given the same answer – a resounding no. It had become a running joke and Martha realised she had made progress when they started to take turns in making the tea.

'Come on, George. Leave Martha alone,' said Jonas. 'You'll all get to hear what Mr John has to say in a couple of weeks. Until then it is work as normal for us all. I promise you'll be pleased.'

For the next two weeks, Martha and Jonas worked hard preparing the artwork and examples to be shown at the board meeting.

–

They worked all day on Saturday and Mr John was happy with the samples. Miss Norton was present, typing lots of papers for the meeting.

It came round to six o'clock and Jonas said, 'We've finished. We can't do any more.'

He went to see Mr John while Martha made sure all the samples and artwork were safely locked away. When Jonas returned, he said Mr John and Miss Norton were staying until all the papers were finished. Jonas had offered them their help, which was respectfully declined. After all they were no office workers.

When they got outside the weather was still warm and they made a beeline for the fish and chip shop on the High Street. They sat on a bench and ate their food out of the newspaper. After all their hard work, it was delicious.

Afterwards, they took a walk around the town and over to the park.

'Don't you think it's marvellous, all these beautiful flowers, such colours. That's what my designs are about, Jonas. It's probably a long time since you did anything so simple.'

'I still spend a lot of time drawing and painting. I try to paint by mood. It's surprising how much you can discover about an artist by the depth of colour and the light and dark.'

'Yes, we did some of that at the art school. It's so strange to know I'm not going back. I loved the whole experience. I've learned so much about the world and our industry. I want to carry on discovering more.'

Once inside the park gates, Jonas threw his arms around her and kissed her and she didn't want him to stop.

Remembering where they were, she reluctantly pulled away.

They carried on walking, her arm linked in his, smiling broadly. By the time they arrived back at Park Terrace, the sun had dropped behind the buildings, but some of the walls were still in sunlight. The whole scene had a hypnotic crimson glow.

'D'yer fancy going to Trentham Gardens on Bank Holiday Monday? The Besses-O'-Th'-Barn Band are playing and they're really good – won quite a few prizes. There's boating on the lake and refreshments and even a soda fountain. We could make it a proper day out. What d'yer say?'

Martha's eyes shone. She didn't know anything about music, but she loved hearing the unique sounds of a brass band. She rarely had enough money to spend on such luxuries. 'Do we have to pay?'

'It's a shilling each for a ticket – but you've no need to worry – it'll be my treat.'

'I can't let yer pay.'

'Like I said – it'll be my treat. I asked yer, didn't I? Now – d'yer want to go.'

'Yes please!'

–

'Good news. They've approved it!'

Mr John came into the modelling room after everyone had left and Jonas and Martha were alone.

'It was unanimous, so it's all hands to the pump.'

Chapter Thirty-nine

The story of Mrs Parker's Pies continued. It was around this time last year that Michael and Issy came up with the idea of selling hot pies outside factories at breakfast and dinnertime. Michael had come up with a way of keeping the pies warm by renting Mr Gianelli's bicycle with its ice cream container mounted on the front. He and Issy had proved that pies could be kept warm just as well as ice cream could be kept cold. He believed in it so much he said he would give up his job in the fruit and veg shop and run the deliveries himself to prove it.

Issy had been excited about it and was keen to try it out. Mr Gianelli was willing to rent them a cart during the winter when he didn't need it. Warm oatcakes would get people parting with money even when they didn't plan to, Michael had said.

Martha could remember to this day her mother's laughter as she beamed at Issy and Michael and said, 'Why do I feel as if you've already decided this for yourselves?'

–

Their day out at Trentham Gardens was every bit as glorious as Martha had hoped, and the band was as good as Jonas had said – if not better, from sad and sentimental to jovial and happy. She was able to put work out of her mind for once. They walked through the extensive formal gardens and beyond. She linked his arm with hers and felt comfortable, as if she had known him all her life.

'I'm glad we decided to come here, Jonas. I would never have come otherwise.'

-

On the first day back after the holidays, Mr John called a meeting of his managers to discuss the requirements for the project. He asked Jonas and Martha to be there. Everybody seemed to be involved: paintresses, decorators, jiggers, jolliers, casters, kiln workers, labourers, glaze shop, pattern makers, mould makers and even Emily Norton to look after the administration.

Mr John went over his plans and announced that Jonas, as Chief Designer with Martha assisting, would take responsibility for the new lines. Mr John then showed the meeting the sketches which had been shown to the board before the holidays.

-

The following day, Martha, Vera, Mr Higginbotham and Jonas met to decide the number of decorators required. They would be mostly paintresses. Initially, it would only be two, but would increase steadily as production increased.

'Well,' Martha said, 'we need to be able to work together and not mind putting in extra shifts if needed – at least until after the trade show. After that, we'll have to wait and see.'

'You're beginning to talk like a boss, Martha,' Jonas was pleased to point out.

'I am not!'

'Yes, you are – and that's a good thing, if this project is going to work.'

'Now I'm feeling worried again.'

'Don't be. I have faith in you and so does Mr John – otherwise he wouldn't have let you take it on.'

'I hope you're right.'

'I know I am. Takes one to know one!'

She punched his arm gently and they sat at her bench to decide who to put on their list of required workers.

Following advice from Vera, they chose five of the current paintresses to start with, including Bridie O'Connor and two girls Martha had had her eye on since the project had become more than just a dream.

For now, she had a trade show to prepare.

Chapter Forty

Martha and Jonas worked hard throughout the week on the project, but left Friday evenings free for themselves. They took it in turns where to have their tea: one week at Park Terrace, one week at Jonas's home. Jonas used to call it their home-and-away fixtures, just like the football. Once the meal was over, the rest of the evening was theirs. The only rule was that they did not speak of work.

When Martha and Jonas got home from work one particular Friday, there was a thick envelope with Canadian stamps on it.

'Good. Letters from Daniel,' said Martha.

The family did not eat until half past seven on Fridays so that Mother and Issy had time to close the shops and change.

'D'yer think your grandma has a piece of fruit cake?' asked Jonas. 'I'm very hungry.'

'Go and ask her, I'm sure she will. Can't have you fainting on us.'

Jonas left the room and Martha settled in a chair and opened her letter.

8 November 1922

Dear Martha,

Congratulations. Your work went down very well at the art school exhibition judging by the cutting from The Sentinel Mother sent with her last letter. It certainly sounded as if you've got the reporter on your side. Even better news is Paradise Pottery's decision to manufacture your designs for the big trade show in London. Who'd have thought my sister's work was being shown in London. Mother said the trade show might be visited by Queen Mary.

Mother's so proud of you. I guess you will be working hard in preparation for this event. Let's hope it's a big success.

I was also surprised to hear in Issy's last letter that Michael has joined the staff of Mrs Parker's Pies and there's now a shop in Burslem. Michael sounds as if he's an enterprising lad. But they don't sound any nearer to romance. In her last letter she said Michael felt like a brother to her. Keep an eye on the girl, just in case brotherly love turns into something else.

I haven't yet started building my house. Catriona persuaded me that I needed to make sure I had the correct buildings for the cattle and I've spent hours erecting fences to create paddocks and fields. I did find time to build a cabin on the land. It has one room and a wood-burning stove. The rest of the facilities are provided by Mother Nature and a shovel. Although I have spent two years training, it made me realise how much I didn't know. This got me depressed and I was starting to think that I had bitten off more than I could chew. But Catriona persuaded me I was being too hard on myself. She said they had lived on this farm and in this valley all of their lives. It was in their blood in the same way as mining is in mine. She said that with the right help I would soon become a good farmer.

We spent loads of time planning how the land was going to be used and the whole of the MacLeod family seemed to get involved. She's so good at planning and so patient with me. She is also very wise for her years. She went to agricultural college in Halifax and is now qualified, so she knows what she's talking about.

She calls me the Quiet Englishman. We've talked about our families, and she knows all about my father. I thought it was good to get things out in the open. I don't suppose it'll come as a shock that we are going to get married in a few weeks. Before you ask, it is not in the same circumstances as Peter! Catriona is a lovely girl, with dark red hair. She is very practical but also very sensitive. We love each other very much and are looking forward to making our home together.

We have been walking out since she returned from Halifax and I wanted to get my land settled before asking her. We had been marking out some field boundaries when it started to snow, we returned to my cabin and she prepared to return home. We stood on the porch with the view of the valley and hills now covered with snow. She said the cabin would make a good place for a home. I asked her straight out if she would marry me. We have set the date for 21 December 1922. It so happens that date is also her twenty-first birthday. I will miss not having any of you with me on the day, but I know I will be in your thoughts – which is good enough for me. We shall have a traditional wedding. The MacLeods have lots of relations so it will be a rowdy affair and I think plenty of whisky will be consumed.

We have arranged for a photographer to take pictures at the wedding and will send you copies once they are ready.

I even thought you might beat me to the altar, and it looks like I have won that race.

All my love, dearest sister,
Daniel

Martha let out a scream and ran to the door just at the same time as Jonas was returning with a piece of cake. They ran into each other. Jonas managed to save the plate, but his cake flew through the air and landed on the hall floor.

'What's wrong, Martha? Bad news?'

'No! It's the best news there could be. Daniel is getting married to Catriona on 21 December.'

'Oh, that's good,' said Jonas, smiling.

At that moment, the front door opened and Mother and Issy entered, and by this time Grandma and Grandad had made their way out of the kitchen. Six adults were in the hall and once Martha had told them the good news, there was lots of hugging. Martha smiled at poor Jonas holding his empty plate and looking regretfully at the remains of his fruit cake on the floor.

Chapter Forty-one

February 1923

It was getting closer to the trade show and like all projects it looked as though nothing would be ready. Martha was getting very edgy and Jonas, despite his calm exterior, was the first to admit he was worried. Even their Friday nights had gone by the board. They were living in a never-ending cycle of work, eat and sleep. Mr John had moved a camp bed into his office to save making the journey back home at all hours in the winter.

Mr John had recently bought a surplus lorry from the war department. It was nothing more than an automobile with a flatbed on the back, which was used to collect things. But on nights when he worked late Jonas used it to get home to Goldenhill.

–

At the beginning of February, the family received a parcel of photographs taken of Daniel and Catriona's wedding. The whole family came together to look at them. Tears were shed and toasts drunk to the absent bride and groom.

Martha wrote back to Daniel.

> *4 February 1923*
>
> *Dear Daniel,*
> *We were all waiting for your letter and photographs to come.*

We are all glad that the wedding was a success. It sounds as if the evening party was so much fun, even though you had a headache for a few days. You look very handsome in your suit and Catriona is very pretty. I thought her dress looked lovely and was impressed that she had made it herself. It's so nice to see all the people you talk about in person, so to speak. The one I like the best is of you stood by the door of your cabin. You look the part of a farmer and you look so happy. I am not surprised when I see the picture of what you were looking at — the view is spectacular, especially with the snow on the ground and no smoke from kilns and chimneys.

It was so nice to get a letter from Catriona telling me all about herself. She sounds as if she really loves farming, and when she told me she had taught you to ride a horse, deliver a calf and shear sheep — I was, quite frankly, amazed, dear brother!

I don't know anything about farming, but it sounds as if you are happy that you have all your animals and fields ready for the spring. I was surprised your winters are so long and that most of it below freezing. But your description of the summer made me long to see it. I'm sure I could produce some lovely designs with the inspiration of those summer and autumn colours.

Jonas is well and we are very busy at work. It is not long — two weeks — until the trade show. I'll write to you to let you know how it went.

Lots of love,
Martha

-

All in all, the girls in Martha's little group got on rather well, for which Martha was thankful.

Her stipulation was that the girls chosen should all be enthusiastic about the new styles: sharp but beautiful designs, that made a person smile.

Martha was amazed at the group's dedication. Their work was now complete and the trade show just around the corner. She thanked the girls for their hard work and commitment to the project.

Bridie stood up and asked to say a few words. 'I think I speak for all of us when I say this, Martha. You have been an inspiration to us all. We've seen yer working, and yer do work hard, Martha, there's no mistaking that. You've shown us that women can make a difference. That women can become designers and planners for the future. We would never have thought it possible cos we've never seen nobody do it before.'

Martha's face reddened. She wished it didn't do that when she wanted to be seen as such a woman, creating prestigious ware to decorate the tables of the rich and the not-so-rich.

'Thanks, girls. Yer don't know how much that means to me. I've enjoyed working with all of yer. Whatever happens at the trade show, it'll be business as usual for all of us. We are taking Paradise Pottery forward and it's thanks to all of you.'

–

Mr John put Jonas in charge of getting the trade show stuff together. It was all individually wrapped in tissue paper and cloth. The whole lot took up three packing cases, which would be transported by passenger train to White City.

Martha and Jonas oversaw the operation. As expected, the covered van arrived on the Thursday morning to take the cases to Stoke station. The cases would travel on the express to London along with Mr John and the rest of the trade show party. Jonas had decided to travel in the goods van to look after the precious items.

Martha and Jonas's excitement was obvious to everyone, though Martha had to admit her temper had been a little short as the deadline approached. She had been waiting for so long, and now it was here, she felt it had been no time at all. It was exactly as she'd felt over the art school exhibition.

It was almost time for the trade show team to leave and Martha had mixed emotions. No one had asked her to go along. She wasn't sufficiently experienced in talking to the trade. It was Jonas, as Chief Designer, who would go this time but, if it all went well, then Martha would accompany them to the next trade show.

'I wished I could be there, but supposing it is a terrible flop, and nobody likes it because it's too simple – I don't know if I could cope with that.'

Jonas grabbed her shoulders and forced her to look at him.

'Martha, darling. You've nothing to worry about. You trust me, don't yer?'

'Yes – course I do.'

'And I've told you lots of times that your work is good and deserves to be shown in the big world outside of Paradise Street?'

'Yes, but—'

'No buts, Martha. You are good and it's time you believed it for yourself.'

She nodded. 'But—'

He held up his finger and placed it gently on her mouth. 'We are nearly ready to leave.' They kissed and received a round of applause from the onlooking workers.

The cases were loaded, paperwork signed, and the future of Paradise Pottery pulled out of the gates and started its journey to London, White City and the British Industries Fair.

Once the men had left, Martha immediately regretted not going with them. At least she would have known what was happening. Now she could do nothing but wait until they returned at the beginning of March.

Throughout the days that followed, she tried to put the trade show out of her mind, but she couldn't do it. She had come so far and that might just be a little too much. The whole factory continued to produce small amounts of the design while waiting for news. Most of their time had to be spent on the old designs that would keep them going.

Martha and her paintresses had a reasonable amount of ware to work on, keeping their minds off the events in London.

–

Mr John left instructions with Miss Norton to organise a small party for the people involved in the project on the middle Sunday afternoon of the trade show. It was to take place in the Decorating Shop.

Miss Norton had arranged for outside caterers to prepare basic food consisting of sandwiches and cakes. She said, 'I'm sorry we are not having pies and oatcakes, but your mother doesn't open on a Sunday and in any case, it would seem too much like a working day for everyone.'

'I hope we don't jinx the trade show by having a party so soon.'

'No, don't think of this get-together as a premature celebration but as a thank you from the company for everybody's work, no matter what the outcome is. Oh, and by the way, Martha, as the leading person left from the project, Mr John would like you to say a few words on his behalf.'

Martha gulped, went red, gulped again, but suddenly, looking at the faces of the people, she knew what she wanted to say.

'We've all worked very hard for the project, and we should be proud of what we have achieved in a little over six months. New shapes, new designs, new patterns and most of all, new colours. Colours we hope will make people want to buy our ware. We've gone through a lot during my time here though unfortunately some people are no longer with us. Let us hope that this is the start of a new era in Paradise. Thank you.'

'I'd prefer to know as I had a job when he comes back, if yer ask me,' came one response.

'Oh, shut up with yer moaning. Are yer never satisfied?' said another.

Martha grinned. A steady job was what they were all looking for, but some people were better at controlling their feelings than others.

'We all want to keep our jobs,' she said, 'but we can allow ourselves a little celebration on what we have achieved. We've done our bit and now it's up to others to do theirs. We must have faith.'

'Martha's right,' said Bridie. 'We've been lucky to be involved in this project. I, for one, couldn't be happier. Here's to *Sea, Sand, Sun*. Happiness in a pot – or a saucer!' She stood up and raised her glass. Everybody joined in and cheered.

The talking grew louder. People were singing and dancing and, at first, no one saw Miss Norton leave or return. She stopped in front of Martha.

'A telegram for you, Martha.'

Martha's face lost its smile as she held out her hand and took it. That's when everyone noticed the scene. Suddenly, the room was silent. Faces turned to look at one another, not knowing what to do. All eyes went to Martha.

She opened the envelope with a trembling hand and read the contents. Then, she read it again. When she looked up, her face was beaming.

'Listen, everybody,' she called, waving the telegram in the air. 'It's from Mr John.' She read it out.

SEA SAND SUN GOING VERY WELL STOP
ENJOY THE PARTY STOP
MR JOHN STOP

A cheer went up after her closing words. Bridie and Vera and a couple of the others began a barn dance around the benches. The kiln man, Dave Trenchman, twirled Miss Norton around the floor, much to her surprise. Martha raised her eyebrows, but Miss Norton was enjoying herself as much as everyone else.

'We shall have to wait for more news – but I believe we will need to step up production as soon as Mr John gets back.'

The caterers cleared the remains of the food and Vera called for quiet. 'Everyone, we need to tidy up the shop and get it ready for the morning, bright and early. I can't be the only one who needs to make me money. Perhaps our colleagues from the dirty end would care to assist us?'

The woman who had moaned about how she'd rather have a job caught Martha at the sinks.

'I hope as yer dunner think I weren't grateful earlier, Martha – cos I am. It's just that it's bin a bad year for us and I've got another kid on the way. It's all very well for us to look at doing new things, but who's going to put bread on the table when things go wrong?'

Martha looked into the anxious face with concern. 'I'm so sorry for your grief, but I can say that we've shown some samples round and everybody has been very interested and wants the ware to do well. People from all over the country will be looking at it at the trade show today.'

A tear rolled down the woman's cheek. 'Now I'm on me own and I've got nobody to talk to, I worry all the time about what'll happen if I lose me job. I conner stop.'

Martha put her arm around the distraught woman just as Vera appeared next to them. She'd heard their conversation.

'Now listen, Wendy, it's thanks to Martha and the others that we may all keep our jobs. I know how yer feel. I felt very much the same when my Eddie was taken in the war. But life goes on and we learn to survive. Here – there's another paintress, about your age, what lost her husband to the flu when he got back. She took it hard. Him staying alive all through the war and then losing him when he got back on English soil. I'll introduce yer both. Have a chat with her. She's a nice girl.'

Wendy allowed herself to be led back to the others looking calmer now, then Vera came back to Martha. 'I thought as you'd still be here,' she said.

'There are times when I wonder if I'm doing the right thing, Vera.'

'Being in charge of summat is always a bit scary. We just have to do our best. And try to help those what aren't as strong as us.'

Martha burst out laughing, which very nearly turned into tears. 'Thank you, Vera. How many times have yer helped me out in the past with yer wise words?'

'Dunno, duckie, but as long as we're all there for each other, we conner go far wrong, can we?'

Chapter Forty-two

March 1923

The trade show ended on 3 March and Martha couldn't wait for Jonas to arrive back. She had all sorts of questions for him but, more than anything, she wanted to be in the safety of his arms. When he wasn't around, it brought home to her how much she relied on his encouragement, support and love. How she had grown used to having him at her side to give her ideas and answer her questions. She had missed him so much.

The van trundled into the courtyard just after five in the afternoon. Jonas jumped down from the seat at the front and spoke to the driver before heading into the building. Martha had heard the van's engine rattling. She hoped he'd come up to the workshop before doing anything else. She wasn't disappointed.

She was still at the window as he came rushing in. A cheer went up as he took her in his arms and planted a kiss on her cheek. She thought she should tell him off but couldn't bring herself to. Who cared that they had been seen? They were engaged, after all.

'We've done it, Martha. *Sea, Sand, Sun* went down very well. We've got a full order book and we can sell plenty more.' He turned to Martha's band of workers. 'We are going to be very busy. I hope you're all ready for it!'

-

Mr John came back from London brimming with enthusiasm at the achievements Paradise Pottery had made in the two weeks of the trade show. Their new designs sat well against Susie Cooper's Gloria Lustre ware, one of the highlights of the show. All the shop floor workers had made their contributions to the project by keeping the potbank going with their usual day-to-day ware – the 'bread and butter' stock of the company.

Just before the bell went for knocking-off time, Mr John walked into the Decorating Shop followed, a few paces behind, by Mr Higginbotham and called for everyone's attention.

'To show our appreciation, we have decided to reintroduce the Summer Dance. Those of you who have worked for us for a number of years will remember the dances we held in the Floral Hall. After 1916, with the losses we sustained, it was felt to be inappropriate to celebrate when our men overseas were going through such a terrible war. We lost many good men. We are now trying to rebuild ourselves and look to the future. It started with our success at the British Industries Fair and our new lines, courtesy of Jonas Gray and Martha Owen. We aim to go from strength to strength and you will be the ones to get us there. So, to mark our appreciation, the Summer Dance will take place this year, and hopefully will become an annual function in our calendar. Friends and colleagues, you are all invited.'

A cheer went up with everybody clapping. Martha glanced at Jonas, clapping and grinning. Someone called for three cheers for Mr John.

'I thought it would go down well with you all – but I'll say it once again: you all deserve it. The dance will take place on 23 June – commencing at half past seven. Miss Norton will put something on the noticeboard tomorrow. I look forward to seeing you all there and thank you for your attention.'

He gave a swift nod and walked out, no doubt to visit the next shop on his list. It was just like him to visit all the shops personally. How good of him, thought Martha.

Everyone buzzed with excitement on the walk home.

'How good of Mr John to bring back the Summer Dance,' said Vera to Martha and Jonas. 'We had such a marvellous time at the last one, knowing everyone. Mind you, I don't think as anyone sat out without a partner back then. We were one big happy family.' The smile slid from Vera's face momentarily.

'That's a big problem these days. So many men not coming back. It could be quite upsetting for some,' said one of the younger paintresses, who got a sharp scowl from a woman twice her age and a warning about being insensitive.

'I don't think as I'll be going this year – but it's good of him to reintroduce it,' said Vera, blinking to fight the tears that still appeared when she thought of Eddie.

'You've got to go, Vera. You've earned it as much as anyone.'

Vera shook her head. 'No, Martha. It wouldn't be right without my Eddie.'

Martha squeezed her hand. 'You'll never forget Eddie, Vera, and you wouldn't want to. But you have to move on. You can't not enjoy yerself ever again.'

'Who shall I go with then?'

Martha could only look blank. What Vera said was true. She couldn't, offhand, think of anyone.

'We'll think of somebody, Vera. Just don't decide not to come. Not yet, any road.' She changed the subject smartly.

'Cassie and Peter are talking of moving out and renting rooms when the new baby comes. They didn't think it was fair to me to have two young 'uns. I told them I was happy for them to stay. Their rent comes in useful some weeks, but I can't say as I blame them. They'll not be moving far, they say they want to stop in Tunstall. We can stay in touch. I'll miss young Andrew. He's coming on a treat, isn't he?'

Martha nodded. 'Yes, and he'll be ready for school next year.'

'Did yer know that Adeline is a regular visitor now? A proper granny she's turning into.'

'Peter mentioned it. How's she faring with Mr Mellor? I can't imagine him being too pleased.'

Vera laughed 'He's not. But Adeline's warned him that if he tries to prevent her from seeing her daughter, she'll leave him. She's got more backbone than I thought she had.'

Martha covered her mouth to stop the laughter spewing out. 'Looks like women have learned quite a bit during the war about speaking up for themselves. The world will be better for it, in my opinion. Congratulations to Adeline.'

Chapter Forty-three

June soon came around. Martha hadn't asked Vera who would accompany her to the Summer Dance. She had suggested that Jonas put on his thinking cap when she hadn't heard from Vera. She was sure her friend would've said something by now if she had chosen someone. Martha didn't want to give her any opportunity to excuse herself.

Out of the blue, the week before the dance, Vera popped her head around the door to the modelling room and motioned to Martha to follow her. When Martha joined her, she was surprised to find Vera beaming.

'You'll never guess, Martha,' she said. 'Guess. I want you to guess!'

'How can I guess if I don't even know what you're thinking about?'

'Suppose I say it's about the dance?'

'About the dance?'

Vera nodded. 'Come on, Martha. You aren't usually this slow.'

Martha began to shake her head… and then… 'You've got a partner for the dance, haven't yer?'

Vera broke out into more smiles. 'I wanted to tell you first.'

'Go on then – who is it?'

'Dave Trenchman.'

'The kiln man what helped us on the project?'

'That's right. Asked me on the way home last night.'

'And what did yer say?'

'I said as I'd have to think about it.'

'Oh no, Vera. You can't do that. He's a nice man.'

'Dunner werrit, Martha. Of course I said yes.'

Martha jumped up and hugged her.

'I shall still feel strange about dancing with a man other than Eddie.'

'But you have to start somewhere, Vera. Eddie would've wanted that.'

'And you don't think it's too soon?'

'It's bin seven years, Vera. No one would be expecting yer to mourn forever.'

It was the night before the Summer Dance and Martha was surprisingly nervous.

Mother frowned. 'What's the matter, love? I thought as yer'd be proper excited.'

'I was just thinking about Jonas. He's such a good man. Gentle and caring and so thoughtful. I've learned so much from him, Mother. He lets me go at my own pace, and I'm so glad he took no notice of me when I said I wasn't interested in finding a man. That's why I chose him.'

'He knew that was the voice of a woman who hadn't made up her mind. If he'd given chase at that time, you'd have probably run a mile. He let you choose the right time and that's precious, Martha. A man to hold onto.'

'How's Issy getting on with Michael Dean? They're both strong characters.'

'I can't believe the change in our Issy since she took over our shop in Burslem. She's another one who has taken charge of her own life. All that trouble in the past has brought out the best in her. The Longton shop is almost ready for opening. Issy's thriving on it all, and now that Michael's taken charge of delivering hot food to potbanks and manufacturers, she's delighted. I believe the two of them could take over the business – when I'm ready to let it go. Not that I'm planning on retiring just yet!'

Martha laughed. 'I should think not! Mrs Parker's Pies are the best pie shops in Stoke-on-Trent, and long may they continue, I'd say.'

'I thought as them two might get together one day. She was quite keen on him. These days they each have their jobs to do and they both get on with it.'

Mother tipped her head to one side, thinking, and then caught Martha's shoulders. 'I am so proud of my girls. You've both achieved everything you could wish for and more. Your jobs suit yer perfectly and bring out the best in yer both. Look at you – not only did you become the paintress you wanted to be, but you're now designing the patterns that the other paintresses are working on. Betty may have bin the brightest in the class, and she's done well – after a bad start, bless her. But you and our Issy have done so well too. All my children have given me more than I could've hoped for. Daniel and his new life in Canada and Peter as the family man. I'm so lucky.'

Martha watched the tears build up in her mother's eyes. 'It's us that owe you. You're the one who set us on the right road and made sure we stayed there. You could've given up at any time, Mother, but you didn't. You gave us the strength to do what we did.'

'In the bad days I thought, so many times, that I was letting you all down – so you couldn't have said a nicer thing to me. Thank you, Martha.'

–

Martha had made a new dress to wear especially for the occasion. She was becoming quite a dressmaker, out of necessity rather than choice. She'd seen a pattern in Burton & Dunn's in their basic design range which would suit the moment perfectly. Dropped waist, square collar, three-quarter sleeves, and a flouncy skirt to just above her calves. Having considered all the bolts of material they had to offer, she had chosen a beautiful violet. To go with her outfit, she had made a lace scarf to tie around her short, bobbed hair, or to throw round her shoulders if the evening should turn cool.

'You look beautiful, Martha,' was Issy's comment when she walked down the stairs, all done up. She'd popped down to Park Terrace to do Martha's hair for her.

'Aye, lass. That man of yours won't be able to take his eyes off yer,' was Grandad's comment.

'I'll borrow it next time I go somewhere posh,' said Issy, all smiles.

'No yer won't. I'm saving it for special days.'

'Then you'll have to make one for me an' all.' Issy licked her tongue out to press the point but smiled all the time.

At that moment, there was a knock on the door.

'I'll go.' Issy shot off to the door before anyone could stop her. 'She's waiting for yer, Jonas. And she's so looking forward to it.'

Martha heard Issy's words as she led him in. She stood in front of the fire automatically, although it wasn't lit and it wasn't cold.

Jonas stood still and stared at her. 'You look... wonderful.'

'You think so?'

'I know so. I'll be the envy of every man at the dance.'

Issy grinned. 'Best get off. Too many compliments. You'll never get there.' She kissed Martha and spoke in a quiet voice. 'Have a great time. I mean it. You pair were meant for each other.'

They set off for the Floral Hall at a slow pace, meeting Vera and Dave on the way. Dave had spruced himself up well and looked particularly proud. Martha would have been happy to have Jonas to herself for as long as possible. She almost wished they weren't going to the dance but was positive they would have a good time.

'Hiya, you two. We're going to have a great night. I can feel it in me bones,' said Dave, grinning broadly.

Martha glanced at Vera who looked striking. She had obviously made an effort to look good and had even arranged her hair in a style Martha hadn't seen before. It suited her very well. Dave seemed to be doing all the talking, but Vera was quick to take notice and nod appropriately. They both looked nervous, like a couple of school kids going out for the first time. Martha grinned and crossed her fingers that they would both relax once they got to the dance.

Bridie and Raymond joined them on Station Road.

'This is going to be the best night ever.' Bridie clapped her hands. 'I've bin thinking about it ever since Mr John told us, haven't you lot?'

'You're a one for the dancing, darling.' Raymond grasped Bridie's hand and together they did a pirouette.

There was a great deal of giggling as they walked through the park towards the Floral Hall, with its welcoming lights. They drew closer, heard voices talking, laughing and generally louder than at work and with much more abandon.

Martha was glad the workers were all coming together as they used to, and that she had Jonas at her side.

'I'm looking forward to this, Jonas. We're so lucky to have workmates who are such good friends. I'd be lost without them.'

'And I'd be lost without you, Martha.'

She blushed as his soft tone did strange things to her insides. She carried on, hurriedly. 'I remember Dave helping us with the project. He seems very nice.'

'Yes, he is. I think he's been wanting to ask Vera out for a while now but he felt awkward – what with him being an old friend of Eddie's.'

He stopped walking and drew her towards a tree that would shelter them from prying eyes.

'What are—'

'Stop talking and listen to me.'

334

She stepped back, surprised at the strained look in his eyes. 'What's up? Are you feeling all right?'

'There's summat I need to say to yer.'

She felt his intake of breath.

'Darling Martha. You mean everything to me, and always will. I'm so glad that I asked Eddie and Vera to introduce me to you. It was the best decision of my life.'

Martha was overcome by the earnestness she could see written on his face. She had no doubt at all in his words. She had been excited when they got engaged. It had been a long engagement so far, but there did not seem to be any obstacles in their way now. The next step could only be… oh, my word!

'Dearest Martha, would you do me the honour of marrying me as soon as possible? I don't think I can wait any longer. Tell me if you need more time, but I have to—'

She threw herself into his arms. 'Yes! Oh, yes, Jonas. As soon as we can arrange it.' She'd had enough of waiting too. Jonas had helped her through her working life and now she wanted to marry the love of her life. She knew, had known, for longer than she cared to admit, that there had never been anyone else for her.

'How about Potters' Week?'

'This August coming? Could we arrange it so soon?'

'We can try. And if not, we'll go for the earliest date possible.'

She took his hands in hers. 'I do love you, Jonas Gray.' She pulled him towards her and kissed him, gently at first, then growing more urgent. She was a woman of the new world. It was about time she took responsibility for her own feelings.

When she eventually let him go, he looked dazed. 'Martha Owen – I think we'd better arrange the wedding as soon as ever we can.'

She laughed, throwing her head back, delighted with the sense of abandon that flowed through her body at that moment.

They entered the Floral Hall to find Vera and Dave waiting for them. Bridie and Raymond were already on the dance floor.

'Martha Owen!' Vera said. 'We thought you'd changed your mind about coming tonight when you disappeared but, judging by the colour of your face, you obviously had something on your minds!'

Martha turned quickly to Jonas. 'Oh, can I tell her?'

His smile broadened. He nodded. 'I don't suppose – for one minute – that I'll be able to stop you.'

She picked up Vera's hands. 'We are going to set a date for our wedding – hopefully for August.'

Vera squealed. 'Oh, my love, that's wonderful news. Mind you – we have been expecting the news ever since you got engaged.'

They hugged each other, twirling and dancing. After that, there was no point in keeping anything quiet. All her friends – and she didn't realise she had so many – came forward to wish her well. One of the first was Emily Norton.

'I wish you all the best in the world, Martha. I'm so pleased for you both. You and Jonas make a lovely couple.'

'Thank you, Emily. It's kind of you to say so.'

'I must tell you that we've been running a sweepstake on when you two would get married. And I am happy to tell you that I was the one who drew out August 1923.'

'We never knew anything about it.'

'It was started after you got engaged but we were getting worried that we would need to add more months, or even years, as the mould maker Cecil suggested, but that is not going to be required now.'

'I don't know how you managed to keep that quiet. You can't keep anything secret on a potbank.'

'Oh, you can,' said Emily, with a knowing wink.

'Does that mean what I think it means?'

'I'm saying nothing more.'

'Have you anyone with you?'

Emily shook her head. 'No. I just wanted to show my face on such a wonderful day. I'll probably stay for an hour and then go home.'

'Oh, no you won't. You'll sit with us and enjoy yourself.'

'Oh no. I couldn't intrude.'

'You'll sit with us tonight and we'll all have a wonderful time, after all, you have organised the event, you should enjoy it with us.'

'That would be very nice.'

'In any case, if you don't sit with us how can I find out your secret?'

A couple of loud knocks on a table soon stopped the talking. Mr John was on his feet calling for everyone to be quiet.

'Good evening, everyone – and I hope it will be a good evening for us all. Today, we find ourselves with plenty to feel good about. When my father passed away nearly two years ago, I had a tough act to follow. He had built C. Rhead & Son into a company well respected in our industry. We have much to thank him for.'

'I'll drink to that,' shouted one of the clay-end men.

'Hear, hear,' came a woman's voice.

'Thank you.' Mr John smiled. 'However, the war presented our company with problems. While the home market was doing well with no German imports to compete with, industry itself was changing and we had to change with it. We were ready for the challenge. You' – his arm swept around the room, taking in everyone – 'have made it possible with our mix of old and new. And I salute each and every one of you.'

More cheers.

'I would like us to take a few minutes to remember those of our friends and colleagues who gave their lives for their country, not forgetting the injured – both in body and in mind – who have to bear the results of those labours every single day.'

Standing next to Vera, Martha could feel her friend's body shaking and her heart went out to her. It was the last thing Vera would've wanted – to draw attention to herself in such a manner. Martha squeezed her hand gently and cast a quick look at Dave. He too had noticed. She turned back to Mr John, hoping that his speech wouldn't go on for too long.

'I like to think of Paradise – as we lovingly call it – as a family of which my father would be proud. Orders for the new line are looking good, and along with our existing fine china, the company's future is looking more secure.'

More cheers followed and he waited for them to settle down again before continuing.

'On a lighter note, Jonas and Martha, join me if you will.'

Surprised, Martha passed Vera to Emily, hoping they would look after each other, and went to join him. Jonas arrived at her side at the same moment.

'These two young people decided, as you know, that they don't spend enough time together and got engaged – some time ago. According to the word circulating among you, I am led to believe their wedding will take place in August.'

The cheers were deafening, causing even Jonas to blush furiously.

'I am sure you will want to wish them every success in their future together.'

After the cheers had faded away, Jonas said, 'Martha's an amazing woman, and I'm looking forward to the day when we can become man and wife. Thank you, one and all.'

'About bloody time.'

'Thank you, George.' He lifted his glass to them. Then he turned to Martha and lifted his glass to her. How proud she was of him. She hugged him, no longer worried what others might think. He was hers, and that was all that mattered.

'So enjoy yourselves this evening,' Mr John finished. 'You deserve it. But don't be late on Monday.'

Guffaws of laughter followed.

Once they returned to their friends, Martha noticed Vera was missing and immediately made her way to Dave.

'I haven't seen her since Mr John's speech. She said as she was going to the ladies' room. She was upset after what he said about the fallen.'

Martha nodded and pushed her way through the dancers to the ladies' room. Two women were washing their hands and checking their appearance. Martha's eyes went to the one closed door. She waited until she was alone.

'Vera? Vera, are you in there?' she whispered.

There was a sound, something between a sob and a breath.

'Come out, Vera. I'm here now. I know you're upset.'

The door opened and a dishevelled Vera appeared.

'I'm sorry, Martha. I had to get out of there. I think about Eddie all the time. It's not getting any easier.'

Martha put her arms around Vera, taking on some of the tears herself. Tears for this woman who had become very dear to her.

'Dearest Vera, no one is going to judge you for being upset. You lost the man who meant more to you than anyone else in the world.'

Vera nodded, attempting to dry her eyes with an already damp handkerchief.

'Mr John wanted to thank the likes of Eddie when he spoke, including his own father. You wouldn't have wanted it any other way.'

'I know. But whatever will Dave think of me – running out on him like that?'

'If he's half the man I think he is, he'll recognise your distress for what it was – a woman who is still recovering from a tragic loss.'

'He won't want anything to do with me if he thinks I'm not over Eddie, will he?'

Martha shook her head. 'You can't know that. No one can take away what you and Eddie had. You will always be in love with Eddie. But eventually you'll have room to give some of your love to another, who will come to love you as much as Eddie did. Dave is worried about you because you're upset. You need to go out there and show him that you found Mr John's speech overwhelming but you are ready to move on now. Dave's a good bloke. He'll understand.'

Vera tidied herself up and the two made their way back to the dance floor. It only took Martha one look at Dave to see how much he was affected by Vera's heartbreak. He took her hand and led her to a quiet corner where they could talk, smiling at Martha and miming a thank you. She smiled back. Yes, Vera would be well looked after with Dave. Of that, she had no doubt.

The music had grown louder and the dance floor was packed when they returned. The latest dance sensation, the foxtrot, both slow and fast, required a seat at the end, to enable dancers to recover before returning to the dance floor for more of the same.

Jonas tapped Martha's shoulder and pointed to Mr Higginbotham, who was talking to a couple of the older male painters. His fondness for a drink was well known. Martha remembered the day he'd turned up at the pub to tell her she'd got the job at Paradise Pottery and had stayed afterwards. It was plain he knew her grandad well. Since then, she'd discovered that he often took the opportunity to enjoy a drink when out on his own without his Temperance wife monitoring everything he drank.

Having a few drinks inside him made him merry and he smiled and giggled like a schoolgirl. It appeared that he'd decided to visit every table and to say a personal thank you and share a drink. When he arrived at Martha's table he looked considerably worse for wear. His bow tie was crooked and his glasses were hanging precariously on the end of his nose.

'Are my favourite des... des... igners enjoying themselves?'

Already his stance was precarious, as he concentrated on getting his words out.

'Certainly, Mr Higginbotham. Are you?' asked Martha, trying to hide a grin.

He giggled and tapped his nose. 'What the wife doesn't know about she can't complain about, can she?'

He had to grab the table to avoid sliding to the floor. Then, his eyes went to Dave. 'What are you doing here, Mr Trenchman, sitting with my designers?'

Dave began to explain, but it was obvious to them all that Mr Higginbotham wasn't listening.

He got up as if he was leaving. He must have realised that his brain was not capable of processing the movement of so many body parts at the same time. He spun round and said to Martha, 'Is this seat taken?' then slumped onto it without waiting for an answer.

'Mrs Higginbotham's not with yer tonight, Mr Higginbotham?' asked Martha.

'No, no, no. The demon drink is present and there is enjoyment abounding. Too much excitement for my wife. And you may call me Wilfred tonight, my dear.'

'You're going to be in trouble when you get home, Wilfred,' laughed Jonas, lifting his glass.

'I know, but I will have enjoyed myself getting there. Better get my tin hat on. Mrs Higginbotham will not be pleased, and I shall be sleeping in the dog's kennel!'

He never actually left the chair, for he fell asleep minutes afterwards, his head resting on his arm now attached to the back of his chair.

When Martha and Jonas stood up for the final dance, she saw that Mr John was already there. At his side was Emily Norton. It was both a surprise and not. At work, Emily had been his secretary ever since she had left The Potteries Tramway Company, four years before. Martha hoped they had continued their friendship from that day Jonas and her had seen them on the train. It was very likely they might have discovered feelings for each other. Martha saw her look into Mr John's eyes and witnessed the emotions written there – longing and loneliness, love and need. Emily was wearing her heart on her sleeve. Mr John was smiling and happy, unlike at work when he tended to be too busy to show any feelings preferring to focus on the matters in hand. She saw him take Emily into his arms and found herself hoping that Emily might have a new friendship to celebrate before too much longer. She believed she had discovered Emily's secret.

The next couple to arrive at the dance floor was Vera and Dave on their first outing together. Vera looked well recovered from her troubled visit to the ladies' room. Her and Dave had spent plenty of time sitting talking and things looked to be going well. She hoped so. Vera deserved to be happy. Maybe she was witnessing the dawn of a new friendship for her dearest friend Vera, too.

Martha slid into the arms of her intended and he guided her round the dance floor, her head resting on his shoulder. It was so good to be in his arms, his strength supporting her. She couldn't have been happier. She had been so lucky – a job beyond her expectations and a forthcoming marriage to the man of her dreams. What more could a girl wish for? She felt Jonas's lips brush the top of her head and closed her eyes to savour the moment.

As the dance came to an end, Martha's eyes turned to Wilfred Higginbotham still in the chair where he had settled earlier. He looked glum, but more sober than he had been.

Bridie joined her and followed her eyes to Mr Higginbotham. 'He's a sad old man, isn't he?'

Martha nodded. Yes, she did feel sorry for him. He obviously enjoyed having a good time, but it sounded as if his home life was far from happy.

'At least he's enjoyed himself tonight. Some people should never be together if you ask me.'

Never was a truer word spoken, thought Martha.

At the end of the evening, Mr John had to find someone who would be able to take Mr Higginbotham home just in case he collapsed somewhere. Whoever was going to take him would have to be prepared to sober him up a little bit first to avoid the wrath of Mrs Higginbotham. This action fell to Vera and Dave. It was hoped that Vera, knowing Mr Higginbotham's wife personally, would get into the least amount of trouble when they returned him to his home.

Martha and Jonas walked out of the Floral Hall holding hands. It was a lovely summer's evening with a warm glow in the sky. Martha thought it was coming from the setting sun, but Jonas thought it might well be coming from the Shelton Bar steelworks. They laughed and agreed that whichever it was, it was romantic.

'You know summat, Jonas? Tonight we've seen some of what the war did for us, both good and bad. Do you ever think of what life might've been like if there had been no war? I mean, if it hadn't been for the war, I might still be working at Jackson's, and we may never have met. If my father had lived, I couldn't have gone to art school. He was dead set against spending good money on the future of any woman. Mother wouldn't have had Mrs Parker's Pies because he wouldn't have let her go out to work. I wouldn't have made so many wonderful friends. I thought I only needed one good friend. It turns out that we all need friends – different friends at different stages of life.'

'To answer your question – I've not thought about how I'd feel if the war hadn't come along. I couldn't bear to think of us never meeting, Martha. I can't get past that. My family was lucky – we all came back. I'm glad it's all over and we can get on with our lives, working together, living together. The war is over. May we never see the likes of it again.'

'I shall so look forward to planning our wedding, Jonas.'

'I'll help you. We make such a good team.'

'Best get off home to tell Mother we're setting a date.'

'I've got a confession, darling – I might've already told her!'

'Jonas!'

A letter from Lynn

It is with great excitement that I send out the latest of my Potteries Girls sagas. Living with characters such as Martha and Jonas is a privilege, and getting to know them is like watching a film running inside my head. For that moment in time when I write about their trials and tribulations, they are my friends, and I want to wish them well – most of the time!

If you have read my previous books you will recognise Martha as Betty Dean's friend from *The Potteries Girls on the Home front*, but her story is very different. Martha's story takes the reader back to the pottery industry and to a character with many challenges to face.

In writing Martha's story, I called upon the knowledge of former pottery workers who could point me in the right direction for making the story as close to what it was like working in the industry. Although the industry has benefited from new technology and updated working regulations, much of the work is done using traditional methods.

This book is a work of fiction as are all the characters who reside in it. The names of the towns making up The Potteries are all real. The businesses are fictional although there is passing reference to some of the well-known pottery manufacturers. Many of the street names are real although the actual addresses mentioned are not. Some of the buildings referred to, e.g. The Floral Hall, the covered market in Tunstall and the Victoria Hall in Stoke did, or do, exist. The British Industries Fair did take place in 1923 and Susie Cooper was exhibited. By including all of this, I hope readers who might visit Stoke-on-Trent may benefit from a closer relationship with the area.

Art schools were important to the pottery industry and one existed in each of Burslem, Tunstall and Longton towns to prepare young local workers for jobs. I chose Burslem School of Art for Martha to attend as it was the principal school in the area, although the curriculum was fictional based on information I had picked up in the course of my reading.

I do hope you have enjoyed meeting Martha, her family and friends in The Potteries.

Acknowledgements

Once again, my thanks to the lovely Keshini Naidoo at Hera Books for her ongoing support. Her thoughtful suggestions are always a great help, especially during times of crisis when characters refuse to act in the manner I have chosen for them. My thanks also to editors Phil Williams, Jennie Ayres and Jenny Page for their valuable contributions.

Getting feedback from someone who isn't as close to the work-in-progress is really important. It's so easy to miss elements that don't quite fit or points where a simple change could enhance the story. My thanks also go to my beta reader, Jacquie Rogers, and to my sisters Carol Blood and Pat Beresford who, once again, were both beta readers and guides to the workings of the pottery industry. My niece, Nicola, a former paintress herself, offered some great suggestions, for which I am grateful.

In the writing of this book, my heart must mention the part played by my dearest husband, Michael. He has provided never-ending support and has been promoted to research assistant, admin assistant, and has gone above and beyond the call of duty. Thank you, Michael. Have I told you that I love you recently!

Finally, my heartfelt thanks to all my readers, for without you, my novels would not see the light of day. You are wonderful. If you would like to review this novel, or any of the previous three in the series, I would be very grateful.